WHAT CRITICS ARE SAYING ABOUT

THE
PURPLES

2011 AMAZON BREAKTHROUGH NOVEL SEMIFINALIST

"The rich detail of the multifaceted characters bring realism to this well-crafted tale. The author reveals that not even the most hardened gangster is truly good or evil as gang violence erupts and the story reaches its fitting conclusion."
—*PUBLISHERS WEEKLY*

"Read this book because it's fun. Berger captures the spirit of Detroit when it is small enough to walk around and when the whole city administration can easily fit into a gangster's hip pocket." —*THE HISTORICAL NOVEL REVIEW*

"Tense, exciting, and extremely satisfying.... The appeal of *The Purples* is universal." —*LL BOOK REVIEW*

"Best gangland tale ever! And the most entertaining book I have read in a very long time." —*WENDY BERTSCH, AUTHOR* "ONCE MORE FROM THE BEGINNING"

"A historical legend come to life." —*READERFAVORITE.COM*

THE
PURPLES

a novel by

W. K. BERGER

RINGER
BOOKS

Visit www.ThePurplesBook.com for more information on the story and the author.

RINGER BOOKS

FIRST EDITION
Designed by Laura E. Kelly

Printed in the United States of America

ISBN 978-0-615-23170-9

1. Fiction   2. Fiction—Thriller   3. Detroit history—Prohibition era

"And what of the melting pot? The problem is not with the pot so much as it is with the base metal. Some metals cannot be assimilated, refuse to mix with the molten mass." ∗

"This American system of ours, call it Americanism, call it capitalism, call it what you will, gives each and every one of us a great opportunity if we only seize it with both hands and make the most of it." ∗∗

∗ Henry Ford

∗∗ Al Capone

ONE

"So how did it start," they all want to know. Then, before you can answer: "Didn't it all start at the Cream of Michigan? On that night when the ghost of Joe Bernstein walked into the diner?"

As a matter of fact, no. If you want the truth, it started four years earlier, during the Palmer Raids. Of course, people don't want to hear about things they'd rather forget. What they want is a ghost yarn or a gangster tale, and if they can get both at the same time, even better.

So they always start with that night at the diner—the night I strolled, big as life, through the front door of "the Crime," as it was known back then. It was quite a moment, I'll admit: The place was filled with forty of the mouthiest guys you'd ever want to meet, yet they all went dead quiet soon as I entered. Art Goldman actually let out a tiny squeak, like a mouse. He told me later that the moment he saw me, he pictured being eaten alive and that caused the squeak.

The amazing thing was that nobody reached for anything. The only motion came from a guy named Meltzer, who had been constructing an igloo out of sugar cubes on one of the tabletops (yes, this is the kind of productive work that was done back then). When he saw me, Meltzer's hands went limp and crashed down on his igloo, spilling cubes onto the floor.

After coming through that door I stopped and looked around

at all of them as they huddled in the diner's ten booths. I held my hands up in the air, palms out, to show I was unarmed.

"Hello, fellas," I said. "Been a while."

Not a sound from any of them, not even another squeak.

So I continued: "I am not here to make trouble. I am only here to make a suggestion."

I explained to them that a new time was beginning in Detroit. It was something big, and they could be part of it if they so chose.

I then moved towards Art, figuring he was the closest thing to a leader this decimated group had left. I extended my hand as I approached. Art seemed to be studying the lower part of my face. He was trying to get a look at my teeth, he told me later—wanted to see if they were pointed. Imagine that.

Art slowly reached out to meet my handshake, not knowing whether he was going to touch something solid or not, or if the hand would be cold as death, or maybe wet with river slime. But he got a warm handshake from me, and that seemed to change things.

At that point, the forty men in that diner began to ease up. For the first time in months, they could relax a little—knowing that I was right there in front of them, instead of lurking behind them or above them or who knows where. And upon hearing my offer—"Why not come be a part of this purple gang of mine," I said—they began to see the possibility of a future wherein they could once again go to a movie or even just take a piss without having to worry about being pierced in the back by a blade or, worse, chewed to small pieces. They saw a fresh chance to start a new life.

And half of them were right about that. Whilst the other half ended up, over the next three days, in various sections of the Detroit River.

But I get ahead of myself.

To understand any of it—why those men reacted to me the way they did, how I came to be in a position to dictate the future for them and for a lot of other people in Detroit at the time—you have to start at the start. You must go back to Palmer: four years earlier, on the night of the second day of 1920.

On that bitter cold night I was stretched out on a mattress on the floor, looking up at the ceiling of a drafty little Hastings Street apartment. I was 19 at the time and my brother Max, 17, was sleeping like a baby in the apartment's only bedroom. Somewhere in the middle of the night (whilst I was just lying wide awake the way I do) I heard footsteps out in the hall and then creaks in the floorboards, just outside the apartment door. Then began a light tapping on that door—once, twice, three times, four, five, six. Only an idiot would tap so many times, so I figured it must be Solly.

Whatever bad things I may henceforth say about the Original Solly Levine—and there will be many—let it be noted that he was the one who, that night, knocked on my door and brought me the news.

"Joe, you will not believe it," he said as I opened the door.

I hate it when people try to predict what I will or won't believe.

"Just spill it," I said.

"I just couldn't believe my eyes, " he said.

"Well, I wouldn't trust them either," I remarked.

I should mention here that Solly wore thick glasses that made his eyes look like big dark marbles. Behind the lenses, the eyes were so crossed and cockeyed it was hard to tell if he was looking at you or at something on your chin.

"There is nothing wrong with my eyes," Solly said to me.

"Then you wear those glasses because they make you look so good?"

He folded his arms. "Want me to tell you what I saw or not?"

I rolled my hand, meaning *get to the point.*

Like me, Solly was a lackey at the time for the local Sugar House Gang. His real name wasn't Solly Levine—he took the name from a local gangster who died years earlier (this was sometimes done back then as a tribute to the dead). As Solly started using the new name, someone once asked: "Are you the *original* Solly Levine?" Being the liar he was, Solly couldn't help answering, "Yes, I am the original Solly Levine." We caught him doing it, and then made fun of him by calling him the Original Solly Levine and it stuck.

He proceeded to tell me what he saw, though it took a while. At

one point I had to take a hold of his ear and give it a short clock-
wise twist—just from 12 to 3 o'clock—to encourage him to keep
the story moving ahead. After I did that, he kept his hand cupped
over the sore ear as he continued talking, and it made him look
like one of those radio announcers.

The story was that he was driving down Hastings and noticed
a commotion in front of the apartment building where my girl
Rachel lived. He saw two guys escorting her into a car.

"Were they cops?"

Solly shrugged. "They wore regular clothes. Feds, maybe."

I had my hand on the doorjamb and found that I was squeezing
it so hard there was a tiny cracking sound as my fingernails dug
into the wood. But otherwise I was calm.

"How did she seem? Was she putting up a fight?"

"Hell, yes," Solly said. "I think she bit one of the bastards."

Solly smiled after he said that. As if amused.

"And while she's fighting, you're watching? You're just a
spectator?"

His little smile uncurled. "Christ's sake, Joe, what am I supposed to do? Against three Feds?"

"You said two."

"I said two held her. A third behind the wheel. What, I'm supposed to take them on? I played it smart." He tapped a finger
against his cranium. "I tailed them. Saw where they took her."

I lifted my hand off the door-jamb and laid it upon Solly's col-
larbone. I clenched firmly, but nowhere near hard enough to snap
the bone.

"If you saw where they took her," I said, "then *that* is the point.
And now is the time to get to it."

We left shortly thereafter. Before we did, I tiptoed through the
apartment, past my mattress on the living room floor and over to
the bedroom door. I cracked it open. Max was still asleep, curled
on his side with his hands tucked between his knees under the
blanket. His mouth was wide open as if he'd discovered a surprise.
Maybe in his dream he had just invented a new engine that would

put Heinrich Ford's to shame. I crept quietly to the bed and something made me want to touch his shoulder. I did it lightly, the way
you'd touch a bubble that might burst. His breathing shifted a little—in his sleep he must have felt the touch. For a second, a
thought popped into my head: *What if I never see him again?*

As Solly drove me downtown in his Ford T—and I hate Fords,
which is just one more reason why the ride was unpleasant—we
bumped and bounced on streets that were mostly still cobblestone.
It was cold in the car and Solly's breath formed little white clouds
as he told me how he'd tailed the car carrying Rachel all the way to
Cadillac Square.

"They took her inside the Federal," he said, his big eyes giving
me a sideways glance whilst he drove.

He was talking about the old Detroit Federal Building, the one
used be in Cadillac Square. It's not there anymore; they tore it
down sometime after the night in question. Maybe they were all
ashamed of what went on in the building that night in 1920. So a
couple of years later they leveled the place with a wrecking ball.
Today, a lot of people don't even know about what happened—
you mention the Palmer Raids, you get a blank stare.

Of course, at the time, I didn't know anything myself. I sat
there in the passenger seat of Solly's car, my heart pounding and
the rest of me bouncing to the bumps in the road, and I tried to
figure why they'd grab a poor girl in the middle of the night and
toss her in that building.

If they'd taken me, that I could understand: I'd been breaking
the law one way or another since I was recruited, at age 12, right
out of the schoolyard by a member of the Sugar House Gang. The
guy stood outside the fence and asked, "Who wants to make half a
buck?" And me, a boy who never once raised a hand in class, shot
my arm straight up. From then on, I carried things for the gang,
passed them, swiped them. As I grew big enough to do damage, I
did my share.

Now, at 19, I was still a grunt doing odd jobs for the Sugars,
earning enough to pay for the lousy apartment. I mostly kept to
myself, didn't carouse or engage in loose talk, didn't mess with

politics, had no use for unions. So there was no reason for someone like me to be wise to this whole Palmer mess.

"Did you talk to anybody at Cadillac Square to try to find out what the hell's going on?" I said to Solly as we drove.

"I talked to a couple of guys. They said the cops were just grabbing people from all over."

"Jews?" I asked.

"All kinds."

"Who ordered it?"

Solly shrugged. "Nobody knows."

"For what reason?"

"No reason. They were grabbing people for no reason at all."

I knew that couldn't be true—there's always a reason. I found out later what it was: The raid was a response to a bombing by some crazy anarchist who tried to blow up the house of a guy named Palmer, the Attorney General in Washington. The government got spooked and decided to round up "troublemakers" everywhere. Raids were going on that night all over the country. But the one in Detroit was big: Some say they grabbed close to a thousand. I cared only that they grabbed one.

When the car got to Cadillac Square, I told Solly to drop me.

"You're doing this on your own?" he said, in a tone that struck me as very hopeful. "You sure, Joe? Because you know I would go with you. If you want."

"I'm sure you would, Solly. Just give me your tie." I figured I should look proper—didn't know what I might be called on to do.

Solly took off his tie and handed it over, loosened but still knotted. I slid the little noose over my own head and tightened it at the throat.

"Keep the engine warm," I said. "I don't know how long this will take."

"What if you don't come out?"

"Then don't forget to visit," I said as I opened the car door.

Cadillac Square was jammed. It looked as if everyone in Detroit had lost their minds and decided to go sightseeing in their pajamas. This was four in the morning on a night that would freeze the snot in your nose, and yet there were hundreds of them out in the square, just shuffling along in furry slippers. I mingled amongst them, hands in my pockets and head down, just trying to get a feel for what was happening and what I was going to do about it.

People kept pointing at the big white Federal Building, located just across from the square. I figured these shufflers were all in the same boat as me: Hunting for a loved one who'd been snatched in the night and tossed in that building. But the place was guarded like a fortress, cops all over the entrance, so there wasn't anything much that these wandering idiots could do. They just went round and round crying, *"Bwah-hah, where's my Louie?"*

As for me, I circled that square with a purpose, looking for my opening. For a good half-hour, my eye was trained on the building and its broad marble staircase and those giant pillars that glowed white in the dark. I watched the cops huddled in front of the entrance. They formed a circle whilst they smoked and tried to stay warm. Now and then, they'd part the circle to let someone into the building. They didn't seem to be letting anyone out.

I was watching that entrance when I saw opportunity arrive, limping on a cane. I'm talking about the gimp, of course. I noticed him before the cops at the door did. He hobbled right up to them and barked something. When they turned to him, he flashed some kind of I.D., which he then returned to the inside pocket of his overcoat (I took note of that). The cops gave each other looks as he passed between them and went inside. One cop, behind the gimp's back, put on a little act for the others: He grabbed his own leg like he was trying to drag it, and the asshole cops all laughed, though the gimp never turned back.

About fifteen minutes later, he came back out from inside the building, hobbling through that same entrance. Down in the square, I was waiting and ready. I calculated the angles, worked out the timing of his limping down those steps. But first, he paused at the top of the stairs and looked around at all the chaos in the square. He pulled a hanky from his pocket, wiped his forehead. He wasn't much older than me, in his mid-20s, but I saw his shoulders sag like an old man's as he wiped his face and exhaled. He neatly folded and pocketed the cloth, then started down the steps— angling his body sideways, stepping first with his right foot, planting the cane, then bringing down the left leg, which was stiff and clearly a fake.

"Move it, Peg, I don't have all night," I muttered.

Halfway down the steps, he stopped—I thought he was just taking a breather. Then I realized he saw the woman with the nose. And I thought, *Oh, for shit's sake, this is gonna be a while.* The woman was sitting on the steps, about the same level as the gimp was standing, but maybe ten yards to the side. She quivered as she sat, her hand cupped to her face. Blood seeped through the fingers. Some heartless prick of a news photographer stood nearby, popping her picture. Earlier, she'd tried to rush past the cops to get in the building, and one cop pushed at her face; the bridge of her nose must've gave way (women's noses will do that). Now she just sat there quaking.

The gimp came toward her, moving sideways across the wide step like you'd creep along a ledge. When he got to her the first thing he did was reach with his cane toward the photographer—he pointed that stick right at the camera lens and gave a sharp little poke, and the photographer scrammed. When it was just the gimp and the woman, he said something to her but she didn't seem to hear. He fumbled in his pocket for that hanky again and gently stuffed it into the woman's hand, still cupped against her face.

I thought he'd never be done with his good deed. When he finally resumed coming down those steps, I shifted gears. The further down he got, the faster I walked. By the time he was all the way down and a few paces out into the square, I was approaching like a gust that blows in from nowhere.

My shoulder collided with his, muscle against muscle, and it stopped him cold. He'd have tumbled backwards but I gripped the shoulder of his coat with my free right hand and steadied him. Then we got tangled up with each other and did a little clumsy dance; I could feel his hard unnatural leg against my knee. When he pulled himself back from me, the look on his face was not so much startled as suspicious. I could see now that he was fair-skinned and soft of chin, but the eyes were hard.

"Sorry, it was an accident," I said.

He glared for a moment, then moved on.

And so did I, his wallet in my own coat pocket now.

Soon as I had some distance from him, I peeked into the wallet and saw the badge. It was silver metal; next to it in the wallet was an ID card from the Wayne County District Attorney's office.

When I saw his name—Harry Riley—my first thought was: Can I pass for a mick? And do I really look like someone who works for the D.A.? I knew my age might give me away, or the cut of my coat, or my shoes, or the way I walked. There are lots of ways to tell who belongs and who doesn't.

I couldn't stop to think about all that. I headed toward those cops guarding the entrance. I approached with a confident stride, which is the way I walk anyway. When I got to them, I flashed that badge without saying a word. I barely acknowledged them, acted as if I considered them beneath me (and that didn't require much acting).

And then, just like that, I was through the front entrance and inside. It was faster and smoother than expected. But then again it is always easier to get into trouble than out of it.

TWO

The inside of the Detroit Federal Building had a high-domed tile ceiling, slick marble floors—all very grand. But I only cared about one room, and it was easy to see which one it was. There was another gang of cops standing guard at the door, just like outside. Five of them stood in a semi-circle, smoking. The double-doors behind them were chained shut at the door handles, with a padlock big as a fist. I noticed the chain and the lock jiggling— someone was pushing on those doors from inside.

As I walked up to the group, I reached in my pocket for a cigarette and put it in my mouth but did not light it. When I arrived and the heads turned to face me, I decided to open with a pleasantry—no easy thing for me.

"What a night, huh, fellas?"

No one said anything back, though a couple of them nodded.

"Got a light?" I said to one of the smoking cops, the oldest-looking one, who handed over a lit cigarette and waited whilst I rolled the glowing splint against the tip of my own cigarette.

I handed back the cop's smoke and said to him: "Hate to make you open those doors again, but I gotta go in."

For a couple of seconds, no one answered.

I took the badge from my pocket and showed it to the older cop, who squinted at it.

"You don't want to go in there," he said. "It's no picnic."

I shrugged. "Orders," I said. "There's a girl inside needs to be fished out, now. Never should have been grabbed—she's somebody's niece."

"Aren't they all?" said the older cop.

"Well," I said, "this is one uncle who could have us all fired."

The older cop seemed to chew on that. Then he slowly pulled a jangling key ring off his belt.

"Lemme show you something," he said, and then head-signaled the younger cops, who stationed themselves with shoulders braced against the doors, two cops on each door, whilst he put the key in the lock and popped it. He pulled the chain off and looked back at me.

"Come poke your head in, and tell me if you think you could find anybody in there," he said.

They gave me a wide enough opening so I could look, but I just announced, "I'm going in," and pushed my shoulder right through. The cops didn't try to stop me—they just let me go in and shut the door behind me. Before it closed the older one yelled, "Let us know when you want out."

Inside, it was pitch black, no air to breathe, no room to move, bodies on all sides and even underfoot. The stench of sweat, pee, vomit, all mixed, made me gag, just once. I heard moaning, praying, whispering, screaming, but I couldn't see who made these sounds; the only thing visible was a thread of light along the bottom of the closed doors behind me.

Before I could take my first blind step, someone grabbed me by the lapels of my coat and shook, yelling something I couldn't make out. The guy must have been half-gone and I felt bad for him but still, he had his hands on me. I reached in the dark and found his throat whereupon I squeezed his apple with my thumb and forefinger until the two fingers nearly met. He dropped quickly and I let go the apple soon as I heard his knees hit the floor.

The next thing I did was reach in my pocket for a match, wondering if there was even enough air in this room to light it. When I struck, it flared and that gave me my first look: I saw wall-to-wall people, many down on the floor, either huddled up or laid out, some conscious and others not. I saw wide hopeful eyes turn to me and my match, whilst others kept their heads down, as if afraid to see anything. The loon at my feet was still holding his throat, looking up at me with bulging eyes. I gave him a little nod: no hard feelings. I kept moving the match from side to side until it burned my fingers, at which point I dropped it, grabbed another and struck again. Then I sucked in as much foul air as I could and let it all out, in the loudest yell of my life:

"*Rachel!*"

I tried a second time. My voice cut through the hum of crying and groaning; I was sure it could be heard through the entire room. But nothing came back. I figured she must have passed out, or maybe she was trapped in a corner, trying to call back but without enough air in her lungs to make a sound. I didn't want to dwell on such thoughts so I kept moving, stepping carefully into holes in the human carpet, my heel landing on a hand once. All the while I held up my little match until I felt the burn and even longer, because burnt fingers did not concern me at the moment.

I was down to my last match when I found her—on the far side of the room, against the wall, curled up in a ball like a little cat. Even in the match light, I recognized her shiny black hair and her nightgown (her *nightgown*—the pricks didn't even let her get dressed). The way she was curled up, I couldn't see her face. Could not tell if she was breathing.

I kneeled down, put my hand on her forehead and then on her cheek. I slapped it ever so lightly. Her eyelids moved, as if they were about to open. But before they did, the match already scorching my fingertips went out and I lost sight of her.

In the darkness, I felt her face and found her mouth, and with my fingers I gently parted her lips. I put my own mouth on hers— something I'd done many times before but it felt different now: the lips were dry and there was no warmth. I tried to push the little air I had in my lungs into hers. Then I lifted my head, opened my mouth, sucked in hard, and returned to her mouth a second time to give her another breath, then another after that. There was nothing at first, and then her whole body shifted and her arms started moving.

I gathered her in my arms to lift her. The only way out of the room was back through those doors, with me carrying her. I had just straightened up on my feet, with her in my arms, when I looked over my shoulder and saw light coming through the partially opened door, and a cop pushing his body halfway in and holding a flashlight level with his head. The light scanned the room, blinding me when it hit my eyes, then moving past me to continue searching.

"Riley!" the cop yelled.

Maybe my brain was starved of air, because it took a moment before I realized the name he was calling was temporarily mine.

"Come on, Riley, where are you?"

I just stood there with Rachel in my arms, not feeling her weight. The flashlight, coming back around the room, stopped on me, blinding me again. "There you are," the voice behind the light said. "You found her, good for you. Now come on, we gotta get you out of here."

The cop wasn't offering to come inside—he stayed wedged halfway through the door and kept the flashlight trained on me. I stepped over and between the bodies, following that beam of light to its source. When I got near the door he grabbed my shoulder and pulled me through the opening; I had to be careful to squeeze through without Rachel hitting her head.

Coming back into the bright hallway, I blinked hard as I looked down at Rachel's face, my first look in good light. She started to open her eyes, then put her hand over them, the light too much for her after that darkness. With the hand covering her eyes, all she said was, "Joey, what's happening? Where are we?"

I was looking down at her in my arms and also seeing the floor around me, and all those heavy black cop-shoes. I noticed one pair differed from the rest—finer and more polished; and the left shoe looked smaller, less full, than the right. Coming up from between those two shoes was a smooth honey-colored cane; my eyes followed the cane up to the hands folded on top of it, then up to the face.

*

Riley didn't say anything and neither did I. The cop who fished me out was the one who spoke.

"Mr. Riley," he said to me, "I'd like you to meet Mr. Riley. I think maybe you took something of his, didn't you?"

Riley stepped toward me. "She okay?" he said.

He looked down at Rachel's face. Then he laid a hand on her arm and patted. "She may need to see a doctor. Why don't you hand her over to me? I'll see she gets looked at."

The thing to know about me is that I was trained in certain things at an early age, in the Hastings Street ghetto. I learned that when you're surrounded and there is nowhere to run behind you, you attack what's in front of you. And that if an outside person, someone not of your circle, tries to reach in and touch someone within your circle, you are entitled—no, expected—to lash out. You do it with bare hands, and if those hands are not free, you use legs and feet. This is what made me kick out at Riley as he touched Rachel.

Of course I didn't mean to kick him in the peg leg but it was the one closest to my right foot, so there you have it. The leg came out from under him, and he looked at me in disbelief whilst toppling over sideways like a tree in a storm.

Down on the floor, Riley seemed more embarrassed than hurt. The peg was still inside his pants leg but must have come off its moorings and Riley was clutching it through the pants, trying to maneuver it back in place. A couple of cops bent down to help him, whilst another cop drew his gun and pointed it at my face, and still another circled behind me, no doubt to point a gun at the back of my head.

Riley said, "Get your hands off me," to one kneeling cop.

I felt bad. I don't apologize for much, but I thought about doing so then. I was also thinking about the mechanics of taking out five cops with my hands, elbows, and feet—not easy, not impossible. But I would've had to let go of Rachel and I didn't want to do that. So I stood holding her, looking down at Riley fixing his leg, then looking up at the gun pointed at me, and also wondering about the other one behind me. I was waiting to feel that cold muzzle touch the back of my neck. Instead I felt the crack of a nightstick against my skull.

My legs wobbled under me, but I didn't let go of Rachel. I looked at her face and she'd pulled her hand away from her eyes and was looking into mine. She must have seen them go glassy and I wish that was something she never had to see. Everything started moving in slow motion as I set her down on the floor. Then I lay down myself and curled up beside her, as if we were back home on Hastings Street, safe in her little bed.

They could have just dragged me a few yards, tossed me back into that pitch-black room, and re-chained the doors. But they have different boxes to hold different kinds of people. I was taken to a downtown Detroit police station and I stood there woozy as they booked me on charges of petty larceny, trespassing, impersonating an officer of the law, and assault. After I was fingerprinted someone slapped a bandage on the back of my head, and they took away my belt and my tie (or rather, Solly's tie) and put me in a holding cell. By the time I settled in, it was sunrise, another bright new damn day in Detroit.

I sat there, head pounding, until noon when word came I had a visitor. As I entered the visiting room I saw my brother Max sitting on the other side of the glass divider, hands folded in his lap like a good school kid. Max had my black hair and blue eyes, but he was smaller and skinnier than me—at seventeen, not quite filled out yet (though he never did fill out). He was also paler than me and with that hollow darkness around his eyes, he could look like a little vampire at times. But his eyes burned with pure smartness. Max was the most intelligent person I knew, even moreso than myself.

He put his fine-fingered hand flat against the glass divider as I came to my seat. I put my hand flat against his, and I swear I felt the warmth of his blood right through the glass. With our hands lined up like that, mine seemed like a big protective glove over his. We didn't say hello because when you're as close as Max and me, you just start in mid-conversation.

"They feed you?" he said.

I laughed, food being the least of my worries.

"Don't laugh," he said, "you've got to eat and keep your strength up. Be careful of the john, though. Prisons are notorious—you pick up twelve kinds of disease, right off the seat."

"If I don't eat I won't have to crap," I said.

"Well, but if you do crap, keep your cheeks raised, that's all. It's what I do in any public john."

"I don't want to hear about your ass. What do you know about Rachel? Is she okay? What the hell happened last night?"

Max shook his head. "You're asking me? I was asleep in my bed and missed everything. Somebody didn't even wake me up to tell me what was going on."

"I didn't want you involved," I said.

"You never want me involved. You know what—I'm involved. Just being your brother makes me involved."

It was true that I tried to shield Max. There were reasons for it. Our father died when Max was still a toddler. On top of that, he inherited sick blood. I always looked out for him growing up and when he was fifteen and his mother caught the flu and died, he became my charge. Notice I say "his mother" because whilst the woman also gave birth to me, she never wanted any part of the trouble I brought and finally disowned me at sixteen. The word came down that I was to be shunned by the community—and she went along. I didn't hold it against her then and bear her no grudge today. But if she didn't wish to acknowledge me as her son, then I guess I won't acknowledge her as my mother.

As I say, Max's mother assumed "the community" would take care of him after she was gone—that's what they did for widows and orphans. But I made sure they didn't get their hands on him. I brought him to live with me in my drafty little apartment. Made sure he stayed in school. And I kept him away, as best I could, from anything connected to the Sugar House Gang.

Which is why I didn't like it when Max brought up Buster Weintraub's name. Buster was the head of the Sugars.

"Maybe he could help with all this," Max said. "He's connected to everybody, isn't he?"

"Don't even talk about Buster Weintraub," I said. "Don't even utter his name."

"I could go see him on your behalf," he said.

"Out of the question. You do not go near him, ever."

I knew what a gang boss like Buster would do if he got hold of a brain like Max's—he would squeeze it dry and drink the juice. Besides, I didn't want to ask Weintraub for help anyway; didn't think he'd call in any favors for a flunky like me. And if he did, that would be bad, too—because he'd own me then. Buster was a last resort in my mind.

I wanted to try other possibilities first. Though before I could do anything, I needed information. Max had some.

He knew—everyone did by this time—about all the people being locked up in Detroit during the night, all because of that fucking so-called anarchist and his bomb. The anarchist, by the way, was a Wop, an oiler—and yet they responded by rounding up a very large proportion of Jews. You figure it out. This aspect of the story wasn't covered in the newspapers, but it was the talk of Hastings Street. Some wondered if Heinrich Ford was involved.

"Sure he was," I said to Max as he filled me in.

"Who knows," Max said. "What I hear is that the order came in from Washington to round up troublemakers. And then it was up to the locals to decide who fit the bill. A lot of this was directed by the Wayne County DA—guy named Thompson."

"That would be Riley's boss," I said.

"Whose boss?" Max always perked up when he encountered new information, which is a good quality I believe.

"The guy whose wallet I picked. I think it was him arranged to have Rachel sent to the hospital after I got knocked out."

We knew Rachel was in the hospital because Max had asked around that morning. It was one of the first things he told me through the glass and I was relieved to learn she wasn't put back in that black room. But I was less relieved to learn they'd sent her to the Henry Ford Hospital.

Max felt there was no reason to worry. "It's a hospital, it doesn't matter whose name is on the door."

"We'll see about that," I said.

"So this Riley," Max said, "he's the one pressing charges against you? What was he like?"

"What do you mean, what was he like?"

"I mean, did he seem like a reasonable guy?"

I could see right off where Max was going with this. "Don't even think about it," I said.

"What am I thinking?"

"You're thinking you'll go talk to this Riley and tell him some sad story about being an orphan."

"I *am* an orphan."

"You're seventeen years old. That's too old to be calling yourself an orphan. And too young to be acting like my lawyer."

"Somebody's gotta look out for you," he said, to which I replied, "Ha fucking ha."

THREE

Of course as soon as he left, Max went straight to talk to Riley. I figured he would. When Max got to the DA's office, Riley was busy at work doing whatever his kind does, and wouldn't talk then but offered to buy Max a cup of coffee later. Max said he couldn't drink coffee because of his condition, and Riley asked what condition is that, and Max said it's a long story.

So Riley said, "Fine, I'll buy you a glass of warm milk, or does that make you nervous, too?" And right away Max knew he was dealing with a guy that had sharp corners.

At the coffee shop, Riley insisted they sit at a certain table and told the waiter that the table needed a wipe with the rag. Then he ordered tea and said, "Don't forget my lemon wedge."

Max sipped a Howdy and tried to sell Riley a story about how he and his brother were two lost lambs, trying to get by. And that it wasn't easy for two orphans, especially when the younger one had a nervous condition. He said his older brother had never been in trouble before that night and just wanted to help his girl, who was snatched for no good reason.

"Your brother runs with a gang, that I know already," Riley said. "The girl I don't know about—maybe you can educate me."

Max said she was a sweet girl, lived on her own in a little apartment on Hastings, no family and no one to count on but Joe.

"She belong to any groups, unions, that kind of thing?"

"If you're asking if she's a red, the answer is no," Max said.

Max asked Riley about the raids, and Riley said he had no part in the whole thing until after it broke. It was true: His boss, Thompson, had kept Riley in the dark. That evening before the raids, when Riley finished up his workday, all Thompson said to him was, "Goodnight, see you tomorrow."

Max noticed that Riley put one spoonful of sugar in his tea followed by a second, which he carefully measured so that it was exactly half a spoonful. ("He's a peculiar fellow," Max would later comment, to which I said, "Look who's talking.")

At one point Max asked Riley, "Did they grab the girl just because she's a Jew?"

Riley seemed puzzled by the question and shook his head as if such a thing was not plausible. "No, no, she had to be on some kind of list of troublemakers," he said. "Lot of the people they rounded up belonged to groups. The idea was to break up the groups, stop trouble before it starts." Then he shook his head. "They thought they'd raid these little meeting halls and apartments and find stockpiles of guns and bombs. Of course they found nothing. The whole thing is a travesty."

Max saw his opening. "If it was a travesty," he said, "then how can you blame my brother for trying to do something about it?"

Next day I was sitting in my cell waiting for another visit from Max. But at noon a guard said, "Come along, Bernstein." I expected the worst, perhaps a beating for what I'd done the night before (there was a misunderstanding with my cellmate and somehow he ended up in the infirmary). But to my surprise, I was told they were letting me go. No explanations, no goodbyes: They just handed me my wallet and my belt. "How about the tie?" I said, but the tie was gone as was my overcoat. This was how it worked back then in Detroit prisons—they kept what they liked.

I stepped out into the bright sunshine of a crisp winter day. It was cold, especially without a coat, but I was happy to be out in the open air. I started ankling down the street and saw myself in a store window, and brother was I a sight—hair standing up, unshaven face, shoes flopping like slippers because they took the laces, blood stain running down the back of my white shirt. People were giving me a wide berth, which was fine by me.

I got the sense someone was tailing me, and whipped my head around to see a familiar Ford driving slowly in the street behind me. The car pulled alongside me and Solly leaned his head out the window. "Scuse me, mister," he said, "need a lift?"

Max had alerted Solly that I might be getting sprung around noon. Soon as I got in the car, Solly asked about his tie. I gave his ear a little twist because when somebody's just been through hell, you don't greet them by asking about your goddamn tie. Solly then held the wheel with one hand and cupped his ear with the other whilst he drove me, as ordered, to the Henry Ford Hospital.

At the front entrance of the hospital, Ford's name was engraved in big letters on a sign over the door. I thought, *It's not enough he owns all the cars we stick our fannies in, he also has to own the beds we get sick in. He'll probably own the caskets next.*

"Fucking Ford," I said out loud as I came through the entrance. A security guard heard that and gave me a queer look and I gave it right back to him.

At the desk I said I was there to visit Rachel Roth and a fat woman smiled at me and started looking up the name in her chart. I noticed her smile went away as she saw something on the list. She looked up at me and said, "Will you wait here a moment, Mister —?"

She was expecting me to give her my name I guess, but I saw no reason. "Okay, I will wait a moment," I said.

She left the desk and came back with a doctor. His eyes widened as he saw me in my present state and he stopped at a distance. He looked past me at the guard by the door and I heard movement behind me—the guard getting out of his chair. Then the doctor looked back at me with a phony smile and said, "And you would be Mister —?"

This was beginning to annoy me. I didn't see why I had to give my name to go visit someone in the hospital.

"I *would* be Mister J. P. Morgan," I said.

"Oh, you would," he said, glancing back at the guard.

"Yes that's who I *would* be, given my choice," I said. "And now I *would* like to see Rachel Roth."

"I'm afraid that's impossible," the doctor said.

I felt the muscles tensing up in my neck and that is never a good thing for people who happen to be in my vicinity at the time.

"Why is it impossible," I said.

"I'm afraid she's just been transferred to another facility."

The guard was directly behind me now, close enough that if I thrust my elbow straight back it would have doubled him over.

"And what facility would that be?" I asked the doctor.

He answered with a word that sounded so sweet—a cute little girl's name. "Eloise," he said.

That was when I elbowed the guard in the gut, and then cut his feet out from under him with a backsweep of my leg. I looked back at the doctor and the fat nurse was hugging him for dear life.

I walked out and went straight to Solly's car and plopped into the seat. "Well, they went and put her in the nut house," I said, and Solly's big marble eyes got even bigger.

Max was waiting in our apartment for Solly to bring me home. He thought I'd arrive happy because I'd been sprung. He even had a whiskey bottle and two shot glasses out for a toast, wherein I could thank him for talking to Riley and getting me out. But when I came through the apartment door, I slammed it so hard the noise made Max bolt upright in his seat. Then his whole body shook and I knew I had to try to calm down, lest I trigger one of his fits.

"It's okay," I said. "It's okay."

I sat down opposite him, landing hard in the chair. I didn't bother with the glass, just took a long chug from the bottle and felt it burn its way down my throat.

"You okay?" Max said, almost whispering.

I nodded and put my head between my hands so the heels of my palms pressed on my temples. I told him about Rachel being moved from the hospital to Eloise. He wanted to know why and I said he wasn't the only one. I told him that somebody must've had it in for the poor girl. Maybe the DA. Or maybe Heinrich Ford himself, who knew?

Then I brought up Riley. "He must know more than he told you," I said. "He's got to have at least *some* idea why this is happening to her."

"I could talk to him again if you want," Max said.

"No, this time I'll do it myself. Do me a favor, get in touch with Abie—let him know I might need his help later."

"Might need his help with what?"

I hesitated to tell Max. "I might have to bust her out tonight."

Max looked up at the ceiling and started breathing funny again.

"Don't get all worked up on me," I said.

He took a deep breath and then looked back at me. "You saw what happened when you tried this the other night," he said.

"This would be different. I'll be more prepared."

After cleaning myself up, I tracked down Solly so I could borrow his car. Solly hated lending it and offered to drive me but I said no, it's okay, I'll drive myself. Then he made the offer again and I again declined. When it looked like he was going to offer a third time I reached down in the direction of his groin. He flinched, but all I did was help him locate the keys in his pants pocket.

It was mid-afternoon, too early to go see Riley, but I had another destination in mind. I started driving west out of the city, leaving behind the factories and the street vendors and the dingy apartment buildings of downtown, moving off the paved streets till I was out on a dirt road in what seemed like the wilderness.

The car jangled every time I hit a pebble in the road, and fought me when I put my foot down all the way on the gas. "Fucking Ford," I said, more than once on that ride. I never had my own car back then; figured a man with two good legs should make use of them. I ankled all over Detroit in those days. When I had to do a job I was more effective on foot—people never heard me coming, as I do not sputter like an engine. But Eloise Hospital was six miles away and I didn't have time for a stroll like that.

Half a mile away, I could see it on the horizon: big stone walls, iron gates. I'd heard about it before—everybody knows somebody who ended up in Eloise. The grounds spanned a thousand acres, with all the amenities of a small town. The nuts had their own post office, their own power station. There was even a pig farm on the premises. It was said that at night, you could hear the hogs squeal as the inmates screamed.

I parked alongside a wall, scaled the side and peeked over the top. I didn't see pigs running wild, nor any living creature; just a bunch of buildings with each one looking like the other—flat and boxy, plain brick, three stories high. Years later I would come to find out that whilst the buildings looked separate, they were actually connected by underground tunnels and passageways. And through these tunnels, patients sometimes were led from their beds to a laboratory where tests were conducted using the latest unproven methods and untried pills. As I peered over that wall I didn't know any of these secrets yet, and neither did anyone else except the powers that be.

I slid back down the wall and drove up to the front gate, which had an armed guard posted. I got out of my car and walked up to that guard. I used the same trick again of needing a light for my cigarette—yes I know it is old and tired but it works because even the surliest bastard will not a refuse a man a light. The guard lit me up and soon we were chatting like chums.

"Never seen a place like this," I said. "Is it the state university?"

He got a chuckle out of that and told me proudly that it was the biggest hospital around (he neglected to mention the loony bin aspect). I asked him about all the different buildings and eventually learned that the women were in Buildings C and D, which was good to know.

I also asked him if it was lonely being the only guard in such a big place and he laughed again and told me there were guards in every building, and I said "You're kidding, how many?" and he said three per building. I said, "Huh, I never realized a hospital required so much guarding, is it because people are dying to get in or dying to get out?"

He laughed at my little joke and by the time I left I knew his name was Oscar and I was thinking to myself, *Oscar you're alright and I sure hope I don't end up having to kill you tonight.*

It was dusk when I drove back into downtown Detroit. I was annoyed by how much traffic there was at that hour of the day. Being a guy with two good legs who doesn't mind ankling, I hadn't realized the car situation had gotten so bad in the city. I almost had two smack-ups with people who refused to yield to me. Then I bumped someone from behind, intentionally, at the new flashing traffic light on Jefferson. The guy in the car had refused to move—he just sat there waiting because the light was red. After I bumped him (not that hard), the squirt hopped out of his car red in the face, and I must admit the sight of him gave me my first laugh in two days. He said, "Can't you see it's a red light?" I told him a red light is just a suggestion. Then I pressed the gas lightly and started pushing his car further out into the intersection whilst he stood there in disbelief. "Better get back in, your car is leaving without you," I said.

As if all this wasn't headache enough, I then discovered it was impossible to park at Cadillac Square because all the curbside spaces were taken. I had no choice but to park the car up on the sidewalk. When I got out, somebody said, "Buddy, they will haul your car away," to which I replied, "It's not my car and I'm not your buddy."

My plan was to go sit in the same little coffee shop where Max had sat with Riley. It was across the street from the Square, and offered a view of the building Riley worked in so that I would be able to spot him when he came limping out. I sat near the window and sipped coffee and watched. When Riley appeared off in the distance I noticed right away. He moved at a different pace from everyone, and his head was a good six inches above the others.

He was coming along the sidewalk leading to the coffee shop and would be passing the window soon, so I took my last gulp of coffee; the idea was to get up and follow him on the sidewalk after he passed, then catch up with him. But he surprised me by turning to come in the coffee shop. He didn't see me in the window; he didn't seem to see anything, in fact. He was moving like a man in a trance, doing something he'd done a hundred times before.

He came in and nodded at the guy behind the counter and then went straight to a table in the corner and I would bet it was the same one where he sat with Max. It occurred to me that this must be Riley's life after work, coming into this lousy diner and eating alone. It took him a while to sit himself down in the chair, and even more time to get comfortable; he had to shift and fuss. When he got settled, he pulled from his pocket a worn little book. He rested his forehead in the knuckles of one hand and started reading whilst the waitress quietly put a cup of tea down in front of him and placed a wedge of lemon on the saucer.

I walked to his table and stood there until he looked up. When he did, I pointed down at the chair opposite him and said, "Mind?"

He exhaled and nodded toward the chair as if to say, *Go ahead it's a free country.*

The first thing he said to me when I sat down—and I have to say, it rankled me—was, "You don't have to thank me."

"That's good," I said, "because I wasn't planning on it."

I could see that conversation between us was not going to be easy and that it would be up to me to move it ahead. I asked him a simple question: "Why don't you tell me what the hell's going on?"

"Could you be more specific?" he said.

"My girl was sent to Eloise and I want to know why. Also why did you send her to the Ford Hospital? And why didn't you press charges against me? Are you trying to punish *her* for what *I* did?"

Riley put up his hands to stop the questions. "One at a time," he said. "You'll have to be patient with me because I'm used to asking questions, not answering them."

I wasn't sure if that was a joke, but I didn't laugh. I was staring at him pretty hard. To his credit, he didn't look away.

"First off," he said, "I dropped the charges because it occurred to me that you didn't break the law that night."

"Oh, I didn't?"

"When all those people were rounded up without just cause, and without counsel, and locked away without so much as air or water—at that point the law was broken, you see? You couldn't break something that was already that badly broken."

I didn't know what to say to all that.

"Besides," Riley added, "your brother asked me very nicely."

"Fine," I said. "What about the girl? Why's this happening to her?"

Riley pushed aside his teacup, put his elbows on the table and leaned toward me. "I honestly don't know why she was rounded up in the first place. And I'm not sure why the cops took her to the Ford Hospital. I handed her off to them and said 'get her to a hospital;' I never specified Ford. As for her being transferred from Ford to Eloise—well, that is strange. That is not good."

No kidding, I wanted to say.

Riley seemed to hesitate before continuing. "I'm going to try to ask this delicately. Is the girl... does she have problems?"

This bothered me. It was not an appropriate question. "I would say she's got a hell of a problem, seeing as she's locked up in a goddamn fucking mental ward."

"Yes, but I mean..."

"I know what you mean," I said. "She's as normal as anyone. She does not belong in the nut house."

"And what about her politics," Riley said.

"You want to know how she votes? What's next, her favorite color?"

"A lot of those people were rounded up because of their politics," Riley said. "Does she belong to any groups?"

"She's a Jew, does that count?"

Riley didn't like that, I saw it in his eye. "That's not what this is about," he said.

"Oh, really?"

Riley didn't want to discuss this aspect. I brought up Heinrich Ford, and he dismissed it. I asked if his boss Thompson answered to Ford; he scoffed and said of course not, to which I said, "Then he would be the only person in Detroit who doesn't."

"I don't know what to tell you," Riley finally said, "but I will try to look into it in the next couple of days, see what I can find out."

"The next couple of days? I want her out now. Do you know what goes on in that place?"

Of course he didn't know and I didn't know either, not yet. But I had my suspicions.

"I'll do what I can," he said. "This may be beyond my authority."

"What about Thompson?" I said.

"What about him?"

"Is it beyond his authority? Or did his authority make all this happen in the first place?"

Riley didn't answer right away. Then he said, quietly as if to himself, "At this point, I'm not sure what that man is capable of."

That cinched it for me. Just like that, the plans in my head began to take shape.

I got up from the table and started to leave. Riley said to me, "Don't do anything foolish. I won't give you a second free pass."

I didn't care for that remark. I did not need some gimp a few years my elder talking to me like a stern father. And I do not need a free pass from any man. But I didn't say anything as I left, because there's a point at which words don't matter anymore and you just have to take action.

FOUR

Late that night I found myself ankling the empty streets of Cork-town, a wealthy Irish neighborhood (Well, it was back then). The only sound on the street was my heels clacking on the sidewalk, giving a beat to my furious thoughts. As I passed by mansions with bushy yards in front and private driveways for the Packards, I looked for a number on a door. I knew I'd found the right house when I saw one with no number at all. This made sense as a man like Thompson would not wish to announce his address to outsiders. Nor was I surprised that there was a tall and pointy wrought-iron fence around the house. There might even be a guard dog inside; I was prepared for that possibility.

I grabbed one of the bars—my hands bare for a better grip, though I had to worry about my skin freezing onto the cold iron—and started hoisting myself up, hand over hand. I reached the top, eight feet high, and swung my legs over the spike points, feeling a tingle as one of the points grazed my crotch during the flyover. I hung by my hands then let go, my shoes landing on frozen dirt, hardly making a sound. I crept round the side of the house to the back, with just enough moonlight to see where I was going.

In the shadowy back yard, I looked up to see a large second-story balcony—the master's bedroom, I presumed. A branch on a nearby tree reached out to that balcony as if to touch it. I shimmied up the trunk and grabbed onto that branch and hung from it, then moved along it hand-by-hand. When I could go no further, I was still a good four feet from the balcony. I swung my legs a couple of times for momentum and on the third swing forward I let go the branch and flew like a bird to a perch, catching hold of the railing and pulling myself onto the balcony.

I stepped lightly on the smooth balcony tiles until I was in front of a pair of glass doors with curtains on the inside. I turned the knob and pushed the door slowly open; it made a small creak. Then, from inside, I heard a single low *woof*—the sound a dog makes when he's been woken up. I froze, still outside, and kept the door as it was, slightly ajar. Then I heard the dog's paws land heavy on the floor; he must have jumped down from a bed. His nails clicked on the floor as he walked to the balcony door, not in any big hurry—he must've figured there was nothing there, but being a dog he would go check anyway.

As he got closer I reached in my pocket and pulled out a balled-up hanky with a few thick chunks of raw steak inside. I dropped one chunk onto the tiles as the dog, a German shepherd gone old and soft, came waddling through the open door. He saw both me and the meat. He chose the meat.

He started to chew, looking up at me whilst I softly pulled the door shut again, so that it was just the two of us on the balcony. I dangled a second piece of meat to let him know there was more. By the time he swallowed the first chunk, I was kneeling down and holding the second piece behind my back; he would have to snuggle up to get it. He started poking his nose at my elbow and wagging his tail, and I gave him a peek at the meat, then hid it again. I pet him softly on his smooth head and moved my hand to his scruffy neck and gave him a rub. I have never been much for dogs, but he seemed like a good old one. I wished things could have gone differently but these were difficult times.

I showed him the meat again and as I let him taste it I also wrapped my free right arm around his neck in a loose, gentle headlock. The dog seemed confused by this and tried to back up but I held him steady and patted the top of his head with my left hand. He kept chewing and the petting seemed to calm him. From the back of his neck I took a firm fistful of fur and in one hard motion I pushed on the back of the neck whilst I tightened the arm lock in front. The piece of meat flew out of his mouth and landed splat on the tiles, half-chewed. He tried to make a sound but his air was cut off so he just gurgled. I stood up with him in the hammerlock so his feet were off the ground and he couldn't use them to try to escape. But the legs still moved fast in the air, in spasms; it made me think of a marionette. It was probably just a matter of seconds but it seemed like ages before the body went limp.

I whispered to him, "Rest easy, boy, your work is done now," and I laid him on the tiles, gently. There are worse ways for a dog to go, trust me—a dog can die slow and hungry in the street, instead of fast and with the taste of prime steak on his tongue. I tried not to look at his face as I snatched up the chewed meat and then opened the glass door and stepped inside.

The bed was fluffy and white as a marshmallow in the moonlight. I could see where the dog had snoozed moments before—a little nesting place curled into the thick blanket. A body that I assumed to be Thompson's was under the blanket, snoring away. I walked alongside the bed and kneeled down beside it until my face was right in front of his and I could feel his breath, and smell it, too. He was old, smelled like decay. I had the chewed meat still in my hand, slimy with saliva, and I gently placed it against Thompson's parted lips and then pushed it into his mouth.

He jerked in the bed and squealed a little and tried to spit out the meat but my hand was clamped over his mouth. With my other arm I pinned his shoulder down onto the bed.

"Don't move," I said. "Don't try to talk. Just listen."

Thompson's eyes looked hard at me, trying to make out my face, maybe trying to figure out if I was real or a nightmare. Then the eyes darted left and right, probably looking for the dog.

"There is no dog," I said. "There is nothing to protect you now. Understand?"

He started to move his head in a funny way, like he was signaling. I realized he was pointing with his head to the bureau next to the bed. His wallet lay there.

"That's not why I'm here," I said. "I'm here because of something you did to a girl named Rachel Roth. You had her picked up in the raids. Then you had her sent to Eloise."

Thompson tried to shake his head no.

"Don't shake your head—I'm not interested in denials. I want an answer. When I pull my hand away, I want an answer."

I lifted my hand and the first thing he did was spit the meat out, and it slid off his cheek onto the pillow next to him. Then he coughed, and started gagging. He took a couple of deep breaths before he spoke. "I don't know the name," he said. "I don't know any of the names. The lists came from Washington. It wasn't me."

Thompson started to kick his legs under the cover—maybe it was nerves. I reached down and grabbed a bony foot and felt for the little toe, holding it firm in my fingers, through the blanket.

"I can break this off and it will hurt you more than anything has ever hurt you," I explained.

He nodded and stopped moving the leg.

"Now answer me a question," I said, still holding the toe. "Why would a girl from Detroit be on a list from Washington?"

"I don't know," Thompson gasped. "I didn't make the lists. Was she in a group?"

It made me laugh. "Everyone asks that, Thompson. What the hell does it mean? A group? Isn't everybody in a group?"

"I don't understand it, either. This is all coming from above."

"From God?" I said.

He seemed confused by that.

"Or maybe you mean Ford?"

He shook his head. "Palmer is the one you need to talk to."

"But you authorized the arrest, Thompson."

Thompson didn't try to deny that.

"So that makes you responsible," I said. "And now you are going to fix the problem."

"What do you want me to do?"

"You're going to get her out of Eloise—immediately, no questions asked. You are going to tell them it's all a mistake."

Thompson shook his head. "You don't understand, once she's in a place like Eloise…"

I twisted the toe and that cut him short. "You're not going to tell me you don't have the authority. Don't tell me that."

Thompson's eyes were shut tight now. He took a breath. "If she was committed," he said, "a doctor had to be involved. And a judge had to sign the order. I can find out who the judge was, and speak to him. It may take some time."

I gave the toe another little twist. "You don't have time. You've got a deadline of noon tomorrow. If she's not out by then, you will be held to account. Do you know what I mean by that?"

Thompson nodded, still wincing.

"If she's not out tomorrow, I'll be back for you. I won't just put a little bomb in your mailbox—you won't be as lucky as Palmer. You will get me. And I am worse than a bomb."

Thompson nodded again. He had become very agreeable.

"There is no way to hide from me. And no way to find me, even if you think you know who I am."

I released the toe and stood up. "Remember: Noon tomorrow. Now turn over on your stomach."

I hog-tied Thompson's feet and hands with a piece of rope from my pocket. Then I went back out those doors and across the balcony, trying not to look down at the dog. I leaped down to the ground, climbed over the gates and soon was once again ankling through Corktown. The car was parked several blocks away, but I took my time. I knew it would take a good half-hour for Thompson to flop around and get loose and maybe call the cops. Or, maybe Thompson would heed my warnings and not call the cops at all—if I was lucky.

As I found out later, he never did call the cops. But that didn't mean I was lucky.

Afterwards, I couldn't go back to the apartment—if Thompson *did* call the cops, they'd look for me there. I drove to an empty lot behind a boarded up factory near the river. I tried to sleep in the car but the cold bit my fingers, even when I put them under my armpits. So I just stayed huddled in a ball on the back seat, picturing all kinds of outcomes. It's funny how no matter how many outcomes you picture, in the end you never get it right.

At sunup I left Solly's car there in the lot and walked to Hastings, where the market stalls were just setting up for a new day. I went straight to the butcher shop run by the father of my trusted pal Abie Zussman. Mister Z (as I called the old man) was putting fresh cuts of beef in the glass counter; he gave me a big hello and said "Abie's in the back," meaning he was in the so-called abattoir, which is a nice word for a lousy place. It was a cold back room where slabs of meat hung on the walls. Abie was working at a chopping block, cleaver in hand.

Abie was no older than me, just a kid really, but he towered over everyone and had hands like baseball mitts. He was always a giant, even back at the Old Bishops School, where we became friends. I did not make friends easily back then (or now, come to think). People would follow me around and do what I asked, but that didn't make them friends. I chose Abie to be my friend because I liked that he didn't try to take advantage of his size—just kept to himself, reading. Some boys in the school took this for weakness; once a couple of them picked on him and Abie grabbed one with each hand and lifted them, pinning them against the fence. "Do not bother me," he said, then put them down and went back to his book. I was tickled by this and introduced myself. I had a motive, to be honest—it pays to have a guy that size around.

As I got more involved with the Sugar House Gang, Abie stayed clean. His father was upstanding and religious, and Abie was trying to follow that model. But he was restless, like all of us. He only half-believed the religious stuff. And he didn't want to be a butcher. He wanted something more (who doesn't?).

He didn't say hello when I walked into the so-called abattoir; here again, we were too close for hello. "Did he like the meat?" he asked, without looking up from the chop block.

"Sure he did, what's not to like about prime," I said.

"You'll see, that dog will be your friend for life. Next time he sees you, his mouth will start watering."

There was no point telling Abie there would be no "next time" for the dog. That was the kind of thing that would upset Abie.

"You think the guy will do what you asked?"

"If he knows what's good for him," I said.

Abie glanced up at me whilst separating a cut. "You look like hell," he said. "You get any sleep? Had any breakfast?"

I shrugged. I don't know why people care so much about food.

"Papa!" he yelled. "Got any coffee for our Joe?"

Before you knew it, Mister Z was feeding me like a prince. After I ate, I took a little nap in a chair amongst the hanging carcasses, a blanket tucked up under my chin, whilst Abie chopped and talked about who-knows-what. It was a nice in-and-out drifting sleep, and I almost forgot my troubles for a while. Then Abie came over and sat next to me. He patted my knee with that big hand but didn't look at me—we didn't look right at each other much. "Whatever happens," he said, looking across the room, "I am here. You need me to help bust her out, say the word."

It was good of him to say it. But the best thing about Abie was that he didn't even have to, because I already knew.

By the afternoon, I hoped to hear good news. Max rode out to Eloise with Solly at midday. They learned that Rachel was still in there. And she was not allowed to see visitors.

I am a fair man and I understand that it can take time to do something. So I said, "Give Thompson another day and let's see."

I gave it another day, but nothing changed. By now I was feeling the pressure. I had an urge to break something and it's a wonder I didn't hurt some passerby just for crossing my path. I was sleepless and unwashed, having stayed on the move between the apartment, the butcher shop, and Solly's car. Mostly I roamed the streets of old Detroit: the smoke-belching factories, the construction sites, the crowded fish markets. But I didn't see any of it. I was deep in my own head and it was not a cheerful place.

I checked in at the apartment in late afternoon of the second day and Max finally had some news, though not what I expected. "One of Weintraub's guys came by earlier," he said. "Buster wants to know why you're in hiding. Wants to talk to you."

I was going to ignore it; I did not need to get distracted by work right now. But Max stayed after me. "Go see him," he said. "Tell him the situation. What can it hurt?"

Max didn't understand about Weintraub—that anything you got from him would have to be paid back for the rest of your life. But I wasn't in a position to be choosy.

"He is waiting for you at the Crime," Max said.

Buster Weintraub liked to eat his supper at the Cream of Michigan diner, surrounded by other members of the Sugar House Gang. There was nothing special about the place. It had chipped tile floors, and the booths had wooden benches with worn seat cushions. The Sugars were the diner's best customers. They were also its only customers, because once they started coming regularly, everybody else stopped. The newspapers in all their cleverness began calling it the "Crime of Michigan." Didn't bother us; we thought the name was funny and we embraced it.

The booth in the corner furthest from the front door was Buster Weintraub's. He was so wide he took up almost the whole bench himself. He usually had his bodyguard, Baldy Klein, sitting opposite him. Klein was also big, especially around the shoulders, and had a full head of wavy hair, which made his nickname confusing (he got it as a kid when his father made him shave his head). The only time Baldy got out of that opposite seat was when somebody else came to talk to Buster. Then Klein would take a seat in the adjoining booth, with his back to the visitor.

When I came walking toward Buster's booth, Klein was studying a crossword puzzle whilst Buster was reading the paper and spooning barley soup into his wet mouth. Buster never looked up but knew it was me coming. He said to Klein, "Move it."

Klein vacated his seat, giving me a look. Then I stood waiting for the signal. Without looking up Buster flicked his pudgy hand in the direction of the empty bench. That meant it was time for me to sit.

He then raised the hand in the air and snapped his fingers; it always surprised me that fingers so soft could make such a sharp sound. A waiter came rushing up, an old hunched-over guy.

"Get him a soup," Buster said.

"Nothing for me, I just ate," I lied.

"You should have a soup," Buster said, his eyes still on the newspaper. "It settles you. These idiots come in here and guzzle coffee and then wonder why they get *shpilkes*. If you are gonna hang around a coffee shop all day, soup is your best bet."

With a guy like Weintraub, you're supposed to go along with whatever bullshit he feels like talking about, so I guess I should have said, "Yes, Buster, you got that right, nothing beats soup, that's for sure." But I had neither the time nor patience for that.

"I have a situation," I said.

Buster took a big loud slurp of his soup. He still wouldn't take his eyes from the paper, which was his way of putting me in my place. I would not get a look from him until he was ready.

"Yes, I heard all about your situation," he said. "Your honey is in the nut house, and your balls are feeling blue."

Now he looked up and gave me a little mocking smile. A grain of barley sat on his fat lower lip.

"Can you help?" I asked.

"What, with your balls?"

This was a joke and then again maybe it wasn't. Since I joined the gang as a teenager, Weintraub always made remarks like this to me, and sometimes put his hand on the back of my neck in a way that didn't feel right. There were rumors that he liked boys, though he had a wife at home. With me, at least, he never took it beyond little soft pats and sly remarks. I wouldn't have stood for more and he was smart enough to know that.

"Can you help with the girl?" I said.

"The girl, the girl, what about the girl," he said, imitating me now. And I was thinking about things I could do to his throat, if ever I could locate it under the triple chin.

Weintraub folded his hands on the table between us; the fingers were so swollen they could only cross at the tips, no further up. "Okay, you want my help, is that what you want?"

I thought it was pretty fucking obvious, but I went along, and nodded. This was not enough for him.

"Ask for it," he said. "You want my help you gotta ask."

I was pretty sure I already had, twice. But no matter, I had been eating shit from the time I sat down at this table, and another helping wouldn't kill me.

"Can you help me?" I said.

"You should ask it right. Not *can* I; *will* I."

"Will you?" I said.

"Will I what?"

I heard Baldy Klein chuckling behind me, at my expense.

"Will you help?" I said.

"Of course, Joey." He reached out and pinched my cheek. "All you had to do was ask."

He asked me if I wanted to bust her out and I said yes. He asked when and I said the sooner the better.

"Well, how's about midnight tonight?"

My stomach tightened when I heard that.

"I will provide you a truck and three goons," Buster said. "That good enough for you, my Joey?"

I left a few minutes later, dismissed by Weintraub with a wave of the hand. It was all set: I was to meet up with a crew of his men, at midnight, on an abandoned riverside pier off Riopelle Street. I would be picked up by a truck fully stocked with arms and explosives. From there, we would proceed to Eloise, whereupon we would storm the nuthouse, grab Rachel, and, who knows, maybe set all the crazies free to wreak havoc on Detroit.

FIVE

It seemed like midnight would never come. I killed some time by sneaking into Rachel's apartment. The door was unlocked; in fact the chain lock was broken. Soon as I walked in, I could see how she'd struggled—a chair was toppled over, a blanket strewn on the floor. They'd pulled her out of bed. Imagine being yanked from your bed by strangers in the dark. The pillow was still dented where her head lay; I put my face to it and smelled it, and the scent of her hair filled me up.

I gathered up a pair of her socks, her coat, and a scarf. I wasn't going to carry her out of that place in just her nightgown. I rolled up the coat, with the socks inside, and used the scarf to tie up the whole package.

Later, at around 11 pm, I made one quick stop back at my own apartment.

Max jumped when he saw me. "I've been worried sick about you," he said.

I filled him in on what I was doing. Of course he started to fret and fidget and ask questions: Why so soon, why is this necessary, etcetera. Finally he got round to the question uppermost in his mind the whole time: "What if you don't come back? What then?"

I sat him down in the chair and put my hands on his shoulders.

"You think I would ever leave you behind?" I said.

He didn't answer; he was looking down at the floor.

"There is nothing on this earth that could keep me from coming back," I said.

I poured him a shot of whiskey and one for myself, and we drank a toast to our dead father. "I remember the way he used to hold you," I told Max. "Like you were the most precious thing, like he never wanted to let go." I saw a tear in Max's eyes and I knew I better cut the sob stuff and get on my way.

As I was leaving, Max said, "Abie's been by a couple of times, looking for you. He said he doesn't know what you're doing but he wants to be part of it. What should I tell him?"

"Tell him we'll all meet for breakfast—steak and eggs."

I ankled down to the Riopelle pier, arriving early. I looked out on the black river; moonlight glinted off its oily ripples. I paced back and forth on the wooden dock, Rachel's balled-up coat under my arm like a football. At a quarter past midnight, the truck still hadn't come. Then I heard footsteps.

In the dark I could make out three men, all wearing hats. I was pretty sure one of them was Baldy Klein.

"So where's the truck?" I said.

"Change of plans," one of them answered—yes it was Baldy's voice. With him was a guy I recognized as Art Goldman; the third man was a stocky goon known as "Gottasmoke" (he got the nickname because he constantly bummed cigarettes by asking "Got a smoke?"). I didn't know any of the three that well, but I knew all three were killers. Art was particularly known for his skill with a knife.

Art and Gottasmoke fanned out so that they were on either side of me; Baldy was dead ahead. Behind me was the river.

I dropped the balled-up coat to free my arms. After that, no one moved. I guess they were waiting for me to run, but I stood perfectly still. It wasn't easy because I had so much juice pumping through me, but the best thing to do in such circumstances is wait, and then counteract. They must have been thinking the same thing, so we had a standoff.

In that long moment, I had a burning feeling inside and it

wasn't fear—it was anger. And whilst I had plenty of people to be mad at, I was mainly angry at one person and that was myself. I've never thought of myself as stupid, but it occurred to me now that it was stupid to believe that Weintraub could be trusted. And stupid to think it was possible to bully a DA who was, in fact, better connected to the gangs than I was. It was stupid not to realize that such a corrupt DA would no doubt be owed a favor by the likes of Weintraub; and that he would collect on that debt by calling Weintraub and saying, "There is a man in your employ who has threatened me and killed my dog and I want him taken care of." All of this was crystal-clear to me now on this dock, but of course that is the mark of the stupid man: By the time he wises up, it's too late.

Baldy Klein made the first move—stepping forward, drawing a silver blade from inside his coat. I lunged right at him and thrust the heel of my hand straight into his nose, whereupon I heard the bridge crack. Art was meanwhile coming at me from my right, in good position for a side-thrust elbow. The elbow hit his face at exactly the same time his blade penetrated my side, just under the ribs. Art staggered back, leaving the knife stuck in me. I should have left it—it had already done its damage—but instead I tried to delicately draw it out of me, and whilst doing that I felt a sharp point rake across my back, thanks to good old Gottasmoke. I spun to face him and grabbed his wrist but as I did I was slashed on the side again, this time by Baldy, whose nose was gushing. I reached for my newest wound and this freed up Gottasmoke's hand, and he slashed me again across my chest. Then Art, coming from behind, grabbed the knife still embedded in my side and yanked it out, which set off a gusher—I tried to cover it with my hand, keep the blood from escaping. Then I got slashed again, in the shoulder, and this time I couldn't even tell you who did it because I was starting to see less clearly now.

They took turns slicing me. They could've just run me through and ended it, but they didn't. This was a conscious decision on their part, or maybe an order from Buster Weintraub. At some point I dropped to my knees but that didn't stop the slashing—it only made it easier for them.

By this time, the three of them were blurs, circling me. The only thing sharp was the feeling of the blade each time it crossed my chest, back, shoulders—they were putting so many stripes on my body that I had a vision of myself as a tiger. I heard one of the voices above me say, "Baldy, let's finish this." And then I felt one last penetration, deep this time, through the middle of my back, and into my very core. After that I got smacked hard in the face and I thought maybe it was a baseball bat. But it was just the boards on the wooden dock, hitting me in the cheek as I landed face-first. I lay there with one eye open but seeing nothing, and what I heard with my ear to the dock sounded like gentle raindrops on a pond—which was almost comforting until I realized I was hearing my own blood dripping through the slats on the dock and into the shallows of the river below.

I thought the men were gone but they weren't. I could feel tugging on my jacket, and hands reaching in my pants pockets. I assumed the bastards were robbing a dead man, but no, what they were doing was jamming heavy rocks in all my pockets. Then my body seemed to levitate, like something in a magic show—I was up in the air, and would have thought maybe my spirit was rising up to heaven, except I do not believe in such garbage. After rising up, I felt my body swinging from side to side. And then I went sailing through the air and that, I tell you, was a thrill, even in my sorry condition. But that was followed by a splash and a descent into the cold—a cold I had never felt before. Down in the water I was like a baby in the womb, the only difference being that a baby in the womb is headed one way and I was headed the other.

For some crazy reason I thought of my dead father and had the distinct feeling I was about to run into him. And I thought, *How will he recognize me? He has not seen me since I was five.*

You may wonder what it's like to find yourself at the bottom of the Detroit River with rocks in your pockets. Not many who've been in that position are able to tell of the experience. But I can.

First off, I never did see a light at the end of that tunnel everyone talks about. Probably because there *was* no tunnel at the bottom of the Detroit River (though in later years, we would do our damnedest to build one). Down in that water, I saw nothing and felt only that I was in limbo, waiting for someone or something. As I said, my father was foremost in my thoughts for some reason. So I was not surprised when I felt his big hands take hold of me under my arms.

I was facedown in the muddy floor of the river and couldn't see him but I could feel his strength as he started to lift me out of the in-between world. Of course I welcomed this—at first. But then it occurred to me that if I went with my father, I would be leaving behind Max, who needed me, and Rachel, who needed me even more. I struggled in his grasp, twisting my shoulders. But he wouldn't let go and kept pulling and I started to feel myself rising up out of the muck.

Then I had the distinct feeling I wasn't in water anymore—but there was no air, either. I was not breathing, and I was blind and deaf. I was still in limbo, though it now seemed like a drier one. Suddenly I felt a tremendous force pressing down on my chest, which caused water to surge through my lungs and out my mouth. The water must've gone straight up and come right back down in a splash on my face. In that instant, all my senses returned to me. I was breathing, and could hear my own gasps. My eyes popped open and I could see again. And what I saw was a face looking down at me from above. Not my father, no—it was Abie.

"You're alive," he informed me. He had a smile on his big face.

Then everything went black, for a good long time.

The next time I opened my eyes, I was surrounded by dead meat—bloody carcasses hanging on all sides of me, whilst I was laid out on a chopping block. If I didn't know better I'd have thought I was in some stage of hell, but of course I knew very well I was in the Zussman family's butcher shop, or more precisely in the rear of it, in that so-called abattoir.

Abie took my body there because he didn't know where else to bring it. Whilst I was out cold, they sewed and bandaged me up right there on the chopping block—Abie, his butcher father, and a neighborhood woman with training as a nurse. They were all out of the room when I woke up but Abie was the first to return.

"You pulled me out of the river?" I asked, and he nodded with his head down as if embarrassed.

"But how did you know I was *in* the river?"

"Max told me you'd gone down to the pier alone, on a mission," he said. "I had a bad feeling so I went down right away. When I got there I saw the blood on the dock—I touched it and it was still warm. Then I jumped down into the water and started wading. I almost tripped over you."

He leaned in a little closer to me now, as if to share a secret. "When I pulled you out, your face was blue—I was sure you were a goner. I pushed down on your chest. Then I said a prayer over you, and pushed once more. And just like that, you came spitting back to life. God saved you, Joe."

I was not buying any of that. Some people suddenly discover God when they're close to death, but not me.

"No, you were the one who saved me, Abie," I said. "You did it with your own two hands."

"But how did I know just where to step in the water so I'd stumble on you? And how'd I know enough to push that water out of your lungs—I never did anything like that before. Maybe I was God's instrument. His agent, sent to save you."

I smiled. "Abie the Agent," I said.

This would become my name for him forever more. People would hear the name and not get what it meant. Some thought he was named after a Jewish comic strip hero from that era, others figured he got the name because he was stealthy (which he sure was). But the truth was that Abie was an agent of God, destiny, or whatever you wish to call it. He could give life, as he did for me, or quietly take it away, as he did for so many others.

I had trouble staying awake the next couple of days. It was touch and go because I'd left a lot of blood in the river. The only reason I survived at all was because of the good work of a former war nurse named Myra. She was a mother of four living on Hastings who risked a lot to help me, just because her friend and butcher, Mr. Z, knocked on her door and asked. (I would never see the woman again, but in later times she would open her mail to find a mysterious unmarked package containing a large sum of money.)

She closed and stitched every one of those openings all over my torso, working for hours on end. Abie's father stood beside her, in his butcher's apron, helping to seal the wounds and tend them. I should have been in a hospital, but if they took me to one, people would have known I was alive—and that the job of getting rid of me still needed finishing.

They had to be careful to keep me a secret. When my brother Max came to the butcher shop to see me, he did so in dead of night, because the Sugars were watching by day to see how he'd respond to his brother's disappearance. When Max first laid eyes on me, all bandaged and breathing funny, he got very upset. Right off, *he* started breathing funny, and I said, "There's only room for one sick person in this so-called abattoir, and I got here first."

He smiled a little but then all of a sudden he broke down and started crying. He was embarrassed and tried to hold it back, but couldn't; he just sat in the chair next to me and buried his face. "I thought you were gone," he said into his hands.

"You didn't listen," I said. "I told you I was coming back."

When Max stopped crying, I asked about Rachel. "Any news?"

He looked down whilst shaking his head. But then he looked up at me with eyes still bleary though also a little hopeful. "One good thing—you'll never guess who's trying to help us," he said.

"You mean the gimp?"

SIX

Whilst I was busy getting myself sliced and drowned, Riley had been taking a more productive approach to the Rachel situation. Some of the details of his actions were not known to me until many years later, when he divulged them during several visits to me in prison. I was surprised to learn how much he tried to do back then. Didn't mean I was grateful—because how can you be grateful to a man who takes from you all that he eventually took from me?

Still, back then, in January of 1920, he did do a few things. He got started the day after I met with him in that coffee shop. He went to his office determined to ask his boss about "the girl." But Thompson did not show up in the morning as usual. He did not arrive until afternoon, and when he did, Riley observed that the old man looked shaken. Asked about it, Thompson said his dog had died tragically in the night.

Riley waited an hour to show respect, then went back into Thompson's office to try to get answers. He asked if Thompson knew anything about a Rachel Roth and of course Thompson denied it. He told Thompson about the girl being taken in the raid and then mysteriously transferred from the Ford hospital to Eloise.

"How in the hell would I know about such things?" Thompson

barked at him. "And why do you care? What is this to you?"

Riley said he didn't want to see an innocent girl get put away in a nut house, or words to that effect, and Thompson said, "How do you know she's innocent? And how do you know she's not crazy? And how do you know her in the first place?"

Riley explained that it was all bound up with the pickpocket incident—Rachel was the pickpocket's girl.

"I see," Thompson said, getting more and more steamed. "So it was not enough to drop the charges and let that criminal off the hook. Now you're going to solve all his problems. And you're doing this on my dime."

The conversation just got worse from there, and it ended with Thompson telling Riley in no uncertain terms to "leave it alone."

But Riley did not. He went to the Henry Ford Hospital, to inquire about why the patient Rachel Roth was transferred to Eloise. They hemmed and hawed, but he put his foot down (his real one, I'm sure) and said, "I want to see any papers that were signed, and I want to see the person who signed them."

They brought him to the office of a man named Ernest Liebold. Riley did not know this, but Liebold was Ford's secret right-hand man, involved in everything from Ford's newspaper, *The Dearborn Independent*, to Ford's hospital. The funny thing about Liebold was that he had no knowledge of newspapers, or hospitals, or the car business. His area of expertise was *The Protocols of the Elders of Zion,* of which he'd made quite a study. For those who still don't get it, here it is plain: Liebold hated Jews.

He had a heavy accent and a thick mustache that covered his mouth. As soon as the meeting began, he tried to turn the tables on Riley by asking *him* questions: Vot is your rank in the DA's office; vot does your boss say about all this; are you questioning zee medical practices of zee most reputable hospital in Detroit, and so on. Riley waited him out and then asked Liebold just two questions: Are you saying you're unwilling to tell me who approved the transfer of this girl? Are you trying to hide that information?

Liebold finally told Riley that he himself had approved sending the girl to Eloise, based on "consultation" with the doctors in attendance. He said the girl had become uncontrollable. He also said they'd followed standard procedure of having a judge sign off on the order to have her committed; the judge was named Patterson. Riley knew that name—an old crony of Thompson's.

Riley noticed that at one point when they were speaking of Rachel, Liebold referred to her as "the Jewish girl" and Riley interrupted him and said, "What does her religion have to do with any of this?" Liebold just tilted his head and gave him a little tight-lipped smile under the big mustache.

After he left Liebold, Riley tried to see Judge Patterson, but Patterson wouldn't talk to him. He ended the day by going to his coffee shop to have his lonely little dinner.

Next day when Riley went into work, Thompson was waiting to pounce. "So it seems my good friend Dennis Patterson had a visit from you yesterday…"

Before Thompson could get any further, Riley said to him: "I am an investigator. And that means I investigate. Are you telling me that certain things are off limits?"

"You investigate what I tell you to," Thompson said. "This is not even a case. You're not here to help criminals, you are here to help me put them away!"

"And what about the innocent," said Riley. "Am I supposed to help you 'put them away' as well?"

It went on like that for a while and then Thompson laid it on the line: "Maybe you need to stop and think about whether you wish to keep working here or not."

Riley didn't say anything to that. He got his hat and left, with the assistant DA, Teddy Baird, following him outside. "Harry, hang on, let's talk about this," Baird said, but Riley kept going.

Riley spent the day doing research on Ernest Liebold, and on the newspaper Liebold put out for Ford. He'd seen the *Independent* before, with its headlines about "The Jewish Problem," but he'd always ignored it; now he spent three hours reading back issues.

By the time Riley returned to the office, Thompson was gone— off to some swank dinner party, according to Teddy Baird. "But you should speak to him and patch things up," said Baird, who was the kind that always tries to make peace even when no one wants it. "You should talk to him first thing tomorrow."

To which Riley said, "Why wait? Tell me where the party is."

The party was in an upstairs ballroom of a mansion with a grand staircase. Riley was halfway up the stairs, slowly taking it one step at a time, when he felt someone watching him. He looked up and at the top of the stairs saw a girl of about twenty, holding her girl-friend's arm, smiling at him, then whispering something in the girl-friend's ear, without taking her eyes off him. He figured she was making a silly girl's joke, maybe about how slowly he moved. She was tall with long legs and shingled red hair. Riley had developed a habit of not looking in girls' eyes too much, afraid he might see pity. But he did look long enough to notice that this girl's eyes were green and had a curious sparkle in them.

By the time he reached the top, she'd shed the girlfriend, and was waiting alone for him. Riley had already taken his handker-chief in his hand to mop his sweating brow before he noticed she'd thrust out her hand for a shake—an unusual thing for a girl to do. He wanted to accept her handshake, but he had the cane in one hand and the handkerchief in the other. When he tried to put the cloth away he dropped it between them.

"Damn," he said, and that just embarrassed him even more.

The girl easily stooped and swooped up the handkerchief, as he tried to say, "Don't bother, really…" Then she dabbed his fore-head twice and his cheek once, before neatly folding the cloth and handing it back to him.

"What a ridiculous staircase," she said. "It's supposed to make an impression on people, I guess."

"It sure made one on me," Riley said, catching his breath.

She told him her name was Nan, and asked if he needed a drink after all that climbing. He said he didn't drink, other than a ginger ale now and then. "That can be arranged," she said, and took hold of her arm and pulled him into the party.

*

What I know about that night Riley and Nan met comes more from her than him. In her letters to me, many years later, she seemed to recall every moment. At the party, they stood against a wall in the upstairs hallway, revealing themselves to each other bit by bit. Riley told her about his job, sounding none too thrilled. She said she was a dance teacher, which she loved. Then he felt *he* should talk about something he liked; he brought up swimming. She said she loved cards, and Riley snapped his fingers: "Cards— now we're talking."

Riley was a wallflower at parties, but Nan was like a magnet that drew people to them. As each person came up, she would intro- duce Riley as "my new pal from the District Attorney's office." Riley got a kick out of the girl calling him a "pal."

One of the men who approached was a real showboat. He placed his hands against his heart as he neared Nan. "Do my eyes trick me," he exclaimed, "or are you even lovelier than last we met?"

He was a smallish guy with an oversized and very round head, like a baby. He took hold of Nan's hand and whilst he lowered his big head to kiss it, Nan shot Riley a look with her brow raised— they shared their first little unspoken joke, at this blowhard's ex- pense. She introduced the man to Riley as Jerry Barkley and he shook Riley's hand and announced, "I work for Ford. The man himself, not the company."

Riley, fresh from his reading that day, decided to take a shot: "Do you have anything to do with the *Dearborn Independent?*"

Barkley winked and said, "I have something to do with most everything." Then, turning back to Nan, he started speechifying about "this great city of Detroit" and about how the future looked bright for all, but especially for him. He kept mentioning "the Man Himself," as in, "I know all this good stuff I'm telling you because I got it straight from the Man Himself."

Riley noticed Nan's eyes starting to glaze over and he cut in, saying to her, "I hate to interrupt but there is something I must show you." He took her elbow and led her through the crowd to the other side of the room, whereupon he just stopped and leaned back against the wall.

"So what did you want to show me?" she said.

"I wanted to show you what it would be like to be free of that windbag," Riley said.

Later, Riley caught sight of his boss across the room. He excused himself to Nan and walked over. "I have to tell you something," he said to Thompson, who was startled to see him. "Join me on the terrace?"

Thompson followed him outside. It was freezing cold but a group of revelers were out there, huddled up whilst one poured shots for all out of a glittering platinum flask. They were high-society types, the women wore furs—yet here they were sneaking out in the cold to drink, giggling, loving the mischief of it. The man holding the flask raised it high when Riley and Thompson came out, as an offer. The fool had no idea he was inviting the local DA to partake in an illegal act, but it didn't matter because Thompson and Riley just ignored him and proceeded to the other end of the terrace, where it was empty.

"I thought about our talk this morning," Riley said when they stopped. "You're right—if I'm not willing to play by your rules, I should find myself a new game. I'll clear out my desk tomorrow."

Thompson no doubt had walked out on that balcony expecting an apology. So he took this as a sharp slap on a cold night.

"You brought me out here—in the middle of a party—to tell me you're quitting on me? You have a hell of a lot of gall."

"I just wanted to get it over with," Riley said. "Didn't mean to spoil your good time."

Thompson looked away in disgust, shook his head, then looked back with his lip curled. "I gave you a job in the District Attorney's office—the *District Attorney's office!* I could have picked a hundred guys with more experience. But I picked you."

"Well, for that I thank you," Riley said with a nod and started to walk back toward the door, where Nan was just now poking her head out looking for him. She smiled when their eyes met.

As Riley limped toward her, Thompson yelled from behind: "You know why I hired you? I felt sorry for you, that's all."

Riley saw that Nan stopped smiling and that made him look down. And as he angled past her in the doorway, he muttered that he really had to go because it was late.

Riley made his way down the stairs and out to the sidewalk but didn't get far before hearing footsteps from behind. He turned and there she was again. She stopped as he faced her, folding her arms tight under a fur wrap.

"I've had enough of that party," she said.

He nodded but didn't speak, so she went on, with a little hesitation at first. "What that man said to you... I'll bet it's a lie. That man never felt sorry for anyone in his life."

Riley said, "You're probably right about that."

"I don't feel sorry for you," she said. "You were the only real man at that party, do you happen to know that?"

Riley didn't know what to say. He couldn't imagine that he'd presented enough evidence to merit a judgment like that. But it seemed like she meant it.

"You know who I *do* feel sorry for?" she asked.

He shrugged.

"Me—I am cold and desperately in need of someone to take me for a hot cocoa. Think there's any hope for me?"

SEVEN

On the third day of my second life I felt horrible, which marked an improvement. I knew it was time to leave the abattoir behind. It was too risky staying, and besides I was tired of living with slabs of red meat. I thought about it long and hard, and said to Abie: "I need to go away someplace and get better. Get in touch with Grabowski in Hamtramck."

Abie was taken aback. "Grabowski? Hamtramck? You sure?"

The little burg of Hamtramck wasn't far from downtown Detroit, but it may as well have been another country. It was a boiling cauldron of Polack immigrants who didn't trust the government and were pissing mad about Prohibition. The Ford and Dodge plants were the twin engines that ran the town during the day. But at night the immigrant workers spilled onto streets and hell broke loose. The Jewish gangsters had always steered clear of the town and its crazy Poles, as did the oilers. But here was the kicker: Even the law itself had given up on Hamtramck. The Governor tried to bring in state police to tame it and when that failed, the cops cleared out and said, "Let the animals fend for themselves." It was just the kind of haven I was looking for.

Later that night, Abie and Max laid me across the back seat of Mr. Z's Ford. Max bade me goodbye whilst Abie took the wheel. The whole drive, Abie talked to me over his shoulder—about religion, psychology, philosophy, all that crap. I don't recall the particulars because I kept drifting in and out, waking painfully each time we hit a bump in the road; I felt those bumps in every one of my many slits. At one point, I awoke to hear Abie talking about wolves, or so it seemed—an offbeat subject even for him.

"...And when the wolf swallows a piece of bone, his digestive system wraps the bone in hair. To protect the intestines. Can you beat that? As Grabowski says, 'I wish *I* had their guts!'"

I was going to ask Abie what the hell he was talking about, but I nodded off before I could get the question out.

The car pulled up in front of a house with cracked windows and peeling paint. Abie put my arm over his shoulder and walked me toward the house. I saw a man and two women sitting on the porch. The women looked me over with made-up raccoon eyes. The man, big and barrel-chested, stood up.

"Somebody drink too much beer!" he yelled, looking at me. He grabbed one of the women by the arm and lifted her out of her chair. "S'no problem. She gonna make you stand up straight."

"We're not here for that," Abie said. "We're going to see the man downstairs."

The woman looked relieved and sat back down. The man spat on the porch floor. "He focking crazy, that one," he said. "You tell him I say so. He don' scare me."

Abie ignored the man and led me around the side of the house, to a backyard littered with broken bottles and what looked like animal bones. We stopped at two large metal basement doors that slanted up from the ground, the kind that pull open from above. Abie told me I better keep back, and positioned me ten feet away.

"What, is the door booby-trapped?" I said.

"No, it's the wolves," he said.

"The wolves?"

"I told you. In the car. They're not wolves, really. Well, they half are."

"What the hell are you talking about?" I said.

Abie got a solemn look on his face. "Joe, I have to tell you that things have gotten a little strange with Grabowski," he said.

I said, "Yeah, well, Grabowski was always nuts."

"That's true," Abie said. "But now... more so."

Just then the metal door started to open from below, but just a crack. A yell came through the opening: *"You fuckin' whoremonger,"* a deep, phlegmy voice announced, *"if that's you hangin' around my door you're gonna get eaten."* Along with the voice there was a rustling of chains, and a growling sound that was low but still worrisome.

As the door opened wider the first face to emerge had pale eyes that glowed in the dark and fixed on me. The snout was long and white; the lips parted to reveal fangs. It was not a good face to welcome a man to his new abode. Then Grabowski's head poked through the opening and to be honest, *his* face wasn't much better.

Some explanation about Grabowski is in order here, because people have always tended to assume he was some kind of monster who was just born that way. The truth is, he was once upon a time a normal human child. It all changed when at an early age he caught chicken pox, which led a few years later to a severe case of shingles. His skin became scaly, patchy, and inflamed; he walked around like a boy on fire. Such a condition can make life hell for a school kid. In Grabowski's case, it also had the effect of making life hell for those around him.

He was one of the few kids in the Old Bishops School who wasn't Jewish, which made him even more of an outcast. He began to prey on the students, one by one. He would leap out from nowhere and ambush a boy, beating him senseless and taking his possessions. He had a particular fondness for trinkets, rings, or anything shiny. I knew he would try to jump me or Max one day, especially since Max had a nice pocket watch.

Grabowski went after me first—probably figured he'd save the easy prey for later. I was 14, and just starting to absorb street-fighting lessons from a Sugar Houser named Imi Hechtenstein, who knew the art of the elbows, imported from the Bratislava ghetto. When Grabowski pounced, I delivered a few choice ones—if I recall, elbow number 2 to the chin, then number 5 to the gut, concluding with number 7 crashing down on the back of the neck. It was lights out for Grabowski. But he never held it against me. It was almost as if in pummeling him I had been the first person in a while to touch him in any meaningful way. He began to hang around me and Max and Abie, without asking. Max was uneasy about it, but Abie took a shine to Grabowski and so did I.

We formed an alliance that crossed all lines—Grabowski not only was a Catholic and a Pole, he seemed to be of a different species altogether. Our group became known throughout the school, the Hastings neighborhood, and even the far reaches of the city. We did steal occasionally, yes; Grabowski in particular. And the mere sight of us on the prowl scared many in the Hastings neighborhood, though it should be said that some of those people tended to scare easily.

The merchants started to blame us for everything bad that happened to them—every window broken in a storm, any apple that rolled off the pile and went missing. One of the merchants declared that we were "tainted," like red meat that had spoilt and turned purple. That was when we first started hearing the "Purple Gang" name applied to us, though we just laughed it off at the time.

For Grabowski, the breaking point came when, at age 17, he saw a jeweled ring on a boy's finger and decided he had to have it. But the ring was tight and wouldn't come off, so Grabowski cut off the finger to get the ring.

Everyone was on the hunt for poor Grabowski after that, so he beat it out of town on foot, made his way upstate, got himself locked up somewhere in the boondocks, broke out, hid in the woods for a long time, and finally ended up in Hamtramck, amongst what he called his "native people."

When he rose up out of that basement door it was the first I'd seen of Grabowski in two years. He had the one beast in front of him, barely restrained by a chain twisted around his hand. The second animal, also on a chain, skulked behind him, peeking out at me from between Grabowski's knees. Grabowski's hair was long and wild, and his cheeks and nose were covered with those familiar scaly red blisters. Always barrel-chested, he'd grown thicker, especially around the waist—his gut stretched a soiled undershirt, which was all he wore as he came out into the winter cold. He had several rings on the fingers of both hands.

He went to Abie first, and handed him the chain leashes. The beasts knew Abie, who'd been coming to visit Grabowski for some time. With his hands free, Grabowski threw his big arms open wide and rushed straight at me and I braced for the impact.

"Ya fuck, I missed 'ya," he said. "I'm gonna take care a 'ya."

The bear hug was painful; I felt it in every one of my cuts. But at the same time, it wasn't so bad.

Grabowski led us down the steps into his basement lair—a windowless concrete room lit by a couple of lanterns. He'd created a wire-cage area in one corner with a gate on it; he herded the two beasts into the little pen and shut the gate. But even after they were locked inside, they would not stop pacing and eyeing me.

"Take a load off," Grabowski said, nodding at a couple of folding chairs in the middle of the room. With Abie still helping me, we had to step between empty bottles underfoot. The room was full of junk, including all kinds of weapons—long thin knives and short fat ones, a sword, a billy-club, even a medieval mace.

Grabowski reached down and started picking up bottles from the floor, discarding a couple of empties before finding a half-full one. We sat in a circle in our folding chairs and passed around the bottle. The whiskey burned when it hit my shredded stomach.

"Good stuff," I said, meaning the booze.

"I got my own bar," he told me.

"*You* got a bar? Where?"

"Trunk o' my car. I park outside the gate at the Ford plant. Sell 'em shots when they get out on break. Ya should see 'em line up."

"Heinrich won't like that," I said. "He likes his slaves sober."

"Ford don' know shit about it," Grabowski said. "I got an understandin' with the plant manager. Two-shot limit, so nobody gets too drunk to work. Plus, I do favors."

"Favors?"

"Scare off troublemakers."

By that I guessed he meant labor organizers. "How do you scare them?"

"I bring 'em down here. Sit 'em in that chair you're in. Then I give Ono and Ogod just enough chain to get about two feet from the guy's balls. No more trouble after that."

"Ono and Ogod," I said. "That's their names?"

Grabowski smiled wide—I could see his tonsils through the gap of his missing front teeth. "Some guy I dragged down here, he named 'em that," he said. "They were comin' at 'im full-speed, so he looks at the one an' says, 'Oh no,' then he looks at the otha and says, 'Oh God.'"

When I asked Grabowski where the hell he got two wolves, and for that matter, *why* the hell did he get two wolves, he told me the story. He'd broken out of prison and ended up in the woods Up North, finding his way to a logging camp. The loggers were wary at first but when they saw how strong Grabowski was, they agreed to let him haul logs for food. Grabowski didn't see the beasts right off because they were locked in a cabin; but he heard them howl. When he asked about it, the loggers explained that the area had been lousy with elk that chewed bark and ruined trees. These same woods had wolves that would sometimes kill elk but you couldn't bank on it—couldn't train them to do it. So the loggers tried to build a better wolf.

They brought in Alsatian dogs and cross-fucked them with wolves. The offspring, two pups, were just reaching maturity when Grabowski arrived at the camp, and the loggers were pleased to find that the wolf-dogs were very trainable and adept at killing elk. But one day the pair turned on a logger and almost tore him to pieces. Seeing their mistake, the loggers thought it best to hack the heads off the wolf-dogs. Nobody wanted to do the deed, however, so Grabowski volunteered.

He took the two of them into the woods, tied each one to a tree, raised his hatchet in the air. But when he looked in the pale eyes of the one that would later be called Ono, Grabowski saw something that stopped him—if you ask me, he recognized a kindred spirit.

"Instead 'a choppin' his head off, I reached down an' gave that pup a hug," Grabowski said as we sat in the folding chairs. I glanced over at Abie whilst Grabowski was telling the tale and noticed a little welling up in Abie's eye, which almost made me laugh but I suppressed it. Anyway, Grabowski and the two beasts took off in the woods and had been together ever since.

"So you went on the lam and ended up with wolves," I said, making a little joke but of course these two did not get it.

"Not wolves," Grabowski corrected me.

"No, only half," Abie added.

"Mattafact, betta than a wolf," Grabowski said. "A wolf would be scared'a people. And wouldn't pay me no mind. With these, I got the best'a both breeds—think like a dog, eat like a wolf." He looked over at the cage. "They're my babies," he said.

We talked and drank for about an hour after that, whereupon Abie got up to leave, saying, "The old man worries about me."

I couldn't get up from my chair to say goodbye, so I gave Abie instructions from where I sat. "Talk to Max first thing in the morning. Tell him to go down to Eloise again, try to get in to see her. She has to know we're gonna get her out."

After Abie was gone, Grabowski helped me into a little cot in the corner. I passed out, but my sleep was feverish. Sometime in the night, I half-woke to the sound of footsteps, scratching, and harsh whispers. I wasn't sure if it was a dream. I looked across the room and saw, by candlelight, Grabowski pacing back and forth, naked. He looked down as he paced, and trailing him was one of the "babies," staying a step back as it followed, the pale eyes looking at him and then down at the floor, then up again, then down. In the half-light, Grabowski's skin seemed to glow with inflammation as he furiously scratched his arms, his shoulders, his chest. And in that fierce whisper, he spit curses and accusations: *Mothafucka*, and *The hell you will!* and *Who says? Who?*

He kept on scratching and as he did, patches of dried skin came loose and fell to the floor. The beast at his heels licked up the skin flakes and swallowed them, then looked back up, waiting for the next morsel to drop.

Whilst I lay there unable to move my wrecked body or even turn my head away from this spectacle, I had the brief thought that if this was to be my new life in Hamtramck, maybe I was better off dead in Detroit.

It was weeks before I was on my feet again. How many weeks, I could not tell you because you lose track of time when you're laid up in a windowless basement in Hamtramck and your only companions are either inhuman or crazy or both.

I did not care for his babies—didn't like their eyes on me, nor the sound of their chewing, nor the gamey smell that wafted over to my little cot. Grabowski wanted us all to be friends, trying to get me to pet them and talk baby talk. I told him I would rather die screaming than talk baby talk to anything, especially a pair of mangy mongrels. "Okay, then don' blame me if they bite ya some time," he said. I then told him that if anyone or thing ever tried to dine on me, it would be their last supper. Grabowski gave me a death stare, standing over me whilst I lay in my cot. I returned the stare and finally he shook his head and walked away saying, "I don' know if I like havin' a roomie."

The worst part of it was the nights. Grabowski was gone much of the daytime, selling his shots out of the car trunk, so I had time to read whilst the babies snoozed in each other's arms. But at night Grabowski would bring home whores. Soon as they stepped inside that basement and saw the babies in the cage and me in my bandages, their eyes would bulge and they'd say, "Whoa, whoa, whoa," and then turn to leave. But he would haul them over to his bed and then I would have to stare at the ceiling and listen to him pumping them and cursing them at the same time. He liked to slap them too sometimes, but I would yell, "Cut it out," when he did that—the whores were human after all.

One time when he finished with a girl he brought her to my cot and said, "Joe, I have a gift fer ya." I said I wasn't interested and the girl, a chubby one, took it the wrong way. "Well, you're no prize yourself, you look like The Mummy," she said. This made me laugh and next thing you knew she was getting a rise out of me, and it was good to see that part of me was not dead. But after she was done I felt bad because after all, poor Rachel was locked up and no one was touching her (or so I hoped). I said to Grabowski later, do me a favor and don't bring me any more offerings.

The one good thing about being laid up in bed—or being in prison for that matter—is that you have time to think. In that cot, it occurred to me that in all my previous 19 years I had been waiting for things to come to me. Waiting for lousy odd jobs to be offered by Buster Weintraub; waiting for someone to give Max the opportunity he deserved given his brilliance; waiting for my path in life to be made clear. And more recently, waiting for Thompson to do as promised and release Rachel from Eloise; and then, finally, waiting on that dock for a truck that was never going to come. I decided as I lay there that henceforth, there would be no more waiting on others. I would control my own destiny, and that of the people who depend on me. I would act sooner rather than later.

With regard to regaining my strength, I could have taken months, maybe years, to rest and recover. But I pushed things: I stood on my two feet faster than I should have. Soon after that, I was struggling to do push-ups on the concrete floor. The straining of my muscles made my cuts bleed fresh. The blood mingled with my sweat and dripped to the floor beneath me. But gradually it got easier. Before too long I was doing the pushups with one hand, and then doing one-armed chin-ups on the rusted exposed pipes of the basement ceiling.

I asked Grabowski to bring home a mirror. ("I hate 'em," he confessed, but to his credit he got one anyway.) I'd fight myself in the mirror, relearning the old moves. Each day that opponent in the glass got a little faster and more muscled. Watching me one day, Grabowski said, "Can ya show me the elbow thing? The thing

ya did to me in the schoolyard?" After all these years he still remembered and I was touched. I said sure, and tried to share those
secrets that Imi Hechtenstein brought to Detroit from Bratislava,
where the Jews fought enemies coming at them from all sides. But
Grabowski was a poor student with no discipline, and he decided
in the end, "I don' need this shit, I just go wild an' it gets the job
done."

Whilst rehabilitating my body, I did not neglect the mind. I read
more in Grabowski's basement than I did in my entire life before
that. And in doing so I experienced another of those connections
that click together in the mind: I suddenly understood that all the
things I was learning now—about knowledge and power, about
who has it and why, and how it works—had been kept from me
during my years growing up. And it was clear to me now that such
things were purposely withheld from the kind of kids who went to
the Old Bishops School. We were meant to be cogs in the wheel
of Heinrich Ford, so they had to keep us small-minded, had to
control what went into the heads of poor boys. But there were no
controls or filters now, and I devoured everything that Abie
brought me: books on psychology and religion, on business, war-
fare, strategy. I took notes whilst I read. I was planning to use it
all, even if I didn't know exactly how yet.

EIGHT

Eventually, I was ready to go out into the world again, or at least that part of the world called Hamtramck. I wandered out one afternoon and it was like walking through a ghost town. Then the five o'clock horn blew at the Dodge plant, and the day-shifters soon filled the street, shoving each other, yelling, laughing, singing Polish songs. I got swept up in a tide rushing toward the bars, and there I drank, made a few fast pals and, wouldn't you know, got into a scrap. I'll skip the details except to say it was over in a flash and it ended, as ever, with elbow number 7.

After the scrap, I was toasted by my new Polack pals. As I was leaving the bar, the manager, a cigar-chomper named Nowak, stopped me and said, "That was nice handiwork." He offered me a job as a bouncer.

The place was called Zabawa and I worked with another bouncer named Kowalski, known as the Gorilla. This Gorilla Kowalski was the biggest man I have known—aside from Abie, of course. He was very strong but that was not the only reason for his nickname. He also had an uncanny ability to climb—he could shimmy up a light pole, or scale the side of a three-story brick building. He used this skill to win a few bar wagers (with me in charge of taking bets).

After collecting a pot one time, I patted him on the back and

said, "Gorilla, someday we will find a better use for your talents."
He thought I was just talking.

I worked through the nights at Zabawa and enjoyed the company of these rough men. Some of them called me "brot," (which
sounded like "brat" but I knew it was Polish for "brother"—
Grabowski, too, used to call me that). I did not mind the constant
fights because it kept me busy. The one thing I didn't like was the
way drunk Polacks liked to hug and slobber on you; I have never
been one for that kind of thing. A sharp poke in the ribs was
sometimes required to remind someone that, after all, I was not
really his "brot."

But if you think I was standoffish, you should have seen
Grabowski. I invited him to Zabawa one night and all he did was
stand at the end of the bar downing shots, spitting on the floor,
and glaring at everyone. I tried to keep an eye on him but I had
work to do. Later that night, someone came for me and said,
"Brot, you pal's outside, cuttin' somebody." Out in the gutter,
Grabowski sat on top of a man, his knees pinning the guy's shoulders. I couldn't see the man's head beneath him, but I heard the
screaming. When I got closer I saw that Grabowski was using a
small knife to shave a layer of skin off the man's forehead—doing
this in a workmanlike manner, the way you might peel a potato.
The man had made some crack about Grabowski's scaly skin, and
Grabowski was asking over and over, "Whose skin is peelin'
now?" After that I did not bring Grabowski to Zabawa anymore.

Each night I walked home, bloody knuckles in my pockets, just as
night was turning to day. But a couple of times each week, I quit a
little early, borrowed Grabowski's car, and drove to Hastings in
dead of night. I would steal into my brother's apartment and
watch him sleep a little, then wake him gently. I'd put coffee on
the stove—the smell filling the apartment—and we'd sit together
at the table as first daylight streamed through the window. But I
had to leave quick before the merchants came out. I was a dead
man, you see, and therefore couldn't be seen in the light of day.

During those morning coffees I would ask, "So what is the latest?" and Max knew what I meant. He always answered, "No news." This went on for two months. But one morning I crept in and Max was already awake, and couldn't wait to spill the news.

"She is getting out," he said. "Because of Riley."

After quitting the DA's office, Riley had continued to poke around regarding Rachel. You may choose to believe he cared about the girl. My feeling is that he was simply the kind who gets hold of a case, any case, the way a dog takes possession of an old shoe—he will shake it, chew it on all sides, and will not let go. The master can take the shoe away, but soon as he turns his back the dog will be chewing it again.

Riley did not know if there was a connection between a Jewish girl being locked up and all of those Jew-hating screeds he'd read in the *Dearborn Independent*, but knowing Liebold had a hand in running both the hospital and the paper, he wanted to learn more about this Liebold. He didn't think he'd get far talking to the old Kraut himself. So he staked out another source.

Riley drove himself over to Dearborn and parked outside the offices of the *Independent*. He waited in the car until he saw the man he was looking for—the blowhard with the big baby head.

Jerry Barkley was headed for his own car when Riley came hobbling up and said, "Mr. Barkley, can I have a word?"

Barkley gave him the once over from head to shoe. He did not seem to recognize Riley from the party—just assumed he was a gimp beggar. Barkley dug into his trouser pocket and pulled out a quarter.

"Here you are, my good man," he said.

With his thumb he flipped the coin in the air between him and Riley—Riley was supposed to catch it like a trained animal, I guess, maybe with his mouth. Riley was dumbfounded by this little stunt and watched the quarter bounce on the ground. Then he looked back up at Barkley and said, "Don't you know the difference between a word and a coin?"

Riley reminded him that they'd met a few nights back, and Barkley's attitude changed upon realizing he was dealing with the law. But he remained jokey. "Uh-oh," he said. "What am I in trouble for now?"

"That is what we need to sort out," Riley said.

Barkley suggested they talk in his car, a shiny new Model T. It had the softest passenger seat Riley had ever sat on, with its plush velvet cushion. "Custom-made," Barkley told him. "Got this car as a gift from the Man Himself."

Here we go again, Riley thought.

Whilst Barkley took them for a spin, Riley said he was looking into the case of a girl who may have been wrongly arrested, then shipped to a mental institution. "Could be a serious matter," Riley said. "If it turns out fraud was committed, people could go to jail."

"I know nothing about any girl in a mental institution," Barkley said. "Though I know a few who belong in one." He winked again at Riley.

"Don't do that," Riley said.

"What?"

"Don't wink at me," Riley said. "It annoys me. You don't want to annoy me when I'm in the middle of investigating you."

Barkley would not stop smiling, even now. "Investigating me? I'm flattered. Nobody has ever before investigated little old me. Tell me, what deep dark secrets have you unearthed?"

"Well, here is an interesting thing," Riley said. "You work for the top teetotaler in Detroit. Who fought to make this the first dry city. And who spies on his workers to make sure they don't drink, and uses you to do the spying. And yet—here's the curious part— it turns out you are a bootlegger, Barkley."

Barkley tried to keep smiling even as the car swerved.

Riley had gotten the scoop on Barkley from Nan. That night of the party, as the two of them chatted over hot cocoa, Barkley's name came up. "I might have an interest in that fellow," Riley said.

"The gas bag?" she said.

"He might have inside information on a case I'm working on."

She looked at him with raised eyebrows, and he corrected himself. "A case I *was* working on."

"Well, then, why don't you talk to him? He's the talkative type."

Riley gave her a little smile and looked down at his cocoa. "I need some... leverage," he said. "Something that would encourage Barkley to be helpful."

Nan's eyes lit up. "You need dirt! Oh, this could be a hoot!"

Over the next two days, she talked to her girlfriends, including one who'd been "friendly" with Barkley. Turned out Barkley was moonlighting in booze—paying small-boaters to bring it in from Windsor, and even financing a little bar in the rear of a candy store. Riley smiled at the news; many were doing such things, but not many were doing it right under the booze-sniffing nose of Ford.

Once Riley told Barkley that he knew about the bootlegging sideline, the smart remarks stopped and information started to flow. Riley learned that at the *Independent* Liebold decided what would go in the paper, and Barkley's job was to "make it sound reasonable."

"I see," Riley said. "He attacks Jews and you make it *reasonable*."

"I don't necessarily agree with it," Barkley said. "I am a mouth-piece for others. Though some of the views have merit."

Working on the newspaper was just one of Barkley's jobs at Ford. He also worked in the company's so-called "Sociology Department," which spied on workers, poked into their personal lives, and tried to turn them into model employees. Lastly, Barkley was involved in something called "public relations."

"This means you're in charge of slanting things so Ford gets treated well in the press?" Riley asked.

"I would put it this way: My job is to make sure that people get a full and accurate view of the Man Himself."

Barkley signaled a left turn, and then another, heading back the way they had come. The little tour of Dearborn was nearing an end.

"Okay," Riley said, "then let me ask you: Wouldn't Ford be better off without having to deal with some investigation about a poor mistreated girl? Something that could end up in the papers?"

"What are you saying to me?"

"I'm saying this whole thing can go away—and I will go away—if this girl is released from Eloise. No more questions asked. You need to convince Liebold that this whole thing could lead to bad... *public relations*. Tell him you've heard rumblings in the press, someone is threatening to make noise—tell him what you want. Just get him to release the girl."

As he spoke, Riley fiddled with the latch on the car's glove box and popped it open.

"What are you doing now?" Barkley said.

"I'm an investigator, remember?" Riley answered, pulling out a small gold flask from inside. He unscrewed the top and took a whiff. "Smells Canadian," he said.

Barkley didn't answer. Riley put the flask back in and shut the glove compartment, saying, "Oh, well, it's none of my business."

It took Barkley a week to find the nerve to talk to Liebold. It was another week before Liebold would give him an answer, which Barkley relayed to Riley: "He said he'll do it, but not right away."

"Why wait?" Riley said. "If he's going to release her, just do it."

"It's not that simple," Barkley said.

Riley was waiting for an answer and Barkley let out a deep breath and said, "You didn't hear this from me."

"Okay, go ahead."

"They're in the middle of something with her at Eloise."

"Something?"

"Some kind of test, I don't know. They test things on people there. Anyway, they can't release her until the tests are done and they get her... back the way she was. Could take a few weeks."

Riley was speechless. He was the kind who assumed he knew what was going on in the world around him—but there were things he had no inkling of, and Eloise was one of them.

As it turned out, it wasn't a few weeks but more like a couple of months before Rachel was finally released. And as for getting her "back to the way she was," that was another matter altogether.

When the time came, Riley was the one who told Max about

Rachel's release. He limped over to Hastings and knocked on the apartment door. Max was shocked to see him. Riley said she'd be getting out in a couple of days and he inquired if the girl had any family and Max said no. Riley asked what had become of me and Max told him I was amongst the missing and maybe the dead.

"Can you look after her by yourself?" Riley asked, and Max nodded. They agreed that Riley would drive Max to Eloise the coming Thursday, and together they would sign her out, and then bring her to Max's apartment.

As Max told me all of this over our morning coffee, he expected me to be thrilled. But it killed me that I was not the one bringing her home—and that I had to rely on some lame do-gooder like Riley to take care of my business.

Max must've seen it in my face, and he said: "You're supposed to be happy about this."

"I am happy. Don't I look happy?"

Before I left I told Max I would visit the night she came home. "I will arrive at three in the morning," I said. "If you could give us privacy for an hour or two, it would be good."

"You want me to leave? At that hour?"

"It would be good," I said.

"I guess I'll have to walk the streets," he said, and I nodded.

When Thursday arrived, I was jumpy as a tadpole. I told Grabowski what was going on and all he could think to say was, "Bet ya can't wait to plow 'er." That was not foremost in my mind at all, though there was no point trying to explain it to him.

Hastings was deserted when I arrived at three a.m. I parked and crept up the stairs of the apartment building. I stopped to listen at the door to see if I could hear her voice inside. It was quiet except for the *ee-aw* of Max's rocking chair. When I opened the door and went inside, Max was sitting there, rocking to and fro. He had his winter coat folded up in his lap.

"Where is she?" I whispered.

"She's asleep. In my bed."

"Is she okay?"

Max shrugged. "I guess. I can't tell. You going in to see her?"

"Of course."

"Well, I'll be on my way then," he said, and then got up and put his coat on, and then his gloves, and then started wrapping a big scarf around his neck and on up over his face.

"It's not that cold tonight," I said.

"We'll see," he said from behind the scarf, as he left.

I stood alone in the living room, looking at a closed bedroom door. Before going in, I went into the bathroom, splashed water on my face and looked in the mirror. I tried to see if I would look different to her; I'd nearly died since last she saw me. My blue eyes, which had always been watery, seemed moreso as I looked at them now. Maybe some of that river water was still in me.

When I went into the bedroom, she was under the sheets, with the pillow over her head. I tried to lift it off gently, but she woke with a start and looked up at me alarmed. The dark brown eyes were familiar but at the same time not: There was less of a gleam in them. It took her a moment to figure out where she was, and who I was. Then her body relaxed, and she said, "Oh, it's you," as if no big deal, as if she'd last seen me maybe an hour before.

"Is it three o'clock?" she said. "Max said you'd come at three."

"It's three o'clock. Are you tired? I'm sorry I woke you."

"It's okay," she said. "I was having a bad dream. I was dreaming that I had to deliver the uniforms and I went to the Highland Park plant and it wasn't there. It was gone."

She used to be part of a delivery team that brought the cleaned workers' uniforms from a dry cleaner on Hastings to the Highland Park Ford plant. But that was in the past.

"I walked up and down looking for it," she said. "We had the uniforms and we needed to deliver them. And I asked people, 'What happened to the plant?' and they said. 'What plant?'"

She smiled at me. She'd always had a smile that could melt me, but this was kind of a sad, confused smile. She looked into space and shook her head, then looked back at me. "It's still there, right?"

"Still there," I said.

"Good thing," she said. "I have to be there in three hours."

"No, you don't," I said.

"Oh," she said. "Is it Saturday?"

"Yes, it's Saturday," I lied.

Rachel lay there quietly for a minute, then said, "I think I might sleep for a while, would that be alright?"

"Sure," I said.

"Will you lie beside me?"

She moved over and I crawled into the little bed with her. We both faced sideways and I draped my arm around her and put my belly against her small fanny and wedged my knees into the back of hers, like so many times before.

"I missed this," she said. All I could see now was the back of her head. "I missed having you in bed with me," she said.

"Me, too."

"Did you forget about me?"

"Of course I didn't forget about you," I said.

"They said you must have forgot me. That's why you never came."

I raised myself up in the bed and gently took hold of her chin and turned her face to look at me. "Who said that to you?"

"I don't remember," she said. "It doesn't matter. I'm a sleepy-head." She smiled and turned her face back into the pillow.

"Anyway," she murmured. "I forgive you."

NINE

The following spring was a time of rebirth: The flowers opened up whilst my wounds finally closed. I was at full strength once again, and had no worries because Rachel was home and safe with my brother. Even dreary Hamtramck became more pleasant—people still got drunk and fought constantly, but at least they could do so without being encumbered by heavy coats.

I began to gather steam. I suggested to Nowak, the manager of Zabawa, that he broaden his business with my help. He laughed at first. "You're a bouncer," he said. "Whatta *you* know?"

So I told him for the first time about my history with the Sugar House Gang of Detroit—about how I handled various duties and assignments. One of which was to help out sometimes with the operation of two gaming houses.

"We could set up a little gaming house in the back of Zabawa," I said to Nowak. "Just knock out a wall to make room, and I'll take it from there. I'll show you how to do it like the Sugars do."

Nowak had reservations. "There's already a gambling house in town," he said, telling me nothing I didn't already know. "They're not gonna like us cutting in."

I said I'd handle all dealings with the competition. Then he said, "Besides, the slobs that come in here don't have money."

"Then you lend it to them," I said.

"And how do you get them to pay it back?"

I explained that the Gorilla and myself would wait outside the Dodge and Ford plants come payday. The debt would be extracted from the worker's wages, like a tax. It was all so obvious I could not understand why Nowak even needed to be told.

The Zabawa gaming house was an overnight success and here is why: We were tough but compassionate. If a guy was out of control in the craps game, we cut him off before he could lose more than he could ever repay. If a guy had a sob story, we gave him an extra payday to settle. We also encouraged a tradition of sharing the wealth. Each night, the biggest winner had to buy a round of drinks for the whole bar. It made the winning guy feel like a hero; made the other customers feel they had a stake in his winning; and it meant the bar got back a lot of the money he just won.

As Nowak predicted, the competition did not like competition. They came up with a genius plan to send over a bunch of guys with sledgehammers after we closed, to demolish the gaming house. But they made the mistake of talking about it the night before; you never talk about how you're going to hit someone before you hit them.

When they arrived we were hiding inside—me, Grabowski, and the Gorilla. We disarmed the four goons who showed up, but we needed to do something that would leave an impression. We used their own sledges to pulverize the left hand of each man (ruining their good right hand would have been cruel). Now, the competitor would have to hire all new bouncers, unless he wanted to keep one-handed freaks who couldn't scrap.

Nowak had started giving me a 25 percent cut of Zabawa's profits soon as I opened the gaming house, but after the hammer incident, I told him I needed 50 percent. And I told him we'd need to buy guns. Also, we needed to provide a salary for our part-time special enforcer.

"We don't have no special enforcer," Nowak said, and I told him we did now, and his name was Mr. Grabowski.

He grumbled about all these conditions, and I suggested that if he felt they were unfair, he could always take it up with my chief negotiator. "He too is named Mr. Grabowski," I said. It was a joke, kind of, and he kind of laughed.

This additional money was welcome because there were unsuitable living arrangements that needed fixing. I'd had enough of being in a basement with Grabowski and the babies. Our conversations always seemed to end with Grabowski threatening to turn them loose on me, and me daring him to do it.

Meanwhile in Detroit, Max had started to complain about being in the same apartment with Rachel. He said she was like Jekyll and Hyde—that something seemed to build up in her, and she'd get mad and start hitting him with her little fists for no good reason. Then she would storm out and disappear for hours. She'd come back later, happy as can be, at which point she was liable to twirl around the apartment and might even take off her clothes in plain view (which seemed to be what horrified Max the most). I believe he was exaggerating, but still, she needed her own place.

The solution was to take over the upstairs of the house Grabowski was in, so Rachel and I could have the upper quarters. We had to buy out the filthy pig who owned the house and used it for his whores. I offered him fair market value for a Hamtramck house, which amounted to slightly more than nothing. Of course he complained as people often do when you try to be square with them, so I told him if he really wanted to stay in the house I did have a room for him. Then Grabowki and I brought him down to where the cage was and stuck his head inside for a spell. All Ono and Ogod did was to sniff his ears, but it spooked him so much he left without even remembering to ask for the money I was fully prepared to give him.

Since I now had leftover money, it occurred to me that I should use it to buy the house next door for Max and Abie. I went over and knocked. It was a nice old Polish couple, so I offered them twice what I was willing to give the whoremonger.

"But where would we go?" they said.

I said, "Figure it out, and wherever it is, I'll also pay for the move and get you set up." They were reluctant but I continued to give them encouragement. They ended up in a cottage Up North, from whence I received holiday cards for several years thereafter.

Max moved into the house next door soon as it was empty, whilst Rachel moved in with me. Both of them were full of complaints from the outset, but I'll get to that. What troubled me more was that Abie did not want to come at all. He wanted to stay with his father at the butcher shop on Hastings.

To which I said, "But Hastings is a dead end."

And he said: "So is Hamtramck."

He had me there.

Then a few months later, something happened that began to change Abie's mind. For years, Buster Weintraub had collected protection money from the Hastings shops, including Zussman's butcher shop. Supposedly, Buster was protecting the Jewish merchants from Irish cops and oilers and also from the Klan, which was big in Detroit back then (the mayor himself was a Klansman). But over time, it became clear that the merchants were really paying Buster for protection from Buster. Still, everyone went along, as it was not excessive. Then in the fall of '21 Weintraub decided to jack up the rates.

There was grumbling on Hastings, with Mr. Z being the most vocal. He told other merchants the jack was too much, and they should stand together against it. Buster took umbrage and decided to make an example of the old man. He sent a couple of goons to ambush him on the street and beat him. Of course they did it when Abie was not around, being the cowards they were.

For the next two days, Abie sat with his father in the hospital and prayed for his recovery. Between prayers, he made it known he was planning to go after Weintraub, even if he had to take on an entire gang to do it. I got word to him at the hospital to come out and see me before doing anything rash.

*

Soon thereafter, the four of us—me, Max, Abie, and Grabowski— were together in Grabowski's basement, sitting on the metal folding chairs. The babies were asleep as we worked our way through a bottle, passed hand to hand. Abie had just told us that his prayers must have been answered; his father seemed to be on the mend.

"That's good news," I said to him. "But there is still the matter of retribution. Are you going to leave that to God, too?"

"I have been thinking about that," Abie said. "I'm sure God will punish Weintraub for what he's done to my father, and what he's done to you. But it may take a while before He gets around to it. Unless someone helps speed it along."

"An agent," I said, and Abie and I then shared a smile.

Grabowski looked at us. "I don' know what yer talkin' about, but if it's about killin' that pudgy fuck, I'm in."

Max, meanwhile, started to rock in his chair, which wasn't a rocking chair. "This is serious," he said. "This is very serious."

"It is," I said. "It's more serious than you can imagine."

I explained to them all that I was thinking about setting out on something long-term and large: It would probably start with Weintraub, but would then extend to the whole Sugar House Gang. From there, we might have to take on even larger forces—maybe the whole city of Detroit.

"That's crazy," Max said. "We're four little people, sitting in a basement."

"He ain't so little," Grabowski said, pointing at Abie.

Abie meanwhile was lighting up with some kind of thought. "It could be like Gideon," he said to me. Then he turned to Max and said, "He had very small numbers and it worked in his favor."

"That's right," I said. "Now tell us who the hell Gideon is."

Abie explained that Gideon was a guy who used an army of a few hundred Israelites—"a small, select, unified group," Abie said—to take down an enemy ten times bigger in number.

"Because they were small, they could be stealthy," Abie said. "They could sneak up on the enemy in a way that a big army couldn't."

"Write that down, Max," I said. "Stealthy. A word to live by."

Max wrote it down on a little notepad, but also shook his head, saying, "This is crazy."

"So when do we get goin'?" asked Grabowski, already eager.

"There's no rush," I said. "We're going to take our time. Develop a strategy. We'll work it all out in the house next door—our new headquarters."

I looked directly at Max, who was still rocking whilst scribbling something on the pad. "We're going to need your brain to figure out a lot of this, Max."

He didn't answer or look up, just kept rocking and doodling.

"So we're a gang now, huh?" Grabowski said. "What name?"

"The Bernstein Gang," Abie volunteered.

I shook my head no and said, "We'll get to the name later." I was surprised they'd forgotten we already had a name—I hadn't.

We drank a toast. Abie felt there should be a ceremony.

"Somethin' with blood?" Grabowski asked.

"I don't know," Abie said. "I'll think of something."

I asked Abie when he was going to move into the house next door, joining Max. He looked down, embarrassed. "I don't want to leave my father," he said.

"Of course you don't," I said. "You'll bring him here to live with you in the house."

"What?" said Max, looking up from his notepad with alarm.

Abie asked, "What about the butcher shop?" and I told him we'd open a brand new one for his father in Hamtramck.

"Will Polacks buy meat from a Jew?" he wondered.

"They will if they know what's good for them," I said.

Later that night, Abie said he'd figured out a ceremony for us, but wouldn't say more. I had something in mind, too. I stopped in at Zabawa and asked at the bar, "Anybody know any painters?"

Next morning Abie woke us all at the crack of dawn and said, "We're going to Detroit." He had a loaf of bread under his arm.

We rode in Grabowski's car with Abie behind the wheel, no idea where we were going until we got to the Riopelle pier—the very place where I had been sliced and diced.

"Are you kidding me?" I said as Abie pulled the car to a stop.

Abie walked out onto the dock, with Grabowski and Max trailing him, and me reluctantly bringing up the rear.

On the dock, the blood stains remained—reddish-brown and faded. There was one big long smear.

"That was where they dragged him," Abie explained to the other two. Then he pointed to a spot in the water, a few feet out from the dock. "And that was where he lay."

"Thank you for the memories," I said, still standing back.

"Everybody still talks about it on Hastings," Abie said, looking back at me. "They think you're still down there in the water."

"Let them keep thinking that," I said. "Meantime, we shouldn't hang around here."

"This won't take long," Abie said and took the bread from under his arm and started breaking it into pieces. He handed us each a chunk.

Abie said to me, "That spot in the water, where you were—just toss your bread there."

It was crazy but it seemed to mean something to him, so I tossed the bread and it plopped on the water and floated.

"That's your old life, thrown away," Abie said to me. "Now you can start fresh. And we're going to follow. Wherever you lead us, Joe."

Abie threw his piece in and it landed right next to mine.

Grabowski shrugged and said, "Fuck if I know what it's about, but here goes," and threw in his piece. Max hesitated, then was embarrassed to be the only one still holding bread. He threw it awkwardly and it ended up apart from the rest, but no one cared about that except maybe him.

"Zat it?" Grabowski said to Abie.

"That's it."

"Now we'll do my ceremony," I said, and we got in the car and drove back to Hamtramck and went to Zabawa. The place was usually closed at this hour of mid-morning, but it was open for us. There were cold cuts and rolls and fresh fruit, all laid out on the bar. There were four fancy crystal glasses, with the whisky already poured. There were exactly four people there besides us, and each one was a pretty girl. The girls hand-fed us fruit, re-filled our glasses, laughed at our jokes, cheered as we threw the crap dice, and sat in our laps (except for Max's), whilst we had a fine time. There is nothing like having a bar all to yourself in the daytime.

When we got back home, the painters were just finishing up on the house next door.

"Holy shit," Grabowski said. "I never seen nothin' like it."

Neither had the others, nor myself for that matter—none of us had ever before seen a house that was entirely purple.

Whilst we were starting something new in Hamtramck, things were changing rapidly in Detroit. I was hearing about it second-hand at the time, and it factored into the plans forming in my head. But Riley was witnessing the change up close.

After leaving the DA's office, he was blackballed by Thompson and couldn't get another job on the government side, so he took one with a Detroit law firm. Riley's job—and the only thing anyone at the firm seemed to work on—was defending people charged with violating the Volstead Act of 1920.

Riley did not like the work, but he was good at it. Not that it was hard to get bootleggers off; most of them either walked free or were slapped with a $20 fine. But the ones that needed a lawyer were the bigger fish—people using large boats to bring in heavy cargo from Canada. This included members of gangs, but also a lot of enterprising citizens who jumped into the smuggling business in 1921 because everyone said it was "the future."

By the summer of that year, Riley was handling a half-dozen cases a day for clients mainly concerned about losing their boats. The Detroit cops liked to put the seized boats up for auction and Riley's task was to argue that his client "needed the boat for his livelihood," or some such. It was easy to win because the judges just wanted to move the cases along.

Riley had little respect for the judges, the prosecutors, or his own clients. But he did admire one old codger who showed up in the courtroom often to testify against Riley's clients. The man, Howard Blakemore, was a Customs agent who patrolled the river and hauled in more bootleggers than the entire Coast Guard did. Blakemore had a handlebar mustache and wore a wide-brimmed hat that made him look like a sheriff out of the Old West.

Riley was leaving the courtroom one day after getting some runner his boat back when he heard a voice from behind, saying, "Feel good about what you're doing?"

It was Blakemore, lighting up a smoke.

"Just doing my job," Riley said.

"Uh-huh. Yep, we're all just doing our jobs," Blakemore said and then moved on.

They started to chat regularly after that, always on the way out of the courtroom. One day Blakemore made Riley an offer: "Want to see what it's like out there on the river? What I'm up against?"

Riley was surprised, but answered, "Sure, why not?"

A couple of nights later, they were sitting facing each other in a little motorboat with the engine idling, a full moon overhead. They'd taken off from the Detroit side and cruised the short mile across to the Canadian shoreline in minutes. Blakemore cut the engine and drifted, parallel to the shore.

There was tall marsh grass between them and the land. In the dark, with only the sound of ripples slapping the boat, they passed a series of narrow swaths cut into the marsh grass—little pathways, each leading to a dock or boat slip. Blakemore maneuvered the boat through one of the openings and they floated between tall reeds on both sides, heading toward a dock. Blakemore lit his flashlight and pointed it at a clothesline strung between two trees behind the dock; a red shirt was clipped to the line.

"That red shirt's a signal," Blakemore said.

"What's it mean?" Riley asked.

"Damned if I know," he said. "Could mean the filling station is open. Or closed. They change signals all the time, I can't keep up."

At docks all up and down the Canadian shoreline, distillers kept cases of whiskey in storehouses. A boat could pull into one of the stations, fill up with liquor and be gone in minutes. When the boat got back to the Detroit side, a team was usually waiting to load the cargo into a truck. Then it went to warehouses where it was cut with water, before being shipped to the blind pigs—and there were thousands of those opening in 1921.

When the big shipments were coming in, it was no secret—and yet the Detroit cops were nowhere to be found. They tended to call in sick at these times. The cops got more in "sick pay" from the bootleggers than they earned in salary.

This was the situation as it was developing in Detroit that year, and Blakemore was right in the center of the action, which mostly took place in dead of night on the Detroit River—"Bottle Creek," as Blakemore called it. Just in the short time he and Riley were on the Canada side, several motorboats took off for Detroit, each one loaded to the gills, no doubt.

"Shouldn't we chase them?" Riley said.

Blakemore laughed. His little boat had no chance against the big fast ones, some of them designed for professional boat racing. The one thing Blakemore did have going for him was patience. "I hide my boat in the marshes over on the Detroit side and just wait, for hours sometimes," he told Riley. "Till somebody wanders into my web." Whenever that happened, Blakemore would point both his flashlight and his handgun at the pilot, and that was that.

After showing Riley the Canadian coastline, Blakemore turned the boat around and headed back to the Detroit side. There, he slowed the boat and again drifted parallel to the shoreline, giving Riley a close-up view of little sheltered coves and sunken houseboats. One houseboat had a light on; a silhouette of man was in the window. "He's watching us," Blakemore said.

There were dozens of dark little entry points, obscured by bush or marsh. "It's a smuggler's paradise," Riley said.

They idled along the coastline whilst Blakemore softly hummed a tune. Then he stopped and put a finger to his lips, signaling for quiet. Without saying a word, he pointed back out to mid-river, but Riley couldn't see anything. The two of them stayed very still in their boat, and soon Riley could make out a small rowboat coming closer, with two figures just barely visible in the moonlight—one large, one very small. The large one was rowing.

As the rowboat got closer, maneuvering toward one of the coves, Blakemore fired up his engine and cruised over to the rowboat. The rower just drew in his oars and sat waiting. Riley gradually made out that the small passenger was a boy about ten years old. His whole body was shaking. When they pulled right next to the rowboat, Blakemore reached out and grabbed the side of the boat with his left hand and flashed a badge with his right.

"Little late to be out with the boy," he said.

The man pointed at a couple of poles on the floor of the boat and said, "Fishing."

"What'd you haul in?" Blakemore said.

The man shrugged and tried to force a smile. "Guess they weren't biting tonight."

Blakemore studied the floor of the boat, looking for compartments; he could spot them by the mismatched floorboards. Then his eye moved to the boy, who was trying hard not to look up. He was a fat kid, or at least seemed to be.

"Son, would you mind taking off that jacket," Blakemore said.

The boy looked at his father, who nodded, and then took off his jacket. Underneath he was wearing a large rubber life jacket.

Blakemore reached out and poked a finger into the middle of it, then smiled. "Whyn'cha take that off too, and hand it to me."

There was a swishy liquid sound as the boy handed over the life jacket. Blakemore quickly found the cap, opened it, and poured the liquor over the side of his boat. It took a while to drain what must have been a few gallons.

He turned back to the boy, who was crying now. The father just sat there with his head down.

"Now raise your pants-leg up," Blakemore said to the boy.

There were two flasks taped to his calf. Blakemore took the flasks, then checked the other leg and found the same. After he laid the flasks down in his own boat, he turned to the father.

"I could lock you up for this," he said. "And take your boat."

The man didn't answer.

"Your boy's already been scared enough tonight," Blakemore said. "For his sake, I'll let you go home with a warning. But don't let me see you out here again."

The man nodded. The boy was looking down and sobbing. Riley felt sorry for him and reached over and patted the top of his head. The father glared and said, "Don't touch my son." Then he grabbed the oars and started rowing away, still eyeing Riley.

"That's the way it is now," Blakemore said to Riley, unscrewing the tops of the flasks. "Every man an outlaw. And the women and children, too."

He emptied one of the flasks into the water, then handed Riley the other. "Go on, dump it," he said. "Feels good."

An hour later, Blakemore let Riley off the boat at the pier on First Street, then cruised back out onto the river alone. Riley got in his parked car to go home, but he had something on his mind— something he'd been meaning to do for a while, and now he was in the right neighborhood. It occurred to him he should get it over with—just stop in and see how she was doing. So he wouldn't have to wonder about her anymore.

He drove up a couple blocks over to Hastings. He parked and went into the building and up to the apartment and when he knocked on the door, an old woman answered.

"I'm looking for Max Bernstein," Riley said. "Or Rachel Roth, either one."

"Oh, they moved out a while ago," the old woman said.

"Know where they went?"

She shook her head. "Nobody knows about those two, and nobody cares. They were trouble, along with the older brother. He was worse."

"And what about the older brother? What became of him?"

She pointed down at the floor.

"Downstairs?" Riley asked.

"In hell," she said.

Riley left the building, figuring, "Well, that's that—guess I'll never know what became of them."

By the time he got home to his own little apartment, he was tired and had a throbbing pain where his leg used to be. He climbed slowly up the steps, went inside, shut the door behind him but didn't turn on the lights—had no desire to see the bare, half-furnished place. He walked to the window and stood looking out.

Then he felt something, a presence, come up from behind, and he froze. Two hands clamped over his eyes and left him blind.

But it did not worry him because he knew from the small soft palms whose hands they were.

"Guess who?" said the voice from behind.

"Is it really you, Mae West?" he said.

"Guess again," she said.

Riley lifted the hands from his eyes, turned round to face Nan, and kissed her for a good long time. After which he said, "What are you doing, sneaking around here?"

"Can't a girl be alone in the dark with her fiancé? Is that against the law, too?"

"Well, if it is," Riley said, "they probably won't arrest you here in Detroit."

TEN

We made our move in 1922. In late April, I gathered my faithful at the purple house, which was where we held our meetings. We used the living room on the upper level—Max's part of the house—because Max requested it. After being resistant at first to my whole scheme, he began to warm up to it and especially liked the idea of planning and plotting things. He got hold of a big blackboard, the kind used in schools, and attached it to a wall so we could draw diagrams. Often the board was used by Abie and Grabowski to play tic-tac-toe, and when they did this Max would get sore and say, "That's *not* what the board is for."

On this particular day, I wrote a couple of things on the board as soon as we all gathered. First I wrote *Buster Weintraub* and underlined it. Then I wrote, *What do we know about him?*, and I put down the chalk. Right away Grabowski got up and grabbed the chalk and wrote, in a kid's scrawl, *Hes a Fat Fuk*. He put the chalk down and wiped his hands as he went back to his chair.

This annoyed Max, who said, "If you're going to write something on the board it should be important."

Grabowski got up again and said, "Okay I'll write somethin' important." He took the chalk and wrote *Fuk Yu Max*, then wiped his hands again and returned to his seat whilst Abie laughed.

"This is a meeting," I said. "This is not a joke." I decided at that point to stop using the blackboard for a while and just talk.

"What we know about Buster is that he is rarely alone," I said. It was true: He surrounded himself with his own private army at the diner, at the Sugar House's main warehouse, and even at his big home on Chicago Avenue.

"But there is one time when he leaves most of the guards behind," I said. "That is when he goes to the pictures."

Max objected as I thought he might. "You can't put a guy on the spot in a movie house," he said. "Not with all those witnesses."

"You can if you do it quiet," I said. "A gun is out of the question, of course. And if you strangle him, he'll struggle. But if you were to use a blade, in the right way, at the right moment..."

I looked directly at Abie. He was surprised. Then he seemed to accept the responsibility I was putting on him, which was large and perhaps unfair. But he was a butcher boy and nobody else in the room, not even Grabowski, knew how to cut as cleanly and efficiently.

After first saying nothing, he nodded and said: "Tell me more."

We agreed that we'd need to get inside details on Weintraub's schedule ahead of time, and that the best person to do that was the Original Solly Levine. I had reservations about bringing Solly into the gang—wasn't sure I could trust the googly-eyed bastard. But Max noted that Solly was unhappy with the Sugars. "He feels that Buster takes him for granted," Max said.

"Maybe Buster has good reason," I said, but then I gave in.

Leaving the meeting, Abie seemed quiet so I pulled him aside. "Are you up for this?" I said. "I don't want to push you into it."

He said, "Can I think about it tonight and talk to you in the morning?" and I said sure.

Next morning I saw him sitting on the front steps of the purple house, which seemed to glow in the early light of sunrise. I was coming home from a long night at Zabawa, where I was now running the place since Nowak decided to retire (after I suggested it to him). I sat next to Abie on the steps and said to him, "What's the verdict?" And he said, "Joe, I have decided that every life has its own destiny, and every guy has a purpose. I think Weintraub's destiny is to die in the dark, and my purpose is to make it happen."

A few days later, it was all set: A new film, *Nanook of the North*, was playing at the Empire Theater on Woodward Avenue. Solly Levine told us which showing Weintraub planned to attend—at 2 pm on a Thursday afternoon.

It turned out to be a warm sunny day, a strange time to be going to an Eskimo movie. Abie seemed calm at the house before he left, except for when he snapped at Max. It was Max's fault: He was stating the obvious when he said to Abie, "You should get there early, before he sets foot in the theater." To which Abie said, "What a genius you are, Heebie Jeebie." To which I said, "Don't call him that." It didn't go any further.

Abie got to the Empire Theater a half hour early, and headed straight for the john. He locked himself in a stall and began to take things from the pockets of the long overcoat he was wearing. There was a book by Freud (Abie had gotten very interested in psychology of late); he planned to read it to pass the time. But first he laid the book on the floor, opened it, and took out a small stack of pictures of naked girls. After that, he pulled some cotton pads and a roll of tape from his pocket. He taped the pads to the bottom of his shoes so he could enter the theater quietly, like a big cat.

Weintraub and Baldy Klein arrived at the theater whilst Abie was in the john. And wouldn't you know, they came in for a pee, which didn't surprise Abie much. He made sure the latch on his stall was locked and just sat quietly. He could hear them pissing in the urinal; he peeked through the crack of the stall-door hinge and saw them standing side by side, one tall and one squat.

Baldy said, "What's the movie about, boss?" but Buster ignored him. Baldy finished peeing first, then buttoned up and turned—coming right back to where Abie was sitting. He opened the door of the stall beside Abie and tore off toilet paper. Then he returned to the urinal just as Buster was taking a step back and saying, "Okay, wipe me." Baldy reached down in front of Buster and must have used the toilet paper to dry his boss's dick—at least that's how it looked from where Abie sat. Then Buster buttoned up and washed his hands, and they both went out the door.

Abie's plan was to wait until about ten minutes after the movie start time, then go inside. But before leaving the john, he took that stack of dirty pictures and left them in plain sight next to the sink.

The theater was about a quarter-full. In the dark, Abie spotted the two of them right away: Buster was in an aisle seat halfway down, with Baldy seated directly behind him. That was the chair Abie needed to be in, but there was no rush. He found himself a seat in the back corner, and sat watching—one eye on the Eskimo movie, the other on Baldy. The movie wasn't bad, Abie informed me later: "It made you realize Detroit winters aren't as rough as they could be," he said. But Baldy seemed bored by the movie. Half an hour into it, he leaned toward Buster and must've said he was going to the john. Buster shushed him and waved a hand behind his head as if shooing a fly. Baldy then marched up the aisle, never seeing Abie in the corner.

Within thirty seconds of Baldy leaving that seat, Abie was in it—and Weintraub never heard him arrive. Abie figured he had time; Baldy would probably have a smoke, then go in the john and crap at his leisure. And if he found those pictures, he'd spend even more time in that stall. Abie reached inside his overcoat and pulled out the last item he'd packed—a very long and thin knife, one of his father's favorites. Abie started by poking the blade very lightly against Buster's seatback, just to get a feel for what he was up against—thin plywood backing a plush cushion. He pressed the point against the plywood and began turning the blade in a circular motion. He kept his upper body hunched forward and perfectly still and his eyes on the screen; to anyone behind him, he looked like a guy on the edge of his seat. It didn't take long for the knife point to twist its way through the plywood; now there was just a cushion between Buster and the blade.

The blade burrowed through the cushion. But before it broke all the way through the other side, Abie stopped and waited. He wanted a little more noise as a cover in case Buster yelped. The movie soon obliged with a scene where the music stirred up whilst the Eskimos were going through more of their never-ending hardship. As the music built to a peak, Abie's big left hand reached around and clamped over Buster's mouth, whilst the blade in his right hand shot forward like a piston firing—piercing Buster all the way through. Buster never said anything more than a small, muffled "umf." Then his body slumped in the seat, his head resting on top of the seatback. Abie withdrew the blade through the seat and slipped it back inside his jacket. Then he sat back and took a deep breath, surprised at how easy it was.

He was out in the foyer and halfway to the lobby when he saw the bathroom door opening and Baldy coming out. Baldy had his head down and was stuffing something inside his jacket—the dirty pictures no doubt.

Abie kept going straight to the lobby and was out of sight by the time Baldy looked up and started walking back to the theater room. From the lobby, Abie watched, through the glass door, to see if Baldy was going inside. If so, he'd find the body pretty quick. But Baldy didn't go into the theater—he opened the door, looked inside for a while, and then turned around and came out. He must've seen Buster with his head on top of the seatback, "sleeping"—and so Baldy decided to extend his break. He walked straight back from whence he came, the john. And as he reached for the knob to open the bathroom door, he looked back to see if anyone else was coming, whilst also reaching in his pocket for those pictures. He went inside and shut the door behind him.

Abie relaxed and turned to leave, taking his sweet time now. As he passed through the lobby, a kid who was sweeping up said to him, "Is it over already?"

And Abie told him, "It is for some."

We were waiting for him back at the purple house. He didn't come in right away. He sat on the front steps, looking a little lost. I didn't even know he was out there—we were upstairs in the meeting room, with an open bottle and cold cuts all laid out. Max had even written in big letters on the blackboard, *Congratulations*. It was Max who looked out the window and saw him sitting there.

"I wonder if he messed up," Max said. "And he doesn't want to come in and tell us."

I said, "He did not mess up," and went down to get him.

He smiled when he saw me come out on the steps and said, "Hi Joe. Can you beat this weather?"

"Yes, the weather is good," I said. "How are you?"

He thought about it and said. "Okay, I guess. I feel very light."

I brought him upstairs and he saw the food and said he did not want to eat. But we insisted, and pretty soon he devoured everything in sight—turned out he hadn't eaten since early the day before. He also gulped down whisky, and Abie was not a drinker. "I don't know why I'm so thirsty," he said.

We all raised our glasses and I said, "Here's to Abie the Agent!"

Then I walked over to where he sat and said, "On your feet." When he was standing, I wrapped my arms around him and it was like trying to hug a maple tree.

"First you saved me," I said, "and now you have avenged me."

Then Grabowski came up to him with a smile on his face and a hand held behind his back. "I got somethin' for ya, brot," he said.

The something was long and wrapped in a towel. It turned out to be a dagger, though it was more like a small sword—a good 15 inches of blade. The handle had jewels embedded in it.

"Polish warriors used this," he said as he gave it to Abie.

Abie took the dagger and examined it from all angles. He ran his finger along the blade and, seeing he'd drawn blood, nodded his approval. "I don't know what to say," Abie said to Grabowski.

"Don't say nothin' for a change," Grabowski said, as he grabbed Abie in a bear hug, then pulled me, still standing beside them, into a three-way embrace.

I was the only who noticed Max was still sitting in his chair.

"Max, get over here," I said. He came and stood next to us, not knowing what to do. I put my arm around his neck and pulled him into the pileup and he said, "Careful," but he also smiled.

I wish I could say it was all hugs and smiles, but the truth is there was some tension in the Hamtramck houses. Max did not like sharing a house with Abie and Abie's father. I would ask why and he always had different reasons. First it was, "He makes a racket walking around in those big shoes." Then it was, "Him and his father always look at each other when I walk in the room." And, "He is always quoting from books and doesn't know what the hell he's talking about." But the worst of all was, "He is trying to use psychology on me, Joe."

This last one was true and I could see why it bothered Max. Abie did not understand Max's condition and was always trying to explain it or figure it out. He told Max that the shaking and the twitching and the fits were probably all "in his head."

"You have no idea what's in my head," Max said. "*Your* head would never be able to keep up with what's in *my* head."

"It's obvious you have a complex," Abie said.

"I do not have a complex, I have a condition," Max said. "It is in the blood, and there's nothing I can do."

"How come it's not in your brother's blood?" Abie said.

And so it went, with me often serving as the referee. I finally ordered Abie to stop using psychology against my brother. He laughed and said, "Joe, I'm not using it *against* him—psychology is not a weapon, it is a tool."

I said, "Fine, I'm taking the tool away from you," and he said, "You would have to open up my head to do that," and I said, "Don't tempt me."

Then I went to Max and said, "Why can't you get along with people?" And he said, "It's not people in general, it's Abie," and I said, "Oh, yeah, what about Grabowski?" He said, "He doesn't come under the heading of people." When I pointed out that he hardly talked to Rachel anymore, he just raised his eyebrows and said, "I have nothing to say on that subject."

I do not wish to go into a lot of detail about Rachel, because some things should be kept behind closed doors. I will just say that when Max described her behavior back at the apartment on Hastings, he was not exaggerating as much as I first thought. She started doing some of the same things when she got to Hamtramck—acting restless, sneaking out of the house, disappearing for hours, then returning home all smiles. It did not take long to figure it out: She'd gotten hooked on something at Eloise, and then had to find a substitute when she came home. The substitute she found was opium, available at a few bars in Hamtramck. At first I tried to get her not to take it, even tried locking her in her room. But she pounded on the door and even tried to climb out the window and almost broke her neck.

Grabowski said I should tie her to a tree in the yard for three days—that once cured a pal of his from drinking. But I wouldn't do that to a dog. I tried taking away all her money, but she still went off and got the stuff, which made me wonder what she was doing to get it. Finally, I decided the easiest thing was to buy the opium for her and let her enjoy it in the safety of her home. After all, everyone in Hamtramck and half the people in Detroit were getting drunk every day, so how was this worse?

It would have worked out fine, except the opium fueled another habit she already had—imagining things. She decided she was being watched by someone in the house. I said, "Yes, that someone is me." But she said no, no—someone else.

Rachel hated being in Hamtramck. I tried to tell her we would go back to Detroit soon and the city would be all ours. She would smile sweetly and then tell me that I was a goddamn liar. She said she wanted to be back with her friends and I would simply point out that she did not have any. Again I was called a liar.

"What about Matilda Rabinowitz?" she said. Never mind who that was, suffice it to say that just hearing the name irked me.

"She wasn't your friend," I said, "she used you and got you into all this trouble in the first place. And if I ever see you with that bitch I will cut her throat right in front of you."

So, as I say, there was some tension in the two houses, but the good news was that the killing of Weintraub had lifted all our spirits. And better still, it threw the Sugar House for a loop, as I thought it might.

It wasn't that any of the Sugars were sorry to see him go; everyone hated Buster. But they couldn't believe anyone would have the nerve to kill him. And if someone *was* going to do it, they were expected to come at him with large numbers and loud guns. Instead he was quietly killed by an unseen force, in a movie house of all places. It got people at the Crime talking and wondering. I decided to throw some fuel on that flame.

I instructed Solly Levine, who was still by appearances a Sugar but was actually a traitor in their midst, that he should make a certain casual remark next time everyone at the diner started talking about what happened to Buster. Solly was supposed to say: "Who knows—maybe the ghost of Joe Bernstein snuck up on Buster in that theater." Then he was supposed to laugh it off.

I had a feeling that once the joke was told, it would not remain a joke. A lot of Sugars already wondered why my body never turned up, even as the water around the Riopelle pier was dragged several times for various reasons. Some of the Sugars were superstitious to begin with, so they took to this idea that my ghost might be floating around, looking for revenge.

Buster's lieutenant, Honey Boy Strauss, tried to quash rumors and calm nerves as he assumed leadership. To show everyone he wasn't scared, he announced that he was going to keep going to the movies as much as he liked. Of course, the first time he did, he brought an army with him. He did likewise the second and third time. But eventually, he started to relax, as people do. This is why patience is such a virtue in the killing game.

We waited a year before going after Strauss. By this time, the army accompanying him to movies was just one guy, Gottasmoke, whose job was to sit in the seat behind Strauss. That wasn't always easy to do, because Strauss was, in Abie's words, a "seat jumper."

When Strauss came into the Cass Theater on the day in question, Abie, tipped off in advance by Solly, was waiting in a corner seat. Strauss and Gottasmoke took their seats, with Gottasmoke sitting behind Strauss. The movie was in progress. Right away, Strauss got up out of his seat and moved two rows down and to the left. Gottasmoke got up and followed. A minute later, Strauss got up again, and moved back four rows and to the right. Gottasmoke followed again. When Strauss moved a *third* time, Gottasmoke just shook his head and let Strauss go sit in his new seat by himself. Which was convenient for Abie, though it didn't really matter—because soon Gottasmoke left anyway, heading for the lobby to ask around for a smoke.

Abie crept into the seat behind Strauss. He began twisting the Polish dagger and it worked like a charm getting through the seat-back. He was through the plywood and halfway through the cushion when Strauss suddenly leaned forward—Abie worried that maybe he felt the blade. But no, Strauss had his eye on a seat two rows down and to the right, and he got up and moved again.

Abie later told me he got so mad at Strauss he was ready to walk out without killing him. "But that would've rewarded bad behavior," he decided, so he followed Strauss to the next seat, started all over with a new hole, and this time was able to run Strauss through amid the noisy laughter during a comical scene.

In later times, Abie and I would often joke about this "seat jumper" episode, the punchline being: The guy finally found a seat he liked so much that he never changed seats again.

ELEVEN

After the Strauss killing, everyone in the Sugar House gang swore off movies—no easy thing because they loved them, and needed them to pass the long afternoons that plague men without real jobs. The third man in line to run the Sugars, Myron Fletcher, vowed to avoid "anything where a person can sneak up behind you—that means movies, the synagogue, whatever." (It was pointed out to Fletcher that he hadn't been in a synagogue his whole life and he said, "Then I ain't gonna start now.")

But all of this didn't save Fletcher. He would have had to avoid being alone, ever, for the rest of his life, and that he could not do. At a downtown speakeasy several months later, surrounded by his minions, he made the mistake of taking himself to the john for a pee. Whilst he stood at the urinal, Abie, lurking in one of the stalls, softly closed a worn copy of "The Last Days of Socrates" (because Abie was at that time taking a break from psychology to dabble in philosophy). He quietly opened the stall door and crept up on his padded shoes. Fletcher was giving himself one last shake when he suddenly received a heartfelt surprise.

He fell back dead in Abie's arms, his dick sticking out of his pants and the tip of Abie's dagger protruding from his chest. Abie dragged him into the stall and sat him on the toilet. Abie's book was still on the floor there, and he picked it up but then thought, "I've had enough of this." He left the book resting open in

Fletcher's lap. When the corpse was found, there were two questions on everyone's lips: Who killed him, and who the hell is Plato?

All of this just put more hop into the jitterbug that was going around. One day at the Crime, someone could be heard to say, "I'm not saying it's Bernstein's ghost, but you have to admit that whoever is doing it is invisible and out for revenge." The person who said this just happened to be the Original Solly Levine, but others agreed with the notion.

With three leaders down, there was really only one guy with any brains left in the Sugar House Gang: He was known as Baby Elephant. He got the nickname because he never forgot anything; the Baby part was added on because he was a small guy, and it just was too confusing to call him Elephant. Baby Elephant knew everything about the Sugar operation—how much money it made on what, who was on the payroll, who owed money, etcetera.

In a way, he was like Max; they both knew everything. And so it almost made sense when, during a meeting about what to do with Baby Elephant, Max suddenly announced: "Don't put him on the spot in a theater or anyplace else. Bring him here to me."

Grabowski laughed. "Ya gonna nag him ta death?"

Abie laughed too, and said to Grabowski: "Baby Elephant better watch out. If he doesn't cooperate, Max will have a fit."

Max didn't respond, but he looked at me, and I said, "This is a meeting and it's no time for smart remarks. We'll do as Max says."

We snatched Baby Elephant in broad daylight at Navin Field during the fourth inning of a Tigers game. He was at the game with the two enforcers, Baldy Klein and Gottasmoke, along with the Original Solly Levine, who had given everyone free tickets (they weren't really free; I bought them).

In the top of the fourth, Solly went for a pee and then rushed back to the seats, saying, "The bastards are towing our car!" The four of them went running to the parking lot and when they got there, the car in question was still there, but the trunk was wide open. And there were dirty pictures scattered around inside it.

"What in the goddamn hell?" said Baldy Klein, and Gottasmoke seconded that. They both bent over and reached into the trunk and started looking at some of the pictures whilst Abie the Agent—who had popped out of a nearby parked car—came rushing from behind on his padded shoes. He did not have his dagger this time, he had an instrument more in keeping with the venue, which is to say a baseball bat. He hit Klein first and Gottasmoke second—both in the head, both whilst they were still leaning into that trunk. Then he lifted their legs and stuffed them both inside the trunk and shut it.

Baby Elephant just stood there and didn't even reach for his gun. But it didn't matter because Solly Levine already had a gun pointed at him. When Abie, holding the bat, walked towards him, Baby Elephant said, "Don't hit me." Abie said, "Oh, no, we wouldn't do that. You might lose your memory."

Abie drove Baby Elephant back in one car, whilst Solly drove the other one with the two goons in the trunk. When they got back to Hamtramck, they brought them all down to Grabowski's basement. Baldy and Gottasmoke were still groggy. As for Baby Elephant, he was merely a trembling wreck. Especially when he saw a dead man (that would be me) sitting there in a folding chair waiting for him.

The three visitors stood with hands tied behind their backs. The "babies" were not in the room at this time, nor was Grabowski—because you don't want to overwhelm people with too much, too soon. I got out of my chair and walked slowly to the three of them. At this time you may recall—because I sure do—that two of these men were on that dock the night I was cut up.

First I studied Baldy Klein's face, in particular the bridge of his nose. "You healed up well," I said to him.

"You too," he said. "I swore we got you through the heart."

"That's where you made your mistake," I said. "I don't have one."

I moved on to Gottasmoke and, to be honest, found I had nothing to say to him. But I took a cigarette out of my pocket and inserted it between his lips. "Your last one," I said. "And for once in your life, you didn't even have to ask."

Round about this time, there was a clanking of chains coming from outside and before you knew it, the babies were skulking down the steps, their eyes darting from left to right as they stepped lightly. Then the eyes settled on the three guests, because that's just how the babies were—they had a taste for the new.

Grabowski followed them down, holding the chains. He handed the chains to Abie, and walked right up to the men, without looking at me. At times like this, Grabowski was very focused; he only saw the prey and was aware of nothing else. He pulled a flask from his jacket pocket and offered it to Baldy, who must have been parched by now. Baldy nodded, but since his hands were tied, Grabowski had to hold the flask for him. Baldy took one sip, then pulled his face back and spit bright red, all over his chin and down his shirt.

"Get a load a Nose-feratu here," Grabowski said. "Tryin' ta drink blood."

Grabowski then jerked the open flask at Baldy's leg, and red splashed on his pants. He did the same to Gottasmoke, whose cigarette was now dangling from his lip and jittering.

Baldy wanted to know why he was being splashed with blood, and Grabowski explained: "Ya ever put sauce on yer steak? This is like that."

That was the last I saw of Baldy Klein or Gottasmoke, because I left with Baby Elephant and took him next door to the purple house, where Max was waiting. Max was a polite host: He untied his guest's hands and offered him a cup of tea. He put him in a nice comfortable chair and sat down across from him.

"I'll be honest with you," Max said to him. "We are starting something new here. But we can't do it without your expertise."

Baby Elephant let out a very large sigh of relief. "Of course I'll help you," he said. "I can tell you everything you need to know. It's all up here," he said, pointing at his head.

They talked about everything: Where did the Sugars get their boats; who amongst the remaining Sugars was worth keeping in the gang; what was their strategy for keeping the filthy oilers at bay; and so on. The whole time, Max took detailed notes.

Somewhere along the line, it occurred to Baby Elephant that if he gave up all he knew, there might not be any reason to keep him alive. "What are your plans for me?" he demanded to know.

I was sitting there with Max, and now I chimed in: "We have a job in mind for you right away," I said. "We need you to be an emissary."

Baby Elephant seemed to search his memory for the word.

"It means you're going to carry a message for us," I said.

Next day, in dead of night, Grabowski and Abie went to the Cream of Michigan diner. The place was closed at that hour, but they snuck in and walked to the counter. They put down four brown paper bags, each full and leaking a little from the bottom. Each bag had a name scrawled on it: One was marked "Baldy Klein," another "Gottasmoke," the third "Baby Elephant;" the fourth was marked "The Original Solly Levine." The first three bags contained the remains of those three men—all the parts that the babies could not consume. The fourth bag contained more remains from those same three guys. It only had Solly's name written on it for appearance's sake, because he supposedly vanished at the ballgame just like the other three.

Along with the bags, a note was left on the counter: *"Thank you for the delicious meal. The leftovers are for you. Until next time, Joe B."*

After finding those bags, the remaining members of the Sugar House Gang were in a panic. Their leaders were dead, as were their toughest enforcers. They were afraid to go to the movies, terrified to go to a ballgame, and petrified to take a piss. The ghost of Joe Bernstein was haunting them, stalking them, and now worst of all, eating them and leaving behind doggie bags. They understood ambushes with guns and clubs, but they did not understand this.

They wondered where Joe's ghost would show up next. I gave them a couple of days to shiver. Then came the night I made my dramatic entrance at the Crime.

I walked in, shook hands all around, and extended my warm invitation to join the Purples. I made the offer to every guy in that diner. But the truth is, I was lying to half of them.

It is a funny thing when you think about it: We defeated the toughest gang in Detroit without firing a gunshot. We did it using one thin blade, some sharp teeth, and fear. People think you need size, numbers, a well-stocked armory. But all you need are two things: A plan, and the guts to execute it. It is so simple.

Once you seize power, however, things get more complicated. People ask, "What was it like when the Purple reign first began? How did it feel to sweep into Detroit like a winning army claiming its spoils?" I will not lie: At first, we all felt like we were ten feet tall (or in Abie's case, twelve feet tall).

But in a way, coming in to take over our new operation was like moving into a big new house. You think that just because you were able to acquire the house, your troubles are over. You walk into the place dreaming of how you're going to live in comfort forever more. But right away you notice a leaky faucet. And you go down the basement and see a rat scurry past. And you go to the mailbox and there's already a bill for the electric. And while you're at the mailbox you meet your next-door neighbor and discover that he is an asshole who will have to be dealt with at some point.

It's the same thing when you take charge of a gang—and I mean a real gang, no longer just four guys plotting in a basement. You cannot imagine the complications.

For instance, the hardest thing for a boss is to let people go, and I had to let go of half the Sugars right away. Not that I had anything against these guys. It's just that we were inheriting too many people and had no use for them. Up 'til then, it had been just the handful of us. But the Sugars had forty people—*forty*.

And most of them were dead weight. They sat around the Cream of Michigan diner and slurped soup and built their little sugar-cube igloos. Every so often they'd get off their asses to go stink-bomb a dry cleaner, but otherwise they did nothing of any value.

So I thought, *Why in the hell do we need forty of these guys? We could get by with thirty, easily.*

I ran this calculation past Max and he said, "Forget thirty. How about twenty?"

Now this presented a mathematical challenge: How do you turn forty men into twenty?

Max knew the answer straight off. "You divide them amongst themselves," he said.

So I had this in my head as I approached each of the forty Sugars that night in the diner. I invited them all to join the gang, but I really only wanted to keep half of them—let's call that bunch "Group A." Those were the guys I arranged to meet with privately, later on. Whereupon I told each "A" guy that in order to get in the gang, he'd have to kill a corresponding guy in Group B.

Granted, this sounds severe. But stay with me and you'll see that it was pretty reasonable.

First of all, it was a way to allow the members of Group A to immediately demonstrate their loyalty and their ability to carry out a task. We were giving these men a chance to prove themselves and make a good start in their new place of work. Who wouldn't want that?

As for the ones getting killed, that was hard luck and I won't deny it. But Abie, with his grasp of psychology, pointed out something important to me. "By doing it this way," Abie explained, "we are sparing the members of Group B from the humiliation of being told that they're not wanted in the gang—and you know, Joe, there is nothing worse for a gangster."

"That's true," I said to Abie, "but won't they realize they're not wanted round about the time they start getting stabbed?"

"They probably will," he agreed, "but by that time they'll have other things on their minds."

It made sense to me. And besides, supposing we had rejected the Group B guys but allowed them to go on living? They would have formed a rival gang, with a particular beef against us. And it would've been the worst kind of gang—one filled entirely with rejects. So in doing this, we not only spared ourselves future problems, but we also did a favor to the society at large. Because who can say what terrible and stupid crimes Group B would have perpetrated, given the chance?

Bottom line, the process resulted in twenty deaths in a span of three days, and became known as "the Detroit crime wave of late '24." And these killings were of course attributed to the Purple Gang, but that is simply not true. Because each of the killings was committed by a guy who was *not yet* in the gang. It was only *afterwards* he was granted membership.

Naturally, these new people who survived to join us—the A group—were uneasy because now that they'd killed off the B team, they didn't know what we'd make them do next. I assured them we intended to welcome them with open arms, in our own fashion.

Some might think our welcoming process was harsh, but every person who went through it was appreciative afterwards. They suddenly appreciated how good it is to be alive, and to be able to breathe the air. They even began to appreciate the simple things, like a wool blanket you can wrap yourself in, or a good bandage that will stanch the bleeding.

Here is how the welcoming procedure worked. We took the twenty surviving "A" guys down to the Detroit River, to the pier on Riopelle to be precise. It was the middle of the night; not a soul around except our group. This was in January, and the river wasn't frozen but was chilled. We made each guy strip to the waist, and tied his hands behind the back. I asked Abie, using his dagger, to slash each man twice across the chest—leaving two stripes to represent courage and loyalty, which is all I ever asked of any man. When one guy complained about scars that would be left, I stripped off my own coat and shirt to show him the dozens of crisscrossing stripes on my torso, saying, "And you're complaining about a mere two?"

After they were slashed, they were pushed into the water. It was not a baptism (we were Jews, remember, and did not go in for that). I just wanted them to wash away their old life, like I did. Also, it was a way to see if they could take the cold—because when you're a gangster in Detroit, much of your life will be spent out in the cold.

We left each man in the water for a minute, then fished him out, bandaged his cuts, and wrapped him in a blanket. The nineteen men who survived (one caught pneumonia and later died) joined the six existing Purples: myself, Max, Abie, Grabowski, the Original Solly Levine, and Gorilla Kowalski, who I brought over from the bar in Hamtramck. We were the "core" Purples, and didn't have to go through any welcoming process. Though Abie did ask me to slash him twice across the chest so he could "earn his stripes" and I was honored to do it.

The Gorilla also felt he should do some kind of test to prove himself, and I said why don't you climb up the side of the Sugar House building, using just your hands and feet. He did so whilst we all stood by and cheered.

Speaking of the Sugar House, it was all ours now. The headquarters of the old gang was a brick warehouse with the front part dedicated to processing corn syrup. The back part of the warehouse—hidden and walled off from the rest, accessible from outside only via a back alley—was a distillery where the Sugars made their own homemade whiskey, sold on the cheap to speakeasies. It was possibly the worst booze ever made.

The first time we went in to look at what we'd inherited, Max walked around shaking his head. "What a bunch of crap," he said. "This all has to go. We've got to clean this place out."

Max thought the Sugars had it all wrong. They were using the sugar factory as a cover, but the truth was you didn't even need a cover in Detroit; you just needed grease. If you greased the cops and the city inspectors, you had nothing to worry about. As for the cheap homemade liquor, Max said, "That's amateur stuff."

He'd decided back in Hamtramck, whilst scribbling on his blackboard, that we were going to make money in Detroit three ways: By distributing fine Canadian whiskey, which commanded a premium even after you diluted it; by getting in on the action at the top speakeasies; and by getting a piece of the car business.

As we walked around the Sugar House, Max said we could use the hidden area in the back for our "cutting factory," to dilute the Canadian. As for the area in front, he said, "After we get all the damn sugar out of here, we'll use this space for our offices."

Now it may seem strange for a gang to set up offices, but Max had become a student of how business was being conducted in Detroit, and he observed that everybody had offices. "You need a place where someone can come talk to you," he said.

So in this big warehouse space he set up a few little desks. He even put a tiny sign on the front door that said, "Bernstein Enterprises." I thought he was crazy, but a few days after he did this, our first customer came knocking on the door.

TWELVE

That first guy who came to see us owned a dry cleaner and his name was Applebaum. "I have a business proposition," he said, and Max invited him into the "office." Their footsteps echoed as they walked through the empty warehouse to Max's little desk.

"What can we do for you?" Max said, then started rocking in his chair and scratching his arm. He'd never had a customer before.

The man leaned forward and said in a low voice, "You are the Purples, right?"

"We are Bernstein Enterprises," Max said.

"Yes, but... you *are* the Purples, am I right?"

"We are Bernstein Enterprises, and what can we do for you?"

Whilst saying this Max had a shiver go through him and it caused a twitch in his face, which Applebaum may have taken as a wink. In any case, Applebaum proceeded to lay out his needs. He ran the biggest wholesale cleaner operation in Detroit and had decided it was time to raise the price of cleaning a suit. In fact, he wanted to triple the price. He worried that if he charged three times as much as everyone else, he'd lose customers.

"That's a valid concern," Max agreed.

So Applebaum wanted to make sure all the other cleaners in the city got in line with the price hike. "It's good business for all of us," he said. "But some people are going to need persuading."

"What made you come to us?" Max asked, as any good businessman will.

"This was the kind of thing the Sugars used to handle," Applebaum said. "But I'm told the Sugars are no more, and now you have to go to the Purples."

"The Purples?" Max said.

"I mean Bernstein Enterprises," Applebaum said.

He put us on his payroll at a thousand a week and had only one request: "Please don't hurt anybody, just scare them."

This was the beginning of what would come to be known as "The Cleaners and Dyers War." The Detroit newspapers made it sound as if bombs were dropping at every laundry shop in town. But the truth is, the bombs were only a last resort.

Max and I developed a persuasion process that went like this: The first visit to a cleaner, you used logic: "A price hike benefits all." Second visit, you came to the shop in the middle of the night and left a "burnt stick"—a piece of dynamite with the fuse half-burnt, which was supposed to send a clear message. If that did not work, you just stink-bombed the whole place.

Our persuasion process worked like a charm—too well in fact. Before long, most cleaners were charging the higher rate and Applebaum figured he didn't need the muscle anymore. He came to the office one day, and this time I was there with Max. He handed us an envelope stuffed with two thousand dollars.

"There's your final payment with a little extra," he said. "Maybe we'll do business together again some day."

I counted the money in the envelope. "It's as if you read my mind," I said. "Just this morning I was thinking it's time to raise our fee to two grand a week."

Pocketing the envelope, I said, "See you next week, Sam."

I thought I'd given Applebaum a clear message—more plain than a burnt stick, even. But he didn't receive it, and failed to make the next two payments. So we busted into his warehouse and filled one of our trucks with fine white shirts and nice suits—hundreds of them. Then we sent a ransom note, saying if you want your clothes back, give us $4,000 in missed payments and put us back on the payroll. He agreed to do so, and we returned the suits—but not until I had picked out 25 suits and 25 white shirts, one for each Purple.

In addition to being on Applebaum's payroll, we collected a smaller fee from each of the other cleaners. Abie was concerned about all this—he did not think we should be jacking up merchants the way Buster Weintraub used to do.

"But these are not merchants," I said. "These are cleaners."

"What's the difference?" he said.

I had to think about that. "They don't even make anything," I said. "They give you back what's already yours, and charge you a fortune."

He didn't seem convinced, so I said: "And remember, they started it—they came to us."

"But we wouldn't do this to a fruit stand or a butcher, right?"

"No," I said. "We're better than that."

On that subject, Abie's father had returned to Detroit with us when we all came back and we set him up with a whole new butcher shop on Hastings, after previously setting one up for him in Hamtramck. Now here is a funny thing: After worrying about whether the Polacks would buy meat from him, Mr. Z's shop ended up doing just fine in Hamtramck. But when he came back to Hastings and re-opened, it seemed like nobody was coming to him.

"What do you think is going on?" Abie asked me.

I pointed out there was another butcher in the neighborhood, and that maybe we should encourage the guy to relocate.

"No, no," Abie said. "My father is a better butcher than that guy. And people know him from way back. He should be able to compete with that guy. I don't get it."

I got it, but I didn't wish to tell Abie. Though he found out for himself, soon enough.

It happened on a day that started with so much promise. We'd decided to put on our new Applebaum suits and parade through the neighborhood—not the whole gang, just the core six of us. We got dressed at headquarters, where the 25 suits were being stored. When we were all dressed, with our white shirts buttoned tight to the throat and our matching jackets, we looked very sharp indeed, except we didn't have ties. Solly offered to run out and get a batch.

"No," I said. "I like how this looks. Besides if we ever get arrested they will keep our ties. Let's not do them any favors."

Before we left to begin our procession march, Abie said he had to make a quick stop at his father's shop. We waited, and he returned looking extra bulky under his buttoned suit jacket. I had my suspicions about what he was planning, but I let it go.

When we walked down the bustling Hastings Street market, it parted for us like the Red Sea. The street merchants and their customers all stopped what they were doing and looked at us. Our buttoned-up white shirts gleamed in the sun. We walked shoulder by shoulder and spanned the width of the street. We walked at the same pace. It seemed like we had the same heartbeat. I have never felt so connected to five other people in my life.

Abie was on the end and he suddenly stopped and said, "Give me a minute, fellas." He opened his jacket and it looked like a brown paper lifejacket was wrapped around his stomach. He took it off and tore open the paper. The meat was beautiful—the finest prime cut you've ever seen. It was in big chunks and Abie held up a couple of the pieces, one in each hand.

"This is a free sample from Zussman's butcher shop," he announced. "Divide it amongst yourselves and enjoy it."

We continued the march through Hastings and when we got to the end of the market I bought apples for all, and gave the guy at the stand five dollars for a half dollar's worth of fruit. We stood around eating and I asked the man, who I did not recognize, if he was a greener—meaning, fresh off the boat. He didn't answer.

"You're a quiet man," I said. "But don't be afraid to tell me if anybody gives you trouble—the Klan, the cops, anybody."

We turned and went back down Hastings and when we got to the spot where Abie had given away the meat, it was laying there in the road—those big beautiful bright red slabs, now speckled with flecks of dirt. The brown wrapping was crumpled in a ball on the ground, but someone had torn off a piece of it and written in large letters TREYF. The note was stuck on a piece of meat.

Abie bent down and started picking up the meat carefully, as if he was handling something precious. He picked off the dirt with his fingers before putting the meat back into the crumpled paper.

"Who did this?" I yelled, looking around. All eyes were down.

"No, Joe, let it go," Abie said from where he was kneeling. "It's okay, just let it go."

As we walked away from Hastings, we weren't in a line anymore, we were broken into clusters. Abie walked out front and fast by himself, holding the brown package under his arm. Grabowski was next to me and said quietly, so Abie wouldn't hear, "Whazzat word mean?"

I told him it meant "unclean," and Grabowski said, "Are you kiddin'—that was the cleanest cut 'a meat I ever seen."

Later when I talked about it with Abie I told him, "I've been dealing with this my whole life. You have to get used to it."

"But we never did anything to any of them," Abie said.

"Doesn't matter. They decided a long time ago that we were tainted. When they put that name on us."

"I tried to forget about that name," he said. "You had to go and bring it back."

"Damn right," I said. "Fuck them. They think they can put a stain on us? You have to take that stain, and make it a badge of honor. Understand?"

"Yeah, I understand," Abie said.

But he didn't really. It continued to bother him and the Hastings crowd knew it did. The pricks took every opportunity to ostracize him. The worst was when he went to the synagogue with his father. Abie was the only one amongst us who went to that place and we thought it was nuts that a guy in a gang still prayed—sometimes we mocked him for it. But we knew where to draw the line, and when to show the proper respect. The same could not be said for the members of the synagogue, who refused to sit anywhere near him. The pew that he and his father occupied was always otherwise empty, as was the one in front and behind, even when the synagogue was crowded. Abie to his credit never said a word about it, nor did his father.

I offered to go in there with him for solidarity—and you have no idea what a big offer that was by me, given my own feelings about that place and all it represents. But Abie turned me down.

Then one day, whilst he and his father were sitting there isolated, a girl about twenty years old walked over and sat in his aisle—not next to him, mind you, but on the end. Still, it was his aisle. He peeked at her from the corner of his eye; she didn't look back at him. On the way out, he saw her going out the door with an older couple, probably her parents, and it looked like they were scolding her. She kept her head down and didn't talk back to them. But then the next week, she was back in his aisle again, and this time when he peeked over, she peeked back.

She was there sitting right beside him the week after that, and the week after that, and the week after that. And then, the week after that, she wasn't just sitting beside him, she was standing beside him—because they were getting married.

As for my own domestic affairs, Rachel and I moved into a nice big house on Chicago Avenue. It was going to be just we two, but then Max said he wanted to move in with us.

"Don't you want your own place?" I said.

"So you don't want me moving in with you?" he said.

We let him have an upstairs bedroom, plus the entire basement of the house, which became his planning room—with a blackboard, charts all over, a drafting table. He spent many hours there each day, making plans for how we'd infiltrate the car business whilst controlling the Canadian whiskey business. He was anxious for us to get out of the small-change world of dry cleaners. "Whiskey and cars," he said, "that's where we need to be."

His brain was on fire in 1925, and it was beautiful to see. He was like Edison and Ford rolled into one, minus the bigotry. He dreamed up all sorts of inventions aimed at controlling the Detroit

River. For example, he was working on a boat engine that was
three times more powerful than anything in existence. In addition,
he wanted to build a mile-long underwater conveyer belt system,
to transport the whiskey from Windsor to Detroit. At the same
time, he also thought it might be possible to shoot the whiskey
under the water inside torpedoes. I figured he was kidding about
the torpedoes until I saw the blueprints.

I was a little worried about him though—Abie said I should be
careful that Max didn't become "obsessed." I tried to lure him out
of the house in various ways, but the only thing that worked was
when I took him to a Tigers game. I got seats right by the dugout,
where you could see the players' faces up close. Max went crazy
for it, which surprised me as he'd never been much for sports.

So I started getting more tickets, always near the dugout. The
players must've heard about who we were, because they began to
wave to us before the game. Usually when ballplayers look at fans,
their eyes are blank as if they're looking at buzzing flies. But when
they looked at us, you could see them paying attention.

We got to meet the great Ty Cobb, who came over to our seats
once, with a baby-faced blond rookie named Bobby Gates. We
had a nice chat during which I happened to ask Cobb, "So, do you
hate Jews?" (because I'd heard that about him).

"I hate everyone," he said. I laughed and said, "Yeah, me too."

Afterwards I said to Max, "Isn't that Cobb something?"

"He's okay," he said, "but I like that Bobby Gates better."

I laughed—Max just didn't know his baseball yet.

Whilst Max was thriving in the new house, Rachel was doing
surprisingly well, too. The two of us had gone through rough
times in Hamtramck. She spent much of it sedated from the
opium. When she was awake and I wasn't off at Zabawa or having
meetings at the purple house, we sometimes talked nicely and even
made love. But a lot of the time we argued about things that
weren't even real, except to her.

When we moved back to Detroit, though, things took a turn for
the better. She decided she was going to make a fresh start. She

cut down on the opium. She neatened her hair and began to fix up our new house. And she even started talking about getting a job. I reminded her that the last time she had a job, delivering the cleaned uniforms to the Ford plant, it ended very badly.

"I know," she said. "Don't I deserve another chance?"

I said, "Sure, but what kind of job could you do, you have no skills. And you fall apart if there's any pressure."

She said, "You don't have any faith in me. You are always telling me what I can't do, and what I don't have. Maybe one of my friends can get me a job."

And then I simply reminded her that she didn't have any friends, and it made her blow up and yell, "See?"

"See what?" I said, throwing up my hands. She might have been getting better, but she still didn't make sense sometimes.

Max and Rachel got along well in the new house, finding they had a lot in common—headaches, fatigue, me and all my many faults, etcetera. So it was a mixed blessing: On the one hand, they each had someone to talk to, whilst on the other, I had to listen to it all.

For example, one afternoon I came into the house just wanting to sit down and read the paper to see if it contained any fresh lies about us or just the same old ones. As I sat down in the living room, I could hear Max and Rachel talking at the kitchen table.

"When my condition acts up and I can't sleep," he was telling her, "I think about the Tigers."

"I tried that with sheep and it didn't work," she said. "Because I start thinking, what's going to happen to the sheep once I fall asleep and stop thinking about them?"

"When I say Tigers," Max said, "I mean the ballclub not the animals. I picture myself at Navin Field, the sun on my face."

"But I don't like ball parks because of the crowd," she said. "If there was a riot you would get trampled."

"I thought of that," Max said, "and that is why I always take an aisle seat near an exit ramp. I also make sure no one sits next to me. Except Joe of course. I don't mind him sitting next to me."

"Lucky for you, because he would sit there anyway. He does

what he wants, no matter what anyone says."

"But I don't want someone on the other side of me, because I don't want to be crowded. Given my condition."

"How do you make sure no one sits there?"

"I leave a messy smelly sandwich on the seat. Limburger cheese, something like that."

"Uch. If I smell Limburger I get sick."

"Oh, sure, but there's a way to stop that—I mean when you're gonna get sick. You put your head between your knees like this…"

I could hear the scraping of the chair as Max moved in his seat to demonstrate. I could hear this even though I had already put fingers in both my ears.

I had my head down and my fingers in my ears and I was just staring at the paper in my lap, when I noticed a little news item on the page. The headline said: *D.A. Thompson to Retire Next Month.*

I took the paper into the kitchen, laid it down in front of Max, and pointed. "I find that to be an interesting piece of news," I said.

"It's not news," Max said. "It's ancient history, and we should leave it that way."

Rachel tried to grab the paper and said, "What are you talking about, which story?"

I told her, "Never mind, it has nothing to do with you."

But of course it had everything to do with her.

THIRTEEN

Before long, we were firing on all cylinders. Using the spoils from the Cleaners and Dyers War, we imported the finest Canadian whiskey—sometimes importing it from Windsor filling stations, or else importing it right off someone else's boat, at gunpoint.

And there was no way to stop us because we had the two best boats on the Detroit River. These twin monsters were dubbed the "Gar-Max" boats. They started out as racing boats made by the boating champ Gar Wood. Then they were modified by Max, who took Gar's 175-horse Kermath racing motors and juiced up their power even more. Gar himself believed it was reckless to make a boat so fast, and our response was, "You're damn right it is."

We also bulletproofed the sides of the boats, and installed a steel turret, where a gunman could sit protected whilst peering through a visor and firing a mounted Gatling. We put in a false floor on the boat for storing cargo. The boat bottom had a trap door, operable by a lever on deck, so you could release that cargo into the river in case you got caught (as if anyone could catch this boat).

The Gar-Max boats unloaded their cargo at boathouses we'd set up all along the Detroit shoreline. From there, the liquor was trucked to the cutting house, whereupon it was diluted by 25 percent, bottled and slapped with an "Old Log Cabin" label, and then shipped to the blind pigs.

And speaking of speakeasies, we decided to open one of our

own. We started with a vacant space the Sugars owned which had formerly housed one of the worst speakeasies in Detroit. We quickly sold off the rotgut made by the Sugars. We wanted to start from scratch, and do it right. Max soon was approached by someone promising to open the classiest blind pig Detroit had ever seen.

"There is just one thing," Max said, whilst telling me about this prospect. "She is a woman."

I was mulling that over when he said, "Well, there's one other thing, too—she's a dinge."

"I have no problem with them," I said. "They are the only people who've got it harder than us."

All that mattered to me was whether this colored woman, who went by the name Tennessee Jenkins, had the smarts and the means to open a quality place. Max said she seemed sharp, and he'd know. He also said that she had a secret financial backer.

"She won't give a name," Max said, "but she hinted that he's a big shot."

With our booze business coming along, Max—who'd always said we needed to mix whiskey and cars—got us a foothold in the automotive business, too. Not by making cars, but by wrecking them instead.

We set up a little auto repair shop that was really just part of an insurance scam operation. Our customer was the kind of poor sap who'd been taken in by carmakers that gave him a car for nothing upfront, then squeezed him to pay it off. That's when the guy could come to us for help. First, we'd loan him a few bucks to get the dealer off his back. Of course he had no money to repay us, but this is where the insurance came in. We'd crash the hell out of the car, and help the guy file a repair claim. The insurance company would cut a check, which he'd turn over to us. But we wouldn't bother to fix the car. Instead, we'd steal it from the guy—so he could file another claim, this time for the car's full value. When the second check came we got that one, too.

As for the sap, did we leave him stranded? Not at all—you cannot treat your customers that way. We would abandon his stolen car somewhere the cops would find it, and they'd put it in the abandoned car auction. Soon as this happened, we'd tip off the sap that his car was up for bid—we'd even give him a few bucks to bid on it. And since we'd previously done such a thorough job of demolishing the car, it looked like hell and could be had for a song at auction. Bottom line: The guy ended up with a wreck, but at least it was a wreck he could afford.

It was a good business and the best part was that we got to smack up Ford cars on a regular basis. We were so good at it that word spread—all the way out to Hollywood. One day somebody from the Foxman movie studio came to us and said, "I hear you guys are experts on getting into crashes with Ford cars. I may have work for you." Before you knew it we were in the movie business, and I'll get to the details soon enough. But the point is, who would've thought Hollywood would come calling on people like us? What it shows is that one thing definitely leads to another. And also this: Everybody has a need for somebody who will do anything.

With so many things going well, I should have been fat and happy. But I was restless and ornery. I took long solitary ankles through the streets. I yelled at people, including Abie and my brother, for no reason sometimes. I insulted Solly Levine more than even he deserved.

Abie tried to talk to me about it. "Sometimes," he said, "you have to look back in your past to see what's bothering you now."

Being the moody son of a bitch I'd become, I said to him, "Yes, and there are other times when I only need to look straight in front of me to see what's bothering me now."

After Abie walked away shaking his head, I thought about what he'd said. He was right. My trouble was I had an itch that had never been scratched, an itch that went back to 1920 and things done then.

The next time I saw Abie, I showed him the newspaper article I had torn from the paper, months earlier—the one about DA Thompson retiring, which Max had advised me to ignore. Abie had a very different reaction: He looked at the clipping and said, "You kept it all this time? Then it must be important to you."

After that, I couldn't stop thinking about it. I'd never gotten any answers from that son of a bitch. And then he tried to have me killed. I never did anything about it because he was a DA, and you can't go after a DA. Except now he wasn't a DA anymore. He was just an old guy who stilled owed me some answers.

Meanwhile, Abie announced that his wife was going to have a baby. This jerked me in a whole new direction. When Abie told me the news, in our booth at the Crime, tears rolled down his big face. "Now I feel like I really have a future," he said.

It made me go out that day and ankle around, thinking about my own future. All the years I'd been with Rachel I never asked her to marry me. I told myself it was because she was crazy and I was leery of marrying a woman in that condition whilst also being scared to abandon her. So I spent years in limbo. But now I thought it might be time to change that, to make a future like Abie was doing.

She'd recently said to me, whilst crying, "I'm twenty-five years old and I don't have a life like other women—I don't have anything." She was drinking now for the first time, trying to temper the effects of the opium she'd gone back to taking. She was a mess, but maybe all that would change if I finally filled the hole in her life—maybe she wouldn't need these other fillers.

With these thoughts swimming in my head, I walked by a jeweler on Woodward and before you knew it I was inside, buying a ring. Then I was on my way home with the ring in my pocket and a bounce in my step. I hurried into the house, sprung up the stairs, and found Rachel on the bathroom floor lying in her own blood.

She was glassy-eyed but alive. I wrapped her wrists in towels and carried her downstairs in my arms, yelling for Max. He'd been in his basement planning room, oblivious. He came running upstairs and when he saw her, he went white as a sheet.

"Where the hell were you, the one time I needed you?" I said.

I kept going out the door, and behind me he stammered, "Joe... let me... let me come with you."

And I didn't turn around but I knew he was probably starting to quiver, and all I said was, "I don't have time for one of your bullshit fits now."

But he'd followed me out the front door anyway and then I heard a splat on the concrete and I turned, with her in my arms, to see that he'd fallen face first and then turned his body sideways on the ground, putting his hands between his knees. He started to have the big spasms, the kind that made his whole body lift off the ground as if there was an earthquake underneath him.

I sat Rachel in the passenger seat of my car and then went back for Max. I took a handkerchief from his shirt pocket where he always kept it at the ready and I twisted it and put it between his teeth and then checked his forehead, which was cut and bleeding from the fall. The whole time his eyes were wide and looking at me like I was trying to kill him or something. I picked him up and carried him to the car, his body jerking against my chest, and I laid him across the back seat. Then I drove to the hospital. (Detroit General, not the Henry Ford—I am no fool.)

They were put in separate rooms and after a while a doctor came out and told me they were both being taken care of. I decided to stick around for a few hours after that, and to kill time I ankled all through the hospital and into the various departments.

Somehow I ended up in the maternity ward. There was a proud father looking through the glass at his baby. I walked up to him and said, "That's a fine looking kid," and he gave me a cigar. He was a working stiff, I could tell by his hands and clothes.

I said to him, "Let me ask you something, pal. When you got married, did you give your girl a nice ring?"

He said he did the best he could at the time.

Then I pulled the ring out of my pocket and said, "What do you think of this one? Is that a beauty?"

He whistled and said, "Oh, brother. I could never afford one like that. Your girl sure is lucky."

"No, she's not so lucky at all," I said, "but you are."

I left him there with the ring in his hand and his mouth hanging open, as I headed back down the hall.

Whilst I sat in the waiting area, I was filled with uncertainty about Rachel and Max, and what would become of them. I didn't want to think about the future anymore. I was back to thinking about the past, and that old itch that still needed scratching.

Three weeks later, I sat alone in a folding chair in one of our little boathouses, in the light of two flickering lanterns. It was dead quiet. And then through the thin boathouse walls, I heard twigs and rocks crackling under wheels, the squeal of brakes. A car door clicked open, and the soft voice of Abie the Agent said: *"Here, let's get this off your head so you can see... Oh, look at you, all mussed up. We need to fix you up so you look good for Joe."*

I waited for the slanted double-doors, up the steps from where I sat, to open. When they did, I looked up through the opening to see a night sky, full of stars. And then old Thompson appeared in that opening—pale of face and surrounded by all those twinkly stars, looking almost like an angel. He stood with hands behind his back, looking down at me. I think I detected a certain look as it flashed in his eyes—recognition, but of the worst kind.

I couldn't see Abie but he must have given the geezer a shove from behind, because Thompson suddenly came rushing down those steps and right at me as if he couldn't wait for us to be re-united. When his momentum stopped, he stood very still in front of me for a moment. His cheeks were stuffed and a little white corner of a handkerchief peeped out from his mouth, hanging over a trembling lip. Suddenly his knees buckled, and the kneecaps landed hard on the cement floor. From his knees, he looked up at me—like a dog begging. That little corner of the hanky was his panting white tongue.

Abie came down the steps, his big shoes landing softly.

I leaned forward in my chair and reached toward the kneeling old man, which made him cringe. With my two fingers I pinched the white cloth tongue hanging over Thompson's lip.

"Open," I said, like a dentist.

Thompson did, and I pulled the handkerchief out. Then I held the hanky at arm's length, because I did not want to catch whatever disease it was that turned you into a miserable old bastard like Thompson. Abie was standing behind Thompson now, so I held out the hanky for him.

"I'm not touching it," Abie said. "It's got his germs all over it."

I pulled open the pocket on Thompson's jacket and dropped the cloth in. Then I got up from my chair and grabbed under his clammy armpits and hoisted him up—he was so light I could have tossed him in the air. But no, I gently guided him into a folding chair opposite mine and sat him down and arranged him nicely.

"First things first," I said. "Would you like a drink?"

I offered him Old Log Cabin uncut and fresh off the boat. Many would salivate at such an offer, but all Thompson did was drip sweat from the tip of his nose.

"You should sample it," I said. "It has more kick when it's uncut. You could probably stand a good kick, Thompson."

"I will do whatever you ask," Thompson said. "I can tell you who to see about ransom."

I placed a hand over my heart, as if wounded.

"Ransom? You think I'm a kidnapper? You hear that, Abie? He thinks we're kidnappers."

Abie shrugged. "Well, technically we are. We did abduct him."

I gave Abie a look, then said to the old man, "This is a reunion, that's all."

I brought my face right up to his. "Look in these baby blues, Thompson. Now think back, to a night six years ago in your bedroom. Just me and you, looking at each other in the dark. One dreading what the other might do next. Like a bride and her new husband. Is it coming back to you?"

I could see the wheels turning in Thompson's head—*Should I play dumb? Should I beg? What might the Jew want? What would he accept?* He was weighing the options, I could tell. Finally he nodded. "I remember," he said.

I took this as a sign that maybe he was going to be straight with me. But then he added, "I don't know what you think I may have done. I didn't do anything to you. Or to her, I swear it."

"*Her?*" I said. "Funny you would bring up *her*, when I had not even gotten around to that. But all right, you wish to talk about *her*. Then let's do."

Thompson and I sucked down some of the Log, in a glass tumbler we shared. The old man had politely declined to drink but I said, "No, I insist," even holding the glass for him and pressing it against his lips whilst gently prying his mouth open with my free hand. The first gulp made him cough, as did the second. The third went down smooth.

"See, you get used to it," I said.

We sat facing each other in the folding chairs. Across the boathouse floor and apart from us, Abie balanced on his own folding chair, which looked like a child's seat under his bulk. He was absorbed in a magazine, nodding to himself as he read.

Thompson was sunk down in his chair, as if the weight of the world was pressing on his chest.

"I'm glad you're interested in the girl," I said, "though there are other things we could have talked about. Old friends we had in common, like Buster Weintraub. But let's talk about Rachel."

"I did my best to get her released as soon as I could," he said. "She did get out, didn't she?"

"She did, but not because of you," I said.

"Is she… alright now?"

"I appreciate your concern," I said. "As a matter of fact, she is back in Eloise. After all the fuss about getting her out, she's right back in there now. Isn't that a kick in the balls, Thompson?"

It was true. The hospital wouldn't release her to my custody; they suspected I was drugging her. They said she needed "extensive special care," and there was only one place could provide it. The doctors got a judge to sign the order; if I didn't know better I'd have sworn I was dealing with the Ford Hospital all over again. But I didn't really fight it because, believe it or not, she wanted to go. She said to me from her hospital bed, "I am tired of being sick and sick of being tired. I want to be normal, that's all. If that place can make me normal, then that's where I'll go." I felt like I was the

crazy one. I tried to tell her, and the doctors, that Eloise had dam-
aged her, experimented on her, got her hooked on who-knows-
what. Nobody believed me, not even Rachel. What could I do? I
let them put her back in that place, and this time I had no grand
plans to bust her out.

"I'm sorry for her troubles," Thompson said now. "If there is
anything I can do for her... I know some of the best doctors in
Detroit, maybe I can—"

"The only thing you can do now," I cut in, "is tell me the truth.
Because I never did find out why she was taken in the first place."

Thompson launched into the same old line: It wasn't his fault, it
all came from above, he didn't choose the people, and so forth.

I cut him off again. "Do you have the list? The one with her
name on it?"

He said the lists were destroyed at the time.

"Are you sure the list with her name came from Washington?" I
said. "You sure her name wasn't given to you by Heinrich Ford?"

Thompson shook his head. "Why would Ford care about her?"

"She had dealings with his plant workers. Something happened.
He held it against her."

The details were not important, I told him. The only thing that
mattered was the list. I didn't tell Thompson, but I knew if I could
get hold of such a list, I'd have something to use against Ford.

"I need that list," I said to Thompson. "And so do you. That
list is your life preserver. And the boat is sinking fast."

Thompson's brow furrowed; he was thinking hard about something. I hoped maybe he was trying to recall the location of the list
but it turned out he was just trying to spin a theory, to distract me
I guess.

"If she did something at that Ford plant," he said, "maybe one
of Ford's spies was watching her. Some of those spies were with
the APL—they passed tips to the Justice Department. That could
explain how Palmer got her name."

He wasn't telling me anything new: Ford had spies? No shit.
And as for the American Protection League? Everyone knew
about them—local people who agreed to be snitches during the

Red Scare. Didn't get me any closer to what I needed to know.

"Your pet theories do not help me," I said. "I need hard evidence."

On it went like this, until Abie pulled me aside to offer a suggestion. "Maybe you should put him in the chute," he whispered.

He was referring to the underground chute we'd built connecting the boathouse to the river's edge, fifty yards away. It was designed so the boats could unload cargo in a hurry—pull up in the marsh, open the outside door to the chute, and drop in their crates, which slid through and ended up here in the boathouse.

"Why the hell would I put him in the chute?" I whispered back.

Abie quietly explained that if you put someone in a dark place, it could be useful in helping them remember things. He got this from one of his psychology books, I guess. It sounded queer, but I had nothing to lose.

I walked Thompson over to the mouth of the chute—an opening in the wall about two-foot square. I explained to him that the inside of the chute was just wide enough around for him to crawl through. I told him that it led to the riverbank. And so if he crawled all the way to the other end, who knows, he might be able to get himself free.

Thompson shook his head. "Don't make me do this," he said. "I'm an old man."

"What are you scared of?" I said. "It is snug I admit, but there's room for you to slither. I bet you slither very well, Thompson."

He realized he did not have a choice. I gave him another suck of the Log, for strength. Then he put his head and shoulders into the chute, whilst Abie lifted his legs and gave him a boost from behind. Once inside, he started to crawl. It took him a while to crawl the length of the chute. We knew he'd reached the end because we heard him pounding on the small door at the other end—the small door that separated him from freedom. Unfortunately for him, that door was padlocked from outside.

I poked my head in the chute—couldn't see anything in there, it was pitch-black—and yelled, "Sorry, Thompson—it's locked. But we'll come around and open it, soon as you tell us you have the information I need. Now why don't you just stay put and think for a while. And give us a yell when you're ready."

It got very quiet at the other end; Thompson stopped pounding and I guess that meant he was ready to start thinking.

Then above us we heard a car pulling up outside the boathouse. Abie looked at me. "It's probably Grabowski," he said. "I told him we'd be here."

When the double-doors opened, the first feet to come down the steps were white and furry. Ono was pulling on the chain, Grabowski coming down behind him. The other beast was not with them.

"What the hell did you bring him here for?" I yelled.

"Well, hello ta you, too, brot," Grabowski said. "Jeez. Thought ya might need him, 'at's all. Ono is good at helpin' guys rememba things."

Grabowski looked around and realized it was just me and Abie, and we were standing right in front of the chute.

"Is he in there?" Grabowski said. He smiled approvingly.

"We're giving him time to reflect," Abie said.

Grabowski walked to us, whilst Ono sniffed the ground furiously, head sweeping side to side; he'd picked up Thompson's scent.

At the chute, Grabowski hunched and stuck his head in. "Hey, Thompson, ya hear me? Somebody here wants ta say hello."

Grabowski pulled his head out and then bent down to grab Ono under the front legs, lifting him up.

"What are you doing?" I said. "Don't put him in there."

"S'okay, I just wanna let Thompson get a peek at him. I got hold a his chain, don' worry."

Grabowski put Ono's front paws inside the chute and then pushed him all the way in, whilst still holding onto the chain with one hand. You could hear the animal sniffing hard inside; the sound echoed. Then Ono must've lunged because the chain went taut and then slipped right off Grabowski's hand. We heard the jingle and scrape of that chain dragging along the chute.

Grabowski thrust his head inside but it was too late to grab anything. He pulled his head back out, looked at me and said, "Oops."

He maintained afterwards that it really was an accident, that he didn't mean to let go of the leash. I never believed him. But I'm not sure it mattered much because one way or another, we would have had to get rid of Thompson. He'd already shown, years earlier, that he wasn't the type you could threaten and then let go.

When Ono got to the end of the chute, there was quite a commotion as you might imagine. It all reverberated back through the tunnel and came out very loud on our side.

Grabowski cocked his head and listened closely as if to a symphony, whilst Abie turned away quickly and rushed up the stairs and outside. I stayed alongside Grabowski, but covered my ears with my palms. When the sound died down, I leaned into the chute and yelled something to Thompson, though I have no idea if he heard it. I yelled, "Sorry about the dog, Thompson."

"He ain't a dog," Grabowski said to me, but I told him I wasn't talking about Ono.

So that was our one mistake of 1926, at least according to some people. I'm not sure it *was* such a big mistake. Who's to say Riley wouldn't have come after us anyway—or if not Riley, someone else like him. You can't live your life being careful and trying to avoid missteps.

And as I pointed out to Max at the time, Thompson was an old, hateful, out-to-pasture geezer who got what was a long time coming. Nobody was going to miss him, not even his dead dog.

But Max said, "No, no, you're wrong. He will be missed very soon, and we will be blamed."

"Okay, fine," I said. "We've gotten blamed for every bum who's died in Detroit for the past two years."

"But this guy," Max said, "he was no bum."

FOURTEEN

It was two weeks before anyone even missed Thompson. That says something right there about the kind of man he was. The neighbors finally reported it, but the cops didn't know where to start looking—no leads, no suspects, no signs of foul play. Who knew, maybe the old geezer just drove off in his Duesenberg to begin a new life somewhere.

The case probably would have been forgotten soon enough, except that Thompson's successor, Teddy Baird, became very concerned about it. It wasn't that Baird liked Thompson. And it wasn't that he felt a professional obligation to do something. It was simpler than that: Baird was scared. If somebody could make a retired DA disappear, what would stop them doing the same thing to a current DA?

For a week after Thompson was reported missing, this was all Baird could talk about; we knew, because we had a snitch right there in the DA's office, a secretary who was on our payroll. She told us that Baird talked a lot about it—though he didn't seem to *do* anything about it. His excuse heard round the DA's office was that he had "too much on his plate" to begin investigating. What else was on the plate I don't know, but when it came to this course he had no appetite for it. Baird was a puffy man who liked to please and did not want to make enemies, especially not with people like us. He preferred that someone else go down that road.

And so he began to float Riley's name. Baird had a young investigator working for him named Bud Fleischer—yes, a Jew, from the Hastings neighborhood in fact (not all of us became gangsters)—and he said to Fleischer one day, "I think I might know just the guy to help us out on this case."

Baird told Fleischer about Riley—how he'd fallen out with Thompson, quit the DA's office, hung around Detroit for a while and then took a job in a local county DA office up north, where he also found himself a quiet little place by a lake. "I spoke to Riley before he took off," Baird told his young assistant. "He was fed up with all the graft. Said he needed to 'get out of the cesspool.'"

"Scared, in other words," Fleischer said. He was the skeptical kind—the 23-year-old who's seen it all.

Baird gave him a look. "Oh, you think so? Tell me Bud, ever heard of the *Croix de Guerre?*"

Bud hadn't.

"Well, it's a medal and you don't get it for being scared," Baird said. "When it comes to this guy, you don't know the half of it. He went through hell to rescue a fallen soldier. Then he went back and went through hell again—so he could carry a second guy out. He was going back a *third* time when he got hit, and was left for dead in a ditch. You have any smart remarks about all that?"

Fleischer nodded, grudgingly. "Okay, he's a war hero. I get that. But what does it have to do with the Thompson situation?"

Baird said, "I don't know, maybe nothing. But maybe this thing with Thompson is going to lead deep into enemy fire. In which case, you want a guy who's been there."

Baird could've just called Riley on the phone, up at Riley's tiny office in the shithole town of Gaylord. But instead he said to Bud, "Why don't we go visit him in his little cabin. This Saturday, let's you and me take a scenic drive, kid."

They set out from Detroit at dawn. There weren't many cars on the road at that hour, but there was at least one other one, driving well back of them, unnoticed. Behind the wheel of that Ford was

Solly Levine, squinting through his thick glasses as he tried to keep the other car in sight. We'd heard from our snitch that Baird was going to see Riley, and I sent Solly along because I wanted to know if they were going to talk about me.

They drove most of the day, with Baird and Bud stopping for a bite at a roadside diner in Clare. Solly waited in the diner parking lot, watching them whilst they sat in a window booth and ate a nice hot meal. Solly meanwhile had to make do with a little sandwich he'd packed, and he grumbled the whole time. When the cars got up past Gaylord, Baird's car veered right off the main packed-dirt road and took a narrower, rockier path, passing a hand-painted wooden sign that said, *Lake Horicon, 1 mile.* Solly really had to stay back now, and almost lost them on the two-rut trail. Eventually through the woods he spotted their car, parked just outside a cabin set back under a canopy of pine trees. The dwelling was constructed of long dark pine logs broken up by a few windows with flower boxes on the sills.

Solly caught sight of the two men stepping carefully through the woods along the right side of the cabin. He put his own car in reverse and backed a safe distance away, pulling off the trail to park between two trees. He got out and closed his car door softly and began to cut through the woods himself.

Baird and Bud made their way to the rear of the cabin, moving closer to the lake. Then they seemed to hold back, standing in the woods and just watching. They were staring out at the lake, and at first it seemed like there was nothing out there—until a swimmer's head popped up through the smooth surface of the water, only to disappear again quickly. When the head next reappeared it was twenty feet further along. Then the swimmer began doing a crawl stroke, cutting the water very quietly with each stroke.

Baird gave Bud a little head signal and they stepped out of the woods and onto the scruffy, shin-high grass that led down to the lake. They passed a horseshoe pit knocked together from four old boards; a couple of rusty shoes were inside the pit, ringing the stake. Just beyond that was a small dock, but they stopped a few feet short of it. They were just standing there, waiting for the right moment to call out. And that's when she came walking quietly behind them with a rifle held in both hands, pointed at the ground. She stopped ten feet behind them and they still didn't know she was there.

"Want to tell me why you're sneaking around my property?" she said, not in a mean way, but with seriousness.

The two men jumped when they heard the voice. They turned to face her and though the gun was not pointed at them, Baird still thrust his flabby white hands in the air.

"It's okay!" he said. "We're friendly!"

To which she said, "I'll be the judge of that."

She wore an open robe with a swimsuit visible underneath and a pregnant belly protruding under that suit. She was taller than either of the men, owing to her long legs. The sun glinted off her red hair, cut in chin-length layers.

"Ma'am, I am so sorry," Baird said. "I tapped on the door and didn't see anyone. I'm Teddy Baird, the DA of Wayne County."

She let go the handle of the rifle and staked the butt into the ground, holding the barrel with one hand at her side. Her free hand touched her stomach.

"Not good to startle a lady in my condition, Mr. Baird—never know what she'll do."

"Agreed," Baird said. "I just stopped by to talk to Harry. And this is Bud Fleischer, works with me in the DA's office."

She smiled at Bud—she hadn't smiled at Baird—and her green eyes brightened a little as she offered her hand for a shake.

"Pleased to meet you, kiddo," she said. "Nan Riley."

Bud had his right hand tucked away in his pants pocket and kept it there whilst awkwardly offering his left to shake her right. She noticed this and raised an eyebrow but didn't say anything. Then she turned to Baird. She didn't offer him a handshake.

"Now why on earth would the Wayne County DA want to come all the way up here and talk to my husband?"

Baird smiled and fidgeted with his mustache. "Well, you know—just wanted to see how Harry was doing."

She smiled a little, but her eyes made it clear she wasn't buying.

"You didn't drive all the way up here to say hello. I do believe you want something, Mr. Baird." She looked at Bud now, and winked. "Tell me Bud, just between you and me—what does Mr. Baird want with my Harry?"

"Wants his help," Bud said.

Nan nodded. "That's what I figured."

She walked past them, toward the dock, and cupped a hand around her mouth. "Harry!" she called out. "These men want a word with you. Will you come in, or should we make them swim out?"

Riley, who'd caught sight of Baird by now, was already swimming in but was in no hurry to get to shore. Nan didn't look back at the visitors, just watched her husband glide up to the dock. In one motion he gripped the dock-edge with both hands and pulled himself up from the water. His eyes were shut tight as water streamed down his face. A pair of broad shoulders came out of the water along with a rounded belly above a pair of long swim trunks. A bandy leg came down from the right side of the trunks. But all that came out from the left trunk-leg was water, pouring down as if from an open faucet.

Bud was jolted by what he saw or rather did not see, and Baird noticed his reaction. "Like I told you," Baird whispered, "when it comes to this guy, you don't know the half of it."

Whilst he hoisted himself up onto the dock, Riley also spun around, so that he ended up sitting on the edge with his wide freckled back to them. Nan passed him a towel over his shoulder, which he took without looking back. He draped it over his head like a sheik and rubbed the head hard.

Nan bent down to pick up the wooden leg lying on the planks of the dock. She tugged at the tangled straps attached to the top of the leg, freeing them up before handing the leg to Riley. He pulled it into place and began to wrap the straps around his torso—she helped him fasten the small buckles. Then finally, Riley finally glanced back over his shoulder at the two men.

"Looks like my past is catching up with me," he said.

*

Minutes later, the three men were sitting at a pinewood picnic table halfway between the lake and the cabin. Nan sat apart but close by, pretending to knit whilst peeking up at them. As for Solly Levine, he was in the woods fifty yards away, nestled in a tree and looking through field glasses. The voices carried on the water; he heard every word.

"Teddy, I never did congratulate you on your promotion," Riley said to Baird. "You deserve it—if only for putting up with Thompson for so long. You must've thought he'd never retire."

Baird and Fleischer traded glances when Thompson's name came up. Riley caught that and said, "Okay, I promise not to say another word about my former boss."

"Harry," Baird said as he rubbed his hands together, "it's just that... well, there's been a development regarding the old man. Could be troubling." Baird hesitated, and fingered his mustache. "How shall I put this? Thompson seems to have... gone missing. Might be nothing—the old codger's a bit of a loner. Maybe he just went fishing for a couple of weeks."

Riley shot Baird a look that said *not likely*.

"On the other hand," Baird continued, "I can't help but wonder if one of the gangs isn't involved in this. The Purples, in particular."

Nan glanced up from her knitting and raised an eyebrow, then looked down again.

"I assume you've been following their exploits," Baird said. "You do get newspapers up here, don'tcha, Harry?"

"He doesn't read them but I do," Nan cut in. "Aren't they the ones that started bombing all those cleaners last year?"

"That was just the warm-up," Baird said. "We think they've been involved in kidnappings, hijacking boats. What they're really after, I suspect, is control of the pipeline from Canada. Pretty big ambitions for a bunch of guys that came out of nowhere."

Bud cut in, interrupting Baird. "They didn't come from nowhere. They came from the same place I did."

Baird nodded and reached over to pat Bud on the shoulder. "No offense, son. Fine hardworking neighborhood. Though it has produced some of the worst criminals in town. Who can say why."

"If you lived there you'd know why," Bud shot back. His pale face reddened. "I grew up watching the Klan torch the merchants' shops while the Detroit cops did nothing about it. Somebody had to step up and say, 'No more.' That's how the gangs got started."

Riley had just been sitting there looking bored, but when he heard this he shook his head and gave Bud a look.

"They didn't protect and defend," Riley said. "They took. And they killed."

"I know that better than you," Bud said. The redness spread down to his neck now. "All I'm saying is they didn't come out of nowhere, for no reason."

"Our Bud tends to take a *socio-logical* view of things," Baird said with a phony smile. "You and I see apples that went bad. He blames the tree."

Baird reached again to pat Bud's shoulder but this time Bud looked at the hand like he might bite it, so Baird pulled it back.

Nan then raised her hand like a student. "A question," she said. "Why are they called the Purple Gang? No, let me guess: They pelt their enemies with grapes."

Bud explained about the merchants declaring the boys tainted, "like meat gone bad." Hearing this, Baird pulled his head back, surprised. "Really?" he said. "I thought it was because they dropped their guns in purple paint once, after a shooting." Then, for Nan's benefit, he added: "To cover up their prints."

Bud shook his head. "But why would anybody choose purple paint unless they had a reason already?"

Whilst the two argued, Riley lifted himself out of his chair. "All very interesting, I'm sure," he said. "But it has nothing to do with me."

He limped away from the table and Baird spoke to his back.

"We were hoping you'd help us take on the Purps, Harry."

Still hobbling away, without looking back, Riley said: "And why on earth would I want to do that?"

"Because you have a sense of duty, and civic responsibility," Baird said. Then after a beat, he added: "And because we could've put Joe Bernstein away a long time ago, and you stopped us."

Riley didn't respond, just kept walking over to the horseshoe pit. He reached down, picked up one of the iron shoes, and set his feet in place. Then he let fly, his legs remaining planted. The shoe sailed high and then clanked on the stake, a ringer.

Riley glanced back at the table. "Any challengers?"

Baird just chuckled and shook his head. But Bud got up from his seat and started walking over to Riley. As Bud moved away, the smiling Baird turned to Nan and said quietly, "I don't mean to lay the world's burdens on your husband."

"The hell you don't," she replied, keeping her eyes on her knitting needles.

When Bud came up beside him, Riley handed him a horseshoe. As he got set to pitch, Bud held the shoe up in front of his face with his right hand—Riley noticed it was missing the ring finger. Bud then stepped and threw, and the shoe ringed the stake, landing right on top of Riley's.

An hour later, the two visitors were gone. Solly was still in the woods, watching. And Nan was underwater, pinching her nose shut. She crouched on the lake floor, peering through the clear water, past the minnows, up at Riley who swam above her. His movement was smooth as the two arms cut the water in rhythm; the single leg didn't kick so much as bob, like the tail of a dolphin. Whilst he swam, she crept along the lake-floor underneath, tracking him.

Then he came diving down, right at her, his smile shooting out bubbles on each side. He grabbed her in the water and kissed her. She pointed up with her hand, signaling that she needed to go up for air but he wouldn't let her go right away—just kept kissing her. Then she relaxed and inhaled, drawing air from him.

After they resurfaced, they perched on the edge of the dock, their three feet dangling in the water. Riley's peg lay beside him on the dock. He had his arm around her waist and his hand on the side of her belly. They looked out across the surface of the lake and watched a red sunset coming through the trees. Then Riley let go of her and started to lower himself back into the water.

"An Indian summer day is a gift," he said. "Gotta make the most of it."

Nan didn't answer. She was thinking as her feet swam.

"Join me?" he asked, splashing down into the shallow water.

"I'm comfy. You go in without me."

Still turned to face her, he moved out a little deeper, until the water was covering his shoulders. He noticed a minnow swimming just below the surface, cupped his hands round it and held it in a small pool. He had a talent for trapping.

"Harry," she said from the dock, "when you let that fellow off the hook—Bernstein, I mean—you didn't do anything wrong. Teddy Baird has no right to suggest otherwise."

Riley separated his hands releasing the minnow. He looked up at her as he fanned his arms out to the sides and churned the water with each hand.

"All you did was help an innocent man," Nan said.

"He's not so innocent anymore," Riley answered.

"You think he went after DA Thompson?"

"Could be," Riley said. "He blamed Thompson for what happened."

"With good reason?" she asked.

Riley shrugged his shoulders and the tops of them broke the water. "Lots of people to blame for what happened in 1920," he said. "Thompson was just one of many."

Riley pushed off with his foot and began to float away.

"I have more questions," she called out to him.

"I'm sure you do," he said, still on his back and fluttering his arms like wings in the water, his eyes closed.

"I have an observation, too," she said. "I noticed you never said no to Mr. Baird's request."

He stopped the arms and just floated now. "Didn't say yes either," he said. "Think I'd leave this paradise? We're not going anywhere."

Then he turned his body and dove down, disappearing.

"Liar," she said to the bubbles he left behind.

She looked down and patted her stomach. "Oh, you be still now," she whispered. "Detroit isn't such a bad place to be born."

When Riley finished his swim they came in from the dock together, their arms wrapped around each other. They went into the little cabin and he lit a fire whilst she cooked fish in a pan on the stove. They ate side by side in front of the fire, with their feet out and their toes curled to the heat. After that, they sat at the table to play cards, never once talking about Baird's visit. Then they got into their pajamas and snuggled up together in their little bed, and after a while she sat on top of him, with the blanket pulled up over her shoulders, covering them like a tent. Her body moved up and down, just a little and very quietly, whilst they looked each other in the eyes.

And the whole time, Solly Levine was watching through the cabin window.

After they went to sleep, Solly decided he didn't want to stumble through the woods in the dark and then drive all night. So he snuck into the cabin—they'd left the back door unlocked, never suspecting a bug-eyed degenerate from Hastings Street would be in the vicinity. He crept into the kitchen and ate some pie. Then he took a cushion off the sofa and brought it with him into the coat closet, where he curled up with the door closed. He dozed off. But later on, he woke with a start when he heard Riley's voice, screaming.

"*Get it off me!*" Riley yelled. "*Don't you dare cover me up!*"

Solly sat there in the closet wondering what the hell was going on with this wholesome couple—was she trying to smother him? Or were they at it again, and doing it rough? (This is how Solly's mind worked).

What Solly did not know—nor did I, until Nan explained it in her letters years later—was that Riley faced his own death on an almost nightly basis. And it wasn't his sweet wife or some gangster trying to kill him, it was a doctor. Riley did not even know the doctor's name. He recognized him, always, by the footsteps. Night after night, Riley heard those steps approaching whilst he lay there on a gurney, his eyes shut tight, his hands folded on his stomach, his silver-cross medal on a chain wrapped around his hand.

All around him, wounded men moaned but Riley wouldn't open his eyes, even when he heard the doctor coming. He didn't want to see any of it—not the blood, not the other men, and definitely not what was under his own sheet. Then he'd hear the doctor speak to a nurse, saying just what Riley expected, because he'd said it before: *"Nothing more we can do for this one."*

Hearing that, Riley's eyes would pop open as he looked straight at the doctor. "If I'm dying, get me a priest," he'd say. "If not, get to work on me."

The doctor should have been startled by this but wouldn't react at all, ignoring Riley. He'd reach down and start untangling that silver medal-and-chain wrapped around Riley's hand. He'd pull it free and hold the medal in front of his face, admiring it. Then he'd slip it into the pocket of his own white jacket. Finally, the doctor would take hold of the sheet and begin pulling it up, over Riley's chest but not stopping there—he'd keep on pulling that sheet up until it began to cover Riley's face.

And right at this point Riley would bolt up in the bed screaming, as he did on this particular night.

"Don't you dare cover me up," Riley yelled at the doctor.

He kicked the blanket off his leg, stepped out of bed and began to rise—then lost his balance on the one leg and fell to the floor. Nan woke when she heard the thump of him landing, and looked around for him. She got up and rushed over to the other side of the bed, where he sat on the floor.

"Harry? Are you okay?"

"You heard what he said, didn't you?" Riley said to her.

"Harry wake up, it's all right," she said, rubbing his shoulder. "You just took a little spill."

Riley blinked and looked around, and the dark room started to take shape. He touched Nan's cheek, to make sure she was really there. Then he turned and reached for the bedside table, pulling open a drawer. His hand rummaged inside, and came out holding the silver medal on the chain. He looked at it, then put it back and closed the drawer. He leaned back against the bed again, and exhaled.

"Oh, boy," he said. "Sorry."

Nan used the sleeve of her nightgown to pat dry his forehead.

"Don't be sorry. Just a dream. Were you back in the trench?"

"No, the hospital tent in Chateau-Thierry. And that doctor."

"The one who operated?"

"Yeah. But it was before the operation. It was that moment when I first woke up in the tent. I kept my eyes closed because I didn't want to see. I guess he thought I couldn't hear him. He was writing me off."

"Big mistake," she said. "And what did you do then?"

"When I heard myself pronounced dead," Riley said to her, "I figured it was time to open my eyes."

Solly heard them talking for a while, but couldn't make out much from inside the closet. All he'd heard clearly was the screaming.

"Guy's a little wacky, if you ask me," Solly said to me, whilst we were at the Crime having coffee the next day. "But the woman—she's a cute one." He pulled his face a little closer to me and winked one of his googly eyes. "I got a pretty good look," he said.

I told him two things: That when I send him to get information on people, he should respect their privacy whilst spying on them. And that if he ever again winked an eye at me, he would re-open it to find just an empty socket.

FIFTEEN

Riley and Nan were back in the city three months later, the winter of early '27. They took a room in a hotel that looked out on the river. That first night, they sat on the hotel room bed wondering what the hell they were doing in Detroit. It was dark out but a light was flashing somewhere outside the window, and it lit their faces red each time it blinked.

"Doesn't this city ever go dark?" Riley said.

"I miss the loons already," she said, laying her head on his shoulder.

He tried to catch her eye. "You sure you want to be here? You didn't have to come. I'm not sure you should have."

"And let you have all the fun? I want to go to the speakeasies. And dance on the tables."

Riley smiled. "I'll dance with you," he said. "The one-legged man and the big-bellied lady—we can sell tickets."

"Hey, watch it, you," she said, then patted her stomach. "Hardly even noticeable."

"I just don't know if it's safe for you and the baby," he said.

"I'm not afraid of a bunch of rotten fruit."

"You mean tainted meat."

"Not scared of that either."

Riley placed his hand over hers, still resting on her stomach. He was holding back a surprise and let it go now. "Well, I guess there's no way around it," he said. "I'll have to take you to a speakeasy or I'll never hear the end of it. How 'bout tomorrow night?"

She sat forward, clasping her hands. "Really? Truly?"

He nodded.

"Yowza!" she said, and clapped once. "But how will we know where to go? Will we need a password to get in? I'm good with passwords."

"Don't worry, we've got someone to take us around," Riley said. "Fella named Barkley."

Nan covered her mouth and her eyes got wide. Then she punched Riley in the arm. "That's for withholding information," she said. "When did you become pals with Jerry Barkley? I recall a time when you thought he was a 'gas bag.' Change your mind?"

"Oh, he's still a gas bag, all right," Riley said, clutching his arm as if wounded by the blow. "And he's found the perfect job for a gas bag—he talks on the radio."

"He's a radio star?" she said. She punched him again. "Oh, you see what you've made me miss, up there in the boondocks?"

"It was Teddy Baird's idea to put us together," Riley said. "Barkley's quite a man about town, apparently. Knows all the juice joints—intimately. Including one with a very colorful clientele."

"Really?"

"And when I say colorful, I mean purple."

"Oh, my," she said, gasping a bit. "Oh, this is going to be *fun*."

Watching her get worked up, Riley couldn't help smiling. Then he found himself getting annoyed by that flashing red light outside. "What *is* that, anyway?" he said.

Riley took his hand off hers and reached for the crutches against the wall by the bed. He went to the window and saw a huge electric CANADIAN WHISKEY sign displayed above a building on the other side of the river. The blinking red sign shone across the frozen water, beckoning to downtown Detroit.

Riley laughed to himself and shook his head. "Jesus," he muttered. "How's that for temptation."

*

As it happened, that night Riley wasn't the only one staring out at that cold hard water. On the riverbank, Grabowski sat in a Ford, alongside the Original Solly Levine. They were on night patrol (Grabowski didn't mind, being a nocturnal creature anyway), keeping an eye out for bootleggers bringing whiskey across. Hijacking was more profitable than buying it in Canada and bringing it over ourselves. Of course it was more dangerous too, because the bootleggers—the ones worth robbing, anyway—were usually armed. So you had to find clever ways to ambush them in their boats. At this, Grabowski was adroit.

On the night in question, there were no boats because the river was frozen—had been for weeks. But this didn't mean smuggling stopped. It just meant people had to drive across the ice in cars and trucks, listening for crackling under the wheels as they went.

Just before dawn, Grabowski and Solly spotted a truck leaving from the Detroit side and driving slowly across the ice, headed for Windsor. They watched the truck roll all the way across, getting smaller as it went. When it got to other side and was out of sight, that's when Solly started to drive onto the river, heading for an area the truck had just passed through. He stopped the car right there on the ice, about a quarter mile out.

"Need my help?" Solly asked Grabowski, who was opening the passenger door to get out.

"Nah, yer useless anyway," Grabowski said.

Grabowski went around to the back of the car, walking on tiptoes so he wouldn't slip on the ice; he looked almost like a ballet dancer, Solly told me later. Grabowski took an ice pick from the trunk and tiptoed away from the car, out into the middle of the ice. He stopped and looked down at the tire marks left by the truck. Then he raised the pick over his head and struck, making a little hole in the ice.

By the time he was done, there were dozens of tiny holes, perforating an area about ten feet wide. After he finished making the holes, he used his shoe to carefully sweep the surface smooth and clean of chips, so that the work he'd done would be invisible. Then he got back in the car with Solly, who put it in reverse and slowly backed to the shoreline, where they sat and waited.

An hour later the truck reappeared on the horizon, coming slowly back across the ice in its old tracks. The doors on both sides were open—the front of the truck looked like a face with big floppy ears. People often drove with doors open on the ice, so they could make a quick exit if they heard that cracking sound.

Solly and Grabowski waited for the truck to reach the area where the holes had been made. When it did, you could hear the first crack all the way at the shoreline. The second crack was even louder, and then the front of the truck sunk until the bumper caught on the ice and rested there. With the front wheels in the water, the headlights down near the surface, the doors still open, and the rear of the vehicle sticking up above the rest, that big-eared truck face now looked like it was stooping down to lap a cold drink from the water below.

Two men jumped out of the truck, one on each side, and they both immediately slipped and fell on their asses. One got up waving his arms at the other, blaming him no doubt. They walked carefully on the ice to the front of the truck and stared down at those sunken wheels. Meanwhile Solly began to move his car out onto the ice, slowly rolling towards them.

When they heard the car coming, both men reached in their coat pockets. One pulled out a pistol and quickly moved it behind his ass, so all you saw was a brief flash of steel. The other kept his hand inside the coat. They were both peering hard at the car, trying to see the man inside. And yes, it was only one man or so they thought, because Grabowski was squeezed down under the dashboard, out of sight.

Solly waved a hand out the window, and stopped the car a good twenty feet away from them. He came out with both hands waving in the air. The two men saw this small guy with funny glasses and fluttering hands, and must've felt relieved even if they didn't know what the hell he wanted.

He was yelling, "Hey fellas, need a hand?" but they could barely understand because they were oilers and therefore too dumb to know English.

So a lot of pointing and gesturing ensued. Solly pointed down at the wheels in the water and shook his head. They nodded and shrugged. Then Solly pointed one-two-three to each of them and himself, and did a lifting motion with his hands. They did not get it, so Solly tiptoed over to the bumper, grabbed it and then gestured for them to help. The man who had been hiding the gun behind his back kept it out of sight but managed to wedge it into the back of his pants, thereby freeing up both hands. Then both oilers joined Solly at the bumper and together they tried to lift the front of the truck—though Solly was only using one hand to lift, whilst the other was sneaking inside his coat to grasp his gun.

They were all three grunting and groaning with the effort, which may be why they did not hear the tippy toe footsteps of Grabowski coming fast from behind. Solly happened to have his face turned left and got a close-up view as the ice pick went through the back of the oiler's head, popping out one of his eyes. The body slumped face forward right there on the hood of the truck—the ice pick planted in the head, the eye bouncing like a yo-yo on a string.

Solly couldn't take his eye off the eye, so to speak, and just stood there. The other oiler realized what was going on and reached fast inside his coat. Before he could pull his gun out, Grabowski tackled him in the chest and they both fell to the ice and slid, with Grabowski on top. The oiler's gun, which fell when he was tackled, also slid and ended up out of their reach. When the two of them stopped sliding, Grabowski raised a forearm and brought it down hard on the oiler's face, then pounded him a second time, causing a little splash of red on the white ice. The oiler covered his face and curled up his body whilst Grabowski got up and tiptoed over to the dropped gun, then picked it up. He was breathing heavy and he looked at Solly.

"Yer a useless piece 'a shit, ya know that?"

Solly, who had never gotten around to taking out his own gun, tried to make an excuse but Grabowski waved him off, saying, "Shut up and get the ropes, will ya?"

They used a shorter rope to tie the hands of the living oiler, and a longer one to tow the sunken truck, pulling with their car. (And here is where they were lucky that Max is so brilliant: He had fitted their car with "ice tires" he developed himself, with double-edged studs that really took hold in the ice). Once the truck was pulled out, it left behind a big hole in the ice—which had broken off neatly, in one piece. Grabowski hauled that big icecap out of the water and set it down, a couple of feet away from the hole. Then he extracted his pick from the head of the dead oiler, whose eye still dangled. He dragged the body over to the open hole and pushed it into the water.

The whole time, the second oiler was standing with hands tied and head down, mumbling in Italian, saying the word *Dio* a lot. Grabowski grabbed him by the arm and brought him to the hole, saying along the way, "You people betta stick ta the olive oil and leave us the booze."

When they were standing before the hole Grabowski said, "Jump in." But the oiler just looked at him.

"He doesn't understand you," Solly said.

"Okay, lemme put it anotha way," he said and pushed the oiler, who staggered over the lip of the hole and then dropped straight down out of sight. Grabowski grabbed hold of the big icecap, yelling for Solly's help, and together they dragged and pushed the cap into place, neatly covering the hole.

Whilst they looked down at the cap, the face of the oiler who'd jumped suddenly rushed into view under the ice, his eyes open wide, looking up at them. The palms of his hands were flat against the ice trying to push up. It must be hard to push up a heavy object when your feet are not on the ground, but he made the cap jump a little once, then again, and even a third time. Then something changed in his eyes and he stopped pushing after that.

They split up on the ice—Solly took his car home and Grabowski drove the hijacked truck to the cutting house. The ride in the truck was filled with the sound of bottles clinking together in the back, like a thousand toasts being made to the great Grabowski.

He got to the warehouse, turned and drove through the alley and around to the big garage-style door in the back. He knocked twice and twice again. The big door raised slowly, lifted by two men inside. Other than them and another two who sat on folding chairs and threw dice, the place was empty—nobody at the big mixing vats. The men at the door nodded at Grabowski and looked a little wary; everybody was scared of him and why not.

"Get busy unloadin' this shit," he said to them. Then he left behind the truck to get his own car, parked out front, and headed for the Crime—the best place to go after a long, cold night.

We were already there for breakfast and I was happy when Grabowski arrived because I needed a distraction. Abie, sitting opposite Max and me in the corner booth, had just shoved across the table at me a piece of paper with one of those Rorschach ink blobs. He wanted my opinion. He had done this to me once before and I believe I tore the paper in half, yet he was doing it again.

"What does it mean to you?" he said.

"I told you, I don't care about these blobs," I said to him. "They mean nothing."

He shook his head and said, "You don't understand, Joe. You have to put your own meaning into them. It's not there by itself."

That baffled me even more. Just to shut him up, I told him the blob looked like my old dead Aunt Mabel.

He was disbelieving at first. "*That's* what she looked like?"

And I said no but it's probably what she looks like now, having been dead a while.

Right about then Grabowski came barreling in, swinging his arms wide whilst he walked, as was his custom. When he passed behind the guys sitting at the coffee counter, they all knew to arch in their backs so they wouldn't get clipped.

I called out, "Speaking of blobs, look who's here."

Grabowski plopped down on the bench, right next to Abie. "Got a full truck," he said. "Twenty cases at least."

"Oilers?" I said and he nodded.

"Livoli's guys?"

He shrugged. "Who knows. A wop is a wop is a wop."

"What'd you do with them?"

"Nothin.' They done it ta themselves."

"Suicide?" Abie said (he'd been reading about that).

Grabowski nodded. "They jumped in tha water an' froze. What can ya do."

We knew Grabowski was lying. He was supposed to kill oilers as a last resort—it caused bad blood. But with him, last resorts always came first somehow. Max was troubled by his behavior and would make little comments, as he did on this morning. *"Suicide,"* he said under his breath, shaking his head whilst looking away. "That's what you're doing to *us*."

To which Abie said, "You know Max, you have a very negative outlook. You are full of negativity."

"Fulla shit's more like it," Grabowski said.

"Okay," I said, "everyone shut up and let's enjoy our eggs."

Over breakfast, we talked business. I told everyone I wanted them to be at the speakeasy tonight. I'd heard from Tennessee that Riley was coming. I wanted him to get an eyeful of us.

There was another bit of news, announced by Max. "The movie camera arrived yesterday," he said. "So we can start making movies anytime we want."

This was from that Hollywood guy who, as previously noted, came calling on us. Turned out he wanted us to make little moving pictures of Fords crashing, to show how dangerous they were. He was doing this on behalf of his boss, Walter Foxman of Foxman Studios (though I doubt Foxman was aware the guy was coming to the likes of us). Foxman had instructed the guy that his job was to go out and somehow get footage proving Ford cars were a hazard.

Why? Because Foxman, like the rest of us, was sick of Heinrich Ford's tactics. You see, Ford's spies were not just in Detroit—that prick Liebold was even sending moles out to Hollywood, to dig up dirt on Jews at the big studios. So this film footage was to be Foxman's way of saying, "Fuck you, two can play this game." I approved wholeheartedly and wanted to help out, plus we were going to get paid for the films we made. And on top of all that, it gave us another excuse to smash Fords.

Everyone at the breakfast table agreed that it was good to be getting into the movie business, because movies, along with cars and booze, were the future. We decided that if the sun stayed out we should get started that afternoon. And at that point Max was so excited he stood up right there in the diner and announced, "Okay everybody, we're gonna start shooting today," and of course they all wondered who was going to get shot.

A couple of hours later, we were making movies and I must admit I have never had so much fun. We all drove down to the lot of an abandoned warehouse near the river—it was perfect because it was big, empty, and covered in ice.

We arrived in a caravan of five cars, four of them brand new black Fords. We parked and got out and met each other in a circle of five regular-sized men as well as two giants, Abie and Gorilla Kowalski. Everyone stepped delicately on the ice except the Gorilla, whose feet had very good traction even with shoes on. All eyes turned to Max, who had a big black movie camera cradled in his arms like a baby.

"Alright let's get going," I said. "Who's gonna use the camera?"

"Solly will operate the camera," Max said.

Solly nodded behind eyeglasses that were frosted.

Abie shot Max a look. "Why does Solly get to do it?"

"Because I already taught Solly how to operate it," Max said.

"But he can't see."

"There is nothing wrong with my eyes," Solly said.

"If you're such an expert," Abie said to Max, "why don't you do it yourself?"

"Because I am the director," Max said.

Grabowski meanwhile opened the trunk of one of the Fords. He pulled out a football helmet and two big fluffy pillows. Patting his wild hair flat against his head, he squeezed the helmet on.

"You can't wear that," Max snapped at him.

"The fuck I can't. I gotta protect my brains."

"You're going to be on film this time, you have to look normal," Max said, then muttered, "if that's possible."

Max looked over at the seventh member of our group. "Ziggy," he said to Ziggy Selbin. "You will be the star."

"Whataya nuts?" said Grabowski. "*I'm* the driver!"

"That's right, but we need a star to do the set-up. It has to be someone good looking and there's only two like that in this group. And Joe must remain anonymous, so that leaves Ziggy."

I made sure they saw me snicker at that 'good looking' remark.

They stationed the camera on a tripod in front of one of the Fords. Max neatened Ziggy's hair and also straightened the carnation in his lapel (Ziggy always wore a white carnation). The so-called set-up of the film required that Ziggy stand and point a lot, and sometimes shake his head like a very disappointed man. He pointed at the front wheels of one of the Fords. He opened the hood and pointed at the fan belt, and shook his head. He held out his hand with a couple of worn brake pads in it, and pointed at those, and shook his head. Amidst all the pointing and head-shaking Ziggy suddenly burst out laughing and this made "the director" so upset he started waving and flapping his arms, which made everyone else laugh. I even laughed a little, before yelling at everyone to stop laughing.

When they were finished with the set-up, it was time for the action scenes. Grabowski got in one car and the Gorilla in the other; they each wedged pillows between their chests and the steering wheel. They drove to opposite ends of the lot. Then, with Solly rolling the film, they drove straight at each other and crashed. Fenders crumpled and everyone cheered.

Next, the Gorilla turned his car around and drove to a spot where he parked and pretended to innocently read the newspaper. Grabowski drove up from behind acting like a man who couldn't control his car. He rammed the Gorilla's car; the newspaper went flying. There were a couple more scenes involving collisions between those two cars, until the vehicles were unusable.

After the last crash the Gorilla needed help pulling his bent door open. When he got his big body out, there was blood streaming from a cut on his forehead and Max yelled: "Solly, get a shot of that blood!"

After that it was time for Grabowski to do his solo scenes using the other two Fords—a series of spins and skids on the ice. After one sharp turn the car flipped over on its side and then tumbled so it was upside down; Max liked that scene very much.

With three of the cars destroyed, Grabowski walked up to the last one, his pudgy feet stepping on tiptoes. Before he got in the car he turned to me.

"Joe! C'mon an' take a spin."

I looked at him like he was crazy and of course he was.

"Come on—fer old time sake!" Grabowski yelled.

I thought what-the-hell and walked to the car and got in the passenger side. Grabowski drove slowly at first, circling around the lot, glancing over at me.

I said, "Don't go slow on my account."

"Yer right," he said. "It's the movies. They gotta have action."

He pressed the gas pedal and yanked the gearshift, and the car lurched forward. We sped to the middle of the lot over a big patch of ice, and Grabowski reached across the wheel with his left hand, grabbing hold at five o'clock.

He said, "Here we go, brot."

Then he yanked the wheel to the left and the whole car jerked and went into a circle-spin—round and round on the ice, twirling like a top. Grabowski threw his head back and hooted whilst I held the dashboard, shut my eyes and imagined I might shoot straight up through the roof and into the sky.

SIXTEEN

That night, Riley and Nan sat side-by-side in the back of a roomy white Packard. Seated across from them on a pull-down bench was Barkley in a trim pinstripe suit (which only made his big baby head seem even bigger). Two cigarettes dangled from his lips; a match in his hand flared and lit up his moon face. After lighting the two smokes he took one in each hand and offered them to Riley and Nan. Riley accepted, Nan declined, and Barkley took the leftover cigarette for himself. Then he drew back his overcoat to reveal a sterling silver hip flask with his initials engraved.

"You won't arrest me for this, will you Mister Prosecutor?"

Riley shook his head. "Deal's a deal. You show me around, and I'll pretend everyone's drinking Vernors."

Barkley offered the flask but got no takers, so he took a good long swig himself. He twisted the cap back on and tucked the flask away, took a deep drag on his smoke, and then leaned toward them with elbows on his knees. He tried to look earnest.

"Harry and Nan, you are my inspiration," he said, blowing smoke from both nostrils.

Riley shot Nan a glance. She was tickled; he was not.

"Now that may sound like so much banana oil," Barkley continued, "yet I say it from the heart: You're my inspiration, the both of you."

"Mr. Barkley, you are easily inspired," Nan said.

"Oh, not at all, Madam. I've rubbed elbows with the Dodge boys, the Chevrolet brothers, and as you know, with the Man Himself."

Whilst he spoke, Barkley didn't look either of them in the eye— he was staring right between them, at a reflection of himself in the rear windshield.

"…And yet these reputed giants do not impress me," he continued. "Oh, sure, they have power and wealth. They are the arisTOCracy of Detroit. But you two have something they don't."

"Bills?" said Nan.

"I'm talking about integrity, Nan. Dare I say, nobility. Why, just the thought of you two, venturing forth from humble Lake Horamonga…"

"Horicon," Riley cut in, but Barkley paid him no mind.

"…and plunging yourselves into the muck and mire of a Motor City fueled by booze, and lubricated by graft…"

Nan, eyebrows raised, looked at Riley and even he couldn't help cracking a little smile.

"…And why do you do it? Have you come to siphon your own little fortunes from a Detroit River spiked with hooch? No sir! You come to save us all from the purple plague. Well—I say that's damn inspiring."

Riley, cigarette dangling in mouth, began to applaud slowly.

"Actually, I just came for the speakeasies," Nan said.

Barkley stopped staring at himself to give her a wink. "Well, in that case," he said, "you've come to the right man."

"Tell me, Barkley," Riley said, "do your listeners know about your illicit interests?"

"If I told them about all that," Barkley said, "there'd be no time left for jokes and songs."

As they rode along, Riley asked Barkley about his former boss. "Why'd you leave Ford, anyway?"

"Parting of the minds," Barkley said. "Mr. Ford as you know is a teetotaler. Whereas I on the other hand… am not. He heard a nasty rumor that I was funding a speakeasy. Can you imagine? Any-hoo, we agreed to go separate ways. While still having the utmost respect for one another."

"You miss spying for him?" Riley said. "And writing those enlightening articles in the *Dearborn Independent?*"

"Uh-oh," Barkley said to Nan. "Somebody's digging up my past."

"I have to say, those were some clever theories you dreamed up," Riley said.

Nan looked to her husband for a clue but he was too busy staring down Barkley, who in turn saw her puzzled look.

"I think your husband is talking about a few silly editorials I wrote. This was roughly a million years ago."

"Didn't surprise me when the paper brought up the old *Protocols* junk about conspiracies and ritual sacrifice," Riley said. "But when you blamed the Jews for ruining baseball—now that was creative. If memory serves, you even took a swipe at their prizefighters— something about *'the Jewish tendency to avoid pain and conflict.'*"

Barkley wagged a finger in the air. "Now you see Harry, this is what happens when lines are taken out of context. That was an editorial I wrote about the boxer Benny Leonard. I was simply floating a hypothesis as to why Leonard never seemed to get any cuts on that smooth mug of his. I proposed that he'd figured out how to win the fight and take the prize without taking the blows. Honestly, I thought I was complimenting the man and his people on being crafty—but oh, the trouble that came of it, Nan!"

Nan wasn't looking at him anymore; she'd turned her head to the window and the dark outside.

Barkley turned back to Riley. "I even started getting anonymous notes from a Jewish mobster who lived and died by Leonard's fights. He wrote to me: 'How's about you and me settle this man to man—or do you have *a tendency to avoid pain and conflict?*' Isn't that priceless?"

Barkley hooted. But Nan was still looking away, whilst Riley was giving him a cold eye. So Barkley threw up his hands.

"Fine, arrest me," he said. "Flog me in Cadillac Square. Sure I wrote things that were… questionable. I was Ford's mouthpiece, that's all. Nowadays I speak for myself, on my little radio show. And I have a kind word for everybody."

"Clarify this for me," Riley said. "You agreed with Ford's ideas? Or you didn't, and spouted them anyway? Because I'm trying to decide which would be worse."

Nan patted Riley's knee to stop him. "Can we leave off this dreary subject?" she said.

"By all means!" Barkley said. "So many other things we can discuss—I have wide-ranging interests. But first let's take a little stroll."

Barkley nodded out the car window in the direction of a plain brick building; the car was just pulling up in front of it. It looked empty, another downtown factory shut for the night.

Nan looked through the window at the building, then turned back to Barkley. "Place looks kind of dead," she said.

Barkley smiled and said, "Nan, you must keep this in mind about Detroit: Things are never as they appear."

Barkley hopped out and held the car door for Nan. Following behind her, Riley was slow in sliding across the seat and then getting himself up and Barkley, still waiting by the car door, began to whistle a tune (which Riley did not appreciate). They walked to the front of the building. As they arrived at a closed door Barkley stopped and turned back to Nan.

"Tell me—what are you gonna name the little one?"

"If it's a girl, Jean," Nan said.

"Okay, watch this."

Barkley pulled his hat down to cover his face, then knocked on the door. A door slot slid open and two small eyes peered out.

"*Jean* sent us," Barkley said to the slot. He disguised his voice, whilst hiding under the hat.

Just like that, the slot closed and the door opened. A big doorman stepped aside to let the group pass. As Barkley walked past him, he raised his hat to show his face, and winked.

"Oh, Mr. Barkley, I had no clue it was you," the doorman said in a throaty voice.

Barkley took another step and then stopped and turned back to the doorman: "Tell me, Froggy, what if someone said, 'Rin Tin

Tin sent me'—would you still let 'em in?"

"Sure, I love that dog!" Froggy said.

Barkley hooted and waved him off. He led Nan and Riley down a dark hallway that smelled of old beer and was sticky underfoot. The muffled sound of music and voices was getting louder as they approached a pair of oak double-doors. They could feel the vibration through that sticky floor.

"Does this establishment belong to you, Mr. Barkley?" Nan asked.

"Officially Nan, I own nothing more than a smooth voice. But you might say I'm on intimate terms with the proprietor."

Barkley turned both knobs and pushed open the heavy doors. The noise came at them in a blast and Riley's head reeled back as if from a slap. He stood stunned and might have stayed that way forever if not for Nan—who grabbed his sleeve and pulled him through that door into the depths of Detroit and the top of the world circa early '27.

The place took your breath away when you first walked in: A big room filled with Chinese lanterns glowing red and gold, hanging from a deep blue ceiling covered with tiny painted white stars. The lanterns swayed gently as if from a breeze, though there were no windows—the room generated its own swirling air, pumped by pure hubbub. The walls were illustrated with scenes of French girls kicking their legs to show knickers. Beneath those murals were long tables packed with people throwing back their heads to laugh or just swallow.

Out in the middle of the floor young dancing couples kicked their legs and swung each other like monkeys. In one corner of the room, three colored men puffed their cheeks whilst blowing into horns. In another corner, a group of men had arranged their seats to form a circle around a ping pong table, upon which a small white ball bounced back and forth between two women who had paddles in their hands and not a stitch of cloth on their bodies.

There was much for the eye to absorb in that room, but the main attraction on this night and every other was a woman who floated through it in a bright red dress with collar feathers surrounding her long throat. She had smooth skin the color of coffee with cream, and she wore her short black hair lacquered flat against her head, with little sideburns that curled on her cheeks like question marks. Her pencil thin brows arched over big brown eyes.

She didn't stop for more than ten seconds at any table but by the time she left, a round was ordered and everyone was laughing. She was just leaving a table when she saw Barkley stride into the room. She gave him a coy smile. Barkley, with Riley and Nan following close behind, stopped short and clutched his heart, then threw his arms wide. She ankled toward him, hips swaying, in no big rush.

Nan was enjoying the whole spectacle; Riley was still trying to get his bearings. She squeezed his arm. "Isn't it fabulous?"

He shrugged. He was scanning the room when he spied a table full of men in suits and white shirts with no neckties. He tried to focus but his view became blocked by the mocha-skinned woman, who crossed in front of him and threw her arms around Barkley's neck. Barkley clasped his own hands behind the small of her back and dipped her whilst giving her a kiss. This brought forth hollers and whistles around the room. When the lovebirds straightened up, Barkley saluted the crowd. Then he remembered his two guests and turned back to them.

"Harry and Nan, I'd like you to meet the inimitable Tennessee Jenkins. Belle of the ball, the queen of the blind pigs."

"Oh, he *does* know how to flatter a lady," she said, extending a hand with nails that matched her red dress. "I go by Ten. Welcome to my little palace—always good to see a couple of new suckers."

"She calls everyone that," Barkley said. "Term of endearment."

"No, it's the plain truth," Ten said. "When y'all see what I charge for a glass of giggle water, you'll understand. Now you kids get wet. I'll be back straightaway."

She slipped out of Barkley's grasp and he watched her go, then turned again to Riley and Nan.

"Amazing woman," he said. "Came up from the South with nothing, and built all this. She knows the secrets of everyone in Detroit who's worth knowing about. Starting with yours truly."

"The place is something," Nan said. "Where does a woman like that find the resources to do this?"

"A woman like that?" Barkley said with a sly grin. "What ever do you mean, 'a woman like that?' "

Nan flushed and Barkley laughed. "Just having fun with you, Nan. And speaking of which—will you join me on the dance floor? Harry, would you object forcefully?"

Riley looked at Nan, prepared to save her from a fool, but her raised eyebrows seemed to ask permission. He turned back to Barkley and then extended his arm toward his wife in a "she's-all-yours" gesture.

I was watching Riley from the moment he and the redhead wife came walking in with the Motormouth. I sat at a long table with Abie, Grabowski and a few other Purples (Max was home drawing up plans, no doubt).

"Izzat him?" Grabowski said. "Ya neva tol' me he's a gimp."

"Some kind of war hero," I said.

"Yer worried about a guy don' even stand on two legs?"

"Who says I'm worried?"

"Yer watchin' him, aintcha?"

I ignored Grabowski and kept watching. I was surprised Riley would let his wife dance with Barkley. He just stood there whilst Barkley took Nan's hand and pulled her into the midst of the swirl. She tried to take it slow, her hand on her big stomach. But you could see she knew her stuff—her feet moved easily. Barkley gave her a twirl at one point and as she spun, her smiling eyes met Riley's and he smiled back. He kept watching her dance, but his eye also wandered around the room. Eventually it found our table.

He looked at me between all the moving bodies on the dance floor. I gave him a little smile—the kind that says, *I know you're here, and you know I'm here. Now what?*

Riley's eye moved across our table, taking in the lot of us: He knew my face from the past, but it was his first look at Abie, who had his head down reading, and his first gander at the scaly-skinned Grabowski, who had a young girl about 16 beside him, his thick arm headlocking her. Grabowski had been waiting for Riley to look at him—soon as he did, Grabowski raised a hand with the middle finger up. Riley got a bored look on his face, shook his head, and then looked away.

"What's he shakin' his head at?" Grabowski said. "I'll shake that head right off 'im."

"No, you won't," I said. "You won't go near him."

Riley's attention went back to his wife, who returned to him winded and laughing, with Barkley trailing behind. The three of them moved to a table on the other side of the room from us.

"Old Log Cabin whiskey for my friends," I heard Barkley yell at the waiter as they all sat down. "And don't give us the cut stuff!"

I had a couple of "ears" sent over to sit by Riley's table and listen; I did this when someone important came in, but I didn't use Purples—you needed someone inconspicuous. A nice middle-aged couple did it for us in return for free drinks. You'd never suspect them, as they looked like Mr. and Mrs. John Q. Public.

Not that there was much for them to hear: Barkley bragged and made toasts, whilst they all clicked glasses (Riley was drinking ginger ale). Tennessee eventually came to the table and when Nan told her how great the place was, Ten reached out her hand and said, "C'mon with me, honey. I'll give you the nickel tour."

Nan took her hand and walked off, smiling back an apology to Riley who just shrugged and said, "I can't seem to hang onto you."

When Riley and Barkley were alone, the Motormouth started bragging that he knew all the important people in the room.

"Including Bernstein and his boys?" Riley said.

"Oh, I steer clear of those characters," Barkley said. "Ten's the one who deals with them. Pays 'em rent for the space. And buys the booze from them. Otherwise, the place is hers and they let her alone."

Riley leaned forward in his seat, and locked in on Barkley.

"I've got something to discuss with you, Jerry."

"Uh-oh," Barkley said. "You going to subpoena me?"

"You and I could possibly help each other," Riley said.

Barkley wouldn't look right at him. He tried to play it casual—chugging down his drink, signaling for another, glancing all around the room. "Whatever you say, Harry. I try to be helpful to everyone. My, my, take at a gander at that ping-pong gal—ever seen anything like that?"

Riley leaned a little closer. "Look at me when I'm talking to you," he said, in a low, deliberate voice.

Barkley wasn't sure he'd heard right. He smiled at Riley but it did no good. So he stopped smiling and paid attention.

"Here's the way I see you, Jerry. You're like a megaphone. People grab hold of you when they want to get attention. Mr. Ford used you to spread lies."

"Now Harry, I hope we're not going to keep talking about–"

"Let me finish," Riley cut in. "I would like to use you, too, but in a different way. To do something important."

Barkley sat back in his chair, arms folded—quiet for a change.

"There's a lot plaguing this city right now," Riley continued, "but the two worst things are fear and apathy. That's going to make my job very difficult. Nobody is going to testify. Nobody is going to do anything. Because no one gives a damn that this city is drowning in booze and blood."

"Drowning in booze and blood—not a bad line, Harry. Might want to borrow that sometime."

"Feel free. As you said, you have your own forum now. More powerful than the *Dearborn Independent* ever was. Suppose you used it for more than cute gags and songs? What if you were to tell folks what's really going on in this city—the killings, the corruption. Wake 'em up, get 'em mad."

Barkley was sipping his drink, and seemed to snort into it before he put it down and answered. "So. You're suggesting I talk about the gangs—about organized crime in Detroit?"

"I can feed you the inside dope," Riley said. "All kinds of stuff that the newspapers don't have."

Barkley nodded but he wasn't looking at Riley. He was looking down at his glass and turning it round and round with his hand.

"Tell me, Harry, do you happen to have my death certificate handy? Because I probably should sign it *before* I go on the air—in case I don't make it out of the goddamn booth alive."

Riley gently lifted the glass out of Barkley's hand and put it aside. He said, "If you won't do this for Detroit or for your eternal soul, fine. Then do it for fame. You're not gonna make a name crooning or telling jokes—you're not good enough. But if you make yourself the voice of the people—well, that could be your ticket, Jerry."

Barkley looked up at him with an uneasy smile. "Unless my ticket gets punched," he said.

SEVENTEEN

Whilst Riley and the Motormouth conspired, Nan followed Ten through the crowded speakeasy, holding her guide's hand. Revelers saluted and toasted them at every turn. Nan tapped Ten's shoulder and pointed to the dancing girls painted on the wall.

"The Moulin Rouge?" She had to ask loud, over the music.

Ten nodded and smiled. "Good to have somebody with culture in here. Most of these fools don't know France from Flint."

In a back corner of the big square room they reached a door with a small curtained window.

"Lemme show you my *bou-doir*," Ten said.

She turned a key in the lock and led Nan into a quiet little den with upholstered red satin walls, a couple of plush chairs, and a four-poster bed topped with tossed pillows. The room was lit by flickering gaslights. In one corner, a young colored boy was sitting cross-legged on the floor reading a book.

"Arthur, what're you doing in here?" Ten said. "Shoo now, go make yourself useful."

The boy got up, head-down and shy, and started to creep past them. When Nan touched his shoulder, he peeked up at her.

"Can I see what your book is?" she said.

He hesitated, then showed it to her.

"Robinson Crusoe! My favorite."

The boy was looking down again. Nan bent over to his level.

"You like the story?"

He nodded without raising his head. Then he stole a sideways glance at her and asked, "Is he gonna die on the island?"

"You have to find out for yourself, Arthur."

"Go on, boy, leave us be," Ten said.

Arthur broke into a trot and disappeared out the door. Ten pointed at a chair for Nan.

"I look after him," she said. "He's got no family."

"That's kind of you."

Ten shrugged. "I put him to work round here, so we both get somethin' out of it."

She pulled a champagne bottle from a silver bucket and popped the cork. "We call this liquid platinum," she said. "Thirty-five dollars a bottle. But I'm gonna treat you."

Nan held up a thumb and finger. "Just a smidge. Have to be careful in my condition."

"In your condition," Ten said, "it's too late for careful."

They talked for a while, and Nan got the distinct feeling an interrogation was underway. She didn't mind—being married to Riley, she was used to those. Ten wanted to know what Riley was up to, and if he planned to make things tough on the speakeasies.

"His concern is the killing, not the drinking," Nan said.

"Fair enough," Ten nodded. "Nobody wants killings—bad for business."

She wanted to know other things, too; how Nan met Riley, how they came to be together. Nan remembered what Barkley said about this woman—that she made it her business to find out about everyone—but it struck her that Ten was just curious, maybe even lonely for girl talk. So Nan told her about the party, and seeing Riley on that staircase. "When he looked up at me, I was a goner," she said. "Turned to the gal beside me and whispered, 'Now *there* is a man I could marry.' She thought I was crazy. 'But you're a *dancer*! And he's… ' She wouldn't say what he was. 'Well, you know what,' I told her, 'maybe it means my dancing days are done.'"

Ten smiled at that and laid her hand over her own heart. "Now that's romantic," she said. "I like that."

Nan tried to turn the tables on Ten, asking her about Barkley.

"I'm afraid it ain't a romantic story like yours"—that was all she'd say.

She didn't tell Nan about the night Barkley, still a hot shot at Ford, propositioned her at a speakeasy in the Black Bottom neighborhood. Ten managed the place and Barkley was one of a handful of whites who frequented. When he sidled up to her one night, she expected some kind of offer but not the one she got.

Barkley told her he'd been admiring her style and needed someone like her to run the swell joint he planned to open. Said he couldn't run it himself, as his boss would not approve—he'd have to remain a "silent partner." She suspected from the get-go this might eventually turn into more than a business partnership, even though Barkley was married. Her suspicions proved right. And that was the story that she did not wish to share with Nan (though it was shared it with me, years later, in the letters Ten wrote me).

Before they left the so-called boudoir to rejoin the others, Ten said, "Got somethin' for you." She opened a top drawer of a fancy dressing table. Nan could see small trinkets inside. Ten sorted through them and pulled something out, keeping it hidden in her fist. She reached for Nan's hand to put that little something in it.

Hoo boy, maybe it's a bribe, Nan thought. When she looked in her hand, she saw a rabbit's foot.

"I got lots of 'em," Ten said. "You keep it for luck. Maybe slip it into your man's jacket. If he's gonna fool around with those Purples, he might need it."

As Tennessee led Nan back to the table where Riley was still tightening the screws on Barkley, I was at my own table nursing a whiskey. Grabowski had left with his girl; Abie rested his head on his closed book, taking a nap right on the table. I watched the two women walking and saw Ten stop short, looking at the front entrance—she didn't seem happy. Then I saw why: Vivien Clarke was coming through the door.

Clarke was a big beefy cop, in full uniform. He ankled slowly, eyeing the patrons as if he might decide to arrest one at any moment. He stopped at a table along the way—a group of upper crusters in fine suits and dresses—and he snatched someone's whiskey glass off the table and held it up. He wagged his finger at the group as if they were naughty kids. And then he swigged down the whole glass, slammed it on the table, and laughed. The people at the table forced a laugh to appease him.

He kept coming, staggering a couple of times on the way. When he finally made it over to my table, he folded his big arms and stood looking down at me whist I sat.

"Well, well, well," he said. His face was beet red.

"Why don't you sit down, Clarke," I said. "You look like you might blow a gasket."

He didn't sit. He laid his palms down on the table and leaned forward, hovering over me. "If I blow a gasket," he said, "you'll know it."

Abie awoke and lifted his head, seeing Clarke in my face.

"What gives?" Abie said, looking first at me, then at Clarke.

"What gives," Clarke repeated. "That's what I'm wondering, what gives."

I could see in the corner of my eye that Abie straightened in his seat. I patted Abie's knee under the table, letting him know he should take it slow.

"Why don't you sit down, Clarke," I said.

"No, I wanna know *what gives*. Like the big dope here says, what gives? I thought you and me had an understanding, Bernstein."

"Clarke, you should either sit down or you should move away from my table," I said.

"I thought the understanding was ten bucks a week," he said, "not fucking five."

"It's always been five," I said. "And it always will be."

"Bullshit!" Clarke yelled and he pounded hard on the table. That brought Abie to his feet. Big as Clarke was, Abie was a good three inches taller, and a lot more solid. But Clarke was too drunk and stupid to feel vulnerable.

"You standing up to me?" he said to Abie. Clarke straightened up and walked around the table to where Abie was standing and the two of them were chest to chest. "You think I can't handle a big dope like you? You wanna go out the back door with me and we'll find out?"

Abie looked him in the eyes. Then he just said, "No."

"No?" Clarke said. He put a hand on Abie's chest, on his white shirt, and patted him. "Okay. S'okay to be scared, big boy."

"He's not scared," I said to Clarke. "You don't get it."

Clarke turned to me and said, "Oh, yeah? Explain it to me."

"It's simple," I said. "Abie does not wish to slaughter a pig on the Sabbath."

It was true: Abie wouldn't do grievous bodily harm on a Friday night; wouldn't even do it to a fly, in fact. None of us understood it. But he'd always observed the Sabbath with his father, and this was a rule he stuck by. People who were scared to go to the movies in Detroit at that time should have only known: If they went on a Friday night, they were safe in their seats.

"Are you sayin' I'm a pig?" Clarke said, turning toward me.

Abie put a hand on his shoulder to stop him. "If you just want to go out back and talk," Abie said to him, "that I can do."

Clarke pushed Abie's hand off his shoulder, though he had some trouble—the hand did not move easily. "Okay," he said to Abie, "let's go out there and *talk*, big boy."

Clarke started walking toward the back door, unbuttoning his cop jacket as he went. Abie, still standing at the table, took off his own jacket and hung it neatly on the back of his chair, whilst I stood up and peeled off my jacket—jackets were coming off everywhere, it seemed.

"I'll stand in for you on this one, Abie," I said.

But he wouldn't hear of it. "My job," he said, "is to protect you. Not the other way around."

Abie walked off toward the back door and when he did, the whole crowd seemed to jump up all at once. Then there was a rush to that back door as if a magnet was pulling everyone. Meanwhile I noticed Ten across the room, cupping her hands around her mouth and yelling to everyone: "That's right, suckers. We give you a fight a night or your money back!"

I saw Riley and Barkley getting up to join the action. Nan stayed put at the table, and Ten sat with her to keep her company.

I let the crowd squeeze their way through that door in back. When it was clear, I finished the last bit in my whiskey glass and headed out back myself.

The back-door lantern threw enough light on the alley to put a sparkle in the little eyes of rats waddling between garbage cans. The cold air tingled the nose. When I got out there the crowd had formed a circle and in the midst, Clarke and Abie stood facing each other with eyes locked—always the first step in this dance.

Clarke spoke first and revealed much about himself with his words: "Put up your fists, Jew."

But Abie was not one to heed a pig and kept his hands down, clasping them together in front of him.

"You deaf as well as dumb?" Clarke said

"I was just wondering about something," Abie said.

"What are you *wondering?*" Clarke sneered.

"What kind of a man is named Vivien?"

Clarke didn't answer, but his face got even redder than before. Then he shrugged and started to turn away from Abie, but even the rats watching from behind the cans must've known he was setting up a sucker punch. I knew of this punch whilst it was still a thought slowly forming in Clarke's head. When the blow arrived, Abie did not duck or even flinch. He absorbed the meaty fist on his clenched jaw, right on the muscle. The force must have been considerable, as it moved Abie a step sideways—and moving Abie even a little took a lot.

The gawkers heard the splat of fist against skin; some grimaced. I could see Riley and Barkley, other side of the circle— Barkley flinched, Riley didn't. There were several Purples in the crowd, including Solly, who watched with big eyes behind thick glasses, and also Ziggy Selbin (whom we'd taken to calling Handsome Ziggy ever since Max declared him so). Ziggy looked sharp with his white carnation in his lapel, but he also looked agitated: He wanted to intervene, but I caught his eye and shook my head.

The expression on Abie's face—those calm hangdog eyes—did not change at all when he was hit. I think this alarmed Clarke. He realized he would have to hit much harder, and probably wondered if he had it in him. Clarke tried to smile through all of this but his eyes gave him away. He turned his body sideways and then launched himself back at Abie, putting all of his weight behind a punch that sailed a little and landed on Abie's forehead. That was the wrong place to hit Abie—he was very hard headed. The blow moved him back just half a step, and it made Abie smile. As for Clarke, he pulled back the fist and started shaking the hand to get the sting out.

"You okay?" Abie said to him.

That got to Clarke. He put both hands flat on Abie's shoulders and pushed his knee hard into the groin—a place where even Abie was vulnerable. Abie doubled over and soon as he did, Clarke clasped his hands together and brought them down hard on the back of the neck. Abie fell, but not all the way down; his hand stopped the fall and he took a knee, and continued to kneel like that with one hand on the ground steadying him, his head down. He did not make a sound, except for trying to catch his breath.

Clarke looked down at him, unsure what to do next. He did what people do when they've gotten themselves into a fight harder than they expected: He tried to declare victory and get the hell out.

"I'm done with ya now, Jew," he said, and turned and started to walk away. Soon as he did that, Abie managed to get to his feet again, a little unsteady at first, though he found his footing.

He had to breathe deep before he could talk, but he got the words out fine: "You didn't answer my question. What kind of a man is named Vivien?"

Clarke stopped and looked back at him, then around at every-body, still trying to sell that smile of his. Then he looked down at the ground and nodded his head whilst sneaking his hand in his pocket. The bulge in the pocket started moving.

"You must think you're a real hard case," he said. "It's okay, I know how to handle a hard case."

His hand came out of the pocket with a set of brass knucks on it. He turned and started to walk back at Abie, very slowly, dangling the armored hand. As he did, I began reaching into my own jacket whilst shouldering my way through the people in front of me. I was almost through the crowd at the moment Clarke reared back his arm, ready to strike. I fingered the gun handle. Clarke was about three seconds from extinction—then Riley stepped forward.

"Enough!" he yelled.

He hobbled up and planted himself right between Clarke and Abie. He glanced at me—saw my hand in my jacket, I'm sure— and then looked Clarke in the eye. "This fight is over."

Clarke took a step back, slipping the brass-knuckled hand into his pocket. "This is not your business," he snarled at Riley.

"It is now," Riley said. "I'll bring charges against the next man who raises a fist or anything else."

Some in the crowd grumbled. Abie just stood there as if he did not care what happened next. But Clarke was furious. "You gonna stick your nose in every fistfight in this town?" he said to Riley. "Cause if you do, it'll get broke."

Riley stared at him for a long second and did not blink. Then he said, "You're a disgrace to that uniform."

Clarke had nothing more to say. He spit on the ground in front of Riley, then turned and stalked away.

Riley never looked at me, or Abie; he just went back inside with the rest of the crowd.

I walked over to Abie and patted his shoulder. "You okay?"

"I'm fine, why do you ask?"

I said, "Let's go inside," but he wanted to stay in the alley a little longer. I knew why: He was feeling the effects of that knee and didn't want anyone to see him moving funny.

"Tell you what," I said. "We'll stay out here and chat for a few minutes. Just you, me, and the rats."

*

Back inside, Riley said to Barkley, "I guess I spoiled the show," as the two of them got to the table. Nan and Ten were sitting there and laughing together like old pals.

"Nice to see someone's enjoying themselves," Riley said.

Nan grabbed his arm and said, "Harry, Ten was just saying…"

"Oh, this girl's a blabbermouth!" Ten cut in.

"…that it's too bad you don't drink. Because your leg would be the perfect place to stash hooch."

Riley smiled. "That's almost a reason to start."

"No, no," said Barkley, "we don't want to corrupt you. Stick with the Vernors, we need at least one sober man in Detroit. As for the rest of us…" He stood up, held his glass high and looked around the room, and roared, "…Let's get ossified!"

A cheer went up all around, and the sound of it made its way out back to the alley, where Abie was trying to explain something to me, probably about psychology or some such. He saw me turn my head toward the door when I heard the cheer.

"It's okay, we can go back in now, Joe," he said.

EIGHTEEN

Riley being in town didn't worry me. What could he do? There was no evidence we'd done anything to Thompson. There were theories; there was hearsay. But the proof was where—in the bottom of the river? In the belly of a beast (or two)? In the trunk of a torched Duesenberg, sitting in a Hamtramck junkyard? These might've been good locations to search. But Riley did not have the wisdom nor maybe even the stomach to peer into such dark places.

All he did was go around and talk to people. And all that got him was more hearsay and theories. Still, I wanted to keep track of all the useless information he was finding out, so I had Solly Levine tail him his first couple of weeks in town.

First, Riley talked to Thompson's enemies, of which there were plenty—people he'd put in jail, fired, or just plain screwed. When he finished with the enemies, Riley set out to talk to all of Thompson's friends. There weren't any. So he settled for Thompson's barber, his stockbroker, his mailman.

"His mailman?" I said, when Solly informed me. "What the hell is a mailman going to tell him?"

Wouldn't you know, the mailman gave Riley his first solid lead. Riley asked him, "When did you first notice Mr. Thompson's mail being left out in the box?"

The mailman was chatty. "Well, I got concerned when I saw the box hadn't been emptied Friday, though I thought maybe he's taking a long weekend. I still thought that on Saturday, by which time the box was stuffed with three days mail because he hadn't picked up Thursday either, though that didn't worry me at the time because maybe he was just sleeping in after the Wednesday night Houdini show. By Monday, I was thinking—"

Riley rapped his cane on the mailbox to stop him. "Did you say *Houdini show?*"

Turned out the mailman was the only one who knew Thompson was a magic buff and had tickets to Houdini at the Garrick Theatre. Of course, *we* knew Thompson was going to the Houdini show, because we were tracking him and waiting for the right moment.

Once Riley knew about the show, he set off on a new round of interviews, with all the Garrick employees, as well as members of the audience and maybe Houdini himself, I don't know. Amongst all of those people there was only one possessing any useful information—the parking lot attendant.

"Well, a funny thing happened that night," the attendant told Riley. "I remember a Ford pulled into the lot and there was a guy with thick glasses driving and a very big guy sitting next to him. A few minutes later, the car comes back out of the lot, with only the glasses guy in it. I said to him, 'Leaving so soon?' and he told me he only came to drop off his friend at the show. But I thought, why not drop him by the lobby—why in the parking lot? P.S., I never saw that big guy go from the lot to the theater. It was like he pulled a Houdini right there in the parking lot."

Riley could picture the disappearing act—Abie the Agent squeezing himself in the back seat of Thompson's car in the lot, then laying in wait. Riley asked the parking lot guy whether he thought he'd be able to identify the two men if he saw them again.

"Oh, yes," the guy said. "I got a photographic memory."

So Riley left his number and said he'd check back later. Very next day, the guy called Riley.

"Did I mention that the one with the glasses was a Negro?" the guy said over the phone.

Riley didn't know what to say to that. Before he could say anything, the guy on the phone said, "Oh, and the big guy—did I mention he was a Chinaman?"

Riley tried to convince the guy that maybe he was mistaken about this new information. And that he might want to think on it, because a person could go to jail for giving a false description. But the guy held firm: "a Negro and a Chinaman, definitely," he said.

Riley was smart enough to know what had happened: Grabowski paid the parking lot guy a visit shortly after Riley met with him. And in his own persuasive way, Grabowski showed the guy that he had a choice: He could tell a funny little fib and no one could do a damn thing to him. Or he could tell the truth and many things could and surely would be done to him. When it was broken down for people this way, the choice was so simple that there really was no choice.

To his credit, Riley was not easily discouraged. He put in long hours at the DA's office, according to our snitch. He seemed, from day one, as if he was running the place—telling the floundering Teddy Baird what should be done. He also spent a lot of time tutoring his new right-hand man Bud Fleischer on how to dig up leads and pull information from people. He corrected Bud a lot; the kid bristled, but he also soaked up everything.

They went to talk to a lead one day and when they said hello to the guy, Riley noticed Bud doing that odd handshake thing—using his left hand, backwards, to shake the other guy's right hand, whilst keeping his own right hand in his pocket.

"Why do you do that with your hand?" Riley said to him later, in the car.

"What?" Bud said, but he said it weakly.

"Why do you hide your hand? You ashamed?"

"Hell, no," Bud said and to prove it he took his hand out and slapped it flat on his own pants leg. The gray wool from his pants bubbled up in the gap between the pinky and middle finger. His face, turned to the window, was red.

"You should be proud of it," Riley said. "A man who hasn't

lost something hasn't lived. Don't you know that?"

Bud looked out the window. "Can we change the subject?"

Riley pulled the car over to the curb, and Bud looked at him.

"What are you doing? Why you stopping here?"

"I don't like mysteries," Riley said to him. "You should know that about me if you're going to work with me—I like to know everything. I don't like it when people hold back information. Or change the subject."

"Yeah. So?"

"So what did become of that finger?"

"Oh, for crying out loud," Bud said, looking back out the window. "You know," he said to that window, "polite folks don't come right out and ask like that."

"I'm not polite," Riley said. "Who has time for it?"

Bud shook his head and waited a little before answering. "I lost it in a schoolyard fight. That's all I'm going to say. Suppose I start asking you all kinds of questions about your leg?"

"Go right ahead."

"Okay, how'd you lose it?"

"Same as you," Riley said. "Lost it in a schoolyard fight. Guess my schoolyard was even rougher than yours."

Bud paused and then said, "I heard it happened in France."

Riley nodded. "That's true—you must've done a little digging on me. So if you knew, why'd you ask?"

Bud shrugged.

"Good rule to keep in mind," Riley said. "If you already know something, don't bother to ask."

The two of them drove all over town in Riley's car; he used the one good foot on the gas and brake, operating the clutch by hand. He drove fast and always came to a sharp stop when he reached his destination. It used to catch Solly off guard sometimes as he tried to stay at least half a block behind. One afternoon Riley stopped short outside a coffee shop and Bud went in and then came out holding three cups. When Bud was back in the car, Riley threw it in reverse, sped back half a block to where Solly was parked, and got out and tapped on Solly's window. Riley handed Solly a cup of coffee saying, "There's cream in it, hope you like it that way," and then got back in his car and took off.

He went to some unusual places in that car. One day he drove to a ratty old boxing gym, with tattered fight posters over the windows.

"The hell is he going in there for?" Solly muttered in his car.

Inside, the gym was filled with grunting sounds and the smell of middle-aged paunchy men flailing at heavy bags hung by chains.

"Ever seen such a sorry bunch of boxers?" Bud whispered to Riley as they walked inside. "Why are cops always fat?"

"Because muscle goes soft when not used," Riley said.

Clarke was in the ring sparring with a smaller guy. When he spied Riley, he turned away from the other boxer and leaned on the top rope of the ring with both mitts. He had a crooked grin on his face and said, "Good thing you're here—some of these guys have been fighting."

"You and I need to talk," Riley said.

Riley got right to it, asking Clarke, "What are you going to do about the Purples? After what happened the other night, you're on the outs with them. They might come after you."

Riley said that if Clarke would tell him everything he knew about the Purples, Riley could offer protection and relocation.

"*You're* gonna protect *me*?" Clarke sneered. "And from a bunch of Jew boys, no less. That is rich." He leaned further over the rope, bringing his dripping face a little closer. "If anybody needs protection, it's a cripple like you. You can't even defend yourself."

"Shut up," Bud said to Clarke, and Riley quickly reached over and gripped Bud hard on the shoulder to quiet him.

"Lucky for me, I don't need to defend myself," Riley said. "People need to defend themselves from me."

The visit to Clarke did no good. Even though he was still furious at us for humiliating him, there was no way he'd help someone like Riley. But these setbacks did not slow Riley—he would just get in his car and proceed to the next dead end. You never knew where he'd go, but almost every day ended with him making a brief stop at the LaSalle Hotel downtown. The hotel had a radio broadcast booth overlooking the lobby. It was where Jerry Barkley did his evening radio show.

Each time Riley stopped by the radio booth, he dropped off a package of papers: little stories and facts about the crime scene in Detroit.

Barkley shook his head whenever he saw Riley coming and muttered, "Lord have mercy, the man is relentless."

Riley would drop the package on the desk in front of Barkley and say, "Here it is, Jerry. Your ticket to fame and fortune."

After that, Riley would get back in his car and drive home.

He and Nan had moved into a house, which I took to be a sign that Riley was digging in for a long fight. He came home one night to find Nan decorating the mantle in the living room. Soon as he walked in, she took hold of her ready-to-burst stomach and danced between the unpacked boxes on the floor to rush into his arms. His cane dropped to the floor and he felt the ferocious hug of a mother bear with the cub in her belly. Then he gently broke her grip, reached down for his cane, and headed across the living room straight for the radio.

"He's coming on now," he said as Nan sighed.

He fidgeted with the staticky box whilst she returned to the mantle, where she was finding a place for a small statue of St. Jude.

"Oh, for Pete's sake," Riley said, turning the radio knob. "This thing is useless."

Nan spoke softly to the little statue. "You're the patron saint of lost causes, so I have to ask: What can you do about him?"

Then she left Jude and went to Riley. "Here, let me do it," she said. "I don't know why you bother to listen. You just get in a lather when he doesn't say what you want. He's an entertainer, Harry—he's paid to tell jokes. You're the one paid to be all serious and mopey."

She tried tuning first, then gave the radio a sharp rap on top and the sound came in crystal clear.

"This is why I married you," Riley said.

Together they stared at the box like it was a crystal ball.

"This is WMBC," the announcer's voice said. *"And now your host for the evening hour... Mr. Jerry Barkley."*

"Your friend and mine," Riley said.

"Good evening, Detroit," Barkley's voice said amid the crackling. *"My faithful listeners are used to me starting the program with a lighthearted tale. But I must confess, I'm in no mood for it tonight."*

Riley arched an eyebrow and looked at Nan.

"For you see, I have just learned the tale of yet another young man who has disappeared in this city. Name of Ippolito—Italian, I guess, not that it matters. He is one of us: a simple man with a wife and three young kids at home. One day, just like that, he vanishes. And nobody talks about it—no one utters a word."

Riley leaned forward in his seat. Nan was behind him now, standing with her hands resting on his shoulders.

"The police do nothing. The mayor does less than that. Like Nero, they fiddle as the city burns. Allowing the slinking hand of the underworld to pull its strings, and do its dirty work."

"Are we to sit idly as the Motor City becomes Murder City? I say it's time for the common herd to find its voice. And that voice must say to the powerful and the lawless, 'Enough! Enough with the killings, the graft. Enough turning the blind eye.' That voice must declare that Detroit does not belong to monkeys with guns, nor to only the powerful and the protected. This is our city, my common herd—we built it with our hands. And starting now, we're going to take it back from those who would destroy it."

Riley put his own hand on Nan's, still on his shoulder.

"Now we're getting somewhere," he said.

Barkley's radio show was a sensation by 1928. Didn't bother me: He could rant about gangsters all he liked—it was just words in a box. But common slobs went mad for his "voice of Detroit" bit. The more he preached to the powerless, the more powerful he became. Naturally, Abie wondered if Barkley was using some kind of psychology on people—maybe hypnosis via the radio waves. I said, "No, he's just telling the dopes what they want to hear."

Either way, when he took the mike at seven o'clock each evening, the streets of Detroit emptied. In his broadcast booth at the LaSalle, he pulled out his cheat sheet from Riley and talked about crimes going unreported, witnesses disappearing, the indifference of the authorities. At the end of each broadcast Barkley would light a cigar and lean back in his chair with feet up, alone yet thrilled to be in such good company.

He became the star of Ten's Spot, swaggering around the speakeasy like he owned it. (Well, okay he did, but we held the lease.) He was afraid of me, which was probably a good instinct. He never came by my table, but would sometimes send over a round and then raise a toast to me from a distance. I would raise my own glass and quietly say, "Up yours, Motormouth," and everyone at my table would laugh and across the room Barkley would laugh, too, not knowing why.

Funny thing about Barkley: On any given night he'd come in with thick stacks of bills in every pocket, and he'd piss money away. Next night, he'd come in with a long face and a much tighter wad. I have been around gaming houses enough to know this is the mark of a gambler. And since he had never been seen in either of the gaming houses owned by the Purples, that meant he was gambling with Livoli. Didn't bother me—the man was free to do business with anyone he liked, even oilers.

He and Tennessee Jenkins remained a scandalous item, and this, along with my brooding presence in the corner, was good for business because speakeasies thrived on scandal. Customers liked to feel they were in the midst of mischief.

I never did get what Ten saw in the Motormouth—I asked her this once, years later, in a letter. She said, "He gave me my chance, and a whole lot of other things, too."

That was true enough. One day he passed through the speakeasy carrying two big boxes and headed straight for her so-called boudoir in the back. She was inside admiring herself in the mirror whilst the boy Arthur stood behind her, brushing her hair for her. She looked at Arthur in the glass and studied his small delicate face.

The door swung open from a kick, revealing Barkley and his boxes. "Madam, I have a delivery," he said.

Ten played it nonchalant. "Well, I didn't order nothing. How 'bout you, Arthur?"

Arthur thought she was serious and answered, "No, ma'am."

Barkley walked his boxes into the room. "Well, I find this all very strange," he said, "because it says this top box is for one Arthur Nicks."

"And the bottom box?" Ten asked.

"That one we'll get to in due time."

· Barkley put the two boxes down on a chair, took the top one and, with a big phony bowing gesture, handed it to Arthur. The boy looked at Ten and only after she nodded did he accept it. He carefully untied the ribbon, lifted the lid, and pulled out a leather baseball mitt with a ball in the web. Arthur studied these like foreign objects—sniffing the leather of the glove, fingering the red stitches on the ball. He looked up at Barkley with worried eyes.

"I don't know how to play," he said.

"Okay pay attention, Einstein," Barkley said. "You throw the ball in the air. It comes down, you catch it in the glove. *Capiche?*"

Arthur looked like he might try a toss right then and there but Barkley stopped him. "It's an outdoor game, son. Why'ncha go give it a try?"

Barkley nodded toward the door and Arthur took the glove and ran off. But he stopped in the doorway and turned back to Barkley.

"You teach me sometime?" he said.

Barkley had already moved on, reaching for the other box. "Yeah sure, sometime," he said without looking back. "Go on now, kid."

After Arthur left, Barkley handed the box to Ten. She opened it suspiciously, as if expecting a jack-in-the-box to pop out. Instead she found a hat: maroon velvet with an ostrich feather on one side. She turned the hat over to put it on, and a smaller box fell out of it. She picked up and opened that smaller box and it contained a little snow globe with a tiny Statue of Liberty inside.

"Look into that ball," Barkley said. "See the future."

Ten gave him a look. "Gonna snow, is it?"

Barkley smiled and shook his head. He reached in his jacket and took a stuffed envelope from the inside pocket and placed it down on the dressing table.

"Looks like somebody's on a winnin' streak," she said.

He tapped his finger down on the envelope. "*This*," he said, "is going to take us all the way to New York."

Ten gave him a puzzled half-smile, then watched his hand reach for the thin shoulder strap of her dress. He fingered it and slid it down the side of her smooth arm.

"I've got it all planned out, sugar plum," he said, his voice purring now. "I'm gonna broadcast coast-to-coast. And you're gonna run the fattest blind pig on Broadway."

"Uh-huh," she said. She eyed his hand going for the other strap.

Ten's dress slipped to the floor. Barkley ran a finger down the middle of her chest, tickling the bone. She placed the snow globe on the table with the envelope and started unbuttoning Barkley's shirt.

"You're just gonna go and leave everything behind?" she said.

"Except you," Barkley said. "I'm putting you in my pocket to bring with me."

She pulled the shirt off his shoulders, smooth as a boy's.

"Sure you got room in that pocket? You been stuffin' a lot in there lately."

"Oh, I'll make room for you," he said.

He pushed against her and they tumbled onto her bed, whereupon Barkley started doing the only thing that ever shut him up. He had his face over her shoulder and in the pillow whilst she turned her own head sideways and looked over at the little globe with the flakes all falling down.

NINETEEN

It's funny how people worry about the wrong things. Max was so worried about what we'd done to Thompson, and about what Grabowski kept doing to the oilers. What he should have worried about was that goddamn movie camera. It ended up leading to more trouble than any weapon we ever owned.

Things started to go awry when the guy at the Foxman movie studio decided, after getting the first crash reel from us, that he'd seen enough. That's all he said in a cable wired to us from California: *I have seen enough.* Also: *Can I send man to pick up camera?*

Max and I took this to mean we'd provided so much filmed evidence of Ford's malfeasance that the case was made. Still, we wanted to make more movies because it was so much fucking fun.

So we phoned up the studio guy in Hollywood. Max told him we had found new and better ways to demolish Fords, and were looking forward to filming it.

The guy pleaded with Max: Please, please do not send any more Ford movies. He said the feud between Mr. Foxman and Mr. Ford was over, due to Ford's public apology to the Jews some months earlier.

I then wrote him back a note saying: *Are you kidding me? Ford is not sorry. He had a shitload of old Model T's to get rid of and a new batch of 1927 A's rolling off the lines, hence he needed every customer he could get including Jews, and that is why he apologized. Are you too*

simple to get it? We are keeping the camera by the way. If you have a
problem with that, come see me.

So now we had a movie camera but needed a use for it. This was
the kind of challenge Max relished. I came into the cutting house
one day to find him and Handsome Ziggy Selbin building a contraption in the corner. It consisted of the movie camera, on top of
a tripod, fastened in back to a mechanical swivel-arm, operated by
gears powered by an electric generator.

Max looked back at me, saying, "You won't believe it."

"I probably won't," I said.

"Give me another minute," he said, adjusting the swivel arm.
"The torque has to be just right." After that, he switched on the
generator, stepped back and said, "Behold."

As the gear in the swivel-arm began to turn, the camera moved
in a slow and jerky manner, from left to right. Then it stopped and
started moving back, from right to left.

"What do you think," Max said.

"I am speechless," I said and it was true.

"It can go like this for a couple of hours, till the film runs out,"
Max said.

Handsome Ziggy Selbin was nodding. "Look at it," he said.
"Ever seen anything like it?"

I hadn't.

"Isn't Max a genius?" Ziggy said.

I said, "I used to think so, but now I'm not so sure."

But then they explained it to me, and it almost made sense. We
had a lot of liquor in that cutting house, and each night as we shut
down for a few hours, there was always the possibility someone
would be stupid enough to try to rob us. Hence, the contraption
was designed to keep a roaming eye on the cutting house whilst we
were away.

"It's like having a night watchman," Max said.

It turned out Max was right on the mark—because a month
later, somebody did come along who was stupid enough to break
into the cutting house.

They stole many cases of whiskey, but that wasn't all they did. They busted bottles all over the floor, and pounded dents in the big mixing vats. And they scrawled a message on the wall: *Screw you Jews, from your pals the Wops.* I thought this was strange, because oilers do not like being called Wops, so why would they call themselves that?

The worst thing the bastards did was tear up several blueprints Max had left in the warehouse—plans for an underwater conveyor system connecting Detroit to Windsor. He had slaved over those plans. When he saw them all torn up, he started to shiver and shake, and tears streamed down his face.

I said, "Max, you can re-do those blueprints, it's all still there in your head."

But he sighed and said, "Oh, what's the point anyway." When I saw my brother in this state, you can imagine how I felt.

Then we remembered the camera. The filthy vandals who stole our booze and tore up Max's dream had failed to notice it in the corner. Needless to say we were eager to see the film. And when we looked at it, we saw that sure enough, it wasn't the oilers who did this. It was that fat, humiliated, no-longer-on-our-payroll cop, Vivien Clarke. Along with two other pigs, he was caught in the act of busting bottles, hammering dents, and tearing papers. And the whole time he was laughing his head off.

Now you could say the camera was a blessing here, because it informed us of something we really wanted to know. But the trouble is, once you know something, then you have to do something about it.

The Clarke incident stirred debate amongst us. Max said, "Let it go, it does not matter. We don't need trouble with the cops." Grabowski and Abie felt that a little GBH (grievous bodily harm) was called for. I was leaning to their side, but there was no rush. "When the opportunity presents itself," I said.

In the meantime, I had other things on my mind. Rachel was under sedation at Eloise and I worried they might be doing something to her. I didn't want to take her out—what the hell would I do with her—but I wanted to keep an eye on things.

And so the day after the Clarke incident I decided to get away from it all and visit Eloise. I figured I'd spend the afternoon and stay the night—which was against hospital rules, but on the other hand, fuck them. I was paying a lot so that Rachel had her own room, her own nurse, fresh flowers daily. I had a right to come and go as I pleased.

I could've driven out to Eloise in my brand new Duesenberg (you have to do *something* with all that money). But I chose to walk the six miles so as to work off tension; there is nothing like a vigorous ankle as a substitute for doing GBH. I started out in downtown Detroit, where big new buildings were going up on every street. Soon I was out in the wilderness, walking on that rocky road to crazyland.

When I got to Eloise I stopped at the front gate and shook hands with my old pal, Oscar. "You walked here, Mr. Bernstein?" he said. "You're the only guy ever arrives on foot."

At Building D, the two nurses at the desk looked up at me and froze as always. I ignored them and went upstairs. When I got to Rachel's room, I carefully opened the door to peek inside—didn't want to wake her. But she was sitting up in bed, her legs folded up to her chest and arms wrapped around them. Her dark eyes showed no surprise to see me—more like impatience.

"Where've you been?" she said. "We should've left two hours ago. The Steins will be furious."

She got up and started moving toward her little dresser, to get some clothes I guess; she was wearing her nightgown. I took hold of her shoulders and turned her body toward me, then gave her a hug, but she didn't hug me back. She felt tiny and brittle.

"There's no rush," I said. "I talked to the Steins and told them to give you the day off."

It was easier to play along than to remind her that she'd been fired ten years ago. She would remember on her own, in time—reality came back to her in waves, and you never knew when. But those little moments of clarity always did come, and when they did, she would seem to sag under the weight of them.

I stroked her smooth hair and turned her face up to look at me. She had on makeup: lipstick that was too red, blue eye shadow, and pink powder on the cheeks.

"What's on your face?" I said.

She was never one for makeup, didn't ever need it. When I first met her—she was 19, and I was just 17—she had perfect white skin and large brown eyes that swallowed you. Her looks first drew me in, but so did her spirit: She had her own mind, and her own job with the Steins cleaners delivering those Ford uniforms, and her own little apartment (both parents being dead). I also liked the way she got to the point: We'd only met a couple of times, flirting with each other in the Hastings market, when she came right out and told me she knew my whole story—how I'd been shunned by the community and my own mother, how I had no home and slept nights in an empty corner of the Sugar House. She said, "Why don't you come over and take a look at my place. If you like it, we'll make room for you there." At the time, it was the nicest thing anyone ever did for me. And still is.

"Why, don't you like it?" she said to me now, about the makeup.

She explained that the hospital had set up a beauty shop—I could just see it, the crazy women painting each other's faces whilst the attendants stood by and had a laugh. I took a handkerchief from my pocket and gently wiped the red off her lips and the blue from her eyelids.

"You don't need this stuff," I said. "You're a natural beauty."

I folded the hanky, smeared with bright colors, and put it back in my pocket.

We sat on the bed and she asked me what was going on in the outside world. I told her the factories were belching more than ever, construction was everywhere, cars were stuck in traffic, and people didn't care because they were too busy listening to their radios. "It's all going to hell," I said. "You're better off in here."

"A radio," she said. "I think I'd like one of those."

Later, when she nodded off, I went down to the front desk—I'd noticed they had a radio. I said to the nurse, "I'm going to borrow this," and unplugged it and put it under one arm.

I started to go back upstairs, but then I stopped. With my free hand, I pulled out that handkerchief, with the red and blue smears. I held it up for the nurse to see. "This was on her face," I said.

The nurse nodded and explained about the beauty parlor. "It makes them feel good about themselves," she said, smiling.

I reached toward her with the cloth still in my hand and pressed it against her chubby cheek and rubbed hard. It left a streak of red all the way down to her chin. Then I did the same to her other cheek. She just sat there with eyes wide. The security guard stood and took a step but I looked at him and he stopped.

"Now you've had *your* puss painted, too," I said to the nurse. "Does it make you feel good about yourself?"

I left her that handkerchief and went back upstairs with the radio. The rest of the evening was spent listening to cheery tunes on the little box. Rachel mostly slept, her head on my bare chest, and I mostly stared at the ceiling and tried not to think.

Whilst I was away at Eloise, things were happening without my knowledge. Grabowski convinced Abie that they should tail Clarke, to see what the crazy cop might do next. They followed in Grabowski's car as Clarke went to a couple of speakeasies and got soused. Later that night he staggered to his car on an empty street.

"Let's get 'im," Grabowski said.

Abie was surprised: "Joe said we should wait."

Grabowski pointed out that I'd said to wait for the right opportunity. "This looks like it ta me," he said.

Clarke was fumbling with the key in his car door when Grabowski cracked him on the cranium with a black jack. Abie caught Clarke's body as it fell and dragged him to Grabowski's car, where they laid him on the back seat.

The idea was to stash him somewhere until I got back the next day. Grabowski suggested the cutting house. "Let's take 'im back to the scene 'a his crime," he said.

When they got there, a half-dozen Purples were on duty—they were supposed to be cleaning up the mess left by the vandals, but they were just standing around rolling the dice. Grabowski and Abie brought in Clarke, who was just awakening, and sat him in a chair with hands tied behind his back.

Everyone stared at him. Grabowski was the one who came up with the idea. "What night is it, Abie?" he said.

Abie answered that it was a Wednesday night.

"That's right," Grabowski. "So it ain't the Sabbath."

"So?" Abie said.

"So we can re-do that fight between you an' Clarke."

There were yells of approval from the other Purples on the floor. They were anxious to see Abie in action. The only one who wasn't shouting was the only other big person in the room, Gorilla Kowalski. Gorilla knew what it was like to have people expect certain things from you, based purely on your size.

"Don't do this unless you want to," Gorilla said to Abie.

Abie looked around at the other Purples, who were already starting to make wagers on how long Clarke would last.

"I don't mind," he said.

They cleared the broken glass and debris in the middle of the floor to make room. They stripped Clarke to the waist; Abie took off his own jacket and shirt. When Clarke got a gander at Abie's bare shoulders, he immediately tried to sit back down in his chair, saying, "What's in it for me?" and insisting this was a fight he couldn't win even if he won.

Abie walked to the pull-down door and lifted it so that there was a three-foot-high opening. He said to Clarke, "If you can get by me and get to the open door, we'll let you go." Then he looked around. "Everyone understand? He gets by me, let him go."

Everyone agreed. They were almost ready to start when Grabowski's voice yelled out, from the corner of the room. "Anybody know how ta work this?" he said, taking the movie camera off the swivel arm.

Solly Levine said, "I do," and took charge of that damn camera.

The betting line was, could Clarke last one minute with Abie? He started with a big swing but Abie caught the fist in one hand and then squeezed it with both. Clarke's knees buckled and he screamed as the hand was crushed like a sparrow in a vise. That should have ended the fight right there. But Clarke spied a shard of glass on the floor and snatched it with his remaining good hand. He wrapped his arms round Abie's legs like a tackler, and stuck the glass into Abie's right thigh. He was still wrapped around the legs like that when Abie reached down and grabbed the back of Clarke's pants-belt and started pulling him up. Abie lifted Clarke the way you or I might hoist up a sack of potatoes. Clarke ended up in mid-air, backwards on top of Abie's right shoulder.

With his back bent upon that big shoulder, Clarke saw everything upside-down. His legs kicked and his arms flailed—with one hand still holding the bloody piece of glass. Abie ordered him to drop it, but he didn't. Then Abie drove him headfirst down to the floor. Everyone in that room heard the snap of Clarke's neck, including Abie, who let go quickly and stepped back. Clarke lay flat on the concrete, alive but unable to move except for twitching in his hands. His head was perfectly still but his confused eyes darted all around. He didn't make a sound. Solly was filming him and came in for a close-up of his face, but Abie slapped the camera and almost knocked it out of Solly's hands.

"Turn it off," he said.

Then Abie went quickly to get his jacket and shirt from the chair where he'd stripped. Everybody stood watching. He came back to Clarke and hunched down to look him in those roving panicked eyes. "You fought a good fight, Clarke," he said. Then he gently wrapped his shirt around Clarke's head and covered the eyes, still darting and searching. Once the blindfold was on, Abie took the long blade from inside his jacket. He pointed his index finger against the center of Clarke's chest, then ran the blade through that spot, quickly ending his misery.

Grabowski offered to dispose of the body (guess how?) but Abie said he'd take care of it. He told everyone to leave the cutting house except Grabowski and the Gorilla. He asked them if they would please mix up some cement in one of the vats. Then he left.

He returned with two big cleavers from his father's shop. He cut the body into pieces—insisted on doing all the cuts himself. As he handed each piece to Grabowski and the Gorilla, they dipped it in cement and set it aside to harden. Later, they loaded those pieces, each heavy as a cinderblock, into Grabowski's car. They drove to the pier and loaded the blocks onto the Gar-Max, under the floorboards. When the boat got halfway to Windsor, Abie pulled the lever, the bottom opened, and one more batch of illicit cargo sank to the bottom of the river.

TWENTY

Needless to say, I got a big surprise with my orange juice at the Crime next morning. Abie sat next to me in the booth and whispered in my ear: "*Clarke is dead. It's my fault. I broke his neck, by accident. You don't have to worry about the body. It's in blocks, in the river. I'm sorry, Joe.*"

Max was sitting across from me and he said, "What is he whispering? Are you talking about me?"

Abie eyed him. "Why does everything have to be about you?"

I told them both to shut up and tried to absorb the information. I happened to be holding my orange juice and for some reason the glass picked that moment to shatter in my hand.

After the juice was wiped up, I resumed the conversation. I didn't feel like whispering, but on the other hand you can't discuss such things plainly, even at the Crime. So I said, "Okay, now tell me why you decided to do away with your dog Fido. And why last night?"

Max said Abie didn't have a dog Fido and I told him to shut up and listen and I'd tell him about Fido later.

Abie said he didn't want to do away with his dog Fido. He just wanted to hold the dog prisoner. But other people thought he should fight the dog. Then the dog tried to stab him so he accidentally broke Fido's neck. And then the only humane thing to do was spear the dog through the heart. And chop him up with a meat cleaver.

"But why did you choose to hold the dog prisoner in the first place?" I said. "Did anyone tell you to do this? To the dog?"

He said Grabowski thought it was a good opportunity last night because the dog was drunk.

By this time Max was having trouble breathing as he was so frustrated not knowing who we were talking about, so I gave him a hint by saying to Abie, "Was this all because the dog Fido crapped in our cutting house the other day?"

And when I said that, Max looked at Abie and said, "Oh, you didn't. You didn't, did you? You have ruined us, you big stupid ass."

I guess Abie expected me to defend him. When I didn't, he gave me a hard look, then Max, and then got up and walked out.

"You shouldn't talk to him that way," I said to Max.

Max said, "I don't even blame him. He's too simple to blame. It's Grabowski. He is out of control."

I couldn't deny that, though I pointed out that being out of control was also one of Grabowski's best qualities.

Max was even more upset when he learned, later that day, that his camera had been used to film the fight. Here I agreed with him: stupid thing to do. Max went straight to the cutting house, took the film out of the camera, and brought it home so he could cut it into little bits and then burn the bits.

He wanted me to discipline Abie and get rid of Grabowski, but I said no—what's done is done. Max insisted they were violating my authority, but I viewed it differently. "They saw an opening and acted. I can't blame someone for that."

I did give them a stern warning, however: "Do not ever kill anyone unless I tell you." I had to amend that because Grabowski pointed out that sometimes life and death decisions needed to be made in my absence. So I said, "Don't ever kill anyone unless you know in your heart it is the right thing to do. And if you ever do, for shit's sake do not make a movie about it."

About a week after Clarke's disappearance, Riley hobbled into work one morning and glanced in the window of Teddy Baird's office. He saw Baird talking with two men, a tall thin one and a short fat one. The thin one was swimming in a suit too big for him, whilst the fat one wore a loud plaid jacket that came up short at the sleeves. Riley saw Bud loitering down the hallway, and signaled him over.

"Let me guess—the Feds have arrived," he said softly to Bud.

Bud nodded. "Kill a hundred goons, nobody cares. But get rid of one fat Irish cop, they send in the G-men. Get a load of those suits. They must get paid even less than us."

The Feds were rising to leave now, taking a folder from Baird.

"Wonder what's in there?" Bud said.

"Probably all we know about the Purples," Riley answered.

Riley herded Bud into his office as the Feds headed out of the building. When they were gone, Riley put his hat back on and said to Bud, "Wanna go on a goon chase?"

Soon after, Riley and Bud were tailing the Feds' car. They followed it until it pulled to a stop in front of the LaSalle Hotel, where the sidewalk outside the lobby was bustling with women in furs. Staying half a block back, Riley pulled to the curb and watched as the Feds sat in their parked car outside the hotel. In a few minutes, a man wearing a long camel-hair coat strode out from the lobby. He got in the back seat of the Feds' car.

Bud leaned forward in his seat. "Is that...?"

"John Livoli," Riley answered for him. "Mister Black Hand."

"Lemme understand this," Bud said. "The Feds and the Italians are partners now?"

"Looks that way. So we're feeding inside dope on the Purples to the Feds. And they're taking it straight to the Italians. Which means we're in the sack with mobsters now. How's that for a kick in the keister?"

Bud shook his head. "Think Baird is wise?"

"I intend to find out," Riley said.

When Livoli got back out of the car and the Feds drove off, Riley and Bud returned to the office. Riley went straight in and planted himself in the chair in front of Baird's desk, demanding answers.

"I understand how you feel, Harry," Baird said, rubbing his hands nervously as if he was washing them. "I share your ethical concerns. But we're at war with the Purples now, and we need to win any way we can. With any allies we can get."

"This is not England helping France," Riley said. "Do I have to explain to you that Livoli is tied to Capone?"

Baird shrugged. "Maybe so, but Capone isn't killing our cops. Or making retired DA's disappear. The Feds have determined that the Purples are the priority now. Can't say I disagree."

"The Feds should not be playing favorites among gangsters. And we shouldn't be playing along with that game."

Baird shrugged. He was the type who shrugged more in an hour than some do in a lifetime. "Maybe it's smart strategy," he said. "You use one gang to kill off the other. Start with the one that's isolated. They're easier to exterminate."

"Or maybe the one thing the Feds hate more than an Italian gang is a Jewish one," Riley said.

"Well, that's possible, sure," Baird said. "But the Jews are not helping themselves by killing lawmen. The Sicilians don't do these things. They observe rules of engagement."

"You mean they know who to kill and who to pay. Yes, they've been playing this game longer. They know how to survive."

Riley watched as Baird started fumbling in his desk for something. He couldn't believe Baird would have the nerve to pull the flask out right in front of him, but Baird did.

"Forgive me Harry, but this has been a rough morning," he said, unscrewing the cap. "I won't even ask if you want to join me because I know better."

"Okay, fine, I'll take a swig," Riley said.

Baird was shocked. "Seriously?"

Riley nodded. Baird handed him the flask and Riley took it and got up from his seat. He walked around Baird's desk to the window behind it, and lifted it open.

Baird sighed and turned his chair around to watch as Riley reached out the window and turned the flask upside-down, pouring the liquor out. Baird sat there listening to the glug-glug sound

and did his best imitation of a laugh. When the flask was empty,
Riley set it down gently on the desk in front of Baird.

"Just doing my job," Riley said.

"Indeed," Baird said. "My mistake."

As Riley was headed for the door, he said over his shoulder to
Baird: "And don't expect me to share any more dirt on the Purples
until you plug that leak of yours."

Riley walked out and caught Bud in the hall moving away from
the door and trying to look casual about it.

"You get an earful?" Riley snapped at him.

That same evening Riley found himself eye to eye with Nan, wondering when she would make her move. She stared into his eyes,
not giving anything away at first. Then he thought he saw the be-
ginnings of a wicked smile at the corners of her lips—he figured
this meant trouble. He was right. She slowly balled her hand into a
little fist, then rapped her knuckles on the table between them.

"It cannot be true," Riley said.

"Oh, but it is," she said.

"You're knocking with *how many?*"

"Three."

Riley tossed his losing hand on the table and said to her, "Nothing's more tiresome than a person who always wins."

"Then I guess I'll never grow tired of you," she said.

Nan patted his hands as she gathered the cards. "Poor dear."
Then she slapped the deck in front of him. "Loser deals!"

Riley shook his head and did as told. They were in the living
room of the little house on Clairmount, the baby asleep upstairs, a
fire crackling and hissing in the hearth behind them.

Riley kept eyeing the fire, complaining that it wasn't burning
evenly. He got up and grabbed the poker, and then nudged and
bullied those logs until one of them just gave up and tumbled off
the pile and died, making the flame even smaller.

"Happy now?" she said, watching over his hunched back.

Since he'd left the cards half-shuffled, she began to mix them
for him. He came back to the card table and the shuffled deck was

there neat and waiting for him but he didn't pick it up right away. He sat down and leaned back in his chair and gave her a little smile.

"Know what I'd like to be doing now?" he said.

She put on her "bored" voice: "Yes, yes, I know, floating in the lake."

"Not floating, per se."

"Okay, swimming," she said.

"Not swimming, exactly."

"Drowning?"

"I'd like to be in the water with you," he said. "Sans bathing suits."

She raised her eyebrows. "You could go diving for treasure," she said.

He let his jaw drop open. "The mouth on you!"

He dealt the cards so that each one landed softly on top of the last and when he finished, he laid down the deck and leaned over the table to share a secret. "We could skip town tonight and be on the lake by sun-up. Spend Valentine's Day there. Who'd stop us?"

"It's frozen solid!"

"Then we'll skate on it, hand-in-hand."

"Just play your cards, mister."

But Riley didn't; he leaned back in his chair with arms folded, looking at the fire. "I just don't see the point in staying. I can't trust any of 'em except Bud—who doesn't know which end is up half the time."

"Don't you speak ill of Bud. I think he's darling."

"All this double-dealing," Riley said. "Baird, the Feds. And *Barkley*. Man's got so many shady deals going I can't even keep track."

"He's kept his deal with you," Nan said. "Getting folks riled up, going after the mobs and politicians."

"He's cagey, though. He criticizes Mayor Bowles, but won't push for a recall. He attacks some gangsters, but not others."

Nan looked up from her cards, then placed them face down, reached across the table and tapped his forearm. His eyes came over from the fire and met hers.

"Listen. You trust me?" she said.

"In everything except cards."

"Okay, then I have two things to tell you. One, don't worry about what everybody else is doing. You're here to take the Purples out of circulation."

Riley winced a little. "Doing a bang-up job so far, huh?"

"You're building your hand," she said. "When you get the right cards, you'll play them. And here is number two: the lake is not going anywhere. It will be there when you're done."

"Remind me why I ever left?"

"It was the right thing to do," she said. "You couldn't ignore what happened to Thompson."

"Which we never have gotten to the bottom of."

Riley picked up his cards now and looked at them and what he saw did not improve his mood. He laid the cards face down on the table and his eye wandered over to the fire again. "I still think about that girl sometimes," he said. "Heard she ended up back in Eloise, poor thing."

Nan was quiet for a moment, turning something over in her mind before she spoke. "Ever thought of visiting her there?"

Riley scrunched his eye. "Why would she want to see me? She wouldn't even know who I am."

"I know, but... for someone to be alone in a place like that."

"She's not alone, she's got Bernstein," Riley said.

Nan put the cards face down on the table. She purposely kept her head turned away whilst getting up, but he'd already seen the tear well up in her eye. She walked to the fireplace and knelt down in front of it. "Bunch of bastards," she said to the flames.

"Who?"

"Thompson, Palmer, whoever else was involved in that whole mess," she said. "Just look at all the trouble they caused."

The next time I went to Eloise, I found myself stopping short in the hall outside Rachel's room. Her door was ajar; I heard voices inside but couldn't make out the words. I crept up and peeked in. Sitting in the chair by the bed was a woman with bobbed red hair.

It took me a second to place her face from the night at Ten's speakeasy. I decided to stay put and listen at the door.

"Honestly, you don't need to worry about that," she was saying to Rachel, who was propped up in the bed. Very relaxed in that chair, Nan had her coat open and long legs stretched out in front of her. The skirt ended at the knees and her calves were lean and shiny in her stockings. Her one foot played with the other—the toe nudging the heel of the shoe off and back on.

"He should have come," Rachel said. "It was Valentine's Day. Maybe something happened to him."

"I'm sure nothing happened," Nan said. "You'd have heard."

"Heard? I don't hear anything in here. I am not part of the world."

"My husband would have heard, then."

Rachel nodded, seeming to accept this—until a fresh worry creased her forehead. "Does your husband answer to Ford?"

"No, he doesn't," Nan said. "Remember I told you, my husband works in the District Attorney's office."

"I only ask because Ford is out to get Joe," Rachel said.

"Why would Ford be after Joe?"

Rachel stopped and seemed to ponder that. "I don't know why," she said. "But he is."

Nan leaned forward and patted Rachel's hand and didn't ask any more questions. I waited a little longer, then pushed the door hard to make it fly open. The redhead jumped in her seat and the loose shoe came off. Little pink toenails showed through the silk.

"Who are you and what the hell are you doing here?" I said.

To her credit, once she got over the shock she didn't seem scared. She looked me in the eye, then looked down to put on her shoe. "I'm Nan Riley," she said. "I'm here to keep Rachel company for a little while. Is there something wrong with that?"

"He sent you? To get information?"

"If you mean my husband, no," she said, now looking back up at me. This was when I noticed the eyes were green. "He doesn't even know I'm here."

"You can stop wasting your time because she doesn't know anything," I said, looking hard into Nan Riley's face.

Rachel took exception. "What do you mean I don't know any-thing? I know more than you."

"That's not what I meant," I said to Rachel, then I said to the other one, "I think you better leave and not come back."

Nan exhaled and started getting up whilst buttoning her coat. "I'm sorry if I've upset you," she said, eyes down on the buttons. "I heard Rachel was alone here, and thought she might like a visi-tor, that's all."

"She's not alone, she's got me."

"*You?*" Rachel cut in. "The invisible man? Where were you on Valentine's Day?"

"I was out of town," I said. It was true: I had a matter to attend to in Chicago that day, which was nobody's business. Yet I noticed that this Nan woman raised an eyebrow nonetheless.

"I thought you were just on your way out," I said to her.

She leaned down and patted Rachel on the arm and smiled at her, then walked past me, giving me a look out of the side of her eye whilst she passed.

"I don't like sideways glances," I said as she went out the door.

"Well, bully for you," she muttered loud enough for me to hear as she left and turned down the hall to the stairs.

I thought she had a lot of gall but she had even more than I thought. Because unbeknownst to me until much later, she stopped halfway down the stairs and turned around and came back up. She was planning to come back and tell me it was wrong to keep Rachel from having company just because I was scared about spies. She was going to suggest that if I was so worried, I could listen outside the door when she came to visit Rachel next time. She was going to say all that and more—except when she got near the room and noticed it was quiet in there, it was her turn now to creep to the door and peek in. She saw me down on a knee beside the bed, holding Rachel's hand.

"You are absolutely right," I was saying to her. "It was wrong for me to leave you alone on Valentine's Day."

"I thought they'd done something to you," Rachel said. "I thought they'd killed you."

I smiled at her and shook my head. "They can't kill me," I said. "Believe me, they've tried."

Then she told me that her head ached, and still kneeling, I reached into my jacket pocket and pulled out a small bottle of aspirin.

"You'll fix it the way I like?" she asked though she already knew I would.

I took a little spoon from my pocket and tapped a couple of tablets out of the bottle and onto the spoon. From the glass of water on the bedside table, I carefully poured a few drops onto the tablets in the spoon. And then I took a sugar cube from my shirt pocket and rubbed it between my fingers so that tiny white sprinkles fell onto the spoon. I swirled the mixture on the spoon and slowly guided it into her waiting open mouth. She looked me in the eyes as she took the medicine. I kissed her on the forehead.

Seeing this, I guess Nan found she had nothing more to say after all, so she crept away down the stairs whilst using her sleeve to dab the corner of her eye.

After that warning, Nan did not go back to Eloise for several months, but then her heart got the better of her head. One of the attendants, who'd been paid extra to keep an eye out for her, alerted me and I drove over quick and got to the room whilst she was still there. I once again listened outside the door to see if she was trying to get information out of Rachel, but all she did was attempt to play cards with her. Rachel was unable to meet the challenge but that didn't seem to bother Nan as she turned it all into a laugh for both of them. And when Rachel started up with her worries and predictions of doom for all, Nan turned that into a game as well.

"Let's both make predictions and when I return next month we'll see who did better," she said. They each wrote their predictions and Nan took both pieces of paper and put them in her purse before leaving the room.

Out in the hall she saw me standing against the wall, arms folded, looking hard at her. At the time, I didn't know if I should thank her or kill her or maybe do one followed by the other.

She said, "I stand before you and swear to God that I only want to comfort that girl."

When I replied that the girl did not need her help, she said: "But she is so much worse than she was just a few months ago. You see that, don't you?"

I told her that what I saw or did not see was my business. And that if she wanted to help the sick she should be a nurse but do it someplace other than Eloise.

She ignored that and said, "Heaven knows what they're giving her."

I replied it might be wiser to look for that information in hell, and maybe she should get started on the journey.

She ignored that too, and said: "I would never presume to tell you that you should take her out of here and bring her home. I'm sure there must be reasons why you have not done that already."

I told her she had already done quite a lot of "presuming" and that the good intentions of people like her could end with Rachel dead, not to mention others too.

Then she just nodded goodbye and said, "Please forgive me for interfering," whilst she walked past me, close enough that I smelled her perfume. I was looking for that sideways glance again, and was all prepared to tell her to keep those little funny looks to herself. I waited for it, but the look never came my way and then she was gone.

TWENTY-ONE

By the summer of 1929, the Motormouth Barkley was riding high but was doing so on a tightrope. His radio show was more popular than ever, but Barkley had been losing heavy sums of money at Livoli's gaming houses. Livoli agreed to let him to run a tab whilst also giving Barkley fresh wads of cash each month. In exchange Livoli wanted inside dope on the Purples.

Barkley had access to that from two sources. At Ten's Spot, he employed spies to listen in on Grabowski and others in our group who tended to get loose-lipped when they drank. I still had my own hired "ears" in the place and they sometimes would listen in on Barkley and his "ears." So it was spies spying on spies. Once I knew what Barkley was up to, I began to have fun with it—we purposely spread bad information through the speakeasy, knowing Barkley would pick it up and pass it to Livoli.

However, Barkley's other source of information was more reliable—it was Riley. Of course, Riley was giving him dirt for use on the radio show, but Barkley sifted off some of the topsoil involving the Purples and gave it to Livoli.

But it wasn't enough: Livoli was the type who kept squeezing. He started to press Barkley to go on the air and praise Mayor Bowles, who was deep in the pocket of the oilers. Livoli also wanted Barkley to use his radio show to blame every crime in Detroit on the Jewish gangsters.

Barkley was reluctant to take it this far. He had begun to see himself as a man of the people (never mind that he was rich, soft, full of airs, and owned by the powerful). As Ten Jenkins would later tell me, he really started to believe the crap he spewed on the air each night. And he worried that his "common herd" would smell a rat if he boosted the corrupt Bowles or if he clearly took sides in the gang war.

So Barkley came up with what he thought was a brilliant way to free himself from Livoli's hooks: He would forgo the gaming houses and instead take his money and put it into the stock market, where even a lousy gambler like him could come up aces every time (or so it seemed in the summer of '29). By September he was feeling so good about his investments that he told Ten she should start getting ready for a move to New York by year's end. She listened and smiled but she knew better than to start packing just yet.

Of course the plan was blown to hell a month later on Black Tuesday, a crisp and sunny day in Detroit. Late in the afternoon, Barkley's white Packard rolled slowly along, bumped against the curb and climbed over it, and finally ground to a stop on the sidewalk outside Ten's Spot. The car door swung open, but Barkley didn't get out right away. He sat staring at himself in his rearview mirror, which was nothing new for Barkley—except this time, for a change, he did not admire what he saw. The eyes were bloodshot, and the big baby face was wearing a giant pout.

"You pathetic fucker," he said to the mess in the mirror.

He hauled himself out of the car, a flask in one hand and a rolled-up newspaper in the other. He approached that building like a man going to the gallows.

Froggy let him in and said hello but Barkley just waved his hand without looking up. He heard the scuffling sound of his own footsteps in the hallway leading to the speakeasy. When he entered the big room, Barkley stood and took stock of the place: Half the lanterns were hanging crooked, and the paint on the walls was peeling such that the dancing girls were missing various body parts.

Whilst looking around he spotted Ten at a table with a well-dressed butter-and-egg man whose face was buried in his hands. She was reaching across the table touching the man's elbow. When she noticed Barkley coming she looked up at him and searched his face and didn't like what she saw. He nodded toward the boudoir in back and headed straight for it. Ten got up and followed.

In that room, Arthur was reading a book in the corner and when Barkley entered, Arthur took one look at Barkley's face and knew he'd better get going. He grabbed his baseball mitt and glove on the way out, running past Ten as she was entering.

"Where's the fire?" she said to the passing boy, but she already knew the fire was right in front of her. She looked Barkley over as he stood there with a sour smile.

"So how bad is it?" she said.

He tossed back his head as if to laugh at the question but no laugh came out just a snort from the nose. He dropped his afternoon paper down onto the floor near her feet.

"Read all about it, extra, extra," he said. "G.M. is sinking like a stone. And so is everything else."

Ten didn't pick up the paper. "Who cares about G.M., I want to know 'bout you," she said.

"As the market goes," Barkley said with a flourish of the arms that almost made him lose balance, "so goes yours truly."

He trudged over to the bedside table and picked up the little snow globe, and shook it to make the flakes fly. "See this—our future?" He looked closely at the globe. Then he smashed it down hard on the floor.

Ten gasped, but didn't say anything. After a moment, she bent down and started picking up little glass shards with two fingers of one hand, dropping them into the palm of the other. She touched the tiny snowflakes on the floor to see what they felt like, wondering if they'd be cold; they weren't. Then she picked up the tiny Lady Liberty, still intact and free from that little dome prison.

Barkley left without another word, ankling slowly back through the dark inside of the speakeasy. It happened that Solly Levine was coming in as Barkley was going out and Barkley almost plowed into him.

"Watch it, pal," Solly said though Barkley didn't seem to hear.

Solly watched Barkley step out the front door into bright sunlight that blinded him and made him raise an arm in front of his face. Barkley walked to the curb and looked down the empty street—it was the middle of the day, but nothing was happening and nobody was going anywhere; he was seeing the future of Detroit, I guess. He kept looking and finally saw movement, a ways down the street. He staggered towards it, arm still shielding his face. It was only Arthur, throwing his ball up in the air and catching it, then throwing it up again and dropping it.

Arthur saw Barkley approaching and hesitated, then held up the ball. His eyes asked Barkley if he was coming to play catch at long last. Barkley shook his head no but kept coming. When he reached the boy he stopped and leaned over and put his hand on Arthur's shoulder.

"Then he put his lips against that little dinge boy's ear and started whispering," according to Solly. "He whispered for a good long time."

About two hours later and a mile away, Arthur's ball was in the air once more. It was as high up as the arm of a 14-year-old bookworm could toss a ball; then it started coming down fast and Arthur put up his glove to catch it. And since I never once spoke to the boy and cannot tell you what was in his head, I do not know whether Arthur really tried to catch that ball, or purposely let it glance off the big leather fingers of his mitt. The ball bounced on the hard pavement and started to roll along the deserted alley that Arthur had chosen as his play spot. As it rolled, Arthur gave chase, whilst the ball found its way to the side of a building. Though not just any building.

Inside that building, filled with mixing vats and stacked crates, it was a quiet time of day, the mixers and loaders on their supper break. Grabowski leaned back in a chair, lightly dozing. His dreams—if he had any—were interrupted by a soft thud against the side of the building. Grabowski sat up straight in his chair and turned his head quick to where the sound came from. Then he looked around to see if anyone else had noticed it. Abie sat on the other side of the cutting house, lost in a book.

Grabowski got out of his chair slowly and walked lightly on pudgy feet to the pull-down door. He raised the door quietly as he could, just enough so he could bend under it. Outside he walked to the side of the building where he'd heard the sound. He had to turn a corner to get there and just before he did, he heard footsteps coming around the other side. He stopped and reached in his jacket to feel for his gun and rested his hand on it whilst waiting to see what would come around that corner.

When it turned out to be Arthur, both parties were surprised. Arthur froze and his glove and ball fell to the ground. Grabowski took his hand out of his jacket and smiled but it was not a comforting smile. Arthur turned and started to walk away quickly. Grabowski snatched the glove off the ground and yelled after him.

"Boy! What's ya hurry?"

Arthur kept walking without looking back. Grabowski called again, but this time in a different tone that froze Arthur.

"Don't you take anotha step, boy," he said.

Arthur waited, not looking back. Grabowski walked up from behind, circled in front of him, and held the mitt out like a gift.

"You don' wanna leave without this, do ya?"

Arthur shook his head no but kept his arms at his sides as Grabowski held the glove in front of him.

"Why'ncha take it? Scared I got a disease?"

Arthur shook his head no and took the glove from Grabowski.

"Saw ya lookin' around," Grabowski said. "What were ya lookin' for?"

"My ball," Arthur said.

"It's right there in ya glove. No need to look around fer that."

Arthur didn't answer.

"Maybe ya wanted to see what's inside."

"No sir," Arthur said.

"Sure ya do. Yer a curious boy."

Arthur glanced up at Grabowski, then looked down again.

"Not much to see," Grabowski said. "Buncha boxes. We

load 'em on trucks. You know how to load boxes, boy?"

Arthur nodded. Now Grabowski reached into his pocket slowly and Arthur put his head down, not wanting to see what was coming as Grabowski fished around. The hand came out holding a five-dollar bill. Arthur still had his head down not looking, so Grabowski waved the bill under the boy's nose.

"We pay our loaders good. You can get a bat to go with yer ball."

Arthur looked up at him, but was afraid to take the bill.

"Take it. An advance. Ya get another when the job's done."

Grabowski stuffed the bill into Arthur's shirt pocket.

"We load at midnight," he said. "Don't be a no-show—ya took my money, ya better be here. I seen ya hangin' around Ten's Spot. I know how to find ya, if ya don't show. See ya here at midnight—got it? Now scram."

As the boy ran off Grabowski watched him go, studying the skinny body and legs. When he turned to go back into the cutting house, Abie was just coming out to look for him.

"What are you doing out here?" Abie asked.

"Nothin'. There was a little dinge with a ball, roamin' around."

"Didn't hurt him, did you?"

Grabowski acted shocked and hurt. "What do I look like?"

"I'd rather not say," Abie answered.

They both laughed and went back inside.

At midnight Arthur walked slowly toward the back of the cutting house. Crickets chirped at him to go home, but he kept moving ahead in the dark alley, touching the side of the warehouse to guide him whilst stepping carefully so as not to fall in an unseen hole.

When he turned the corner, he saw the pull-down door raised open about two feet from the ground, a thick bar of light coming from inside. The closer he got to that door the slower he moved. When he was an arm's length away, he bent down to look through the opening. He saw the inside of the warehouse, empty but well lit. He thought about turning around and running home—maybe he would have, if he had a home to run back to and a father to protect him. But he didn't have any of that so he went inside.

The cutting house was empty—Grabowski had sent the night workers out for a long break. Arthur looked at the stacks of crates everywhere. He crept into the middle of the big room, by the main mixing vat. After some hesitation, he dipped a finger in and then put it in his mouth. When he got a taste of the Old Log, it made him grimace and spit. Then he heard a sound in the far corner, a low whirring noise.

He followed that sound till he got to the source—a contraption unlike anything he'd seen before. It was a black box with a big glass eye and it moved slowly from left to right, then jerked to a stop and started moving the other way. It took Arthur a minute to absorb that the object moving in front of him was a camera. He looked into the lens and saw a reflection of his head, misshapen as in a funhouse mirror.

"Huh. Movin' pictures," he said to himself.

This shy boy who never smiled now grinned into the camera and even took a bow, the kind of showy move he may have picked up watching Barkley. Whilst he was doubled over, he heard another sound and at first it seemed like another whirring camera somewhere behind him, but then it sounded more like a low growl. Arthur slowly straightened up but he didn't turn around right away. He heard another growl. He froze and it was quiet for a few seconds. But he was a curious boy and he just had to see what was behind him. So he turned around fast, and that was when things got serious indeed.

That night around three in the morning, a half moon shone its light on the black river whilst the Canadian Whiskey sign flashed across the water. It was all very quiet until there was a splash. A large bag was dropped in the shallow water and the one who dropped it was now up to his knees in the muck but didn't care. He just looked this way and that to make sure no one saw him. Then he tried to lift one foot out of the sucking marsh; when he did, the other foot with all the weight on it now sunk a little deeper. He cursed and got agitated and started scratching his face and a bit of dead skin fell off him and onto the water and it stayed there floating above the sunken bag long after he extracted himself and got in his car and left.

When Riley got word that Ten wanted to talk to him, he brought Bud with him. Their car pulled up in front of the building that housed Ten's Spot, and the two of them went inside. The speakeasy was almost empty. The men who were drinking their money troubles away a couple of days ago had run dry and gone home. There were just a few sad souls left and one of them was Ten, alone at a table staring into a drink. As soon as she saw Riley and Bud, she got up so quick she almost fell. Bud ran up to steady her with a hand on the elbow. She nodded toward the back and they followed her to her so-called boudoir.

Inside, Bud was taken with the room, whistling softly whilst fingering the red satin on the walls. Ten sat down right away and looked up at Riley. Her eyes were red and watery.

"I got to ask you something," she said to Riley. She waited for his nod and then went on. "Have they identified those remains found by the river?"

Riley shook his head. "Not enough left to identify, I'm afraid."

Ten nodded as if expecting that answer. "You know about the boy who stayed with me?" she said.

"I believe my wife met him."

"She did. His name is Arthur and he's gone missing."

Saying those words made Ten lower her head and her shoulders started to quiver. Riley was no good at comforting strangers so he just stood stiff and watched her cry. It was Bud who stepped forward and wrapped an arm around her.

"Kids his age run away all the time," Bud said. "They're gone a couple of days and they come back."

Riley should have seconded that but didn't because he had a feeling it wasn't true in this case. And Ten had more than a feeling. She looked up at Riley.

"I have something for you," she said.

She wanted to say more but needed to take a few deep breaths first. Then she balled up her fists in her lap and continued. "There's been some ugly talk around here last couple nights. One story in particular."

She was squeezing her fists closed so hard the color went out of her hands. "It's got somethin' to do with a boy who got killed. And somethin' about a movin' picture that was made. Of the killing."

Bud looked at Riley but Riley kept looking at Ten.

"Me, I didn't know what to think," Ten said. "Sometimes people get loaded and just talk nonsense. But last night *he* was in here, braggin'."

"He?" Riley said.

"The one with the scaly skin. Sayin' to them all, 'I got it right here in my pocket—you wanna see, buy a ticket.'"

Riley hunched forward in his seat now.

"He was gettin' drunker and drunker," Ten went on. "And I said to my bouncer Marcus—he used to pick pockets—I said, can you get what's in that soused fool's jacket?"

She was opening a drawer now as she talked. Riley saw little furry objects that he recognized as rabbit's feet. This made his hand go straight for his own pocket to feel for the one he was carrying, given to him by Nan for luck.

Ten reached past the little feet to the back of the drawer. "And you know what Marcus said to me?"

She had the big round film canister in her hand now and held it up. "He said a pickpocket never loses his touch."

Riley was at a loss for words but his hand went straight for that can. "Do you mind if I…"

"Take it," Ten said as she handed it to him with her head turned so she wouldn't see even the can. "Get it out of here. I don't want to see what's on it. And I don't want to be anywhere near it when that madman wakes up this mornin' and figures out it's gone."

Riley held the can for a minute and then handed it to Bud. His own hands now free, he forced himself to reach out to Ten. He took her squeezed fists in his hands.

"I just want you to look at it," she said, as the tears ran down her cheeks, "and then you can tell me the one thing I need to know."

As he held her fists he realized there was something inside one of them and he knew without looking it must be a rabbit's foot.

TWENTY-TWO

Having been handed this horrible prize Riley now had to open it and see what was inside. He had no means of playing the film himself. The only way to watch it was to make arrangements with a manager he knew at the Cass Theater. Once that was set up, he stopped at home where Nan's quiet day was about to change. He explained to her about the visit to Ten and the film reel. He never asked her to do anything—she volunteered.

"I have to go with you," she said. "How else will you know if it's him?"

"You shouldn't see such a thing," he said.

"Neither should you. If we watch together maybe it won't be as bad."

She got Mrs. O'Brien next door to watch the toddler Jean, and then joined Riley and Bud as they all went to the Cass that afternoon, between shows. The manager led them into an empty theater where the three of them sat near the back, with Bud off to the side. It was strange having the theater to themselves. The lights went out and Nan took hold of Riley's arm with both hands. They sat in the dark for a minute with nobody saying anything.

The screen lit up. There was no sound, and at first it was just scratchy lines onscreen and then it got all blurry. Then the blur became a close-up view of something ugly: Grabowski's face looking into the camera just after he'd just switched it on.

Nan held her hand in front of her eyes and peeked through fingers split apart. "My God, who is that?"

"You don't want to know," Riley said.

On the screen, Grabowski stepped backwards in the center of the picture but the view began to move away from him, as the camera shifted its focus to the left side of the warehouse.

"They must have had it rigged to make it rotate," Riley said.

After the view moved to the left, it started coming back to the right and once again found Grabowski, smaller now and still stepping backwards. Then it kept moving to the right and found more empty space, just crates stacked against a distant wall. When it started coming back to the left again Grabowski was gone from view. For the next few long minutes the picture just scanned the empty warehouse, right to left and left to right, again and again.

On about the fifth swing to the left they saw movement in the back—someone coming through a door, but the camera moved away before they could see who. Riley wrapped an arm around Nan's shoulders and felt her shaking; she still had that hand in front of her eyes, peeking through. The camera view scanned back and Riley felt the jolt in Nan's body. There was Arthur, dipping his finger in the vat. Nan closed the window between her fingers and buried her face in her hands.

"Is that him?" Riley whispered but he didn't really have to ask.

Riley stayed seated—no way to get up fast with the leg—but with a firm grip on her shoulders he helped guide Nan up from her seat as she kept her face covered. He looked to Bud who was already out of his seat and coming to help. Bud took hold of Nan's shoulders from Riley.

"Both of you wait for me in the lobby, I'll just be a minute," Riley said softly. "I've got to see this through."

Bud and Nan left the theater with Nan never looking up. By the time Riley turned back to the screen, Arthur was smiling and bowing for the camera, which then moved away from him to the side of the empty warehouse again. When it returned, Arthur was in the same position but there was movement behind him, in the background and out of focus. Riley tried to see what it was but the camera moved away. He couldn't wait for the camera to come back and he also wished it wouldn't. When it did, that blur in the background became clear: Grabowski was bent down unleashing two dogs. Or *were* they dogs?

The camera moved away again to the calm and empty space and by the time it returned Arthur was trying to run and one of the animals had hold of his pants leg, whilst the other leaped at his outstretched arm. The camera moved away again and when it returned it seemed they'd disappeared but that was because they were all down on the floor under the camera's view, and there were just glimpses jutting up from the lower part of the picture: first a bit of tail and then a pair of pointy ears, a furry back and finally a quick look at the animal's full face, with pale eyes and dark smears on the mouth and teeth. Arthur was unseen. The camera moved away again to the empty space and by the time it swiveled back around Riley was out of his seat and leaving the theater.

In the Cass lobby, Nan sipped a cup of water and Bud had a hand—the one missing the finger—laid upon hers for comfort. Riley joined them and reached for her as Bud pulled back his own hand and put it in his pocket.

Riley held her for a while and they did not talk. Bud stood nearby, then said quietly to Riley, "Maybe I should go tell Ten."

Nan looked up at Riley. "I think she should hear it from you," she said.

Riley nodded. "I'll take you home first."

"Bud can take me. You need to tell her right away."

They waited whilst Riley got the film from the projection room. When he came back he put a hand on Bud's shoulder.

"Stay at the house till I get back," he said. His other hand was holding the film can, which he now handed to Bud. "And hang onto this and guard it with your life."

When Riley got back to the speakeasy, he walked quick as a stump could take him through the front door and down that hallway and into the big lantern room, where he noticed the tables had been abandoned. Then he saw a group of men clustered outside the door of Ten's boudoir, whispering to each other.

"What's going on?" Riley yelled.

One of the men turned around. "Dunno, something happened in there. Lotta screaming, then a scary lookin' guy walks out. She's still in there, but won't open up. I was gonna call the cops, but... hell, this is a blind pig, ya can't call a cop."

Riley pushed past the men and knocked hard on Ten's door.

"It's Riley," he yelled through the red satin padding.

The door opened partway and Ten peeked out. One eye was red from crying; the other was swollen shut with seepage at the edges. Her lower lip had a split in it. She was wearing a beige and black silk dress with a blood smear on the skirt.

"Jesus," Riley said.

"He came back sooner than I thought he would," she said. "So did you."

She let him in and walked to the bed, then let herself down gingerly using her hands for a soft landing. She didn't look up as Riley came into the room and stood over her. He cupped his hand under her chin and delivered the news like God from above.

"I don't know how to say it, so I'm just gonna say it," he said.

"You don't have to, 'cause I know," she said.

"It was Arthur," he said anyway, because he knew she'd need to hear the words spoken before she could accept it as a fact.

She didn't react much, just a sniffle.

"I just wanted to be sure," she said, nodding to herself. "Understand, he was no kin. Don't even know where he came from. He just drifted in. Then he stuck to me like a burr." She smiled at Riley and the split in her lip opened. "Couldn't shake him," she said.

She didn't cry at first but then suddenly the dam burst and she hid her face whilst her body quivered. Riley didn't know what to do with his hand, but then found it was stroking the back of her head. She talked into her hands as she cried.

"Don't know why I got involved with all these people," she sobbed. "I didn't mean to. Just wanted my own place is all."

Riley's eye was scanning the room and surveying the wreckage: A mirror broken, a chair knocked over. There was a little pile of shattered glass on the bedside table and in the midst of it was something that looked like Lady Liberty on her back.

"Where's Barkley?" he said softly. "Why isn't he here with you?"

"Hasn't shown his face in days," she said to her hands.

"And how'd you get rid of Grabowski? What'd you tell him?"

"I told him I just found the film layin' on the floor in the bar. And he said 'Where is it now bitch' and I didn't know what else to say but the truth—that I gave it to you."

When he heard those words, Riley felt a jolt go through his whole body; he even felt it in the leg that wasn't there. And by the time Ten lifted her face from her hands, he was gone and she was alone again.

Whilst all this craziness was going on (again, without my knowledge), I was having barley soup at the Crime with Abie. He kept talking to me about Max, which he did a lot lately. He did not speak directly to Max anymore, nor did he use his name—it was always "your brother."

"Your brother is becoming more and more of what's called paranoid," he said to me. I tried to ignore him and read the paper, which was full of its usual lies. So there was my choice: I could read lies or listen to bullshit.

Abie said, "Do you know what that means, paranoid?"

I didn't have to answer because he'd tell me anyway.

"It means when he looks around he see enemies and threats everywhere," Abie said.

I didn't say so, but it sounded like he was describing me. Or maybe any sighted person living in Detroit.

It was at this point that, speak of the devil, Max came rushing into the Crime. He arrived very jumpy and agitated, which either meant something was wrong or that he was just acting normal. I was tired of listening to Abie and so I was relieved to see Max arrive, though the feeling soon passed.

"We got big trouble," Max said.

And Abie looked at me and said: "See what I mean?"

Max came up and stood beside our table, scratching the inside of his forearm.

"And the scratching is another tell-tale sign," Abie said to me.

Max said to him, "Are you talking about me?"

"I'm not talking to you," Abie said.

"I know, but are you talking *about* me?"

I told everyone to shut up and made room for Max to sit beside me in the booth. Because he seemed agitated, I passed him my glass of water and he started gulping it down. Unfortunately, this gave him the hiccups. He went ahead with his news anyway.

"It's Grabowski—*hic*," he said.

"What about him?"

Then Max started taking deep breaths whilst Abie got up and went to the counter for something.

"Where are you going?" I said.

He came back with a small brown bag in his hand, sat down, and handed me the empty bag. "If you happen to run into your brother, tell him to breathe in this bag to get rid of his hiccups."

I handed the bag to Max, who wouldn't take it.

"That's a myth—*hic*—bags don't work," he said.

It would work if I put it over your entire head and tied it shut at the neck, I thought.

Abie said, "Joe, if you see your brother, please inform him--"

At this point I pounded my fist on the table so hard that some soup jumped out of the bowl.

"Not another word from you," I said to Abie, who then turned his big body sideways in the booth and shook his head.

I turned back to Max. "Now can you please tell me what you came to tell me."

It took a while but Max eventually explained that Grabowski had been drunk at Ten's Spot the night before, was rambling on about a film he had—something about a dinge boy getting eaten. "Then, today I get a call from one of our guys at Ten's Spot. Grabowski came back this afternoon, looking for something. *Hic.*"

"The film?"

"Don't know. But he roughed up Ten Jenkins before he left. And then Riley showed up. And *he* just left in a big hurry."

I rapped on the table to get Abie's attention. "You and I are gonna take a ride, but first you must stop being mad."

"What about me?" Max said.

"You go over to Ten's. Talk to her, see what you can find out."

"What if—*hic*—she won't talk to me?"

"Use your charm on her," I said and then ankled out the door.

A few minutes later whilst riding in the Doozie, I turned to Abie who was driving. "Tell me the truth. Did you know about this?"

"Only that he spotted a dinge boy hanging around the cutting house the other day," Abie said.

"Was it that kid of Ten's?"

"I didn't see him," Abie said.

I looked out the window and we were passing one of the latest downtown monstrosities, these so-called skyscrapers. The bottom half of the building was finished, but the top half was just girders and scaffolding. Pigeons perched on those empty shelves.

"You can't believe everything people say," Abie said to me from behind the wheel.

I kept looking out the window. "But if it's true," I said, "I have my limits."

"He took you in when you were almost dead."

"Still, I have my limits. With anybody."

"Anybody? What if it was somebody who pulled you out of the river?"

"Anybody."

"And what if it was your brother?"

I didn't answer that because it was stupid, so I kept looking out the window whilst Abie got a bitter face and nodded to himself.

At Riley's house Bud kneeled beneath St. Jude on the mantle and finished laying a fire. Across the room, Nan leaned over the rail of a day crib and tucked a blanket around a sleeping Jean.

"I can't understand it, Bud," she said. "To do such a thing to a child. How did these people become such monsters?"

Bud looked back over his shoulder at her. "*These* people?"

Nan was taken aback. "I mean the Purples. Who else?"

Bud poked at a log trying to get it to catch, and in the meantime talked with his back to her.

"You know, when Joe Bernstein was a teenager I looked up to him," he said. "He was fearless. The old Sugar House gangsters who used to snoop around the Bishops School looking for fresh talent—they tapped him right away."

"They ever try to recruit you?" Nan asked.

"No, no I was one of the good kids—star of the basketball team, pillar of the Young Men's Hebrew Association. I moved in a different circle. But still I had to respect Bernstein and his boys. Nobody told them what to do."

Nan began walking away from the crib toward Bud, but she stopped when she noticed something on the wood floor—a tuft of white that she took for goose down from a pillow. She picked it up and put in her pocket. "What changed your opinion of them?"

Bud didn't answer at first. He thought about whether to tell the story or not. He didn't tell it to just anyone but felt he might want to tell it to Nan. She had this effect on people.

"Well, there was an incident," he said. "It was a little thing, really. But it became a big thing."

Nan sat down on the divan, nearby. He stayed hunched by the fire holding the poker, but turned his body to face her.

"This was 1918—Bernstein was seventeen at the time. He did odd jobs for the Sugar House Gang, kid stuff. They had him plant a stink bomb in the shop of some poor guy who crossed Buster Weintraub. Bernstein got skunked by his own bomb—which made it pretty obvious, next day, who had bombed the shop."

"Did they arrest him?"

Bud laughed. "The cops didn't care about some merchant on Hastings. The neighborhood policed itself."

Bud got up from the fire and went to the divan to sit next to her. "One of my teammates on the ball team, it was his father's shop. We felt we had to do something—to show that the good boys, the athletes, could stand up to the troublemakers. So we confronted Joe and his boys."

Bud paused for a moment. Had he heard something—a creak from upstairs? Nan was wrapped up in the story now and hadn't noticed anything and Bud wasn't sure he had, either.

"Go on," she said. "Don't keep me in suspense."

"That afternoon we walked down to the school and I guess the word got there before we did. It was like the Roman Coliseum—all the students pressed against the fence surrounding the schoolyard, which was cleared out except for Joe, Abie and Grabowski. And Max, too—he was sitting on the ground against the fence, rocking back and forth. There were five of us and four of them, but we were a couple of years younger. I led the way and Joe stepped forward to meet me. I remember he smelled like rotten eggs. Grabowski was beside him—scary looking kid. He was staring at my hand. I figured he was checking for a weapon, but I had nothing except a tournament ring on my finger."

Nan couldn't help it—her eyes went straight to his hand, resting in his lap. She quickly looked back up in his eyes, but Bud said, "It's okay, you can look. Anyway, we were all faced off and then suddenly Max—still down there sitting against the fence—started seizing up. And one of the boys in my group laughed and called him a freak. Joe rushed at the loudmouth, elbows flying. Right away, we knew were out of our league—Joe took down one of our guys and then another. Abie took two at the same time and threw them against the fence. That left me. And Grabowski."

Nan shook her head but didn't speak.

"He had me pinned beneath him and when he pulled out the knife I thought he was going to cut my throat. Then it seemed like he was going to slash my wrist. And then I realized he was after the ring. I must have blacked out when he did it—I remember opening my eyes and seeing Abie pulling him away from me. And Grabowski was holding it tight in his bloody hand like a treasure, though of course it was just tin, it was worthless. The ring I mean. The finger, that wasn't worthless, not to me."

Bud swallowed and looked away.

"I'm so sorry this happened to you," Nan said.

Bud shook his head, looking down at the floor now, his neck reddening. "In the end, what was it? A schoolyard fight. No one got killed. But the repercussions—you would have thought it was a mass murder. The newspaper did a big story. And Rabbi Franklin was incensed that someone would do this to one of the Hebrew Association boys. The merchants were all scandalized—that's when that Purple name was really stamped on them."

"Did they arrest Grabowski?"

Bud shook his head.

"He took off—went to hide in the woods up north."

"And Joe?"

"He was never seen around the school after that—Buster Weintraub took him in at the Sugar House. And he got deeper into Weintraub's gang for the next two years. Until the other thing happened, with the Palmer Raids and the girl."

The ceiling creaked—louder this time. Bud and Nan both looked up, and then at each other.

"Okay, that's twice," Bud said. "I better check." He got up and walked to the foot of the stairs.

Nan stood up. "Bud, maybe you should wait down here…"

He put a finger to his lips for quiet and then started to step softly up the stairs. Nan didn't know what to do but found herself going to Jean's playpen. She looked down at the sleeping child in the pen with wooden bars on all sides. She smoothed the blanket.

"No need to fret," she whispered to the child though she was really talking to herself.

She heard a loud thud upstairs. The glasses in the china cabinet rattled from the force.

"Bud! You all right?" she called out but got no answer back.

She looked all around without knowing what she was looking for—but knew when she saw it. She went straight to the fireplace and grabbed the poker. For a moment, she placed her fingers on the St. Jude statue on the mantle.

"Jude," she whispered, "please help that young man upstairs."

Holding her poker, she walked back to the crib and as she got there she saw something at the top of the stairs peeking through the slats under the banister: Pale, eager eyes looking right at her.

Her heart stopped and she felt a rush of heat to her face. She thought she might faint, but only for a second. Then she felt another wave, a cold one, and this one brought clarity and strength. She felt the fight rising in her blood. She backed up and stood in front of the crib, both hands gripping the poker, whilst she kept watch on that staircase. The animal kept looking sideways through the slats as it came down the steps, slow and slouching, the chain round the neck jingling. Following behind it down those steps were pudgy black shoes bursting at the laces.

She turned her face to the ceiling and screamed through the plaster. "Bud!"

"He can't hear ya," Grabowski said quietly as he came into full view at the bottom of the stairs. He held the chain leash firm with both hands and the beast by his knees stood still.

"What have you done to him?" Nan said, low but firm—no quiver in her voice.

Grabowski looked at her and then beyond her, to the playpen. "Y'know, me an' Bud were ol' pals from the schoolyard. But I never forgave 'im for givin' me the finger one day."

He smiled a toothless smile. "That's a joke," he said.

He started moving—not toward her but to the fireplace. The beast followed but kept eyeing her. At the fireplace, Grabowski took the film can from under his arm, opened it and threw the shiny black film onto the fire. It hissed.

"This was not s'posed to be seen by the whole stinkin' world," he said to the flames. "How come people grab what ain't theirs?"

He turned back to face her. "Have ya met Ono?" he said, nodding down at the animal. "Don't be scared'a him. Y'know, his breed are the most misunderstood bastards on earth. Since way back, they been chased, feared... *accused.*"

He let loose a bit of chain and Ono, feeling the slack, lowered its head whilst taking a few slow steps forward. Nan stepped back until she felt the railing of the low crib against her legs.

Grabowski allowed Ono to pull him a few steps toward Nan. She felt the metal of the poker handle slip in her sweaty palms, so she tightened her grip. Then she heard a small sound behind her: Jean was awake now, looking through the bars at the doggie, pointing with her little finger. Ono must've noticed, because the eyes were now fixed on the child, not Nan.

Grabowski reached his hand down to the chain collar. "You'd neva know to look at 'im, but he can almost eat a whole dinge boy. And as fer a baby mick—he'd finish that off, no problem."

"He'll have to eat his way through me first," Nan said.

"Ya hear that?" he said to Ono. "She's invitin' ya to come on over and dine."

Grabowski had just unfastened the leash when Nan heard the front door opening and prayed it was Riley—though she also prayed it wasn't, for his sake. The first prayer was answered, and as Riley rushed into the room moving faster than a man with a cane has ever moved, Ono changed direction in mid-lunge and went straight for the leg that was closest—which was not a real one. As the beast tore the pants leg away and tried to sink its teeth into the wooden peg, it must've wondered if it was fighting a man or a tree. Riley reached down to grab the white fur on the neck and at the same time Ono lunged up, knocking him off balance. In a flash Riley was on his back with Ono above him. The jaws locked onto his arm, and this limb was more to the animal's liking.

Little Jean wailed in her crib whilst Grabowski watched the fight with glee, pulling a blood-stained knife from his waistband. He was so focused on Riley and the beast that he forgot about Nan and that was a mistake. She swung the poker down hard on the hand holding the knife and the blade dropped to the floor right between her and Grabowski. They both looked down at it but only she had the swift feet of a dancer. As Grabowski bent and reached for the knife she swept her foot and kicked the knife toward her husband. The blade skidded across the wood leaving a red smear as it went. It stopped a couple of feet away from Riley.

Riley had a fistful of Ono's throat and was trying to free his arm from its jaws when he saw that knife slide toward him like a missile. He let go of the furry throat and reached and fumbled and then grabbed the knife handle. In one hard thrust he plunged the blade into the side of Ono's neck. The animal did not know it was dead—it kept the grip on Riley's arm even after the pale eyes went glassy. Then its legs buckled and the beast lay gently on Riley's pounding chest as if to nap. He pushed it off him and at the same time pulled the knife from the neck. The head, eyes still open, thudded against the floor.

For a moment all that commotion gave way to stillness. Grabowski stood in shock, looking at his dead pup; Nan looked at Riley to see if he was all right; Riley looked at Grabowski and pondered the next move. Even Jean had stopped crying and gone quiet. Grabowski broke the spell when he reached in his jacket for his gun. As he did, Nan raised her poker again whilst Riley pinched the wet sticky blade of the knife between his fingers and prepared to throw it.

Then all three of them got a surprise as a yell came from the front door.

"Hold it!"

It was the short fat Fed, with his gun drawn and pointed at Grabowski. And coming in the door right behind him was the tall Fed, also with gun drawn. And behind him was a cop in uniform and then another. Grabowski found himself facing four men with guns, another with a knife, and a woman with a poker who knew how to use it. For once in his life he did the sensible thing, bending down to place his own gun on the floor and then raising his hands over his head.

Nan rushed to Riley, whose left arm was bleeding badly.

"Are you okay?" she cried, reaching out to touch him.

Riley's first reaction was to place the palm of his right hand flat upon her stomach and what was inside.

"Are *we* okay?" he asked.

She swallowed and nodded.

"What about Bud?" Riley asked.

She didn't answer, just turned her eyes to the stairs and up them. Riley started to lift himself, his arm dripping and his wood leg exposed and pocked with teeth marks.

"I don't know if you should go up there," she said, but there was no way to stop him.

He went up the steps without his cane, which was still on the floor near Ono. When he got to the top step he didn't have to go further. He could see Bud on the floor in the middle of the hall. He was face down but an arm was reaching out on the floor in front of him, and the hand with the missing finger was clutched, as if trying to grab hold of the floor. One of his legs was bent at the knees. He was in a red puddle made from his open throat, but there was also a long red smear on the floor behind him. Riley saw that, and saw the position of the arms and legs, and knew: Bud had tried, to the very end, to crawl to those stairs. Riley checked the pulse even though there was no need. Then he went back to the stairs and almost fell down them—managing to steady himself on the banister. He slowly came back down holding the rail with both hands.

Grabowski was cuffed and a cop was pulling on his arm, but he wasn't quite ready to go. He waited for Riley to come down. Riley looked him in the eye and saw that even though Grabowski had a grin on his face, his eyes were teary. Grabowski looked over at Ono and then back at Riley.

"I still have one left," he said. "And I swear on my life... he's gonna *devour* your family."

The cop now yanked hard on the arm and pulled him out the front door whilst Grabowski kept his eyes trained on Riley and then on Nan until he was gone.

Nan came over to Riley again. She'd ripped a strip off the bottom of her slip and began wrapping his arm. The Feds also came over.

"Good thing we were tailing you," the short fat one said.

Riley was too numb to answer.

"We saw you pop into the speakeasy," the tall one said. "What'd you stop there for?"

This reminded Riley of something he'd forgotten about. He turned to Nan. "What about the film?"

She nodded over to the fire. Riley could see the last traces of his evidence going up in smoke.

"What film?" the tall Fed asked.

"Nothing," Riley said, shaking his head. "Doesn't matter now."

Riley walked over to the window and peered out. He saw the squad car at the curb, Grabowski climbing into the back seat. He also saw a man in a hat bent over at the driver's window, talking to the cop behind the wheel. He couldn't make out who it was until the car pulled away and then he saw it was yours truly.

I stood staring after the cop car that drove Grabowski away. Then I turned and walked to where Abie was standing and put both my hands on Abie's big shoulders and looked into his eyes. Abie tried to look away—didn't want to hear what I had to say to him. But I made him listen. His head slumped down now, and he nodded. Then I clapped his shoulder and we turned to leave.

Riley was still watching us go when he realized Nan had come up behind him at the window.

"We should get you to the hospital," she said.

"Fine, but then we have to stop by Baird's. Tell him about Bud."

"We?" she said.

"From now on," he said, putting his one unchewed arm around her, "I am not leaving you alone. Ever."

TWENTY-THREE

It was a short ride from Riley's house to the downtown cell where Grabowski was being driven. But a lot can happen in a short ride, especially on Detroit streets. Here is one version of what transpired: Halfway there, Grabowski managed, from the backseat, to kick the driver in the head. The car veered out of control and crashed on the side of the road, knocking both cops in the front seat woozy. At this point Grabowski, still in cuffs, walked out of the car and was gone by the time the cops regained their senses.

That is version A, whilst version B holds that the cops, just before leaving the crime scene, were advised that if they should happen to get into a minor crash and lose consciousness, they would be eligible for a large benefit (without even having to file a claim). Believe what you like, they're both credible—at the time, Detroit cops were equally susceptible to screwups and payoffs.

Riley, upon hearing from Teddy Baird about Grabowski's escape, chose to believe version B. And after all that had happened, up to and including the rabies shots he'd just gotten at the hospital, this latest news became the last straw.

With Nan and young Jean waiting out in the hallway, Riley, his arm bandaged, sat across from Baird's desk. Baird had a drink in front of him and was looking down into it with red eyes, occasionally glancing up to see if Riley was still staring at him.

"Well, don't look at *me*," Baird complained. "I wasn't driving that damn cop car." He peered at Riley. "Say something."

Riley didn't say anything right away; he was busy taking out his wallet and removing his badge and ID from it. He laid them on the desk in front of Baird. "You don't need me, Teddy," he said. "You need a new mayor, a new police force. You need judges who aren't bought and sold. And a Grand Jury wouldn't hurt. And maybe some witnesses who don't have amnesia."

When Riley got up to leave, Baird got desperate. "Harry," he said, "think about this: If you just walk away now, then what did Bud die for?"

Riley just shook his head at that and wouldn't even look back as he said his parting words to Baird: "He isn't even cold, and you're already trying to make hay out of his death."

Later that same night, the moon was full and there was a chill in the air; Grabowski had felt that chill too long and wanted to go home. In younger days he survived in the woods and then in a cold basement, but that was when he had a tougher hide that he'd long since shed, shingle by shingle. These days he liked his comfort and needed some right now. So the fugitive made his way on foot back to his house in Grosse Pointe. (Yes, he lived in that tony neighborhood—in those days they could keep out dinges and Jews, but a Polack with cash couldn't be stopped.)

He slowly and carefully turned the knob on the back door and poked his head in to see if any surprises awaited him. Then he stepped inside and closed the door behind him. He leaned his back against it and let out a deep breath.

"What a ballbusta of a day," he muttered.

Even a man like Grabowski needs unconditional love in his darkest hour and so he called out:

"Ogod, where are ya?"

But the call wasn't answered. Grabowski walked into his dark living room and turned on a light. The beast was sleeping peacefully on a little fleece bed made just for him, right beside an easy chair. On the other side of the chair was another little bed that was empty and when Grabowski saw that, he felt a pang—but only for a second, because someone like Grabowski does not feel anything for long.

He flopped down in the chair, and reached down to stroke Ogod's back. "Miss yer brother already, don'cha?" he said.

Ogod kept sleeping. Grabowski nudged the shoulder and nothing happened. Then he turned and reached down with both hands, cupping them under the beast's head, holding its face up to him. He looked into the open eyes—no longer pale, they were blood red now. Grabowski drew back his hands and the head dropped straight down onto the doggie pillow, the red eyes still staring into nowhere. Then Grabowski sunk back in his own chair trying to absorb what this meant. As he did, a large hand clamped onto his shoulder and pinned him to the back of his seat. He became aware of something in his ear and from the corner of his eye he could see a long blade, which was now inside the ear but not quite touching anything. He didn't dare move his head with the blade in the ear, so he kept still. He couldn't see Abie but he heard him whisper from behind.

"He didn't suffer," Abie said. "I went in through the ear, straight to the cortex."

If this was supposed to make Grabowski feel better it did not.

"Gonna do the same to me?" he asked, still frozen.

"You shouldn't have killed that poor kid. And left evidence."

"I had to—he was spyin' on us. And I took care 'a the evidence. It's burnt."

"And then on top of that you go and kill that basketball guy, all these years after you first deformed him."

"Self-defense," Grabowski said, his head still perfectly still. "He come at me tryin' ta do me harm."

"Were you gonna kill the lady, too? And her baby?"

"Whadda ya think I am? What do I look like to you?"

When Abie didn't answer, Grabowski said, "Yer suppose ta make a joke when I say that."

"This is not my decision," Abie said. "It's what Joe wants."

"But ya know who's behind this don't ya? Max poisoned Joe on me. He never wanted me in, ever. Just cuz I'm a Pole. Just cuz I'm not a Jew."

"I have no choice," Abie said.

"Sure ya do. We all do—you told me that, rememba? Free thinkin.'"

"You mean free will," Abie said.

"Yeah. Tell me about free will."

Abie paused. "Now?"

"No, after I'm dead. Come on, tell me."

Abie thought about it some more.

"Okay," he said. "But afterwards, I'll still have to kill you."

The next day the sun came up for some but not others. But even for those who saw it shine, it was a day when the mood in Detroit was dark and ugly. It was different from the first few days after the crash, when people were shocked and then dejected. Now they'd moved to the next stage—they wanted someone to pay.

Nobody understood this better than Barkley. That afternoon as he prepared for his radio show, amongst his research tools were old copies of *The Dearborn Independent*. He took his notes to the mike at the appointed hour, and after a few introductory remarks, he got to the point:

"My common herd," he said into the mike, *"I know that some of you have asked of me the following: 'Why should we not go all the way—recall the Mayor, replace the police chief?'*

"And I can only reply, it is not the Democratic way to reverse elections. It is wrong to overturn our system in such a way. So I cannot, in good conscience, urge you to recall our duly elected officials..."

Barkley looked up from his script now because he noticed someone coming into the booth. He shifted in his seat when he saw who it was, but still tried to smile and nod whilst continuing with the broadcast.

"... and while I have been critical of our Mayor, he is not the real source of our financial woes."

Barkley used his finger to locate something in the old newspaper beside him.

"As Mr. Ford once advised us in his fine newspaper, we must point a finger at the merchant bankers—the Rothschilds and their ilk. Shyly cutting

*international deals, and selling the ground out from under us… While their
lower-class brethren, with names like Bernstein, traffic in booze and death.
Till we rid ourselves of them… we will have no peace in Detroit."*

When he finished, he turned off the mike and faced his visitor.
It was Riley, in a chair now, sitting in judgment. "Tell me, Jerry,"
he said, "when was it you opted to sell your soul?"

Barkley smiled of course but these days even his smile was
worn down and crooked. "Oh, Harry," he said. "It was so long
ago. Can't recall an exact date."

Riley looked him over and this made Barkley fold his arms and
then cross his legs, like a man caught naked.

"Remember that talk we had back in the speakeasy?" Riley said.
"About how you were going to be a man of the people?"

"Maybe I'm just the man these people deserve," Barkley said.

"And what about Tennessee—does she deserve to be left alone
at a time like this? Do you even care about what's happened to
her? And to the boy?"

The mention of the boy seemed to kill Barkley's smile. "Are
you going to prosecute me now?" he said. "Because there's a
rumor going round that you've given up that game. Which makes
me wonder why you're still asking questions."

"You're right," Riley said. "I have no more questions. All I have
to say is—you've let me down, Jerry."

Barkley tried to laugh it off but nothing came out. "Well, I'll
just have to live with that somehow," he said.

As Riley got up, Barkley extended a hand but Riley just looked
at the hand and then turned and left. And after he did, Barkley
sagged in his chair whilst pulling open a drawer. It had a gun and a
bottle in it. He took the bottle and closed the drawer.

Barkley wasn't the only one with troubles: More and more, the
Purples were feeling blue, for various reasons. The cops were now
reluctant to accept our grease—the blatant Grabowski escape
became an embarrassment to them, and there were still hard feelings about Clarke's disappearance. Meanwhile, the Detroit River
suddenly was full of Coast Guard boats, owing to a federal crack-

down in late '29. Both of our Gar-Max boats were seized, as part
of a massive operation ordered by the Feds. We watched as the
boats were hauled away, hoping they would be put up for auction.
But instead they were repainted and declared property of the Customs Department. Soon our own Gar-Maxes were back on the
river, patrolling against us. And you will never guess who rode
captain on one of them—old Howard Blakemore, who didn't have
to hide in the weeds anymore.

Because of the awful so-called economy, business was down in
every category: speakeasies, dry cleaners, kidnappings, all down.
Companies had to cut what is known as "discretionary spending"
which meant they couldn't even afford to hire someone to stink-
bomb the competition.

As a result, the gangster community saw a big rise in under-
employment (not to be confused with unemployment). Whilst
companies can do layoffs, it is not easy to lay off a member of a
gang: He may sell what he knows to the cops or the oilers. So what
happens is a slowdown, whence everyone remains on the roll except they hardly ever get paid or asked to do anything. They just
spend more time than ever sitting around the Crime of Michigan
and building igloos out of sugar cubes.

Adding to our problems, the oilers suddenly seemed more in-
clined to kill us. There were differing views on the cause of this.
Abie maintained that with Grabowski gone, there was less reason
to fear the Purples (though there were still many Purples adept at
inflicting GBH, Abie chief among them). Abie's point was that
Grabowski was legendary in his own way and that can scare people more than an ordinary goon with a gun.

But I felt the problem was more complicated. Previously, the
oilers had known that Riley would go after them (however ineffec-
tively). But they had no fear of Baird. They also had the Mayor
deep in their pocket, the Feds on their side, and Barkley on the air
supporting the Mayor and denouncing the Jews. This emboldened
them.

At the same time, the oilers were feeling the pinch of that lousy
so-called economy just like we were. They decided it was time to

grab some of our shrinking business and mounted an offensive, striking several times during early 1930. One attack left three of our men dead, including Handsome Ziggy Selbin. We all were upset, but Max took it especially hard—I guess he was closer to Ziggy than the rest of us. For a long time after, Max took to wearing a white carnation in his lapel, in Ziggy's honor.

Gorilla Kowalski was also lost to us in a separate ambush. His remarkable extremities almost saved him. With gunmen in pursuit, he fled out an apartment window and climbed hand over foot up the side of the brick building. He must've felt justifiably proud when he made it all the way to the roof. However there was an oiler with a gun waiting there, so he got shot anyway.

With the passing of the Gorilla, this time it was Abie's turn to be especially morose. "I felt like he understood me," Abie told me. And I thought to myself, *Well, I'm glad somebody did.*

There was one more thing happening in Detroit in 1930 that really bothered Abie, though it was a small thing. The local movie theaters, out of the blue, began to install metal seat backs. The newspapers blamed this too on the Purples, as if Abie the Agent had invented the very notion of stabbing people at the movies. (And even if he did, what about the imitators?) The timing could not have been worse because with all the bad things the oilers had done lately, Abie had developed a strong desire to go see a movie with John Livoli.

One good thing happened in early 1930—I brought Rachel home from Eloise, again. No, I did not do this because a certain meddling red-haired woman had suggested it. I did it because Rachel herself asked me, saying: "I think I'm finally ready to be myself again." I wasn't sure I knew who "herself" was anymore, but I paid off the hospital and brought her home.

I took special pains to prepare the house on Chicago Avenue for her return. There was a good-sized yard she could wander in with a fence so she wouldn't wander too far. There was a nice stove in the kitchen that included an oven, whose door was welded shut. There was a set of silverware with shiny forks and spoons but only the dullest of knives. There was a medicine chest that was locked up more securely than a bank vault.

At first, she mostly stayed in her room as if still confined. She remained lonely. She kept on worrying and writing down all kinds of queer predictions of doom and gloom. I would find them lying around the house. One time I was just sitting on the sofa and felt a crumple where I sat, and from my own ass I pulled a note predicting that Lucky Lindy was going to have a terrible crash. Some predictions didn't even make sense—i.e., something about "The Monkey" and how he was destined to control our thoughts.

She brought home that radio I gave her at Eloise. Like everyone else in Detroit, she was mad for the Motormouth, listened to him every night. Rachel had always been a great believer in the common man, and decided Barkley was the working stiff's hero. I had more than one disagreement with her on the subject.

She would say, "He is a friend to those in need." And also: "He cares, Joe. He really does."

I'd say: "I will make it simple for you: He hates Jews."

When I told her about his earlier work at the *Dearborn Independent*, she said, "Well, can't a person change?"

I said, "Do you know anyone who's changed? Have you changed, or me?" (This, of course, was the wrong thing to say to someone who badly wanted to believe she *had* changed.)

I tried to get her out of the house sometimes and it wasn't easy, but I did manage it one beautiful spring day.

I said, "What do you want to do today, Rachel? The city is all yours."

She said, "To hell with the city, let's go to Belle Isle."

"Okay," I said, "I'll call Abie and he can join us." She rolled her eyes—I guess she thought we'd go alone, but I needed Abie's protection more than ever at the time. I couldn't say that to her, so I told her Abie was an expert on Belle Isle and hence the perfect companion for this trip. She just rolled her eyes again.

When Max came upstairs and learned we were going to Belle Isle with Abie, he wanted to know why he wasn't going. I said there wouldn't be room in the boat for all of us. He wanted to know why there was room for Abie and not him. "He's twice my size," Max pointed out.

He had me there. But then I reminded Max that he always got seasick on boats. And he said, "How convenient for you."

When Abie arrived at the house I guess he had misunderstood, because he thought I was summoning him to a meeting and not a picnic. He saw Max sitting with me in the living room and he said, "So is this where we're gonna meet?"

I laughed and said I was under the impression we'd already met. I said, "I've met you, have you met me?"

And then he was as peeved at me as Max and Rachel were, and they all probably would have joined forces against me if not for the fact that they weren't speaking to one another.

In all the world you couldn't have found a finer place to be that day than in the middle of the Detroit River, on Belle Isle. The bright sun was filtered and dappled by the island's tall elms. Leaning out over the water were weeping willows, all along the banks of the island. In the gentle breeze, their long thin leaves were as easily swayed as a witness with a family.

In the midst of the island was a small man-made lake, filled on this day with canoes. Women with wide-brimmed sun hats sat across from men with sleeves rolled to the elbows. The men held paddles but did not use them because there was nowhere to go. The long boats just drifted whilst their passengers absorbed golden rays and little sips of illegal beer, smiling whenever one boat bumped gently into another.

Abie sat scrunched in the bow of our canoe, his big knees colliding, his long jacket off and his massive white shirt buttoned to the neck and at the wrists, glowing in the sun. One hand held an oar in place; the other propped open a book.

Across from him in the boat, I had my shirt off so the sun could bake my scars. I held up a folded newspaper with one hand, whilst the other stroked the sun-warmed dark hair of Rachel's head, resting against my knees. She sat lower than us, on a red pillow on the floor of the boat. She leaned back on my legs with her pale face to the sun, her skin so smooth that even in that spotlight you could not find a crease. A picnic basket beside her was open; sandwiches cut in half were stacked on a cloth napkin. There was also a bottle of Old Log Cabin whiskey with the cap off.

All in all it was a perfect moment, almost. There was one little bothersome thing: One of the boats alongside us had a sidewinder gramophone piping out songs the owner must have thought very apt: "Blue Skies," "By the Light of Silvery Moon," etcetera.

It wasn't so bad hearing the songs once or twice, but by the third playing it got tiresome. I gave Abie a nod and he took a paddle and steered the canoe over to the musical boat, and gave it a little bump, which made the song skip. The man in the boat let out a laugh when the boats bumped, but when he looked at Abie and then at me and then at my scars, his smile got lopsided. Since it was such a nice day I did not want to be severe so I offered the man a choice: He could turn off the gramophone or else keep playing it under the water. He made the wise choice.

And I guess there was a second little annoying thing, too. In the corner of my eye I'd been noticing another boat nearby; the couple in it weren't talking much and seemed like they might be listening to us. I turned to face them. "That paddle in your hand," I said to the man. "Now would be a good time to use it."

The man paddled away, as did another nearby boater who got spooked I guess. In a few minutes we had the whole side of the lake to ourselves whilst all the other boats bunched up on the other side. For the rest of the afternoon we were joined only by the ducks, who, unlike the other boaters, were not scared of us. We rewarded them by feeding them bread crusts from our sandwiches. We passed the Log back and forth several times—not enough to get tight but just enough to put a soft haze on things.

We just drifted like that, and it is a moment I will treasure: Rachel sleeping in the sun; Abie reading a book with his lips moving; and me stroking Rachel's hair whilst reading the paper.

As it happened, there was a story in the paper about Barkley and the success of his show. And I thought, *There is no escaping this guy*. I showed the article to Rachel when she woke up and she seemed to spend a long time staring at the picture of Barkley.

"*That's* him?" she said.

I said, "Have you ever seen such a big fat head before?"

And she said she had—but couldn't remember when or where.

When we got off the boat we split up because Abie had to get home to his wife and his oversized toddler. I drove Rachel across the Belle Isle bridge in the Doozie. Then she suddenly told me she remembered where she'd seen Barkley before.

"He was the one used to sneak around and watch everyone at the Highland Park Ford plant," she said. "I think he was the one who told the managers about me. About those little pieces of paper."

"Are you sure?" I said. Her memory could not always be trusted.

"Oh, yes, I remember him," she said. "The workers all used to call him the head spy, joking about his big head. He was there the day…" She trailed off.

"The day they threw you out in the street?" I said.

I could see her eyes starting to well up, thinking about the old incident, and I told her let's forget it (though I had no intention of forgetting). She turned her face to the car window.

As we drove, she opened that window and stuck her head out and with her long hair blowing sideways, she looked up at the stone arches of the bridge. Then she leaned her body out further, and turned head down to look into the water.

What she said next—"Oh my God"—I barely heard. She said the words low and they were almost lost in the wind. She pulled herself back in from the window and grabbed my forearm hard.

"Joe, you have to stop the car right now," she said. "Somebody is down there in the water. They must have jumped!"

I had my doubts but pulled the car over anyway. We got out and looked over the side of the bridge down into the river. There was nothing except an old cardboard box floating along.

"Is that what you saw?" I asked.

She shook her head. "It was definitely a person." Her eyes scanned the water.

Eventually I had to lead her back into the car because she wanted to keep looking.

When we were driving again, I said, "It was the box you saw. There was nobody in that water."

She was looking straight ahead with confused eyes. The crease of worry was back in her forehead. "Maybe by the time we looked it was too late," she said. She thought about it some more and added, "Or maybe too soon."

"What do you mean too soon? What are you talking about?"

I looked at her like she was crazy, and of course she was.

TWENTY-FOUR

Riley's body was floating in the middle of the water.

No, that wasn't him under the Belle Isle bridge. Riley was far from Detroit, on his back in his precious lake up north—his body perfectly still, eyes closed, little smile on his face. "Just a little peace," he murmured to himself. "It's all I ever asked for."

He floated for a good long time. Then he heard a distant buzzing sound. And it seemed to be getting louder. He opened his peepers and raised his head from the water, causing his leg to submerge. He started to tread, whilst scanning the wide surface of the lake. Far off, he saw something—a boat, roaring his way.

"Damn," he said. "There are no motorboats allowed on this lake."

The boat was getting closer but Riley couldn't see who was in it. The engine switched off and it began to drift toward him. He swam over and reached up a hand grabbing the side of the boat. Before he could pull himself up to see, that hand felt something— a cold snout against his fingers and then teeth digging into them. He pulled his hand back and saw he was missing the tip of a finger, his ring finger. He pushed himself away from the side of the boat and saw the wolf-dog in it, looking down at him. Grabowski came up from behind the beast, petting it and smiling down at Riley.

"Hiya!" he said.

Riley kept a safe distance from the boat whilst treading the water. He glanced down at his finger spilling blood into the lake, which in turn attracted small circling fish. He looked back up and the beast was poised to jump in the water after him but Grabowski grabbed its collar.

"Stay in the boat, boy," he said.

"What the hell are you doing here?" Riley yelled at Grabowski.

"Kinda far from shore, ain't ya?" Grabowski said.

Riley looked toward the shore and Grabowski was right. It seemed like miles away. He squinted but couldn't even make out the dock or the cabin.

"I must have drifted off," Riley said to himself.

Grabowski started up the engine of the boat, and gunned it.

"We're gonna have a little race," he said.

"A race?"

"See who can get to the cabin first. And the winner gets…"

He rubbed his chin in the manner of a deep thinker. "I know—winner gets the baby."

Grabowski gunned the engine again and the boat sped off, headed for the shore. Riley began swimming with haste and with desperation and with just the one leg. Each time he looked up the boat was further away. Finally he looked up and didn't see it at all.

Then he bolted up in bed. The first thing he did was look at his finger to see if it was there. Then he looked at Nan, curled on her side. And he touched her to make sure *she* was there. The touch was light but woke her anyway.

"What is it?" she said.

"Nothing. Didn't mean to wake you."

Riley pulled off the covers and reached for his crutches, propped beside the bed against the wall. He lifted himself on the crutches and moved to the window looking out on the lake.

"I dreamt I was floating out there."

"Mmmm. Sounds nice."

"It was," he said. "And then it wasn't."

"You didn't dream about *him* again?"

Riley didn't answer. Nan looked at his back and sighed.

*

Riley told me about the dream many years later—shared it with me whilst I took notes (kind of like a patient with his shrink, except when the session was done, the patient walked away free and the doctor remained imprisoned). He needed to unburden himself of bad memories, I guess; whereas Nan, when writing to me about those times in the cabin, focused on the tender moments.

She told me of a day—in that spring of '30, with the two of them still hidden away together at the lake—when she reached up for a coffee cup on the shelf and felt Riley coming up behind her, reaching for that same cup. His cheek grazed against her hair. After placing the cup gently in her hand, he let his fingers slide along the inside of her forearm, knowing it was one of her weaknesses, whilst kissing her on the neck.

"Ah, the accidental encounter in the kitchen," she said to him, her eyes closed. "Every woman's fantasy."

Riley's hands cupped her shoulders and found their way down her arms and round her waist—slender again, first time in months.

"I know what's going on," she said with her head tilted back to him. "This is a distraction because you're losing. When desperate, seduce your adversary."

He gave her a squeeze and let her go. She filled the coffee cup and walked back to the card table whilst Riley wandered to the other side of the cabin living room, which had big picture windows facing out on the lake.

"Here, you've got your coffee," she said, putting the cup down next to his cards. "Now get back to business."

He stood over a large crib near the window. In it, twin baby boys slept. Then Riley felt a tug on his leg from Jean. He reached down to grab her and lifted her over his head. She giggled and seemed to like the view from the top, but Riley soon brought her back down because there was a knock at the door.

He looked at Nan and she lit up.

"Hallelujah," she said. "We got company!"

Riley had a different reaction. He walked quickly to Nan and handed her Jean. Then he grabbed a hunting rifle from a wall rack and went to the door. He leaned the rifle against the wall just out of view, unbolted the door, and opened it only a crack. Through the opening, he saw a sliver of a wide baby face.

"Well, well," Riley said. "What do you know."

Barkley smiled. "Me? I know plenty."

About a half-hour later, they were on the lawn between the cabin and the dock. The trees were green, the hummingbirds hummed, and the wildflowers were wild. In the tall grass, Riley stood very straight whilst holding a horseshoe at his chest. In that upright way of his he let fly, and the shoe arced high in the air, catching a spark of sunlight at its peak, then beginning its dive for the spike. It landed with a shrill clank and yes of course it was a ringer. Barkley stood near Riley but with arms folded, facing out on the lake; his tailored suit jacket hung on a nearby tree branch. Nan sat a few yards away from them, supposedly tending to the kids and letting the men take care of business.

Unlike the last time Riley saw him, Barkley was cleaned up and full of beans once more. He spread his arms out to the lake as if to hug it. "Oh, Horicon," he proclaimed. "I dub thee Paradise."

Riley tossed another shoe and the clank was audible and you can guess the result. Then he held out a horseshoe for Barkley who pretended not to be aware. Riley kept holding it until Barkley finally turned and took it from him.

The shoe had a little soil on it and Barkley used a hanky from his pocket to carefully wipe it off—when Riley saw that he didn't know whether to laugh or cry. Then Barkley took aim for a long time before eventually taking a dramatic step forward. He released the shoe and swept his arm upward in a windmill follow-through. For all that effort the shoe didn't so much fly as flee, hitting the ground too soon and then bouncing and finally rolling away to hide in the tall grass. Barkley winced and scrunched his shoulders though none of this kept him from talking.

"Yes, I'm doing alright, Harry and Nan," he said at a raised volume so as to ensure he would be heard by Nan and all the Upper Peninsula.

"I will confess," he continued, "I was on the brink. But then...
an *epiphany*."

Riley kept his eyes on the stake and tossed again; again there
was a clank. Barkley followed with another soft thud.

"It dawned on me," Barkley said, "that while I dreamed of making my fortune in New York, I had the world in my hands—right
there in Detroit. My people. My common herd. They love me,
Harry. I don't know why, but they do."

"Yes," Riley said, letting fly another ringer. "It *is* a mystery."

"And I let them all down," Barkley said, "and also let you
down, because I dug myself into a hole. And the more I tried to
get out..."

There was another thud in the dirt resulting from Barkley's latest toss.

"...the deeper I was in."

Riley looked away from the stake and at Barkley.

"With Livoli?"

Barkley shook his head and waved a hand as if washing a window. "The details are not important. I see the big picture now. I'm
done with booze, the women, gambling, bad investments—"

"Is there any vice you *don't* have?" Riley inquired but this was
ignored.

"—and most important, I'm done covering up. Done beating
around the bush and protecting people. Know what this means,
Harry and Nan? There is going to be hell to pay on the radio."

Riley looked at him. "You mean you're finally going after
Mayor Bowles? And the Italians as well?"

Barkley gave him a smile. "I'm going after every mother-lovin'
crook in town. And there's no shortage to choose from."

"Could be dangerous," Riley said.

Having given up the game, Barkley now lit two cigarettes in his
mouth as he ankled closer to Harry. He lowered his voice, so Riley
alone could hear.

"Harry, a few days ago I was staring down the barrel of a gun,"
he said. "And I was the one holding that gun. You know what
I decided? Hell, I'm not gonna do the job for them. I'm gonna

make those Wops kill me. If they've got the balls."

He offered one of the lit cigarettes to Riley—who shook his head no and got ready to toss again.

"The thing is," Barkley said to Riley's back, "I could use some moral support, not to mention legal. In other words I need *you,* Harry. I need you to come to Detroit and back me up. With me on the air and you on the ground—hell, there'll be no place for the slime to hide."

Riley hadn't moved and was still holding the shoe. "I've left that world behind, Jerry. I've moved on."

As he said the words, Riley couldn't help glancing over at Nan. Sure enough, she was giving him a look: *Who are you kidding?* Riley then went ahead and tossed the last shoe and this time it landed short with a thud on the grass.

That evening, after Barkley had gone, it was like the calm after the storm, with just the two of them left to pick up all he'd overturned whilst blowing through.

Riley and Nan sat across from one another at the card table, not speaking. She was calmly arranging her hand and sneaking peeks at him over the cards. Riley's cards were laid face-down and he had his arms folded and was staring at her.

"I am not going back," he said. "End of story."

She said nothing, just kept looking at her cards and shooting him those little glances.

"It's crazy," Riley went on. "With the twins now? I can't expose all of you to that risk."

She lowered the cards and gave him a look. "Listen. You don't want to do it, fine. Don't use the children, or *me,* as an excuse."

Riley leaned back and for once did not have a smart response.

"I can handle Detroit," she continued. "I can handle myself, and the kids. What I can't handle is a fellow who mopes by the lake, thinking about what he should really be doing."

He started to answer and then realized he still did not have one. The best he could do was shake his head.

"And one more thing," she said.

He knew what was coming.

"Gin," she said, laying out the evidence in front of him.

Two months passed, by whence the summer of 1930 was blazing hot. The motormouth Barkley was still alive and yapping. This could almost be classified as a miracle because after what I learned on the boat ride at Belle Isle, I had decided to look into Barkley and put Solly Levine on the job.

Solly learned that Barkley had indeed spied on workers at the Highland Park Ford plant. And, he was a member of the APL at the time—which meant he reported any "suspicious activities" he saw to the Red Scare branch of the Justice Department in Washington. The old geezer Thompson had suggested all this to me, though I ignored him at the time because I thought he'd say anything to save his own skin. But now I knew: Barkley was the one who put Rachel's name in play, all because of a little thing he saw her do at the plant, a thing so small, so trivial, it isn't even worth talking about at the moment.

I decided Barkley had to go. I didn't tell Max, because I knew what he'd say: First a former DA, then a cop, now a radio star? I told only two people: Solly Levine and Abie the Agent. Solly was to be the advance man, following Barkley for a while, figuring out his routine and his vulnerabilities. When we had it all worked out, Abie would do the job.

It would be tougher than any we'd done before, because Barkley was a so-called celebrity. And we determined it wouldn't be easy to kill a member of this new species for three reasons:

1. People are always watching so-called celebrities;
2. The so-called celebrity is always watching other people, to see if those people are watching him;
3. It is hard to sneak up behind so-called celebrities because they are usually looking at themselves in a mirror.

It was only after I'd decided to kill him that I became a faithful listener of Barkley's. I wanted to hear him go after the Purples and insult the Jews so that I would get even madder at him, and then would feel even better about doing GBH to him. But I discovered to my disappointment that he wasn't going after the Jews the way he previously did. One time, Barkley even went so far as to say something good about Jewish gangsters—he said we were "easy targets" who got blamed for everything, whether we did it or not. I found myself saying to the box, "Yeah, you tell 'em, Motor-mouth!" I was curious where Barkley was going with all this. So I decided there was no rush to put him on the spot just yet.

Meanwhile, I also got distracted by the escalating back-and-forth of the summer of '30. For example one night in June, the oilers shot out the windows of the Crime. Luckily no one was hurt, but the idea that somebody would go after the Crime seemed like an attack on a shrine and made me mad. And so two nights later the Caffè Roma—a favorite haunt of the oilers—was hit and two of Livoli's men ended up face down in their Roma house salad.

By July 1930 the mood in the city was one of high agitation and then the temperatures began to soar and that didn't help. The only thing worse than Detroit in winter was Detroit in summer. Bad smells from the swampy river and the belching factories all baked together in the heat. As a result, the whole city had a sour puss on.

Much of the bad feeling found a deserving target in the mayor. As the so-called "gangland killings" gained momentum so did the movement to recall Bowles. I was not normally a political person, but even I got worked up about the recall movement. I put money behind a top contender to replace Bowles because the man assured me that he would level the playing field for oilers and Jews. And that was all I expected—not special treatment, just a level field.

The whole mayor's race seemed to hinge on what Barkley said, and Barkley himself was going back and forth like a whore on a swing. Every time he would get too critical of Bowles, he would get a message from Livoli and next day he would pull back. I would listen to the broadcasts and cheer Barkley one time and curse him the next.

But in the final days before the recall it became clear Barkley was caving to Livoli and backing Mayor Bowles. I felt betrayed— after all, I had saved Barkley's life (by deciding to postpone killing him) and this was my repayment. So, the day before the recall vote I summoned Solly Levine and said, "It's back on."

The night before the recall vote Barkley walked into the radio booth at the LaSalle Hotel, opened a drawer and grabbed a bottle of Old Log Cabin, and took a swig. He looked at himself in the glass walls of the booth.

"What's the worst they can they do?" he said. "They will not silence Cicero—even if they should yank out my tongue, and stick it with a hairpin. Ouch."

He took another swig and put the bottle back in the drawer. He sat back in his chair for a second. Then he reached for the phone.

He asked the operator to ring his wife and whilst waiting he opened another little drawer under his desk and fumbled around in it looking for something.

"Janine?" he said into the receiver. *"It's me... No, no reason... You have dinner yet? Yeah, what'd you have?... No I'm not acting wacky, I just want to talk to you, is that so strange?... Well, okay, it's unusual, I'll grant you that. Listen—give the kids a kiss goodnight for me. Tell 'em I love them... No I have not been drinking. I gotta go... Late, very late. Don't wait for me. I love you."*

He hung up; the other was still in the drawer. "There you are," he said as he pulled out the little rabbit's foot. He put in his shirt pocket and said, "I'm keeping you close to my heart."

He picked up the phone again. But he just held it for a second before he hung it back up and pushed it aside. Then he pulled it back to him again and picked up the receiver.

"Yeah, Sally, get me Tuxedo-8860...

"Yeah, hello, is Ten there?... Oh, okay... Nope, no message... It's nobody, okay, Nosey?... Wait a minute, listen. When you see her... just tell her Jerry wanted to say hello, okay?"

Barkley hung up. Right after he did, the phone rang and he grabbed it quick. *"Ten?"*

But it wasn't Ten.

"Oh, yeah?" he snarled into the phone. *"Who the hell is this? Listen, nobody's gonna take me for a long ride, you scum."*

He slammed down the phone and stared at it. Then the radio station manager popped his head into the booth.

"You almost ready? We're on in thirty seconds."

As the manager ducked out, Barkley put a cigar in his mouth and lit it. He cleared his throat, looked for a signal and got started.

"Good evening Detroit," he said to the mike. *"I'm going to get right to the point tonight because there is no time to waste. Already in this 'Bloody July,' eleven people have been killed by gangs in Detroit. I have complained often about the violence and the corruption and about the Jewish gangsters. But I have not gone far enough, wide enough or deep enough in my indictments.*

"My common herd, we have been led astray. And I wish I could say that I have been misled right alongside the rest of you, but I cannot. Because truth be told, I have been one of the shepherds. And so I must make amends, beginning now."

Barkley was looking at the reflection in the glass and saw this man in front of him lean forward in his seat, warming to the fight.

"Tomorrow we have a chance to start fresh," he continued. *"But tonight, we must face some truths about ourselves. The problem in Detroit is not limited to a particular group of people. While there are gangsters named Bernstein, they are also named Livoli. Their partners in corruption have names like Clarke... and names like Bowles.*

"They span all races and religions—and the same is true of their victims. I'm thinking of a brave young man named Bud Fleischer, who recently died serving this city. And I'm thinking of a young colored child... named Arthur Nicks. Whose killing was one of the great tragedies Detroit has known.

"We are all complicit in these tragedies. We've all played our supporting roles. By taking part in things we know are wrong... By looking away, when we should be bearing witness... By keeping quiet, when we oughtta be screaming our heads off.

"We cannot change the past. We can't bring back Bud Fleischer or Arthur Nicks. But we can begin the process of reform in Detroit. And we can start tomorrow.

"How long, Mayor Bowles, hast thou abused our patience? Well, we shall be patient no more. Tomorrow at the polls, forget what I may have said in the past and remember what I've said tonight. Because at long last I am urging you to do what should have been done long ago...

And that is to recall the son of a bitch!"

*

Throughout the rest of the program Barkley proceeded to lay out his case and by the time he was finished, so was Mayor Bowles. It wouldn't become official till the next day's vote, but Barkley knew it that night as he turned off his mike, rocked back in his chair, and puffed on his cigar.

He took the bottle and instead of swigging from it he grabbed a glass, wiped it clean and poured himself a proper drink. Then he put his feet up on the desk and raised his glass. "Here's to Jerry Barkley. Man of the people."

With the weight of his own guilt lifted off him and a future of light and truth ahead, Barkley seemed more relaxed than he had in a long time—or so said the radio station manager, who'd been watching him the whole time and who saw him doze off, right there in his chair.

Below in the hotel lobby Solly Levine was sitting in a plush chair, a newspaper open in front of him—but his googly eyes were look-ing up at the broadcast booth above. He was waiting for Barkley to come down from that perch. Then he'd follow Barkley on the Motormouth's nightly rounds. He would give Abie a heads-up when Barkley was on his way home. The plan was to snatch him in his own driveway.

Solly noticed that a hotel manager seemed to be walking straight at him wearing a goofy smile. Before the guy could get within ten feet Solly barked: "What in the hell do *you* want?"

"Excuse me," the manager said, "are you John Smith?"

"No I certainly ain't John Smith, do I look like a goddamn John Smith to you?"

Soon as he finished saying this, Solly recalled that John Smith was one of his aliases—he hadn't used it in so long, he forgot.

"And what if I am John Smith?" he called to the manager, now ankling away.

"Well, if you are John Smith," the manager said without looking back, "then you have a goddamn phone call at the desk."

When Solly picked up the phone it was me on the line.

"Did you hear the broadcast?" I asked.

"What broadcast?"

I didn't even know how to respond to that so I didn't.

"It's off again," I said.

"Whadda ya mean it's off again?" Solly said.

"I mean it's off again. Which part of that do I need to clarify?"

When Solly hung up he felt even more underappreciated than usual. He had come to do a job and now there was nothing to do. I had my reasons for changing course; Barkley had redeemed himself that night. This did not mean I wouldn't want to put him on the spot next week, because after all he could never take back what he did to Rachel. But based on good behavior, I granted him another stay of execution.

This left Solly standing in the middle of the lobby just looking around and he spied the hotel coffee shop. He thought some soup might calm him. He also checked to make sure he had fuel in his flask. Maybe he'd order some coffee, then make it Irish.

Back up in the broadcast booth, Barkley's slumber was cut short by a ringing phone that almost made him topple out of his chair.

"Hello?" he said to the phone in a voice that was rough, but then it turned smooth and sweet. *"Well, hello,"* he purred. *"God, it's good to hear your voice. Where are you?... You are? What a sweet surprise... Sure, fifteen minutes, in the lobby. I'll be there. Can't wait to see you, sugar plum."*

Barkley hung up and smiled.

"I'm on a roll, no doubt about it," he said.

He straightened his collar and dabbed at his hair, whistling a tune. Then he grabbed his newspaper and left the booth with a spring in his step. Down in the lobby, almost empty by this hour, he picked out a plush chair in the midst of the open floor, right under the big chandelier. He sat down to read his paper whilst waiting for his "sweet surprise." At one point he heard a commotion from the hotel coffee shop—somebody shouting at a waiter.

"Unlimited refills!" the man was yelling. "It's what any decent coffee shop gives!"

The waiter said something back but it was not audible although the yeller sure was. "Never you mind what I put in my goddamn coffee! That's my business. Wanna make it yours?"

When the yeller came staggering out of the shop into the lobby, Barkley recognized those thick eyeglasses and knew it was one of the Purples—Solly Something-or-other. Barkley had no further interest in the man and raised up his paper in front of his face. But he got the feeling Solly Something-or-other was coming his way.

Solly stopped and stood a few feet away whilst Barkley tried to pretend he wasn't there.

"You got no idea how lucky you are tonight," Solly growled.

Barkley lowered his paper a little and peeked over the top. "My friend, you are so right," he said. "But wait'll you get an eyeful of who's coming here to meet me. Then you'll know how lucky I truly am."

"Loudmouth mick," Solly replied.

Barkley raised his paper back up. "And goodnight to you too, sir," he said. "Safe home."

Solly spit in the direction of Barkley's shoes and when that got no reaction, he turned to leave.

And then Solly saw something in the hotel doorway that bulged his googly eyes and sobered him right up. He would later tell everybody that he was certain at that moment he was a goner. Three men burst through that lobby entrance with hats down and guns drawn. And there before them was Solly, smack in the middle of a wide-open lobby with no place to hide.

He turned and made a run for it and the shots started popping whilst he ran. He was waiting for the bite of a bullet in his back but the feeling did not come. "Goddamn if you're going to shoot me, do it already," he thought as he ran and the shots kept firing and not a one hit him. He kept moving without looking back, and then dove behind a sofa near the wall. The shots had stopped now and when he raised his head to peek over the sofa, he saw the men in hats already disappearing out the lobby door.

Solly looked around that lobby and it was quiet and empty except for the hotel manager crouched down on the floor behind the front desk. Solly wondered where Barkley had run to and then he noticed that Barkley's chair had fallen over backwards onto the carpet and yet it appeared that Barkley was still sitting in it.

He knew he ought to scram but Solly could not resist creeping over for a closer look. As Barkley lay there with his ass still planted in the chair and his back on the floor, the newspaper was open and spread out over his chest and face, whilst his fingertips still pinched the sides of the paper. Solly thought he better get away from this mess fast so he broke for the door. But he would remember the sight of that newspaper shroud—with the headline saying *"Recall tomorrow"* and with the blood seeping through all the holes in the stories—for the rest of his numbered days.

TWENTY-FIVE

On the day of the Motormouth's funeral, the common herd turned out in such force you'd have thought someone was handing out free cheese. I found myself in the midst of that crowd of 100,000 people. I was not there to pay tribute—I simply felt like an ankle that day and got swept up.

The casket—blanketed in flowers, though for Barkley it should've been papered with dollar bills—started out at a packed church where a radio priest known for hating Jews urged all people to love each other. Rabbi Franklin was also there and praised Barkley for being a champion of so-called assimilation. There were politicians too, of course, because like vultures they always show up after somebody dies.

More than anything else in the church, though, there were women—lots of them. Some looked a little sad like they'd lost a friend whilst others sobbed like they'd lost a lover. They all tended to have blonde hair except for the one who had skin like coffee with cream. These women all kept their distance from one another just like rival gangsters might, though they peeked up from their wet hankies, spying on each other. And all of them got the evil eye from Barkley's grieving widow.

From the church, the casket was driven to the Mount Olivet Cemetery, where about fifty thousand squeezed in amongst the tombstones or hovered outside the cemetery gates. After they

lowered Barkley's casket into the ground and threw dirt on him, it
was time for more speeches—by the candidates seeking to replace
Bowles (the recall was official but the election of a new mayor was
still to come). On a makeshift platform set up near the gravesite, a
fat little mayoral candidate named Johnston, who had trouble even
climbing up on the platform, said: "And my fellow Detroiters if I
am elected in September, my first order of business shall be to find
the people who committed this terrible crime."

That remark seemed to get things started. You could hear some
laughter in the crowd but it wasn't the happy kind. Then someone
started yelling at Johnston. "We already know who killed Barkley.
It was the gangsters, who else!"

This was a typical ignorant statement you get from the man on
the street—suggesting there was no difference between one gang
or another and that they were all guilty of the same crime. Nevertheless, the remark brought a wave of hoots and hollers from the
crowd. Soon other hecklers were joining in.

"What are you gonna do about the gangsters?" screamed one.

And then: "He's gonna do nothing, like they all do!"

Followed by: "Which one of you two-bit politicians has the guts
to stand up to these animals!"

As the fools got worked up around me, I had myself a good
laugh at them all. When people like this get slapped around, they
always do the same three things. First, they do nothing but take it
on the cheek. Later, they scream and yell. Finally, they go back to
doing nothing. This was the second stage.

Somebody threw a cardboard coffee cup at Johnston and it hit
his chest and splashed brown on his white shirt. He looked around
for help. Down in the crowd, policemen with sticks started to
shoulder their way through.

Johnston used a hankie to wipe his shirt and looked like he
might cry. "This is uncivil," he said. "Why are you attacking me?"

"Somebody give him some cream to go with that coffee!"
another heckler yelled.

There must have been no cream handy but there was a half-
eaten apple and it sailed over his head.

"Mother of God," Johnston said and then was in such a hurry to get off that platform that he slipped and fell to one knee. When he did, no one wanted to get up there and help him. But then from the midst of that crowd, there strode (though it was more of a hobble) a man who reached up and planted his cane like a stake on that platform, and used it to raise himself up onto the stage. To the untrained eye he might have been just one more opportunist getting up to make another speech. But the reader will know by now that we are talking about the supposed hero, and therefore we must presume he took that stage in order to save a fellow man, and perhaps also the day, and maybe whilst he was at it the whole city of Detroit.

Riley helped Johnston get to his feet, patting the fool on the shoulder. The crowd quieted now and no one seemed eager to throw anything at a man with a cane, though everyone wondered who the hell this gimp was. Riley looked out at the faces in the crowd and stared into people's eyes and did not smile or even talk right away; this made everyone even quieter. Finally he cleared his throat.

"My name's Harry Riley," he said. "And as you can plainly see"—now he held his cane up—"I'm not running for anything."

He got some laughs with the line and people stopped talking amongst themselves and began to pay attention, and from then on he had them in his hand.

"I used to work in the DA's office," Riley announced. "And then I quit. Which I am not proud of."

He had the cane planted in front of him now and rested both hands on it and leaned forward.

"I quit because like all of you, I was disgusted with the corruption and the coddling of gangsters. I lost my young partner to the hoodlums. Almost lost my family. And I lost a friend in Jerry Barkley."

There were bowed heads and nods all around when that suddenly sacred name was mentioned.

"I understand what you are feeling," Riley went on. "And why you don't want to hear empty promises from politicians, not on this day. You are right to feel that way."

There were "hear, hears" now, soft and respectful. Then Riley held up a stern finger. "*However,*" he said.

The sheep knew they were going to be put in their place and yet did not seem to mind.

"However," he said again. "This is not a day to hurl insults or objects at people. We all need to show respect on this day. A man is being buried here. He died serving this city and all of you. Let's honor him the right way."

The applause that followed was soft but sincere. Riley gave a quick nod and turned to leave the platform. He even took the first step away. Then he stopped as if he'd thought of something right then and there; whether he did, or whether it was all planned, is for others to decide. But he turned back to the crowd and held up a hand to let them know he wasn't done yet after all.

"One more thing," he said. "Because of Jerry's murder I am returning to the DA's office. If they will have me."

This brought more applause—more bahs from the sheep.

"And I'm going to recommend that we empanel a special Grand Jury—to get to the bottom of the Barkley murder and other killings in Detroit."

The crowd noise was building now.

"With a Grand Jury, we can bring these gangsters and corrupt officials before the people—make them explain themselves. I hope you'll support my efforts to make this happen. Help me put the pressure on. We *need* a Grand Jury in Detroit, and we need it now."

The crowd erupted at that, though Riley didn't stick around to soak it up. He just nodded and left the platform. As he did, someone in the crowd pumped a fist in the air and chanted: "Grand Jury, Grand Jury." Others picked up the chant.

Right in front of me, one chanting fool stopped and turned to another. "So what is a Grand Jury anyway?" he asked.

His pal said, "Dunno, but it sounds like we sure as hell need one."

I watched as Riley descended and moved through people nodding at him and giving him the thumbs-up. He didn't stop or chat, just went in a beeline straight to where Teddy Baird was standing with arms folded, nodding and waiting. Baird had a funny little smile on his face like a man who'd been checkmated and now could only lean back and admire the move.

Riley went up to him and reached out a hand and Baird shook it. Then Riley leaned in and said something in Baird's ear. I didn't have to be a lip reader to know Riley was asking for his job back right then and there. And I didn't have to wait around to see Baird's nod and that hapless shrug of his.

Just a few weeks after Barkley's fancy burial, there was another one in town—this one much quieter, because the deceased was not deemed important. It was at a small cemetery on the east side and I attended along with Max, Abie, Solly, and about 20 other men, all wearing white shirts buttoned to the throat in spite of the sun and the heat. Most of those in attendance were there not because they cared, but only because I requested live bodies so it would seem as if the deceased had more friends than she truly did.

Of course Rachel did not have friends but that is only because you cannot make them inside your room or your own head. Once her parents were gone and her supposed community turned its back on her, she had only me. At the burial the one person who wasn't a gangster was a nervous young rabbi, who'd been reluctant to come and say a few kind words, until he was encouraged. In his eyes (and all the others on Hastings), Rachel was even more of a *schanda* now than before—because the only thing worse than being a living embarrassment is to become a dead one by your own hand. That's how they saw it. But I knew that she took her life only because she could take no more.

I did not blame myself. I had taken every precaution. And if there was one thing I knew from experience it was this: It is hard to keep a person alive when someone wishes them dead. You can employ as many bodyguards as you like, but there will come a time when the person is left alone and unguarded. And at that moment the one determined to do the killing will suddenly show up, creeping on padded shoes. There is simply no way to keep victim and killer apart forever, especially if they are the same person.

She was not the first, nor last, to do what she did. It has been documented that 87 people jumped off that damn bridge to Belle Isle between 1927 and 1930. The Detroit police even created a "suicide squad" to patrol the bridge. And where was the patrolling officer on that particular day? He was taking a break on the island, feeding the ducks. Later, the man felt so bad about his mistake that he jumped off the bridge himself. This I know because Abie the Agent told me, and he knew because he was there, standing right behind the man when he jumped.

Of course, after it happened, I thought about that earlier incident on the bridge, when she looked out from the car: Did she foresee her own jump? Should this have tipped me off? I don't see how I could be expected to think like a crazy person.

I could see only one mistake I made—giving her that radio. She listened to it all through Bloody July, always expecting to hear my name mentioned when the voices in the box talked about the latest killings. When she heard that Barkley was killed, it upset her for a couple of reasons. For one thing, she heard my name mentioned on the radio afterwards in connection with the killing. She came right out and asked me if I did it. This made me mad, and I said harsh things. All I can say in my defense is: It's hard to be constantly accused of terrible crimes, and it is especially hard in those instances when it is not even true.

The worst thing about the Barkley killing for Rachel was that it made one of her predictions come true. This never happened to her before: Lucky Lindy never did crash, "The Monkey" never did take over our minds, and so forth. But Barkley got killed just like she said he would. She saw it as proof of her worst fear—that maybe she wasn't crazy after all. And she worried that her other predictions would soon come true, too.

Then she got one more crazy idea and this would be the last. She never told this one to me—I only knew because of her note.

"*I know you will laugh at me for thinking this,*" she wrote. "*But what if God or fate is making my predictions come true to punish me? Maybe just by saying these things would happen, I challenged fate. If that is true, then there is only one thing for me to do. If I'm not around there is no reason for these things to keep happening. There will be no one left for God (or fate) to punish. Today I gathered every prediction I ever wrote, every piece of paper I could find, and I burned them and they're gone forever. Now all that's left is me.*"

Of course it made no sense, like everything she wrote and half of what she said. But I kept the note and it was right there in my pocket—I touched it and crinkled the paper more than once whilst standing at the cemetery. You can say it was a crazy note and no one could argue, but if you put yourself inside her head and believe what she did, then maybe you see it differently. Maybe she died so Lindy wouldn't crash and the Monkey would leave us all in peace. Of course no one is trying to suggest this would make her a hero because after all she didn't hobble around on a peg leg.

And speaking of Riley but not the one with the peg, it wasn't until Rachel's service was almost over that I noticed her standing there. She was far back from the gravesite, well hidden behind several goons, but I glimpsed a flash of the red hair and when I did I felt the blood rush to my face (because her being there made me mad, I guess). She must have come late and snuck in quiet, and then as things were ending she slipped out the same way. I didn't even see her go. I looked over peoples' shoulders and all around whilst everyone was squeezing my hand and patting my arm and even trying to hug me (something I did not care for even in the best of times). I was a little disappointed she was gone only because I wanted to tell her to get lost. As I was looking around I noticed Solly Levine giving me the eye.

"Who you lookin' for, the Irish dame?" he said.

"What dame?" I said and Solly raised an eyebrow and turned away.

Afterwards, they wanted to take me for a drink—they really wanted to take themselves for a drink and I was a handy excuse.

"No, I feel like an ankle," I said.

"Want company?" Max offered.

"Let him alone," Abie said. "You want to be alone, right, Joe?"

I turned left out of the cemetery and started walking down Gratiot. My eyes were on the sidewalk and my head was full of memories and that's why I went about a block before I even noticed it. She was walking on the same street about two blocks ahead of me. She had a good stride: long legs, no nonsense. I was a fast walker and though I was gaining on her, I wasn't gaining much. But of course I wasn't trying to catch her.

When I got within a block of her and knew I would catch up with her soon (even though I was not trying), I thought about crossing to the other side of the street just so I wouldn't have to pass right by her. And then I got sore at himself for even thinking such a thing: Why should *I* cross the street? I did that for no man, so why this woman? I kept going and as I got closer it was just the two of us on that sidewalk and she never looked back but I could tell she was aware of my footsteps. She was walking a little faster now. So I started walking faster too, not to scare her but just because now I wanted to pass her and get it the hell over with.

All of a sudden when I was a few yards behind her she stopped short and turned around. We looked each other full in the face for a moment and I noticed little pearls of sweat on her brow and then I looked past her like she was nothing and kept right on moving.

"Don't flatter yourself," I said as I passed. "I'm just walking in the same direction as you, and that's no crime."

I thought that was the end of it and then I heard her voice calling after me. "Mr. Bernstein, please wait," she said.

I was not bound to stop for this woman but I did so because I wanted to see just how much nerve she had. She walked right up to me and said she was sorry.

"For what?"

"For your suffering," she said.

"Do I look like I'm suffering to you?"

She didn't say anything, but nodded as she looked at me. I didn't know what else to say so I turned to leave.

"I have something for you," she said.

I stopped and looked back at her. She was opening up her purse and rummaging in it. For a second I thought she was going to give me a hard-luck donation or something. Then she pulled out a little piece of crumpled paper.

"Do you keep the things she wrote?" she said.

I shook my head no but she reached out and held the crumpled piece of paper in front of me anyway, so I had no choice but to take it and for some reason I happened to notice that our fingers touched just for a second.

I looked at the crumpled paper and tugged it straight so I could read the writing on it:

"You will have a beautiful baby."

"Her prediction was half-right," Nan said. "I had two."

The note with that familiar handwriting made me smile a little at first but as I kept looking at it, the crinkles and the small writing must have put a strain my eyes because they got blurry all of a sudden. I folded the note and put it in my pocket with the crinkled letter.

"She usually predicted bad things," I said. "This is different. This one I'll keep."

I nodded to her and then as I was walking away I had the crazy thought she might stop me *again* and sure enough she did.

"You wouldn't happen to know where a person could get an iced tea on a scorcher like this?" she said.

I didn't stop or even turn back, just said over my shoulder, "There's a joint about three blocks from here."

"Could you point me in the right direction?"

"Just follow me," I said, and slowed down to let her catch up.

I led her to the Crime of Michigan and before anyone starts feeling sorry for the innocent lady let it be known that she was thrilled to go.

"I've heard about this place," she said as we arrived at the door. "I don't know if I should dare go in."

"Suit yourself," I said as I went through the door alone. I held it open behind me just in case she was coming and she did.

She followed me to the corner booth and sat across from me. I didn't need extra eyes to know that there were funny looks coming our way. It wasn't crowded because most of the funeral group had gone to the Town Pump Tavern (Ten's Spot was out of the running—nobody could trust *that* place anymore). Only a hardcore few were around. They were no doubt wondering why their boss had come straight from his girl's funeral to sit in the booth with another woman, but of course nobody said anything.

She wasn't bashful; didn't lower her head and hide in the booth. She looked around the place, taking it all in. She paid special attention to the cracks in the mirror behind the coffee counter, which still hadn't been fixed since the oiler attack even though I'd ordered that repairs be done with money from the tzedakah box. (The box was Abie's idea: You were supposed to put in a donation every time you dodged a bullet. The money went to gang widows and other needy causes).

Eyeing the cracked mirror, she said, "Looks like some damage was sustained. Did Al Capone pay a visit?"

I smiled at her little joke. "Yes," I said, "he came and looked in the mirror with that ugly melon face, and you see the result."

The waiter brought two iced teas in tall glasses and set them down. We sat quietly and I noticed her black dress had tiny black beads on it that shined. She looked down at her glass and twirled a long spoon in it. It seemed like she wanted to say something but took a while before she got it out.

"I was wondering," she finally said. "When I spoke to you back at Eloise... I said those things about taking her out of the hospital. And then when she did get out of the hospital..."

"You feeling guilty now?"

"I don't know how to feel, or what to think about it."

I was also twirling the spoon in my glass now, just glancing up at her once or twice. "You don't need to feel bad," I said. "You gave good advice. She was happier after she got out of there. For a little while, at least."

"It's just so awful what happened to her," she said. Now she wasn't swirling the spoon, she was using it to punch and stab a poor defenseless lemon wedge.

"You have no idea what happened to her," I said. "Nor do I."

"Was she alright before they put her in that awful place? I mean did she start out..."

"Sane?" I smiled and shook my head. "She was never what you'd call normal, though they definitely made her worse. She was always a funny one. But she had a good heart."

"I could tell that about her right away," she said

"It's what got her in trouble in the first place," I said.

Her ears pricked up at that. "How so?"

I wasn't going to tell her the story because why was it her business? But then it occurred to me that of all the people at the funeral that day besides me, she was the only who ever tried to befriend Rachel—the only one who seemed to care. So maybe she did have a right to know.

"Ever hear of a woman named Matilda Rabinowitz?" I asked.

She said the name rang a bell. I told her Matilda was a union organizer who made the Detroit papers years earlier when she was thrown out of the Ford plants for trying to pass out literature to the workers. Matilda became notorious on Hastings and Rachel looked up to her. Not that Matilda cared about Rachel—a younger girl, without family or prospects, a girl who was a little odd and who hung around with a young hood.

"But Matilda got more friendly soon as Rachel got a job with the Steins dry cleaners," I explained. "It wasn't that the job was anything special—the Steins took in the dirty overalls of workers at the Highland Park Ford plant and delivered them back fresh to the factory each morning. Rachel made sure they were neatly packed and even went with the truck to supervise the delivery each morning. Like I say, nothing glamorous—but it gave Rachel *access*."

"To the workers, you mean?"

"Matilda convinced her that if she slipped these little papers in the pockets of the overalls—the usual crap, 'come to the rally tonight,' and so forth—she'd be doing the workers a big favor and nobody would be any the wiser."

I briefly stopped the story at that point because I noticed the door of the diner opening. It was a couple of Purples from the funeral. The last one through the door was Solly Levine.

"What a way to waste a day," Solly was saying to no one in particular as he came through the door. Then he spied me and the woman and he did that thing again where he raised his eyebrows whilst he kept moving to his own booth across the room. I was still tracking him when she interjected.

"But I guess somebody did get wise," she said.

"Well, *there* is the big question," I said. "Who got wise? All we knew at the time was that somebody ratted her out to the plant manager. Because one fine morning she showed up with the uniform deliveries and two men were waiting for her at the door. They took her by the arms and threw her in the street whilst everyone just watched. She picked herself up and went home crying to the Steins. And what do you think they did? They shoved her right back out in the street and told her never to show her face at the shop again. Then she walked down Hastings crying, with all the merchants' cold eyes on her—because to them, you see, she was now a *schanda*. Just like me."

"A schanda?"

"An embarrassment. A troublemaker amongst people who were trying so fucking hard to be accepted that they would do anything—cast out friends, eat shit on a daily diet, anything."

She looked down and got a little red.

"Sorry for my language," I said.

She shook her head whilst still looking down. "No, you're right to be upset," she said. "The whole thing was so unfair."

"Oh, but that was just the beginning. After she was fired, she went to her little apartment and curled up, thinking she'd hit bottom. But it wasn't so—the bottom was waiting for her in a big dark room in the Federal Building, a year later. That's another story, and your husband must have told you that one."

She nodded. "He told me how you tried to rescue her from the Red Pen. That was brave."

I shrugged but didn't answer. I was looking over at Solly, who was whispering whilst also looking at us sideways with his googly eye. This was beginning to irk me.

"Can I help you with something, Solly?" I called out.

"No, I'm fine," he replied.

She brought me back with a question. "You think the incident at the plant was the reason they took her in the Palmer Raids?"

I looked at her like she was a slow child and she nodded to herself and said, "Of course, silly." She paused, then shook her head and said, "It's just so hard to believe they would do that to her over a few scraps of paper."

"Well, it was her second offense," I said.

This surprised her. "What was the first?"

"Being born a Jew in the city of Heinrich Ford."

She didn't know what to say to that and why would she? But she nodded as if she understood.

"So do you think Ford was the one who—"

"Ford had people do his dirty work for him," I said. "Jerry Barkley for instance."

"Barkley?" she said, surprised. "I knew he wrote some things, but… you don't think…"

"I do," I said.

I told her about Barkley being a Ford spy at Highland Park whilst also being a member of the APL, passing tips to Justice. I also told her about Rachel recognizing his mug. "If the shoe fits," I said.

She absorbed all this, shaking her head. Then the look on her face went from bad to worse. I knew what she was thinking.

"No, I didn't kill Barkley," I said. "But I will be honest. I thought long and hard about it."

I didn't know if she believed me or not; I didn't care.

"I shed no tears for the Motormouth," I declared.

And she leaned forward, lowered her voice and said, "You want to know the truth? Neither do I."

Then she did something I won't forget. She raised her tea glass for a toast, saying: "There've been enough tributes to Mr. Barkley already. I would like to salute the memory of Rachel Roth."

I clinked glasses with her and said, "Damn straight."

After a little while, she looked at her watch and acted surprised.

"I really should go," she said.

"You're free to leave anytime."

As she started to get up I stayed in my seat and just watched her. She extended her hand to shake and I didn't get up but did take the hand and fumbled at first, which was not like me. She shook hands like a man except the fingers were long and smooth and the palm so small it was swallowed in mine.

"I just want to say again how sorry I am," she said and then turned and walked away whilst smoothing her skirt.

"I would offer you a ride home with one of the Purples," I called after her, "but you might not make it home alive."

She didn't look back, just kept walking.

"That was a joke," I said as she went out the door.

I turned to look across the room at Solly, his head still down. "You can stop pretending not to look now," I said, but Solly kept pretending anyway.

TWENTY-SIX

Life goes on, even without the great Jerry Barkley to help us through the day. Soon after rejoining the DA's office, Riley had a new partner named Pappas, a couple of years younger than the last one and about half as smart. Much of the time, Pappas had a grin on his face for no good reason. Such was the case on the afternoon in question, as he rode alongside Riley, who was behind the wheel. Riley did not like to see anyone too happy so he kept shooting Pappas sharp sideways glances.

"Will you stop smiling?" Riley finally said. "You're making me uneasy."

"Oh... sorry," Pappas said. "It's just—well, to be honest sir, I'm so doggone excited to have this job."

"Really. Fellow who had the job before you got his throat cut. Now isn't *that* exciting?"

Pappas' smile vanished and he looked out the window as he mulled that over. Riley saw how quickly he'd deflated this little balloon and figured he should put some air back in.

"I guess we can use a little enthusiasm around here," he said. "Lots to do."

Just like that, Pappas was grinning again. "I'm ready for anything, sir."

"Your first job is to sit quiet in the car, while I go corner a rat," Riley said.

"You talking about Solly Levine?"

Riley nodded and this made Pappas proud of himself.

"But there's one thing I don't understand," Pappas said, here showing his gift for understatement. "Why meet him on the sly? Why don't we wait and then grill him in front of the Grand Jury?"

"What Grand Jury would you be talking about?"

"Well, I'm assuming…"

"Well, don't," Riley said. "Don't assume anything about the judicial system in Detroit."

Riley slowed the car, pulling up in front of the Empire Theater.

Pappas was surprised. "You're meeting him here—a movie house? Boy, sir, you got stones meeting a Purple in a theater."

With the car parked, Riley shut off the engine and turned in his seat to face his partner. "You play cards, Pappas?"

The kid shook his head no.

"You ought to," Riley said. "Teaches you strategy. Solly Levine is gonna be the ace up our sleeve. I hope."

Pappas nodded as if he understood.

Riley left him in the car and walked with the cane to the theater entrance. He noticed the letters on the marquee above him said "ALL QUI_T ON THE WESTERN F_ONT." This made him pause just long enough to shake his head. No doubt he would have stood with one leg on top of a ladder to fix it if he had the time and the letters.

He went inside the dark theater and looked up at the screen. What he saw stopped him in his tracks as he stood at the top of the aisle. For support, he rested a hand on top of an empty aisle seat beside him and the seat-top felt strange—velvety in front, cold and metallic in back. Riley never took his eye off the movie.

The scene showed soldiers in the trench with explosions going off on all sides. To Riley's eye the trench looked too small and was dug too straight, as if for a pretty picture. And the looks on the men's faces weren't quite right either. The eyes were too wide, as if trying hard to seem scared—they should've been confused, glazed over; that's how he remembered it.

He had to force himself to stop watching so he could continue moving down the aisle again, looking around at the seats. In flashes, the explosions onscreen lit up the empty seats and revealed the odd person—maybe a dozen in the whole theater, scattered and lonely. He saw one man slumped in his chair with his hat pulled down over his eyes and Riley walked over and gave him a nudge. Solly Levine raised his hat and looked up at Riley— the light from the screen flickered in his thick eyeglasses. Riley found himself watching the movie again, this time in Levine's specs; it looked like a man was dying right there in Solly's left eye.

Levine didn't move so Riley gave him another nudge with his knee and only then did Solly slide over to give Riley the aisle seat. Riley lowered himself and settled in before speaking quietly.

"You sure no one saw you come here?"

"Don't worry about me," Solly said. Then he started shaking his head. "I hate this movie. Goddamn sob story's what it is."

"I guess you had to be there," Riley said.

Solly shot him a look. "What's that supposed to mean? That some kind of a slight at me?"

"Take it easy Solly. I'm not trying to bust your shoes. I just want to know why you killed Barkley, that's all."

Being peeved was Solly's natural state, but this remark got him especially worked up. "What?" he yelled whilst turning in his seat to Riley. The outburst made a couple of people whisper loud at him, and this in turn made him turn back to them.

"Who shushed me?" he barked.

Nobody answered and Riley, eyes still on the screen, spoke softly to him. "Don't make a spectacle of yourself. We're supposed to be doing this on the sly, remember?"

Levine turned back around and took off his glasses and wiped off the fog. "What a goddamn thing to say to me," he whispered loud as he wiped the lenses. "A truly false accusation, that is. I could sue."

"So you didn't kill Barkley?"

"You know goddamn well I did not. I was just meeting a broad at the hotel. Wrong place at the wrong time."

"What was the broad's name?"

Solly didn't answer at first, then got a little smile on his face that Riley couldn't see.

"I think she went by Nan," he whispered.

Riley was quiet for a second. Then, "What did you say?"

"No—Fran, that's what it was. Her name was Fran. Who in the hell cares what her goddamn name was."

Riley was done playing now.

"Solly, let me get to the point—I'm thinking about putting you in jail for the rest of your life. How would you feel about that?"

"Goddamn threats now. Nice."

"I'm not threatening, I'm telling you how it is. Here is the situation: You're the only gangster we can put in the lobby at the time of the shooting. Desk clerk remembers you getting a phone call— the kill order being confirmed, no doubt. Then he saw you approach Barkley with *malice*, in his words. And then you step deftly aside as the shooters come in. When it's over you disappear with them. Tell me Solly, how do you think all this will look to a Grand Jury?"

"But I was by myself—I almost got my ass shot off!"

"I know. You see, *I* realize it wasn't you. The Purples wouldn't have sent a bunch of gunmen into a hotel lobby; they'd have quietly made Barkley disappear. That's what I think. But it doesn't matter what I think. What matters is how it looks to the Grand Jury. And I plan to make it look like you're the prime suspect."

Solly turned hard in the seat again. "But that ain't fair!"

"I agree and I'm sorry. Hate to send the wrong man up for life. But I have my career to think about."

Levine was so mad he could not even curse. He just sat steaming and his glasses fogged up again.

"There is another option," Riley said.

Levine had his glasses off again, wiping them, and he looked at Riley with naked eyes and Riley could tell those eyes saw nothing but haze. One looked like it was forming a tear.

"If you give me something I need..." Riley said. "For example if you tell me who *did* kill Barkley..."

"How do I know," Levine whined. "They were Wops, I'm sure. But they had hats over their faces. And I was runnin' for my goddamn life, don't forget."

"That's not much help, Solly. If you can't give me anything on Barkley, you must give me something else."

"I got nothing to give."

"Why don't you tell me a little bit about Abie the Agent?"

This confused Solly, which Riley expected. "You don't need to tell me anything now," Riley said. "Go home and think about it. And when we meet again, you're going to give me details—specific jobs Abie has done, things only an insider would know."

"You tryin' to get me killed?"

"Don't worry—long as we're careful, no one will ever know where the information came from. Now get out of here and start wracking your brain. *Details*, Solly... I need details."

Solly got up and wandered off like one of the shell-shocked men onscreen. Riley stayed behind, planning to leave a few minutes after Solly. But he stayed longer, watching the movie. What it most failed to capture, he decided, was the unbearable noise of explosions—a hundred times louder in life than the sound in this theater. And yet, at some point whilst watching, he ended up trapped in the trench with those men. He started to sweat and just let it run down the side of his face. He was paralyzed in that chair, and only snapped out of it because he felt something behind him.

It was a sensation at first, a feeling that something was lurking. Before he could even turn around he felt the hand on his shoulder and looked down at it. If it had been a large hand with a grip like a vise, this would be the point in the story at which Riley died. But it was a small wrinkled hand, and when Riley turned quickly around he saw an old rummy, who'd crept into the seat behind him.

"I need to eat," the old man said. "I haven't had a morsel in two days. Could you spare something?"

Riley let out a deep breath.

The old man said, "You don't look so good yourself, mister. Look like you seen a ghost."

Riley took out his wallet and removed a dollar bill. "This will get you a meal," he said, holding the bill back. "And that is what you are going to spend it on, right?"

The old man nodded.

"Because if you spend it on anything else, I will know about it. Do you believe that?"

The old man nodded again.

Riley gave him the bill and then hoisted himself out of the chair and moved up the aisle, careful not to look at the screen again.

Next day, Riley was at his desk doing whatever people do at desks. Pappas was at Bud's old desk, teaching himself to shuffle a deck of cards and making a mess of it. Riley glanced up every time he heard the cards splatter on Pappas' desk. He tried to withhold judgment. He was about to break when Teddy Baird came in with a document in hand and slapped it on Riley's desk.

"Well, Harry, the circuit judge approved it," Baird said. "Signed, sealed, delivered. You've got your Grand Jury."

Riley didn't say anything but Pappas yelled, "Holy mackerel!"

Baird and Riley both looked over at Pappas, then back at each other as Baird proceeded. "Twenty-three man civilian jury. We start interviewing prospective jurors right away."

He tapped down on the papers. "And this gives us latitude to question the witnesses about more than just Barkley."

Riley actually allowed himself a smile.

"We'll drag them all in, Teddy," he said. "High and low, big and small. We're going to make them sweat. Starting with Max Bernstein and Abie Zussman."

This was news to Baird. "Okay. Sure. But we have to pull the jury together first."

Riley shook his head, a little smile on his face. "Not for these two," he said. "I want to bring them in here before the hearing. Alone—nobody else in the room. Starting with Max."

"Why Max?"

Pappas raised his hand. "I'll tell you why, sir." Then he parroted something Riley had told him earlier: "Because to break a chain, you start with the weak link."

Riley nodded. "I owe you a cracker," he said to Pappas.

Baird was skeptical. "You think these guys are gonna voluntarily tell you anything?"

"If I play my cards right, they don't even have to say much. They just have to show up here."

"And how do you get them to do *that*?" Baird said.

Riley did little mock-acting here, rubbing his chin. "Gee, I guess someone will have to go and let them know it's in their interest. Someone persuasive. Someone fearless."

He slowly turned his head in the direction of Pappas, whose big grin didn't entirely vanish but did freeze up.

They were in the car that same day because Riley was not one to waste time. As Riley drove, Pappas was looking out the window trying to take in the beauty of the world in case he did not get to see it again.

"You nervous?" Riley said.

"Who me? Nah."

"Because it's okay to be nervous. If you weren't it would mean you're stupid."

Pappas considered that. "Well, I am, just a little. Nervous, I mean. But I can ignore it."

"That's not what you do with fear," Riley said. "Unless you want to end up dead."

"Yeah, but what about…"

Pappas hesitated and Riley signaled for him to spit it out.

"Well, it's just that—well, Baird told me about you in the war. How you went behind enemy lines to fetch somebody, then went back again. You had to ignore your fear when you did that, right?"

Riley slowed down the car and pulled to the curb.

"I didn't mean to bring up the war," Pappas said, nervously.

"It's okay. I just want to tell you something."

With the car parked, Riley turned sideways in his seat to face Pappas. "You don't ever, ever have to be a hero on my account, you understand that?"

Pappas just nodded.

"No, I want to make sure we're clear on this," Riley said, "because I don't want you doing anything stupid. Like going through a door when you know there's trouble on the other side. Or up a staircase. You don't have to prove anything to me."

"I understand," Pappas said.

"What I did in the war has nothing to do with here and now. It was different. If I go back across that line, yes I might get killed; but if I run away, maybe I'm running right at a bullet. And if I lay down and cry, that just makes me an easy target. A situation like that, there's no safe option. So I'm not sure courage even factors into it. You see what I'm saying?"

Pappas just nodded and Riley nodded back and then started the car up again. After a few blocks they pulled up in front of the Cream of Michigan. Pappas looked out the window but was in no hurry to open the door.

"So let me get this straight," Pappas said. "I know there's trouble on the other side of that door. And I'm supposed to listen to my fear, which is telling me to stay outta that joint. And I shouldn't try to be a hero, but…"

"But you still have to go in," Riley said.

"That's what I thought."

Riley reached across Pappas and opened his door, then sat back smiling as Pappas slowly got out.

Inside the diner I was with Max and Abie in the booth when Pappas came in looking petrified. The diner had about twenty Purples in it at the time. Several crossword puzzles were being worked on. There was also a table with a sugar-cube igloo that stood about two feet high. The proud builders were now seeing how many things they could fit inside it, like spoons, a cup, a gun. This is what happens when the so-called economy fails.

Pappas started to make his way over to my corner booth, moving slowly. Everyone in the surrounding booths was watching him, but Pappas kept plowing forward. I noticed him coming and didn't know who he was. Abie started to rise out of his seat but I signaled him to stay put. When Pappas was a few feet away he stopped and stood very stiff with his hands clasped in front of him. He was having trouble making eye contact with me and seemed to focus on the newspaper resting on the table. After he took a deep breath, he cleared his throat before finally speaking.

"My boss Harry Riley sent me. You know who he is?"

At this point a bread roll tossed from a nearby table hit Pappas in the back of the head and laughter broke out. To his credit, he did not flinch.

"I know who he is," I said. "What's he want?"

Pappas thought for a second as if trying to remember lines in a play, then continued. "You know about the Grand Jury? He's gonna call people to testify."

"What people?"

"Everybody," Pappas said.

I nodded. "So, do you have a subpoena?"

Before Pappas could answer a voice yelled from another table: "Yeah, he's got a tiny little subpoena!"

More laughter all around.

"No I don't," Pappas said. "I mean, I'm not here for that reason. I'm here to tell you that Riley is cutting deals."

"That is a good one," I said.

Pappas looked me in the eye now for the first time. "You come in, talk to him in private, all off the record. If he decides you have nothing to say, he won't call you in front of the Grand Jury."

"Isn't that nice of him?" I said.

Pappas shook his head. "Not nice, just practical. He doesn't want to look bad by having guys get up and stonewall in front of the GJ. If you're gonna stonewall, he wants to know in advance."

I was tired of looking at this kid's scared eyes and turned to my paper again. "Well, you go back and tell him I'm planning to stonewall. So he can cross me off the list and we don't need to discuss it any further."

"No dice," Pappas said.

I looked up at him. "What did you just say, kid?"

"I mean, it doesn't work that way," Pappas said. "To get the deal you have to go in, just for five minutes. One way or another, you have to talk to him—either in private or in front of the GJ."

I nodded. "Is that all? Or do you want some barley soup, too?"

"No, but thank you for asking," Pappas said. "I think I'll be on my way now."

He turned around and walked away like a man in a funeral march—eyes dead ahead, slow measured steps. As he got near the door he passed the booth where Solly Levine was sitting.

"Hey messenger boy," Solly said to him. "Tell the bastard Riley, next time he wants to screw us... send that pretty red-haired bitch of his, instead of you."

Pappas glanced down at Levine, just for a second, then kept marching out the door.

Back at the booth, I was looking in the direction of the door and Solly's table whilst Max and Abie were looking at me.

"Might be worth going in to see him," Max said.

Abie's head swiveled toward him. "What? Are you delusional?"

"Sounds like a bullshit stunt," I said, still not looking at either of them.

Max said, "I'd just as soon spend five minutes with the guy if it gets me out of going in front of some 'GJ.' That GJ business scares me. The prosecutor can drum up any charges against you—and you don't even have a lawyer there to help. He can grill you for hours in front of that jury, try to catch you in little lies. I don't need that pressure, with my condition. Why not wiggle out of it?"

"Hold on," Abie said. "If Max cuts a deal, I want one too."

I finally looked at them. I couldn't believe they were serious but at this moment I didn't feel like arguing because I had something else on my mind. "Sounds like a bad idea, but we'll run it by Fitzpatrick and see what he advises," I said, assuming our lawyer would shoot the whole thing down like a fat slow pigeon.

"If we went in, we would say nothing, that goes without saying," Max said.

"I don't want to discuss it right now," I said whilst neatly folding my newspaper. Then I picked up the sugar bowl from our table and held it in the palm of my hand as if to weigh it.

"You okay, Joe?" Abie said. "You seem distracted."

I studied the bowl in my hand. "Anybody using this now?"

Abie and Max glanced at each other and didn't know what to say. Then they watched as I got up and put on my hat with my left hand, whilst the right stilled cradled that bowl. I walked down the aisle toward the door but before I got to it, I stopped at Solly's booth. I looked down at him—he would not look up at me.

"That remark about the wife. Why would you say something like that, Solly?"

"It was a joke, that's all," Solly said, still looking down.

"It was in poor taste."

"Well that's how I am, Joe—a sonofabitch with poor taste."

"Then we need to sweeten you up," I said.

As the bowl shattered against Solly's head the sugar poured down over his face and only after a couple of seconds did the blood follow. Solly remained conscious and mumbled just one word, "Goddamn," whilst he slowly laid himself down on the bench in the booth and kept his hand on his head. I continued on my way out the door and as I pushed on it I noticed my own hand was cut and bleeding. Out in the fresh air, I pulled a handkerchief from my pocket to wrap the hand but first I licked it and it tasted sugary sweet.

TWENTY-SEVEN

Riley's offer was a cheap stunt and normally I never would have gone along with it. But he got lucky on a couple of counts. It so happened that my lawyer Fitzpatrick (who would gradually come to be known as Putzpatrick), was facing possible disbarment after a run-in with a circuit judge Riley knew well. This enabled Riley to strike a secret deal with Putzpatrick: "I will put in a good word with the judge if you will persuade Joe to let Max and Abie come down and talk to me."

Putzpatrick balked at first and then set down all kinds of conditions: "I must be in the room." (No, said Riley, but you can wait in the hall and watch through the office window). "The meeting cannot last more than five minutes." (Ten, said Riley). "You cannot write down or record or document anything said in that room." (Agreed, said Riley). "You must swear in writing that whatever is said in that room cannot be used in court." (Absolutely, said Riley). "You cannot tell Joe Bernstein that you and I are swapping favors." (Do I look like a fool, said Riley).

Once the private understanding was hammered out, Putzpatrick then came to me and advised that maybe it wasn't such a bad idea to let Max and Abie talk to Riley off the record. "It's safer than letting Max appear before a Grand Jury," Putzpatrick said. I grudgingly agreed and a meeting was set for ten days hence.

In the meantime Riley's plan—or I should say plot—required

that he get inside information from Solly Levine to use in the meetings with Max and Abie. And here is where Riley's second piece of luck came into play. After the earlier conversation with Riley in the movie theater, Solly had thought over Riley's offer and decided he'd rather face the Grand Jury on a fake Barkley murder rap than risk his life as a stoolie. But all that changed when Solly banged his head on that sugar bowl.

The accident put Solly in a mood that was foul even for him. He walked around saying things like, "Can you believe he hit me with a sugar bowl? After all I've done." He was of course especially peeved at me but he was also mad at Abie and Max, because they were at the table when I grabbed the sugar bowl and therefore might have intervened, by Solly's logic. So after stewing for two days, Solly got back in touch with Riley and agreed to meet him once again at the Empire, where "ALL QUI_T ON THE WESTERN F_ONT" was still playing to a near-empty house.

When Riley showed up inside the theater and saw Solly sitting there with his bandaged head he said, "I told you to wrack your brain Solly, but you didn't have to go that far." Of course this remark made Solly sore—"You're making a goddamn joke about my head trauma? Nice."—but it didn't stop him from whispering tales of Abie the Agent for the next hour whilst Riley jotted notes.

And so Riley was primed for the meeting with Abie and Max, which took place a week later at the DA's office. That rainy morning, Riley was sitting in his office when Pappas rushed through the door, so excited he could hardly get the words out: "They just pulled up out front in Bernstein's Doozie," he said.

Riley leaned back in his chair and clasped his hands behind his head as if he could not be more relaxed.

"Are Max and Abie with him?"

By now Teddy Baird had crowded into the doorway too and he was as jumpy as Pappas.

"Yessirree, all three of 'em and Fitzpatrick too," Baird said. "We got a whole convoy coming in here."

Riley nodded to Baird. "Teddy, quick—any last tidbits you can give me on Max Bernstein?"

Baird was surprised at being put on the spot. "Tidbits?"

"Yes, tidbits. Give me anything. Favorite soda pop, anything."

Baird rubbed the back of his neck. "You know more than I do, Harry. 'Course everybody knows about his jitters. Engineering whiz, but you knew that. Big-time Tigers fan, not that it matters."

Riley raised an eyebrow at that. "Tigers fan, huh?'"

"Oh sure, big-time," Baird said. "Got a box seat at Navin Field right by the dugout, near the players. Some say he's a bit *too* fond of them, if you get me."

Riley to his credit paid no mind to that bit of fucking slander and just nodded and wrote "Tigers" on a piece of paper.

"You didn't ask me about Abie," Baird said.

"Don't need to," Riley said, raising himself out of his chair. "About him, I've been thoroughly briefed."

As Riley moved out into the hall, we were just coming through the front door. I led the way walking with a swagger, my hat tilted down over my eyes. We were all in our buttoned-up whites under nice jackets, except for Putzpatrick who wore a bow tie. Max was very nervous; he had been asking Putzpatrick questions the whole way over and was still whispering questions as we walked down the hall.

I stopped a few yards in front of Riley and raised up the brim of my hat. It was the first time the two of us had a good long look into each other's eyes since the night of the speakeasy fight. I gave him a little nod, then looked at Baird who turned his eyes away. Then I looked at Pappas and smiled at him.

"There he is. The boy who had no subpoena."

Riley spoke up. "Here's how we'll do this," he said. "I'd like to talk to Max first, in my office over there."

At this point Putzpatrick figured he'd take charge and stepped forward, extending a handshake Riley did not accept.

"Been a while, Harry," he said.

"Seems like just last week," Riley said and Putzpatrick tried to smile as if it was a joke; already Riley had him on the defensive.

As Putzpatrick laid out the ground rules Riley and Joe looked at each other like two boxers in the ring, both nodding after each point. When Putzpatrick was finished Riley asked them all to sit in the hallway. Nobody sat.

Then Riley turned to Max. "Mr. Bernstein, will you join me?"

Riley led Max into his office, closing the door behind him. The top half of the dividing wall was glass, providing a clear view inside the office from the hallway. The soundproofing was good; you couldn't hear what was said in there. Out in that hallway I folded my arms and leaned back against the wall. Abie looked around for a book but had to settle for a magazine.

Inside the office, Riley signaled Max to sit. Max acted as if the chair itself might be a trap and stood for a minute scratching his inside forearm and bobbing his head. "First, before anything else," Max said, "I have something to say."

"Which is?"

"I got nothing to say."

"But you just said you had something."

"Yes, that was it. I just wanted to warn you."

"Fair enough," Riley said. "You've warned me. Now will you have a seat?"

Max started to sit down but before he did he looked back through the glass partition—and saw me and Putzpatrick staring at him with arms folded. This seemed to freeze him.

"Don't pay attention to them," Riley said. "They can't hear us."

"What does it matter if they can hear us? I'm not going to say anything."

"Right," said Riley. "I almost forgot. Let me tell you my situation, Max. See that guy over there?"

Riley pointed through the glass to the adjoining office, where Teddy Baird was pretending to read a paper.

"That's my boss," Riley said. "You might not know it to look at him, but he is one hard apple. I live in mortal fear of that guy."

Max was head-down, focused on a hangnail. "What do I care?"

"It's just that he warned me I better not screw up with these Grand Jury witnesses. That's why he wants me to pre-interview people."

"Uh-huh. And?"

Riley shot a sneaky glance at Baird and then leaned closer to Max and lowered his voice. "I know a smart guy like you isn't gonna talk. To be honest, I don't even have any questions to ask you. But I have to make it look good, okay? So let's just talk about anything for a few minutes—do that for me, and I won't call you before the Grand Jury."

Max looked up from his hangnail. "But we got nothing to talk about."

"People can talk about anything if they make an effort," Riley said. "Let's talk about... baseball. You follow the Tigers?"

"Maybe."

"Go to Navin Field much?"

Max started to answer, then hesitated. Then he nodded to himself. "I see. Trying to place me at Navin on a particular date?"

"No, no Max, you misunderstand. This is just two guys talking baseball. Haven't you ever just talked baseball with another guy?"

Max thought about that for a second. "Not really."

"Oh. Well you should. It's one of the great things about baseball, you can talk about it endlessly without much thought required. It is kind of a shame, though."

"What is?"

"That the Tigers have no shot this year. I mean, we'd have more to talk about if they had a shot."

"You don't think they have a shot?"

"Nah. So maybe we should talk about the horses."

"They're only three-and-a-half games back."

"Do you follow the horses?"

"And there are still eighteen games left in the season."

"Well, I guess. Not quite over yet."

"All they need to do is go twelve and six whilst the Yanks play one game over five-hundred ball and that would force a playoff."

"You've given this some thought, I see."

"Of course I would prefer they go thirteen and five and avoid the playoff game because you know anything can happen in a one-game scenario. You cannot control it."

"But there's one thing you're forgetting, Max, and that's pitching."

"What about it?"

"They have none."

Now Max leaned forward in his chair. "Am I hearing you correctly? None?"

"Zilch."

"I will count them off for you," Max said, holding up a bony fist between him and Riley.

"They got Stanton," Max said.

From the fist he shot up the index finger.

"They got Hillerman."

He shot up a second finger.

"They got Fat Pete Howard."

A third finger went up.

Riley leaned back in his chair nodding and acting fascinated.

Meanwhile out in the hallway me and Putzpatrick were watching and even Abie was peering over the top of his magazine.

"What's he beating his gums about?" Abie said. "Looks like he's *counting.*"

Nobody said anything and Abie gave Putzpatrick a little poke on the shoulder. "Why is he counting?"

"How should I know?"

"You're a lawyer."

"Abie calm down," I said.

I looked at my watch. They'd been in there two minutes so far.

Back inside the office, they dispensed with pitching and moved to the starting lineup. Riley asked whether Max would change the batting order if he were manager.

"That's a good question you ask," Max said.

"So you would change the batting order?"

"Two changes, that's all I would do."

"I've thought about this myself," Riley said. "Let's try something."

He grabbed a notepad on his desk and tore off a sheet of paper for himself, then pushed the pad in front of Max.

"You write down your ideal lineup and I'll write mine. Let's see if they match."

"Sure why not," Max said, and starting writing down the names whilst Riley did likewise.

Soon as we all saw Max start writing, I turned to Putzpatrick and said: "He's writing. What happened to the ground rules?"

Putzpatrick immediately went to the office window and tapped hard on the glass and then started shaking his head whilst also shaking his hand in a writing motion; he looked like he was having some kind of convulsion. Riley nodded and snatched the pad away from Max and put it in the drawer.

"What'd you do that for?" Max said. "And why's he rapping on the glass? Something going on here?"

Max's whole body twitched once in his seat.

"You okay?" Riley said. "Want some water?"

"There's nothing the matter with me," Max said. "But it looks like everyone else has gone nuts."

"No, your lawyer's just doing his job—we're not supposed to write stuff down. But we still have a few more minutes to kill. This isn't so bad, right? Talking baseball?"

Max just shrugged.

"Come on admit it. It's not terrible."

"Okay, okay."

Riley spent the next six minutes getting Max to give him three reasons why the Tigers were actually superior to the Yanks, as well as four reasons why the team was better off without Cobb, and five reasons why Navin Field should not be torn down for a new ballpark. Max got very emotional about that last one and almost looked like he was going to cry, which was just fine with Riley.

When the full ten minutes were up—as indicated by Putzpatrick who rapped on the glass and pointed to the clock—Max was in the midst of talking and did not want to stop. By this time Abie had rolled up his magazine very tightly and was tapping it against his thigh whilst pacing back and forth and peering into the office window. I never budged; I still had my arms folded and my back to the wall.

Riley opened the door and as they came out together Max was still talking about Navin Field and his box seat by the dugout, though we didn't know that.

"From my position I can see everything that's going on," he said as he came through the door.

Abie looked at me but I would not return his glance.

"Yes," Riley said, "that's the benefit of your being right in the middle of the action, so to speak. And now you have shared that firsthand knowledge with me."

"You had it all wrong," Max said.

"I did. You set me straight, and for that I am grateful, Max."

"So I won't have to go before the Grand Jury, right?"

"You did what I asked—deal's a deal."

They shook hands and when Max turned away from Riley he found Abie standing in his path looking not at all pleased.

"What?" Max said. "We were just talking baseball."

Riley let out a little laugh when Max said that and it made Max turn back to him. "What's so funny?"

"Nothing," Riley said. "I coughed."

Teddy Baird had come out of his office now to join the group.

"No, you laughed," Max said to Riley. "Why is it funny that we talked about baseball?"

"Baseball?" Baird said. "You were talking about baseball that whole time?"

Riley acted a little cowed in front of Baird. "No, sir, we weren't talking about baseball. I was conducting an interview pursuant to the Grand Jury hearing. Sir."

Riley then shot Max a look with a raised eyebrow. And Max now remembered that they were supposed to be making Baird think it was a real interview; this was part of the deal. Max was torn now. He didn't want to scotch his deal with Riley, but he didn't want me and Abie to get the wrong idea. Riley of course moved right in when he saw Max hesitate.

"Max do you have anything else you want to add to our interview regarding the Barkley Grand Jury hearing?"

Max looked at Riley. "No, I guess not," he said.

"In that case, let's move on. Mr. Zussman, will you come in?"

Abie was still staring at Max and he held the stare as Max walked in a daze over to me, whilst I was studying Riley.

"Mr. Zussman?" Riley repeated.

Abie stalked past Riley into his office and Riley followed him in and shut the door. Abie sat in the chair and Riley moved round the desk to his own chair and sat. Before anyone spoke, Abie leaned forward and placed his meaty hands on the desk in front of Riley, then laced the fingers. He spoke quietly.

"What did you do with him? Did you trick him?"

Riley leaned back in his chair. "Trick? Do I look like Houdini?"

Abie didn't answer, just stared at Riley who in turn found himself wondering how many men had seen those eyes with that exact look during their final seconds of life.

"Well, do I?" Riley asked again. "You know what Houdini looked like. You saw him when he performed at the Garrick."

"I have nothing to say to you. Nothing."

Riley let out another of those little laughs of his.

"Why is that funny?" Abie barked.

"No it's just... well, that was the first thing Max said when he came in."

"Well, *I* mean it."

Riley nodded as if in resignation.

"That's fine. But I just want to let you know something. I've learned some interesting information. I won't say from who."

"You only talked to one guy so far."

Riley smiled. "Anyway, I know a few things. Such as..."

Riley raised a fist in the air between him and Abie.

"... I know what happened to Thompson the night Houdini was at the Garrick. And who snuck into his car in the parking lot."

Riley's index finger shot up.

"I also know about that fella Strauss—now *that* was an interesting tale. How he kept changing seats in the theater—a 'seat jumper,' I think you called him. And you almost left the movie without killing him. But you stuck it out and finally speared him, and everyone went home happy. Except Strauss. Good story."

Riley shot a second finger in the air in front of Abie, who had pulled his own hands back off the desk and folded them in his lap.

"Who told you that fictional story about Strauss?"

"I can't divulge my source, Mr. Zussman. But it's a reliable one. And this same source told me that you killed Grabowski—after killing his precious pet. You turned on an old pal, just like that."

In a flash, Abie pounded his fist on the desk.

"That's a lie," he said softly. "I didn't kill him. And *I* wasn't the one that turned on him. *That* was somebody else. You're getting this all from Max."

Riley threw up his hands in a helpless gesture.

"Not necessarily. Not absolutely. Look, it's for you to decide if it was Max or, say, the Tooth Fairy. All I can tell you is I have been given this information. And knowing all of this, of course... I will have to call you before the Grand Jury."

Abie could hardly contain himself but tried to do so by folding his arms tightly together.

"You said you were cutting deals," he growled.

"I am. But only with people who talk to me. You haven't said much. Would you like to start talking?"

"I told you I have nothing to say to you."

"Then there is no deal for you, Mr. Zussman. I'll see you on the witness stand."

Riley pushed back his chair from the desk and then turned his back on Abie to shuffle papers on a table behind him. It was very brave of him—or just foolish—to expose his back to Abie at this moment. But Abie was too stunned to do anything except get up slowly to leave.

Before he could, Riley turned back to him and said: "One more thing I forgot to mention. I know what you did to that cop Clarke. Broke the man's neck. Cut him up in pieces. How do you think the Grand Jury's going to react when they hear about that, Abie?"

Abie stood there, his hand on the doorknob but not moving.

"Better yet, how do you think they'll react when they *see* it. On film. Because my source tells me that he kept the film of the incident. He kept it just in case he needed a bargaining chip."

Abie still stood there, hand on the knob. Riley let him stand. Then Abie opened the door and walked out in a simmering daze.

When I saw the way Abie came out of that office, I got worried for the first time since we'd arrived. I couldn't imagine what Riley might have said to put him in such a state.

"Everything okay?" I said.

"Sure," Abie said but he sounded like he was someplace else.

Max was watching Abie too but Abie wouldn't look at him and this made Max uneasy so he thought he'd try levity (which was never his strong suit). "Boy, he sure chased you out fast—did you start talking about psychology to him?"

Abie slowly turned to look at Max now and Max realized he was better off when he was being ignored.

"Well," Abie said, "Guess I didn't have any *baseball tips* to tell him."

Max tried to laugh but it came out more like a hiccup.

"You say something?" Abie said, walking toward him. "Or was that just a little squeal I heard?"

I knew what was coming now and I tried to move in between them but before I could, Abie's hand got hold of Max's throat and squeezed and Max immediately dropped to one knee. I grabbed Abie's fleshy ear in my fist and tightened and then turned until I could hear the skin behind the ear start to tear. Abie knew right away he was in danger of losing the ear because it was known that I had once torn off a man's ear in Hamtramck (with good reason). So Abie released his grip on Max, and I in turn let go the ear. Max stayed down on his knee whilst checking carefully to make sure his head was still attached.

I moved in front of Abie and put both hands on his shoulders and tried to catch his eye though he kept looking past me at Max.

"Why would you lay a hand on my brother?" I said. I didn't say it with anger—I was more hurt than mad.

Abie paused and closed his eyes, trying to gather himself. When he opened them again he began to speak slowly as if to a child.

"*He…*" (Abie pointed to Riley) "…knows things about *me…*" (now he jabbed a thumb at his own chest) "…that only *he…*" (now he pointed to Max) "…could've told him."

I nodded. "Listen to me, Abie." I took hold of Abie's chin and steadied his head. "You listening?"

He nodded like a puppet in my hand.

"You've been duped," I said. "That's all. A little trick by a guy who thinks he can play games with us."

I glanced over at Riley, who was standing in the doorway of his office, both hands leaning on his cane. Then I looked back at Abie.

"Do you get what I'm telling you?"

"What I *get,*" Abie said, looking at me in a hard way he'd never looked at me before, "is that your brother has made a deal that will put me away for life."

"That's a lie!" Max croaked; he was still rubbing his throat.

And it was, of course—but Abie believed all of Riley's piffle, even the crazy bit about the Clarke film. There was no film; Max destroyed it at the time. And Riley knew that, because Solly told him. But Riley gambled that maybe no one had actually *seen* Max destroy the film.

I tried to reach Abie: "Max would never turn against us."

He looked at me with disbelief now, and shook his head. "Are you kidding? He already turned against Grabowski—he turned *you* against Grabowski!"

"Grabowski has nothing to do with this. Forget Grabowski."

"I can't," Abie said to me. "Maybe you can, but I can't."

Abie looked past me at Max. "Your brother can't see what you are, Heebie Jeebie, but I can. I always saw it. You're a sickness."

Max, sitting on the floor against the wall with his head down, started to quiver now.

"And there he goes, right on cue," Abie said. "Psycho-somatic bullshit. Or maybe it's the symptoms of a rat with a guilty conscience."

I had had enough. I shoved Abie hard in the shoulder to get his attention. And then he did something unexpected—he put his big hand flat against my chest. He didn't push me exactly. He moved me back slowly. He separated himself from me. Then he turned and walked down the hall toward the exit.

"Where are you going Abie?" I called after him but he went out the door. As he went out the two Feds, short and tall, were coming in; Abie almost plowed them over.

I glared back at Riley who had a blank look on his face. Then I reached down and took hold of Max's arm and helped him up. By this time Putzpatrick was hovering a safe distance away—I shot him a look, too, and said, "*You've* been a big help today."

I led Max out by the arm. Putzpatrick, keeping well back, skulked out behind us.

After we went out the door, the office was quiet for a moment. Pappas was the first to weigh in: "Holy smokes," he said.

Riley nodded in agreement, then turned toward the two Feds coming down the hall.

"You fellas might want to inform your pal Livoli about the little brouhaha we had here today," he said.

The Feds looked at each other and then looked at Baird, who promised to fill them in. But first Baird, scratching his head, looked at Riley. "You planned all this?"

Riley thought about that. "Yeah, I guess. But I didn't think it would actually *work*."

TWENTY-EIGHT

Whilst her husband was busy laying traps, Nan was sitting at home but not alone. Across from her at the card table was a large cop named Butch Moran. When Nan insisted on accompanying Riley back to Detroit, Riley insisted on a police guard and hence Moran became a household fixture—much like a floor lamp only bigger and not as bright.

She was attempting to play cards with Moran—he was hopeless—and listening to the sound of the horns on the phonograph player when she thought she heard a drumbeat and then realized it was a knock on the door.

Her eyes lit up as she looked at Moran. "Wowza, we've got company, Butch!"

She started for the door but Butch made her wait whilst he answered it. He opened it just a crack and saw Tennessee Jenkins, decked out in a coat with a mink collar, a fine leather shoulder bag, and a hat with an ostrich feather in it.

"Oh," Butch said. "You the maid?"

Ten's head jerked to a tilt. "Do I look like a maid to you? This look like a maid's hat?"

At this point Nan gave Butch a gentle shove in the ribs and opened the door wide. The women exchanged looks. Then Nan stepped forward to embrace her and Ten hugged her back harder.

"I've been thinking a lot about you," Nan said, her head over

Ten's shoulder. She stepped back and took hold of Ten's small hand.

"Please, come in. Come into my *boudoir*."

They both laughed and went inside.

Nan took her coat and hat, but Ten held onto her bag. From it, she pulled a bottle of Old Log Cabin.

"It's on the house today," Ten said.

They sat side-by-side on the living room sofa with the Old Log and a couple of tumblers on the table in front of them. Off in the corner Butch found a more suitable partner as he played pattycake with three-year-old Jean (the twin babies being asleep upstairs). Louis Armstrong blew his heart out on the phonograph.

"Young fella can play a horn," Ten said.

"Maybe you could hire him to play at your place," Nan said.

Ten smiled and then looked down. "No, I'm done with the place—sold it off last week. I'm headed to New York."

Nan's mouth opened and her hand went to her chest.

"No! You mustn't. I won't let you."

"The blind pig business is never gonna be like it was," Ten said. "That party's come and gone. And Jerry always said I belonged in New York."

"But what will you do there?"

"Start from scratch. Like I did here."

Nan reached for the bottle to pour them both another drink.

"Course I may have to come back," Ten added, "if a certain fella calls me before the Grand Jury."

Hearing that caused Nan to flop back against the sofa with her palm flat against her forehead. "Ugh! If I hear the words 'Grand Jury' one more time... And he hasn't even started yet."

"Needs to be done," Ten said. "It's a big mess he's trying to clean up. I know, cause I was deep in it."

"Were you?" Nan asked innocently.

"The way you ask that question," Ten said with a smile, "I'd swear your husband's got you doing his diggin' for him."

They downed their drinks and talked about a lot of things, but especially about Barkley.

Nan said, "Jerry was in *real* deep, wasn't he?"

"Deeper than the bottom of the ocean," Ten said shaking her head. "Just kept takin' more money and doin' more favors."

Ten, her glass empty, tapped on the rim and Nan refilled it.

"By the end, he was real scared," Ten said. "The mob and Bowles put the screws to him. And Jerry played along—until that last night."

Ten smiled, just thinking about it. "He sure surprised 'em that night," she said. "*Recall the son of a bitch'*—I just about fell over when I heard that."

"You ever talk to him that night?"

"Y'mean, am I the one they talk about in the papers? The 'mystery gal' who called and was goin' to meet him in the lobby? No, I didn't call Jerry that night. We didn't speak for a while before that. Ever since... what happened."

Ten's eyes welled up soon as she said those words. Nan leaned closer and tried to wrap an arm around her shoulder. Ten was stiff at first, as if she did not want the comfort. But then a sob jerked her whole body and she knew there was no point trying to be tough anymore. She leaned into the hug and started to cry. She kept talking whilst crying, her voice squeaky and high like a child's.

"You don't know how bad it got for him," she said into Nan's shoulder. "The crash wiped him out. He owed Livoli. He was desperate. He did some bad things, I know. But I just can't believe he would ever put that boy in harm's way."

Then she pulled back and looked at Nan: "Jerry wouldn't do that, would he?"

Using her own sleeve pulled down into the palm of her hand, Nan brushed a tear from Ten's cheek. "He wouldn't," Nan said. "You mustn't think such things. Jerry was a good man."

Ten nodded. "That's what I tell myself. He wanted to do right. Wanted so bad for Harry to respect him. He wasn't like that with anybody else—just Harry."

"Because Harry believed in him," Nan said.

They were interrupted by the sound of giggling from across the room. Butch was tossing a ball to little Jean, who dropped it and then scrambled after it. Ten watched the child and as she did Nan watched her.

Ten was on her way to a new life in New York by the time Riley arrived home that night. He came through the door and saw no sign of Butch and found Nan asleep on the sofa, the half-empty bottle nearby. He went into the kitchen and found Butch asleep too, his head on the kitchen table. Riley rapped on the table with his cane to wake him up, then spoke to him sharply about snoozing on the job and sent him home.

Nan was sitting up rubbing her eyes when he came back into the living room.

He said, "Why are you drinking half a bottle of whiskey on a Wednesday?"

She told him about Ten's visit and he shook his head.

"Booze in the afternoon. Tennessee Jenkins. You turning this place into a speakeasy?"

"Exactly," she said. "All we need is a name. Any ideas?"

Riley wouldn't play. He turned away, looking for his paper.

"How about… the Mausoleum?" she said. "Quietest speakeasy in town. Run by a couple of stiffs."

"Your trouble is you can't ever be serious," Riley grumbled as he sat down with his paper.

She got up and walked behind his chair, then placed her hands on his shoulders and started to rub them. "You're serious enough for the both of us," she said.

He didn't say anything for a little while after that as she kept rubbing the shoulders, whilst he let the paper fall in his lap and closed his eyes.

"I have to be," he finally said. "There's a lot at stake."

After a little while she asked him how "it" was feeling tonight.

"Not good," he said.

"Shall we take it off?"

As he unbuttoned the shirt she worked on the trousers; with the two of them working together he was soon in his shorts. Then he let her open the buckles that pressed against his torso, leaning forward in his chair as she stepped around behind him, unwinding the straps. She paused for a second and her finger traced the red marks the straps left on his back. She came back around to the front of the chair and helped him remove the leg and placed it on the floor. Next, she popped the buttons on the shoulder of her own dress and let it slide down to her feet. She stepped out of it and then climbed into his lap, right there in the chair.

"If this chair should break," he said, gathering her in, "you will be held accountable."

Later on, still curled up in his lap like a cat, she told him about Ten leaving town.

"I know," Riley said. "I feel sorry for her."

"Me too," Nan said. "But in a way I envy her."

Riley gave her a look. "Why?"

"She gets to start her life over again now. New place, new people. She will be fascinating to everyone. A woman with a mysterious past. I think that might be fun."

He laughed and shook his head, not understanding.

They talked about his day and he told her what happened at the office: his little trick involving me, Max, and Abie. He thought she might congratulate him on his cleverness but she just sat quiet.

"You think it was unfair to fool them that way?" he asked.

"I don't know," she said. "Maybe."

"They *are* criminals."

"I know."

Then she asked whether he thought Abie would leave the gang altogether. Riley shrugged. She also asked whether Max would face suspicion within the gang and Riley shrugged again. The only one she did not ask about was me—who can say why.

"So what do you hope will come of your little ploy?" she asked.

"Honestly I don't know," Riley said. "A crack has formed and we'll see how it spreads."

Several months went by and there was no word from Abie the Agent. I figured he would come back once he cooled off, but Max knew better.

"He holds a grudge like it's precious," Max said.

No one saw Abie around town but then he was always good at keeping a low profile. There was no sign of him at his house—his wife and kid were on their own. There was a rumor he'd gone back to chopping carcasses at a so-called abattoir somewhere. There was an even crazier rumor that he'd gone to Germany to practice psychology, or maybe it was philosophy.

Then Solly Levine announced one Thursday afternoon that he'd seen Abie going into the Detroit Public Library.

"And that's not all," Solly said.

He paused for effect and I asked, "Would you like a drum roll before you tell us the rest?"

"I was getting to it," Solly said. "After he goes inside... a couple of Livoli's goons follow him in."

I looked at Solly's eyes behind the thick glasses (which were held together at one corner by masking tape, ever since the sugar bowl accident).

"You sure you saw right?" I said.

"There is nothing wrong with my goddamn vision," he said. "Think about it—it all makes sense. Abie was probably talking to Livoli's people way back when. And they were passing it to the Feds. And from there it got to Riley—that's how *he* knew all about us. Then to cover himself Abie tries to blame poor Max here. What a sonofabitch that Abie turned out to be!"

I looked at Max. "That sound right to you?"

"The pieces do seem to fit," he said.

I said, "We'll have to look into it and see if Solly is seeing right."

"I'll keep an eye out next few days," Solly said whilst wiping his glasses. "If I spot him again, I'll call you and you can come see for yourself."

I was right to be suspicious of what Solly claimed to see—only half of it was true. Yes, he did see Abie go into the library several days earlier. But he did not observe any oilers there; he made that up. Here is what happened (and hold tight, because it's a twisty road): Soon as Solly spotted Abie at the library he passed this information to Riley, who was still squeezing him. Riley then passed it to the well-fed Fed, who in turn passed it to Livoli. The Feds suggested that Livoli offer a job to Abie, who could provide inside dope on the Purples, which Livoli could then pass back to the Feds. Livoli agreed (he could always use an enforcer like Abie— who couldn't?) and he told one of his oilers to watch the library and let him know if Abie showed up. Meantime, Solly was also keeping watch, ready to alert me. Never before or since has the Detroit Library been of so much interest to so many people.

The next Saturday morning, inside the library, children and geezers were sitting around reading and a few down-and-out bums were pretending to, whilst no one made a sound except for the occasional hacking cough. In the midst of this serenity however there was something amiss and it took the form of two oilers wearing pinstriped suits and wandering through the book stacks as if lost in the desert. One of them was sharp-faced John Livoli and the other a henchman.

"Ever been in one of these places?" Livoli said.

"Once," the henchman said.

"Why?" Livoli asked.

"Had to bone up on a mark. Looked up news articles about him."

"And that was useful?"

The henchman shrugged. "Not really."

A loud "shush" was directed at the two men from a nearby table. Both Livoli and the henchman stopped and swiveled their heads toward an old man sitting at the table in question. They glared at him and he quickly put his nose back in the book where it belonged. Then they resumed walking and looking around. The henchman stopped and pointed to the rear of the library.

"There he is," he said.

At a table in the back Abie was talking to a pretty librarian with eyeglasses; she had to bend back to look up at him. She was smiling at him a lot, though he was only concerned with the book in his hands.

"You don't know how much it means to me that you tracked down this book," he said. "I started reading it once before and then lost it. I always wondered how it ended."

The book was called *The Decline of the West*, by somebody named Spengler. Don't ask me why Abie was reading this, I could not begin to tell you. All I know is, he had left it in a movie theater one time whilst doing a job. And for years after, he mentioned that lost Spengler book.

"We don't get many requests for that one except among students," the librarian said. "Are you a student?"

The question seemed to embarrass Abie, who kept his head down. "Me? Nah," he said. Then he thought about it and said, "Well, maybe. I guess you could say that."

In the corner of his eye Abie noticed the two men approaching. He quickly stepped away from the table and then stood facing the men with arms at sides and fingers spread, ready for action.

"Relax Abie," Livoli said and held up his hands. "I'm not here for trouble. I just want to talk."

Abie stood very still. "I have nothing to say to you," he said. "And I don't want to be seen with you."

Livoli was still holding up his arms but turned the palms up to form a shrug. "Who's gonna see us in this place?"

He walked over to the table as the librarian scurried away. He pulled out a chair for himself, and looked at Abie.

"Come on," said Livoli. "Let's squat here for a moment, just us two." He glanced at the henchman. "Why don't you go read up on somebody?"

The henchman headed for a nearby stack.

As Livoli sat down at the table he swept his arm across it and several books were pushed to the floor. He then folded his hands together (his fingernails were manicured it should be noted), and rested them on the shiny wood tabletop. Abie walked to the other side of the table so he was facing Livoli but didn't sit, just stood with arms folded.

"This is not a bad place to conduct business," Livoli said. "Quiet. Lots of room. Lots of wisdom all around."

Abie said nothing and Livoli nodded.

"All I wish to say to you, Abie, is that a man like you is worth a lot. And should be appreciated. Are you appreciated?"

Abie just kept staring at Livoli.

"Now *I* would appreciate a guy like you," Livoli said. "And I would show my appreciation."

There were a few seconds of silence then. Livoli would tell me, many years later, that Abie must've been thinking things over. But all that's really known are his words, which made things clear.

"If you think I'd ever turn on my own people," Abie said, "then you know nothing about me."

Livoli nodded but he also arched his brow. "Seems to me like they've turned on *you*," he said. "You're on the outs, Abie."

"That's temporary," Abie said.

Livoli's finger was drawing little circles on the tabletop. "Is it? You been hiding for a while now. Not so temporary."

"You wouldn't understand. I took some time to go think about things. But I'm back and I plan to patch things up with Joe. So you and I don't need to talk anymore."

"Why go back if you can go forward?"

"Because it's where I belong," Abie said.

Livoli folded his hands on the table now, and gave Abie that little smile of a man who thinks he knows better. "There is no *belong*," he said. "None of us belong here—they'd run us *all* out if they could. But here we are. In the melting pot."

Livoli now opened his hands, in a kind of welcoming gesture. "There is no reason Jews and Italians can't work together these days," he said. "Look at Luciano and Lansky in New York. Now there is a model of brotherhood we can all learn from."

Abie nodded a little, but just a little.

"You see Abie, if you're choosing sides there is really just one question—are you with the winners or the losers?"

Abie nodded once more. Then he suddenly reached toward Livoli, causing this supposedly fearless oiler to lean back so fast that the chair almost fell over backwards. Livoli relaxed when he saw Abie was just holding a big hand in front of him, for a shake.

"At this point I will say thank you as I leave," Abie said.

Livoli didn't take the handshake right away. "You have no interest? Don't even want to hear what I'm offering?"

"I know what you're offering," Abie said. "I guess I'll just stay as I am—I have no desire to melt."

Livoli reluctantly shook the big hand and for a second his own felt crushed though this was just Abie's normal handshake.

"I do appreciate the offer," Abie said. "However this doesn't mean that I might not still kill you sometime in the future."

Abie walked away, nodding at the librarian as he passed her. Livoli shook his head and checked his hand for damage, then put on his hat and looked around for the henchman, who was lost somewhere in the crusades with King Arthur.

As Abie stepped out of the library and into the harsh sunlight he pulled his hat down over his eyes to protect them, as any person might do even if they had nothing to hide. But of course when somebody is under suspicion everything they do looks suspicious.

"Look at him covering his mug," said Solly from the back seat of the Doozie, parked across the street and down the block a ways. In the front seat passenger side, Max was looking through binoculars. He offered them to me, in the driver's seat.

"See for yourself," Max said.

"I don't need those to see what's in front of me," I said.

We saw Abie come down the library steps and turn right at the sidewalk, moving in the opposite direction from us. We watched him shrink as he ankled further and further away.

"He's got a bounce in his step," Solly said. "Sonofabitch must have made a good deal."

"Shut the hell up, Solly," I said.

Max had the binoculars focused on the library entrance again.

"Here they come," he said. "Not sure who that is with Livoli."

"Doesn't matter," I said.

I didn't bother looking at the two men; I was staring off in the direction of the Museum, directly across Woodward, opposite the library. In particular I was looking at the big statue of the Thinker on the front steps of the museum. All around the Thinker, people sat on the steps reading newspapers. I was quiet for a while and then heard myself say out loud to the statue: "So what do *you* think?"

"Who me?" Max said. "I'll tell you what I think. I think there's no choice but to put him on the spot."

"No doubt," said Solly from the back seat.

I didn't look at either of them, just kept watching the Thinker. I found I needed a handkerchief because I suddenly had something in my eye—must have blown in from the open window.

"Set it up," I eventually said and Max nodded. "But listen to me," I added. "Use at least three shooters including a couple of Tommies. If I know Abie, he will not go down easy."

The Doozie pulled out and drove fast down Woodward and there was no way I would have noticed that inside one of the many parked cars we passed was a tall man wearing a baseball cap and sunglasses whilst a short well-fed man in the passenger seat wore a cowboy hat. Soon after our car sped past, the fat cowboy looked out the window through binoculars. He watched Livoli's car pull away from its parking spot in front of the Library. Then he turned the binocs on that Thinker statue and all those people beneath it reading. One of the readers lowered a newspaper and of course it was Riley.

TWENTY-NINE

I have always believed that the more unpleasant a task, the sooner you should get it done. And so the time of reckoning arrived a mere 24 hours later—a beautiful Sunday morning on which men all over Detroit finally found the good sense to abandon their cars and stroll arm-in-arm with women wearing short-sleeved dresses.

Abie the Agent could be found this morning at a small sidewalk café on Grand, a cup of coffee in his left hand and in his right a library book, by good old Spengler. The waitress saw Abie was alone and that his eyes looked sad and he was reading such a smart book, so naturally she was a goner and kept smiling and filling his cup without him asking. He was on good behavior as ever and didn't flirt back, just stayed true to his book. His lips were moving as he tried very hard to absorb an explanation of how each so-called culture passes through seasons that represent something else: i.e., "springtime" is "faith," whilst summer is "intellectuality," and so forth. He made it all the way to winter and almost had it figured out when a shadow from behind blocked the sunlight on his book.

Abie looked up to see the Original Solly Levine standing behind him smiling; the sun was behind Solly, which made him a dark figure. Then he walked around to the other side of the table and plopped himself down in the chair across from Abie without even asking.

"Long time no see," Solly said.

"How'd you know I was here?" Abie said, still holding the book open in front of him. "You tailing me?"

"Happened to spot you here last Sunday and figured you might come back. 'Specially on a beauty like this."

Solly leaned back in the chair, took off his taped-up glasses and turned his pale face up to the sun as if his sole purpose in coming was to get a tan.

"What do you want?" Abie said to the sun god before him.

"You sure get to the point," Solly said. He turned his face back to earth and put on his glasses so he could see how his lies would be received. "Okay. Here it is. Joe sent me. He wants to fix things up with you and Max."

Abie didn't answer right away, just folded the corner of the page so he wouldn't lose his place, shut the book and laid it down.

"Good book?" Solly asked.

Abie explained he'd lost the book earlier and had to get a new copy.

Solly nodded and said, "Oh, that's a sonofabitch when you lose a book halfway through. I hate that."

"You never even read a book halfway through," Abie said. "So what did Joe say? What were his words, exactly?"

"He said I want to fix things with Abie. They miss you, Abie. We all do. You're like goddamn family."

Abie's face turned a little red when he heard that. Solly noticed and should have let it go but didn't.

"Look at you—blushing!"

"It's the sun," Abie said.

"Sure it is. Anyway it's time for you to come home."

Abie looked down at his coffee and nodded. "That's what I want, too," he said. "I thought about just taking off somewhere and starting fresh. But it hit me: Wherever you go, you're still you. You know?"

He looked up to see if Solly got that, but Levine was otherwise focused on the backside of the waitress.

"Huh? Oh, yeah, I get ya," Solly said when he realized Abie was looking at him. "Yeah, we're all ants on the head of a goddamn pin and whatnot. But anyways, it's time to come home, Abie."

"It won't be easy," Abie said. "Things were said."

"If you're talking about the misunderstanding with Max, it's all been sorted out." Solly then leaned forward in his seat and lowered his voice. "We know who the snitch was. It wasn't Max."

"Then who?" Abie said.

Solly put a finger to his lip and the googly eyes rolled around, as if looking for spies. "This is not something to discuss openly," he said. "Joe will explain everything to you. He's over at Collingwood with Max right now. Why don't we go over, have a pow-wow. Straighten the whole thing out."

Abie was taken aback. "Right now?" he said.

"Got something better to do?"

"I was going to go home and see my wife and kid," he said. "Haven't seen them much lately. I thought I'd take them out to the park. But I guess it can wait."

"Sure it can," Solly said. "This will all be over by lunch time."

Solly got up and then Abie did likewise. He slipped his Spengler book inside his jacket, close to his heart. The two men started walking in the bright sunshine.

"What a day, huh?" Abie said.

"Yeah," Solly said. "But I hear it's gonna get hot as hell."

When they arrived at the Collingwood Apartment complex, a four-story yellow brick building with a courtyard, the place looked deserted because it was. Early that morning at Max's request, the building's landlord pounded on each door and told everyone they had to clear out for a few hours because a team of exterminators was supposedly coming in.

"This place looks dead," Abie said to Solly as they went in the entrance. "Where is everybody?"

Levine blamed the mass disappearance of people this Sunday morning on the Catholic church.

Shortly after they stepped inside the building, a car pulled slowly down Collingwood Avenue and yes it was a Doozie. The car came to a stop at the curb and I shut off the engine but did not budge from my seat because I had no intention of going inside. I didn't even want to look at that building, so I looked down the road and noticed, a block away, some kids playing in the street. This was not a good thing for me to see either, because it made me think of Abie's kid at home without a father, which in turn reminded me of my own childhood, if you could call it that.

Whilst I was reminiscing, Solly reached the top of a creaky narrow stair landing, with Abie coming up behind him. This led out into a dark hallway where the ceiling had brown splotches from water leaks. The hallway was too narrow for walking side-by-side so Abie stayed behind Solly and noticed he was walking very slowly and with heavy clumping footsteps. And then Solly started speaking very loud to him, as if he was twenty feet away:

"Well, here we are—we have arrived, Abie," he shouted.

At the apartment door, Solly tapped twice and then twice again. Abie heard movement on the other side of the door. Then Max opened the door and looked at Solly and then at Abie.

It has been previously noted that Max was no comedian and the same could be said of his dramatic skills. He opened his eyes very wide when he saw Abie and whacked his hand against his own chest as if he might have a heart attack. But the act was all wrong: The eyes didn't stay wide long enough and the dead-fish of a hand stayed on the chest too long, and so forth. The words were a problem, too.

"Abie," he said. "You are the last person I was expecting."

By now the alarm bells were no doubt ringing in Abie's head but he did not let on. It is possible he was taking a so-called fatalist view, figuring there was no point trying to avoid what lay in wait for him so he may as well face it and get it over with.

"It's good to see you, Max," Abie said and extended a handshake. Max took the dead fish from his chest and shared it with Abie. Then Max turned, leaving the door open behind him. Abie went in, with Solly following. Once inside, Abie saw that the living room was empty. But his keen eye also observed there were two big ass-dents in the cushions on the sofa. Also, the smell of cigarette smoke hung in the air and this was curious as Max did not smoke (because of his condition). Abie sniffed that air and as he did, a watchful Solly saw the little flare of the nostrils.

"Where's Joe?" Abie said. "Or has he gone to church too?"

Max didn't understand the remark and tried to ignore it. "He's on his way," he said, then gestured to the lumpy sofa with the assdents. "Have a seat, Abie. Take a load off as they say."

"Don't feel like sitting just now," Abie said.

Max nodded. "Well, guess what, I have to use the can," he said and looked to Abie as if for permission. Abie just stared at him.

Max walked to a door and opened it, went through, and then closed it—all very quickly. That door was not open for more than two seconds but there is much that a sharp eye can see in that span of time. Abie saw a mirror inside the room, and a man in the mirror who appeared to be checking a Tommy gun.

Abie was a man whose face didn't give away much, but seeing the mirror must have caused a reaction in Abie that Solly detected. Solly reached into his jacket for his gun—but by the time he pulled it out and held it in front of him, a long thin blade was coming down with tremendous force upon his wrist. It cleanly severed the hand, which dropped to the floor with the gun still in it.

Solly looked down at the hand, not sure if it was his own. He raised his wrist for a closer look and it sprayed like a hose, covering his thick glasses in red. He bent over carefully as if to retrieve the hand and whilst he was bent over Abie raised the blade up again—but before he could strike, Solly gently toppled head-first onto the floor and just lay there with eyes rolled back behind those thick and now rose-colored glasses. Abie nudged the body with his toe and it did not respond. Then he crept on his big cat's feet toward that closed bedroom door.

As he reached the door he saw the knob start to turn and he flattened his back against the wall alongside the doorway. The first gunner came charging through right past Abie and as he did, Abie hooked him from behind with an arm around the neck and ran the blade through the middle of his back. The skewered gunner started shooting anyway, though not at anything in particular; it was just a reflex and it lasted until he died and maybe a couple of seconds beyond. This proved useful to Abie because the dying gunner briefly became both a shield and a weapon at the same time.

With his arm still clamped round the gunner's neck and his other hand still holding the skewer handle, Abie pivoted the gunner's body back toward that bedroom doorway, where the second gunner was emerging with his Tommy blazing. And for the next few seconds the first gunner and second gunner filled each other with holes. The force of the gunfire drove them apart—with the second gunner staggering back into the bedroom from whence he came, whilst the first gunner and his big supporter both fell backwards down the hall, landing on the floor with Abie on the bottom and the ventilated corpse on top. Abie pushed the body off, checking himself for holes. He had none.

There was no shooting now and the whole apartment was dead still. Abie reached over to pull his blade out of that first gunner's back. He took a handkerchief from his pocket and wiped the blade clean. Then he started to get up slowly with an eye toward that bedroom doorway.

"Come on out, Heebie Jeebie," he said as he reached his feet. "Just you and me now."

Abie walked slowly to the bedroom with the blade in his hand. He couldn't see into the room until he got to the doorway. The first thing he saw was the other gunner dead on the floor, his hands still cradling the Tommy like a baby. Abie didn't recognize the man; he was an outside gun brought here to make a quick buck on a Sunday morning. Now as he lay on the floor his mouth was wide open as if to yell at somebody for misrepresenting the job, but all that came out was a little red trickle.

Abie looked up and scanned the inside of the bedroom. There was a well-made bed in the midst of it, and a picture of a happy family on the wall. There was a small writing table with a chair. And in the corner there was Max, leaning against the wall for support and quivering whilst holding a shotgun and looking sideways at Abie. He was trying to hold the shotgun straight but was having a rough time of it. As he shook, the barrel of the rifle went around in tight little circles.

"Don't be nervous now," Abie said as he stepped slowly toward Max. "You might miss."

Max seized up and his shoulder jerked hard and the gun almost slipped from his hands and then when he tried to grab it, it went off whilst pointing low. The buckshot pierced the floor right where Abie was standing. Abie looked down and saw that the top of his black shoe had a red hole in it. As he looked down he also noticed a silver dollar-sized hole in the floor that went clean through, showing daylight. Abie reached down and poked his long finger through it.

"You made a hole," he said. "Somebody will have to pay for that."

Abie was right about that and the one who eventually had to pay was of course me. If it was just a hole in the floor it might not have mattered, but it was also a hole in the ceiling of the apartment below. This wouldn't have mattered either, *if* the apartment had been empty as it should have been, with everyone having been warned about the scheduled extermination. But just because you announce something does not mean everyone will hear it.

In that apartment below, an old woman sat in a chair reading. She didn't hear the gunshots, just as she never heard the landlord pounding on the door earlier that morning. She was near-deaf and wrapped up in her own world. But when chips of plaster started to snow from the ceiling above, *that* she noticed. She looked up from her book and saw the hole. She walked underneath it and peered up and thought she saw a finger moving around in that hole. This concerned her. She went to get her ear trumpet and then placed it in her ear to listen. She didn't hear anything, but that was just a case of queer timing—because as soon as she put the ear trumpet down there was another blast upstairs.

This second shot did not damage the floor or the ceiling or even the walls, because all of the pellets lodged in Abie's stomach. He looked down and saw that his white shirt was half-red already, and he touched the gaping wound and looked at his bloody hand.

"You made a good shot, Max," he said, though he was having trouble breathing as he said it. "Didn't think you had it in you."

Then he took another step toward Max, who fumbled and dropped his last shell, which rolled across the floor. Holding the empty shotgun, Max stood with his back to the wall shaking like an electrified man. Abie took one more step toward him—and then his legs buckled and he dropped to the floor, first on knees and then on his red belly. But his head bobbed up, looking at Max. And he began to crawl toward Max—staking his dagger into the floor so he could pull himself forward. He dug that stake in the floor a second time and dragged himself a little closer.

Max began to slide his back along the wall, hoping to make it to the doorway whilst staying out of Abie's reach. On the floor, Abie shifted course and started crawling toward the doorway where Max was headed. Finally Max broke into a run for the door and as he got there Abie reached out with one hand and grabbed hold of Max's pants-leg. Max could go no further and looked down to see Abie clutching the pants with one hand whilst slowly raising the other hand with the dagger in it.

Luckily for Max, his flimsy pants-leg tore away in Abie's grasp—freeing Max to run out the bedroom door. Whilst Abie lay there propped up on his elbows, he watched Max run through the living room and out the front door.

I was sitting in the parked car and heard the muffled shots and was waiting for Max to come walking out. Instead I saw him running toward the car like a madman with one leg torn off his pants. Max opened the door and threw himself into the car seat, then slammed and locked the door.

"We gotta get out of here now!" he yelled.

"Where's Solly?" I said. "What the hell happened to your pants?"

"Dead. They're all dead."

Max gestured with his hand for me to start the engine but I just ignored that. "He took out both Tommies? And Solly too?"

Max nodded. He kept glancing back at the building entrance as if expecting Abie to come crawling out on the sidewalk.

"But Abie's finished, right?" I asked him.

"As good as," Max said. "He's gut shot."

I just stared at him and he tried not to look at me. "And you're gonna leave him there alive... *bleeding?*"

Max shivered and shook his head at the same time. I pounded my fist on the dashboard. "Can't you do *anything?*" I yelled. "Are you *that* fucking helpless?"

I threw open the car door and got out.

"Joe, don't go in there," Max said to a slamming door.

As I circled round the front of the car and walked toward the building Max rolled down his window.

"Joe, you don't need to go back there."

But I kept going, through the entrance and to the dark stairwell. I climbed the creaky steps and knew I should be hurrying but could not make my legs go fast. I had trouble making them go at all.

Inside the apartment Abie could hear my footsteps coming up the stairs. He had dragged himself out of the bedroom and into the living room, leaving a red smear along the way. He slithered over to the area where Solly was lying and he looked around—then saw what he was looking for. By now my footsteps were out of the stairwell and in the hall, getting closer to the door. Abie reached for Solly's severed hand with the gun and picked up the whole sticky thing. The hand would not let go of the gun. He realized he would have to pry each finger loose and he'd only done two when he heard my voice above.

"Give that to me," I said.

Abie looked up at me, standing over him with my gun pointed down. Then Abie held up the hand-with-gun like an offering and I took it from him and put it in my own jacket pocket. It weighed down the pocket and started soaking through right away.

Abie had his stomach against the floor and was propped up on his elbows. His head was bent back to look at me. He was short of breath. "Now… it's… your turn," he said to me.

I didn't know what he meant. I just stood pointing the gun.

"To lift me up," he said. "To save me."

"I wish I could," I said to him.

He had no fear in his eyes, which didn't surprise me. Abie was a soldier to the end and deserved a silver cross if anyone did. He did not beg. What he did made it harder—he tried to comfort me.

"It's okay," he said, patting the top of my shoe with a bloody hand. "I don't mind. Long as you… take care… of my family."

"Forever," I said.

"And also… my father. Don't forget… my father." He smiled and said, "Use the money… from the tzedakah box."

I asked him a question: "Should we do this now?"

Because it was up to him—whether to end his suffering now, or maybe take a few more minutes.

"I'm in… no rush," he said.

I stopped pointing the gun. I sat down on the floor, against the wall, about ten feet from him. We talked a little, though it was hard for him to get his words out. He told me he was sorry he'd lied to me. And that it was the only time he ever did. I asked him why he did.

"Because… I just couldn't… go through with it," he said.

"Couldn't go through with what?" I said.

By this time, the old deaf bat in the room below was in a panic. White flakes from the ceiling were bad enough, but when she saw the red seeping through she knew it was time to have a word with the landlord. She put on her housecoat, picked up the trumpet again and put it in her ear—just in time to hear two quick shots fired in succession up above. She looked up at the ceiling. She didn't know what to do. Then, with the trumpet still in her ear, she heard footsteps above, running.

She walked with her cane to the front door and opened it just a crack. The footsteps were coming down the stairs now. She kept spying through that thin crack and saw a man come flying down the stairwell. She didn't see him for long but got a good look. He had thick dark hair and blue eyes that looked watery. He had a bloody lump in the pocket of his jacket. And he appeared to be holding a book in his hand.

THIRTY

The so-called Collingwood Massacre (which could more accurately be called the Collingwood Misunderstanding) was the beginning of the end. Not just for us, but for a whole way of life in Detroit.

By the Fall of 1931, a great exodus was underway. Riley had made it clear that Detroit was not going to be a good place for a gangster to ply his wares. The Barkley Grand Jury was finally set to begin in November and before it did Riley made a final offer to any and all hoods: Leave now for Cleveland or Chicago or anywhere that is a good distance from this city, and I will not haul you back to answer for your past. Or as the Detroit News headline put it: *"Riley to Mob: Scram!"*

Many took him up on the offer because there was more than just the GJ to worry about. The new mayor and police commissioner were shutting down many of the speakeasies (which were half-empty anyway—nobody could afford expensive booze anymore). Judges and cops were suddenly becoming allergic to grease. And at long last the cure was found for the ten-year epidemic of courtroom amnesia. It seems the one thing that can trump fear is anger, and the common herd just would not stop being mad about what happened to their beloved Motormouth.

With all of these problems and another nasty Detroit winter blowing in off the river, it seemed a good time to re-locate and start fresh. A number of the oilers (though not Livoli who was determined to stand his ground) moved over to Chicago whilst some returned to roots in New York. And then there was the fellow who opted for a warmer clime.

Max told me he needed to get out because his nerves were worse than ever after Collingwood. We'd heard that arrests were imminent though I assured him, "It will be me, not you. I will protect you no matter what." (This made Max cry and he said to me: "I wish I could do the same for you but I can't. Because of my condition.") But nevertheless, Max worried that if he stuck around, Riley might call him before the GJ.

More than anything else, Max said, he just wanted to get warm. He told me once, much earlier, "The only time I really feel relaxed is when I'm sitting in the sunshine at Navin Field." So I decided to give my brother a map of Florida as well as the Doozie, to get him there. We stood beside the car and hugged. "You sure you want me to take your wheels?" Max asked. I told him: "I never cared about this car. I like to ankle, you know that."

And I ankled a lot in the following days. I strolled through Hastings for the first time in a long while and noticed the merchants (who still wouldn't look me in the eye) were doing brisk business. Maybe you couldn't sell a Ford during a bad so-called economy, but you could always sell an apple or a piece of fish. I was pleased to see, when I passed old Mr. Z's butcher shop, that he had customers—I guess everyone decided the purple taint should be lifted off him now that his shameful son was dead. (Not that Mr. Z had to worry about making money—he had recently come into a large sum, delivered by two distinguished-looking men in suits. They said they were from the life insurance company and that Abie had a $250,000 policy, payable in cash. Of course, the men were a couple of actors hired by me, but Mr. Z never suspected.)

One morning I walked to the downtown post office because I had a box I wanted to mail to John Livoli. Inside the box was Solly Levine's hand (minus the gun). It had been dipped in purple paint. And there was a note, referencing Livoli's failed attempt to hire Abie: *"Next time you want a hand from the Purples, just ask."*

After leaving the post office, I kept going, all the way out to Eloise. The nurses wondered why I was there, but as ever they let me roam free once I gave them a buck and a cold stare. I walked up the stairs to her old room and poked my head in; they had jammed four beds into the room now and from one of them a crazy old hag looked at me and said, "Henry is that you?" I said I wasn't Henry but she didn't care—wanted to talk to me anyway. I poured her a glass of water and told her about the world outside. Spent a good half-hour, and almost didn't want to leave.

On the way out, I said goodbye to good old Oscar at the gate. "Say, Oscar," I said as I was going, "you know who I am? I mean, do you *really* know who I am?"

He nodded. "Oh, yeah, I know all about you, Mr. Bernstein."

"Well," I said, "thanks for acting as if you didn't."

Then I ankled all the way home and despite the twelve-mile roundtrip I remained light of step and mood, and this did not change even as I arrived at my house and saw three cops waiting. I nodded hello to them and they did the same, and we all had a good chat whilst I held my hands behind my back to be cuffed.

They held me without bail. This may not seem fair but when you are deemed an enemy of the state, all is fair. They can drag you out of bed in dead of night and throw you in a dark airless room and chain the doors if they like. Fortunately that is not what happened to me—the room they put me in had plenty of air and light, coming through the bars.

It was here that I first began to jot down some of the stories in my head though I had no idea what I might do with them. And it was here that I resumed the reading life I had started long ago in the Hamtramck basement. I always meant to keep reading but found that life outside of basements and prison cells tended to get in the way of books.

Of course there were plenty of books in the prison library, but the first one I read was the one I brought with me. It was by good old Spengler. It was no easy book to read because the ideas were

complex and the words were large. And the two holes running
through the middle of the book did not help.

Whilst I awaited trial, the Barkley hearings proceeded. Riley
earned a reputation in the press for demolishing people in front of
the Grand Jury. He fired questions the way a Tommy dispenses
bullets, and often with an equally destructive result. It was said that
powerful men went into that GJ room with their chests puffed out
and left with their asses dragging.

But not all the witnesses were treated harshly. Tennessee
Jenkins appeared on the stand in fine New York clothes (the papers called her "the dark mystery woman") and Riley spoke softly
and handed her glasses of water. She cried and cried anyway.

What gradually emerged during the hearing was that all the previous speculation about the Purples' involvement in the Barkley
killing was (as usual) unfounded. To his credit Riley made it clear
that the likely killers were the oilers, who felt betrayed by Barkley
when he turned against Mayor Bowles. Riley got an indictment but
when it went to trial, there was not enough hard evidence for a
conviction. As the verdict came in, the jurors one by one shook
their heads and uttered what some people consider to be the two
loveliest words in the language. Riley sat slumped in his chair at
the prosecution table whilst Livoli and the two oiler suspects cele-
brated with their lawyers.

In the months leading up to my own trial, my communication with
the outside world was limited. I wrote to Max, who'd found a
place down in Florida where the ballplayers held their spring training games and the minor leaguers played year-round. Max said the
minor leaguers really appreciated a good fan like him and that he
had become great pals with an outfielder named Kyle. "My condition is much better these days and I think this place agrees with
me," Max wrote. And this made me smile for the first time in
memory.

I had occasional visitors, such as the lawyer Putzpatrick who assured me I had nothing to worry about, which convinced me that I
was in big trouble. A few of the last lingering Purples also stopped

by, including one bright young kid who told me: "When you get off—and I know you will—I would like to be your new right-hand guy." I gave the kid a two-part test to prove himself. The first job was to find out anything he could about any supposed witnesses to the Collingwood Misunderstanding. The kid came back with the following report: There was an old lady in the building who apparently saw something; she was now temporarily relocated under a 24-hour-a-day watch with a big stiff of a cop named Butch Moran. There was also a rumor about a second witness but no one knew who that might be.

"Do you want me to kill this old lady? Is that the second part of my test?" the kid asked. I shook my head—no point sending a bright kid to be shot by cops over an old lady who'd probably be no good on the witness stand anyway. "No, the second thing I want you to do is something different," I said.

Just days before the trial, I put the finishing touches on a letter. I had worked on it for a long time, even though it was a short note that said only the following:

I just want to thank you for being so kind to Rachel. I have often thought of the day we drank iced tea at the Crime. No matter what I think of your husband or vice versa, I consider you a gem and Riley is lucky to have you. If I lose this trial and end up in prison maybe you will visit me some time. I have good stories to tell anyone who might visit. I am writing them down and who knows someday I may put them all in a book. But if you can't visit I would understand given the situation. Either way I wish you all the best.

When I finished the letter I asked that eager kid to try to get it to Riley's wife. The day before the trial the kid stopped by. "I got her the letter," he said. But there was no way to know if he was telling the truth.

The trial of Joe Bernstein was filled with lies, which was to be expected. And Putzpatrick was useless. When he tried to get tough with the old lady she told him to behave himself and everybody laughed. Meanwhile Riley skillfully manipulated her. As she sat in the witness chair he put his lips to the mouth of her horn and uttered his leading questions, which slid down into her ear. She would answer each time, "Yes, that is right." She even claimed to recognize my face and especially my eyes; she maintained the eyes looked like they were crying as I came down the stairwell. What the old bitch did not know is that I have always had watery eyes.

The trial did in fact have a surprise witness as the rumors had suggested. Riley hauled out none other than the Original Solly Levine and I don't mean his corpse. Back on that Collingwood apartment floor Levine was not dead after all, just in shock and nearly drained of blood. The police got him to a hospital in time to save him and then it was Riley's clever idea to put out the word he'd died, whilst hiding him till the trial. When Solly took the stand and was told to "Raise your right hand" all he could do was hold up a bandaged stump. That right there should have told everyone that his sworn oath was meaningless.

He went on to offer many fabrications, never once looking in my direction. He also provided some of the trial's lighter moments. For example when Riley asked if he was an active member of the Purple Gang, Solly answered: "No, mostly I just sit around." At another point in his testimony he was doing lots of nodding and shaking his head, so the judge stopped him and said: "Mr. Levine, from now on, all your answers must be oral. Do you understand?" He looked puzzled at first and then shrugged and answered, "Oral." But whilst everyone was getting a good laugh, little nails were being hammered into my coffin.

Solly stated that he came to the Collingwood apartment with Abie, expecting a truce. He said on the way into the building he noticed Joe Bernstein sitting in his car parked up the block and was surprised Joe was not in the apartment. He said that when they got inside the apartment everything was calm and quiet at first and then suddenly there was the sound of a loud car horn honking from the street below; soon as that horn went off, two shooters responded to the signal by rushing out from the bedroom. Levine said that he simply wished to defend himself so he reached for his gun, but Abie mistakenly thought he was one of the shooters and so took the understandable action of slicing his hand off. And so on: It was just one lie after another.

As I sat listening it only confirmed everything I'd suspected about Solly and I now understood all of the mistakes I'd made, not just about Solly but about others who are no longer amongst us. When it came, the verdict was no surprise. They polled the jury just as in the Barkley trial but this time each juror nodded his head instead of shaking it. And instead of uttering those two beautiful words they only said one of them—a word which by itself did not sound beautiful unless you happened to be the supposed hero of this story.

Riley to his credit did not celebrate—just lifted himself up slowly from his table whilst behind him a head of red hair could be seen making its way toward him through the crowded courtroom. When she finally got to Riley she threw her arms around him. She rested her chin on his shoulder and I could see she had tears in her eyes. She never once looked in my direction. But what did those tears mean? She acted as if they were tears of joy at the verdict and Riley's victory. But of course she had to act that way, if only for appearance's sake.

Believe it or not, even after all of that, Riley was not done torturing me yet. I noticed that as he shook hands with Putzpatrick he also whispered something to him; Putzpatrick relayed the message to me.

"Riley asked for a few moments of your time. Says he's got something to say to you in private."

I almost had to laugh. I said, "He's taken a lifetime from me already, so what's a few minutes more."

The courtroom cops led me in my cuffs, with Putzpatrick following behind, to a holding room down the hall. I took a seat inside whilst Putzpatrick waited at the door with the cops. Riley arrived shortly.

"He's in there," Putzpatrick said to Riley. "He's agreed to talk to you, though I don't know why he should."

Riley nodded and started to pass, then stopped and turned back to Putzpatrick. "Tell me something, Fitz," he said. "When the big dogs are locked away, what will all the fleas do then?"

Just like during the entire trial, Putzpatrick had no comeback. Riley left him and came into the room, where I sat at a table with cuffed hands folded in front of me. Riley sat down opposite me. Then I raised up my hands and softly applauded whilst the cuffs jangled.

"Three cheers," I said. "To the man who took down the Jews."

Riley sighed and just shook his head in that familiar way of his. "You think that has anything to do with why I took you down? You don't think it might be because your gang killed several hundred people?"

I rocked back in my chair as if hurt by that. "Several *hundred* now? The legend grows every day. Tell me, how many have the Italians killed? But I don't see Livoli in this room with chains on. Maybe he's busy having drinks with the Feds, eh?"

"I can't answer for the Feds," Riley said. "I can only tell you that *I* went after the Black Hand *and* the Purples."

"But you did more damage to one than the other."

Riley nodded; he had no choice as it was a fact. But he said, "Don't worry, I'm not through with Livoli—I'm just getting started. I don't play favorites."

I couldn't dispute that—he was a son of a bitch to everyone. And I say that as a compliment.

At one point, Riley shifted in his seat and I could tell he was trying to say something and didn't know how. Finally he said, "What happened to your girl Rachel was wrong. I guess no one ever apologized. So I'm doing it now."

I shrugged. "I don't blame you for that. You tried to help at the time. It's other things I blame you for."

Riley nodded with eyes down toward the table. "I didn't think the thing with Abie would... go so far," he said. "That was never my intention."

"Well, we all make mistakes," I said, "and sometimes people end up dead because of them."

Riley had no clever retort for that and seemed ready to wrap up. Then he leaned back and folded his arms. "I guess you're never going to tell us what happened to Thompson, huh?"

I just smiled. "Draw your own conclusions. You're good at that."

"You almost got Barkley too, didn't you? That's why Solly Levine was in that lobby at the time."

" 'Almost' doesn't count," I said. "Had good reason to kill him, though. Barkley was a filthy spy. Spied on poor Rachel. Spied on us. Even sent a boy to do his spying for him."

Riley's face got a look that was rare for him: surprise. This encouraged me to go on. "Imagine using a little kid that way," I said. "And the son of the woman you're sleeping with, no less."

"That boy wasn't her son," Riley said.

"Sure he was. But that's another story and your time is up."

I started to get up from my chair to leave.

"Wait," Riley said. "One more thing. It's about Grabowski." He paused. "Did Abie really kill him?"

I had to shake my head at that. "Why does it matter now? Abie's gone—you can't do any more damage to him."

"It's just that..." Riley leaned toward me, almost like he was a little embarrassed about what he was going to say. "Grabowski said he'd get my family. And he's been in my nightmares ever since. I just need to know he's dead."

I was out of the chair now, above Riley and looking down on him. "Then why don't you ask the Feds about him. Or the oilers. With all the eyes you have on us... *somebody* must know *something*."

I turned and left the room, and the guards at the door quickly attached themselves to me. Back in his chair, Riley sagged and blew air from puffed cheeks, then reached down for his briefcase. When he straightened up again he saw that I was back in the doorway, poking my head in.

"He's dead," I said.

Riley was puzzled for a second.

"Abie told me so himself, and Abie never lied," I said. "So you can stop your nightmares."

I gave Riley a nod and ducked out again. Riley sat back and absorbed this. He was good at detecting lies yet did not catch this one—maybe he needed for his own sake to believe it was true.

He turned to the empty doorway and called out, "Thank you."

By the time he said it, I was gone.

It is customary to end stories with the hero and his loved one together looking forward to a carefree life ahead, and though the author has been known to break a few rules in his time he might as well abide by this one. The next day Riley was out for an ankle with Nan and the little ones. They strolled upon a walkway that ran alongside the Detroit River. The day in question was early spring and the river was still thawing. The sun warmed their faces but there was also a nip of a breeze coming off the water. Nan was holding Jean's hand; Riley held the giggling twin boys, one under each arm like a couple of footballs. Nan stopped to look out on the water, and Riley put down the boys and stood next to her.

"Thought I saw a motorboat out on the Canadian coast," she said. "Maybe the last of the Purple pirates?"

Riley looked out on the water and shook his head. "Not likely," he said. "Most of 'em have skipped town or been locked up. Either that or they're dead."

She was still gazing out with a little smile on her face. "It must have been a thrill for them," she said. "Riding on the water late at night, a stash of hooch under the floorboards. Pulling into some little secret cove."

Riley looked at her and did not understand. "You make it sound romantic," he said. "It was just a batch of crooks fighting over this cesspool of a river."

She turned towards him and gave his arm a little punch.

"Hey—I *like* this river," she said. "You're just not a river guy. All *you* want to do is get back to your precious little lake."

Riley raised an eyebrow. She knew that meant something.

"Am I right?" she said.

He still didn't answer right away. Then he glanced at her sideways as she waited with arms folded.

"Well, sure," he finally said. "Of course I want to go back. Eventually. But I mean... there's no rush. Lake's not going anywhere."

She smiled at him as he looked out on the river. Then she took hold of his arm and gave a little tug. "Let's get out of this breeze," she said. "Let's head over to Cadillac Square."

They put the twins in the big stroller and the family walked to the square. As they passed the central post office she stopped and turned to him. "Will you wait here with the kids?" she said. "I need to drop something in the mail."

Alone inside the post office she pulled a small brown package from her bag and handed it to the clerk. The reader may wonder what was in the package (the astute reader will not need to be told who it was for) and so the contents shall be divulged. There was a short note which read as follows:

"I thank you so much for your letter. I also think about that day at the diner. And I think about my visits with Rachel, all the time. I hope you can appreciate that it would be difficult for me to visit you in prison. My husband understands almost everything, but I'm not sure he would understand that. He does not know that I ever went to see Rachel and I believe it is best that he doesn't. But I do not like to keep secrets from him and so I cannot correspond with you beyond this letter. Though I do wish I could. I wish I could hear all of your stories. Maybe someday I will read them in the book that you are destined to write. You must write it—please, please do. It will give you something to live for, and the rest of us something to look forward to. I have enclosed a book that may help you get started on your journey. Take care."

That was all the note said. As for the book that came with it in the package, it was called *Becoming a Writer*. There was much to learn in it yet it was small enough to fit in a woman's purse, and light enough that the postage fee she handed to the mail clerk was minimal.

A moment later she was out of the building and back with her family, ready to move along.

"Who are you writing to?" Riley asked.

She smiled and said, "Just a friend," and for once Riley had no further questions for the witness.

* * *

Epilogue: 1959

When I think back on the Purple Gang, we were a lot like one of those souped-up Gar-Max boats in which we once roamed the river. We were assembled with mismatched parts and cast-off elements. When it all came together, we took off like a shot and seemed, for a while, to be invincible. But even a Gar-Max is bound to sink if it springs a bad enough leak. Once I was hauled off to jail in 1931, the water came rushing in and soon the gang, or the enterprise, or the dream if you want to call it that, was underwater.

But people continue to ask about it. You tell them everything from how it started to how it ended, and they still want to know, *What happened next? Who went where, and what became of so-and-so?* Frankly, I am tired of going over this shit again and again, so I will here, for the last time, provide answers to the five most commonly-asked questions.

1) What became of the Purple Gang after you were arrested?
Short answer: Not much. There were various stragglers still using the name until about 1940, and that was the end of it. But that name won't die. As I write this now, in the year of 1959, I have heard there is a Hollywood movie in the works, coming out next year. In the movie, nobody is Jewish—all the gang members have last names like Smith and Burke. (I know all this in advance because I have a friend in Hollywood, which I'll get to.)

Of course, the gang also got a lot of attention two years ago in '57 due to that song, "Jailhouse Rock."

Before the song came out I took a phone call from this Presley, a real hick. He told me he wanted to sing about my gang. I said, *Do you require my permission to do so?* And when he answered no I said, *Then why the fuck are you asking?* He ended up mentioning us in one line: *The whole rhythm section was the Purple Gang.* I do not know what the hell that means.

2) What became of the Italian mob in Detroit?

The oilers are still in business in Detroit to this day. They did take a hard hit in the early '30s, when Riley prosecuted Livoli and others; Riley kept his word about going after everybody and not playing favorites. His success as a prosecutor led to him being put in charge of the state liquor commission at which point Michigan, first state to go dry, became the first to repeal Prohibition in 1933. Ten years later, Riley was elected Governor, but you probably already knew that.

Getting back to the oilers versus the Jews and why one gang survived whilst the other did not, I have no big answers but I discussed it with Livoli in the prison yard (he's been in here with me since '33). He gave me his theory: "It's because you guys were ashamed of what you were doing and shame is a real killer," he told me. "You couldn't get it in your heads that this was a business like any other. You all worried what the neighbors would think or what Uncle Moe might say. You walked around your own community with your heads down—cut off from local support." Then he added, "Of course, on top of all that, we did shoot a hell of a lot of you."

3) Have you stayed in touch with Nan Riley (and were you in love with her)?

Regarding the first question, after that one little note I got from her in 1931, there was nothing for the next 25 years. Then, two years ago, I let her know I was working on the book and she wrote me several long letters giving her side of the story. Apparently she is a grandmother now—I cannot picture it because in my mind's eye she will always be in her twenties, twirling a spoon in a glass of iced tea and peeking up with mischievous green eyes.

As to the second part of the question, I only loved one woman and that was Rachel Roth. She took my heart into the ground with her and it has been buried ever since. Lately, however, I have begun to think that if I do get out of here alive someday, I just might go to New York and court Tennessee Jenkins. When I was working on the book, she wrote to me and then came to visit sev-

eral times to tell me all about the Motormouth. I have grown fond
of her. I warned her that I might come for her someday and she
said, "Men have been sayin' that to me for a long time, so I won't
hold my breath."

4) How is your brother Max?

Max is doing fantastic. He got into Florida real estate and made a
killing (as they say). He's also co-owner of a minor league ball
team. And on the side, he invents things in his basement—34
patents to his name. I am so proud of him. Kyle is his partner
(on the baseball venture I mean) and I think maybe in some
ways, Kyle is now the brother Max lost when we were forced to
separate. I know there are some who will smirk and say, "Oh,
he's more than a brother" and so forth. All I can say is that those
smirkers should make sure they are never within elbow's reach of
me, because I will not hear a word said against my brother. All
that matters to me is that he be happy—the wherefores and hows
are not important.

5) Did the ghost of Joe Bernstein return to kill the Original Solly Levine?

This is a question I get a lot, and it's no wonder in light of what happened to Solly after the trial. They put him in a witness relocation
program and set him up in Southern California, per Solly's request.
He lasted a year out there and then he suddenly returned one day to
the Crime of Michigan diner but here is the interesting part—he returned in cut-up pieces, stuffed into a brown bag marked "Solly
Levine" and left on the counter in the middle of the night.

   People assumed I did it—as if I could levitate out of this
prison, sail through the sky to California, cut Solly up, bring him
home, and be back in the cell before anyone missed me. Truth is, I
was as baffled as anyone. Until I got a visitor here at the prison a
few years ago.

   They told me my visitor was named Wolfowitz and I said I
didn't know anybody by that name. But I met with him anyway. It
was a few moments before I recognized him: He had new white

teeth, a slicked-back haircut, and something had been done to clear up his skin—he even had a nice tan. The only thing that gave him away was the eyes, still wild as ever. I looked at this person whom I scarcely recognized and said, "Is that you in there, Grabowski?"

I was shocked—never thought I'd see him again. Of course I knew he was alive out there somewhere. Abie told me so, just before he died at Collingwood. Grabowski was the one and only thing Abie had lied to me about—killing him was the thing Abie just "couldn't go through with." When he pulled his blade out of Grabowski's ear, he told him to disappear and Grabowski did. But when Grabowski later found out that Solly had betrayed us—and was responsible for Abie's death—Grabowski spent a year tracking Solly. And an entire night killing him.

Whilst he was out in Los Angeles doing this job, Grabowski took a shine to the place—of course we all knew he liked making movies. So after doing his little drop-off at the Crime, he went straight back to L.A. and started hounding and bullying that Foxman studio executive we knew (how that guy must have rued the day he first looked us up). He got himself a job, along with a new face and a new name.

He's visited me a couple of times since then and when he does, we talk about the old times in that cold basement in Hamtramck. "How far we've come," he said to me once. I gestured to my surroundings and said, "For me, maybe not so far." He still pines for his lost "babies" and I still tell him how much I couldn't stand those beasts and we laugh about it.

Mostly we seem to talk about Abie. "I owe him my life," Grabowski said to me during his last visit.

And I said, "You and me both, brot."

Author Acknowledgments

This book was nearly a decade in the making and I had many collaborators and supporters along the way. It started when Kevin Walsh showed me old news clippings he'd gathered about the radio star Jerry Buckley, whose killing in 1930 was once dubbed Detroit's "crime of the century." Working with Walsh and Brian d'Arcy James, I began to sketch out a screenplay that featured the Buckley crime but focused on Detroit's Purple Gang. The screenplay was the easy part; once I decided to put flesh on the bones of that story by turning it into a novel, that's when the real work began. Thank you to the Detroit Public Library and its abundant archives, to the Detroit News and Detroit Free Press, and to the various historians (including Paul Kavieff, Robert Rockaway, and Philip P. Mason) who've documented what little is known about the actual Purple Gang. Though I used some of that information as a starting point, I want to emphasize that this is a work of fiction. All the characters in it are my own little creations, assembled from various bits and pieces—some of those parts are rooted in fact, but most are fictional. I'd like to thank the literary agents Alfredo Santana and later David Vigliano both of whom believed this could work as a novel and provided great editorial guidance. To the many friends who read the script or the novel, thanks for your time and thoughts. And thank you to those who took part in our crowdsourcing efforts involving the title and cover. To the book editors who read and praised *The Purples* and even compared it favorably to the likes of *Billy Bathgate*, thank you. To the various members of the Berger and Kelly families, thanks for reading and giving strong feedback along the way. Lastly, I would like to especially thank one particular member of the Kelly clan, and that is Laura. She is the one person who has seen this project through with me from beginning to end. She brainstormed with me and edited the manuscript in all its various stages. When the writing was done, she tackled the hands-on design work that resulted in the book you are holding. So in the end, this is not my book; it is *our* book, mine and Laura's—and together we hope you enjoy it.

For More Information

For more about the writing of THE PURPLES or to order a copy of this book visit *www.ThePurplesBook.com.*